The American, embroiled in murder

Anna hadn't thought twice about what she was going to have to do..and now here she was. Halfway around the word. Telling what little she knew to Veli Yaziz, the detective with the national police.

The koreli cop, threatened by revolution

"A revolution would be the best thing that could happen to this country right now," said Yaziz's source, a boy journalist. "If I knew of such plans, I would not betray them."

"Then you would be a traitor," Yaziz said.

"Not if I chose to do nothing."

Doing nothing while knowing of somethng is the same as doing nothing."

While the gypsy danced for the general

At the top of the hill, the gypsy quickly turned the corner from Yesilyurt onto Gunes. Shade trees spilled over the pink wall surrounding the general's palace. Military men thought they could live like kings, did they? She would use her wiles to fool them all.

Blood had already spilled.

And there would be more.

Dancing for the General

Sue Star and Bill Beatty

D. M. Kreg Publishing

DMKregPublishing.com

Cover Design: Renee Barratt, The Cover Counts

In loving memory of Herbert Williamson, who gave his heart and his technical assistance to his many Turkish friends and colleagues.

Acknowledgments

Thanks to the many fine writers who helped with the various stages of this project: the Boulder Lunch Bunch, the Northern Colorado Writers Workshop, the Oregon Writers Network and the Inklings. Special thanks go to the family, who is always there for us.

Dancing for the General

Sue Star and Bill Beatty

Ankara, Turkey
August, 1957

Chapter One

The afternoon air stirred, lifting dust and heat from the stone pavers, swirling the ripe smell of animals here in the heart of the city. A donkey, hitched out of sight somewhere nearby, brayed. Something had startled it.

Anna Riddle paused in the center of the vast, empty concourse and glanced over her shoulder. The back of her neck prickled. Ever since the cab had let her and her eight-year-old niece out at the main gate to Atatürk's Tomb, she'd felt that someone was following them. She hadn't actually *seen* anyone, but she could tell.

She didn't think it was just her nerves, although her nerves had been on edge these last three weeks, ever since receiving that odd telegram from her brother-in-law, the first in a chain of pleas for help about her sister:

Please come stop we need you

Anna hadn't thought twice about what she was going to have to do. They were all the family she had left. It had only taken a little over a week to arrange a leave of absence from the high school where she taught social studies back home in Boulder, Colorado. It took three more days traveling on airplanes, and now here she was. Halfway around the world. In a foreign land.

The dancing wind swished her full skirts, twirling around her knees like a dervish's. As she anchored them against her thighs, Priscilla slipped her hand from Anna's and skipped ahead, oblivious to the way the wind revealed her lace-edged petticoat and panties.

"Priscilla!" Anna called, trying not to sound like the nervous ninny her niece probably thought she was. "Don't go so far ahead!"

If Rainer hadn't died in the war, Anna might've had a child of her own, just about Priscilla's age. She would've known better how to handle someone of this age.

She wasn't accustomed to feeling out of control. Being in a strange place gave her a disadvantage, making it impossible for her to tell if something was truly wrong. She'd felt on high alert all the way up the long promenade of Lions Alley to this broad, open concourse that spread out before the tomb. It helped her state of mind that security guards watched from their little huts that ringed the property. They would intervene in case anyone tried to steal her purse. She hoped it wouldn't come to that. The day had started out so playful, so full of innocence and fun and filled with hope that she and her sister's only child would finally become better acquainted.

Anna was in charge now, and she mustn't let on her feelings of inadequacy. Mitzi and Henry had left their child in her care, while Henry catered to Mitzi's fragile mental health, whisking her away on a much-needed vacation. Perhaps it had been an over-stated emergency, but Anna didn't mind. Coming here was a once-in-a-lifetime opportunity, and she hadn't been able to resist. During her first three days here, after she arrived and before her sister and brother-in-law left, they'd hardly communicated on account of the whirlwind of last-minute details to work out. Anna couldn't imagine what stress they must live under, thanks to Henry's job with the State Department. Nor what it was like living here in a third world country.

But she intended to find out. She couldn't help feeling a thrill of excitement course through her.

Blinking against the sun's glare, she scanned the field of paving stones that stretched out before the tomb. White travertine, her guidebook informed her. As the crowning point atop the pinnacle of the hill, the mausoleum's shape reminded her of the Parthenon. This was a modern version, however, having been completed only four years earlier. And this place was empty of other visitors in the heat of the day. Ankara wasn't exactly a tourist destination.

Then a scuffling sound pulled her attention back over her shoulder. A flash of movement darted behind one of the lion statues at the edge of the concourse. Maybe only a hundred yards away. He or she, Anna couldn't tell from this distance, wore the balloon-puffed pants of a Turkish peasant. He, she decided. He'd ducked behind the statue as if hiding. From *her*? More likely, from the guards.

She whirled around and hurried after her niece. "Priscilla, wait for me!"

Priscilla paused long enough to stamp her saddle shoes in the dust. Red curls bounced to her shoulder as she cocked her head at one of the guards standing statue-straight in front of a tall, narrow guardhouse. He remained impervious to the distraction of her open curiosity and to the heat that surely made him melt under his rough-spun khaki uniform.

"Hello, Oscar," Priscilla said, tipping up her chin at him. He didn't lower his gaze, shaded under a white helmet.

Anna caught up to her niece, bent down to her freckled ear and whispered, in case Oscar understood English. "You mustn't bother him."

"He doesn't mind."

"But he is on duty." *He's keeping us safe from whoever is following us.* Anna took Priscilla's hand and pulled her away, across the field of stone. "Come on, let's go see the tomb itself."

Her heels clicked across the concourse, and she wished she'd worn something sturdier than her sister's fine, Italian sandals. Anna was sensible most of the time, but shoes were another matter.

"Do you know that man?" Anna asked, once they were out of the guard's hearing range.

Priscilla twisted her neck and squinted into the sun. She had a redhead's pale eyelashes that reminded Anna of moth wings, at momentary rest. Creases wrinkled her brow, revealing fine lines of glistening sweat.

"You'd better watch out," Anna said with a teasing laugh, "or a bird will land on your lower lip."

The image of the moth fluttered away as Priscilla opened her green eyes wide and studied Anna.

"You called the guard by name," Anna said, once she had Priscilla's full attention. She suspected it wouldn't last long.

"They're all Oscar," Priscilla said.

"How can that be?"

Priscilla shrugged. "You don't know very much for a teacher, do you?"

Anna winced, tightening her fingers around Priscilla's

delicate hand. She counted under her breath, disowning the hurtful words. But Priscilla was right about one thing. Anna didn't know very much about eight-year-olds. Particularly, she didn't know her niece, her very own flesh and blood.

Priscilla squirmed, twisting out of Anna's grip. It was an easy release with palms as slippery as theirs in this scorching heat. Her niece raced across the open concourse to the hillside of steps.

"Wait!" Anna called, running after the little imp.

By the time Anna reached the base of the steps, Priscilla had disappeared behind one of the squared columns at the top. Mustafa Kemal Atatürk, the founder of the Turkish Republic, lay enshrined within the mausoleum. Anna paused, needing a moment to catch her breath.

Here at the bottom of the grand stairs, stone carvings flanked either side and illustrated centuries of history. The sun-baked stone had been chiseled into rounded shapes that showed the history of Turkey. Anna had a vague idea of Turks rising up throughout time against foreign oppressors, and she felt the familiar catch in her throat that she always felt at the unlearned lessons of persecution. Mother had told the same tales about her ancestry, Anna's father's people, the Lakota.

"Bet you can't find me," Priscilla called out in a sing-song voice from somewhere above.

Anna's attention snapped away from the carvings. Priscilla's voice floated down from the ledge that surrounded the columns, but Anna couldn't see her niece. She saw, instead, a man in a western business suit ducking behind one of the columns.

Anna felt her heartbeat thud. The game had ended, as far as she was concerned.

Leaping up the steps, she told herself everything was all right. It had to be. Probably, it was just another tourist up there.

Still, Priscilla was out of her reach and closer to a stranger than to herself. Anna had slipped up with a momentary lapse of attention, seduced by her passion—history. What kind of a caretaker was she?

"Pssst."

"Priscilla? Did you say something?" Anna paused to shade her eyes, but she still didn't see Priscilla.

An agitated hee-haw split the air, and Anna whirled around. The donkey wasn't there. Oscar swayed slightly at his station, as if something disturbed him, as well.

"Priscilla," Anna called, running up the steps, "come out of there right now."

At the first landing, she heard Priscilla's voice again. This time Priscilla spoke words Anna didn't understand—Turkish, she presumed. In less than a week here, Anna had only learned a handful of Turkish words thus far. Then her niece pronounced one of them.

"*Hayir*," the little girl said. No. The word meant "no."

"Priscilla?" To whom was she speaking, Anna wondered, quickening her pace. The man in the western business suit? Her heart rate picked up and her skirts jiggled around her, tickling her knees with each step.

"*Hayir*," Priscilla said again, a little louder.

A soft pop and a grunt sounded nearby. Then, red curls, sparkling in the sunlight, appeared in Anna's line of sight. Priscilla backed slowly out from the shade of the portico onto the sunny ledge that surrounded the columns.

Anna's heart hammered. "Priscilla! Watch out!" The ledge

16

her niece was backing across ended abruptly at the top of the relief wall. No railing. Nothing to prevent a child from falling over the edge. Anna ran faster, but there were too many steps to climb before she could yank Priscilla to safety.

"Stop!" she called, using her sharpest tone of voice, the one she saved for field trips with her eleventh-grade students back home.

It worked. Priscilla stopped several feet away from the edge. Her hand covered her mouth as she continued to focus on something under the portico.

A soft thud and a muffled cry sounded together behind the columns. Footsteps pattered, crossing stone. Anna ran too, closing the gap between them. Priscilla's freckles stood out against her pale skin.

Finally, she reached Priscilla's side, and she scooped her precious niece into a tight hug. "You gave me a fright, honey."

"I didn't take it." Priscilla squirmed, ducking under Anna's arms. She dropped her hand first to her side, then behind her back. Her wide eyes narrowed. Anna had seen that look of defiance many times before on her sister.

Priscilla's gaze locked onto something just past the columns. Anna turned to look too, and gasped. A man, wearing a western business suit, sprawled face-down on the stone floor. His outstretched arm pointed in Priscilla's direction, and his fingers clutched a piece of paper.

A trickle of blood slid away from the man's mouth.

He was *dead*.

The shock of the realization sent a shudder through her. Anna sprang in front of Priscilla, protecting her.

The dead man held a paper in his hand, as if he'd been

offering it to someone. To Priscilla.

Anna reached behind her, groping for Priscilla. Petticoats swished. She opened her mouth to comfort her niece, but soothing sounds evaporated in her throat.

A Turkish voice shouted at them, and Anna looked up to see Oscar—or his twin—appear at the far side of the portico and run, galloping toward them. The rifle, capped with a bayonet, pointed in her direction.

Anna froze, certain that her heart had stopped. New voices in the distance answered Oscar's shout. The hammering sound of running feet told her that other guards were closing in from all directions.

Her knees gave way, and she buckled to the floor next to the dead man. Next to his outstretched arm. The piece of paper he held was an envelope. A letter. A caricature of Hitler decorated one corner of the envelope—like those she herself had used to correspond with G.I.'s during the war.

Then Anna spied the meticulous handwriting in blue ink that smudged across the middle. She choked, recognizing the careful penmanship, her own script. The letters spelled out her former fiancé's name: "Lt. Rainer Akers."

Her fingers quivered as she snatched up the envelope. *Her* letter. Written by *her*. To her fiancé before he'd died in the war. What was a dead Turkish man doing with *her* letter to Rainer?

Chapter Two

Sitting on her heels, Meryem shifted with impatience behind the wall of lion statues and flicked at a bee that was becoming too familiar with her face. Gold bracelets tinkled from her sudden movement, and she hid her arm beneath the ends of her scarf. Her brother Umit had made her promise to wait here out of sight, but he hadn't said anything about silence. Still, she had to be careful not to show off her gold when she chose to wear her peasant garb.

He should have returned by now. It was supposed to be a quick deal. A matter of business, he'd said. What did men know about being quick, let alone work at all?

He should have cut her in on the deal. They worked together, after all. It would serve him right if she abandoned him. But the Rom did not abandon one of their own. And women of the Rom usually let their men think they were in charge.

She did not like the way the air fell thickly about her shoulders, as if the almighty force that drove the air currents was holding his breath. Waiting with expectancy. Even the *eşek*, who had been grazing contentedly under the cedar tree nearby, sensed something sour in the air. It lifted its head, twitching its nostrils, clinking the copper pots strapped to its sides. The string of blue beads to ward off the evil eye dangled from its harness, and swung with each stamp of its hooves.

Meryem recognized the look of panic that glazed the animal's wide, brown eyes in the instant before it laid back its ears. There was no use trying to silence it. Its lips curled open, releasing a gush of brays. Meryem covered her ears, but that did no good, either.

It was Umit's *eşek*, and the two of them spoke to each other through their hearts. Was the animal calling to her brother now? Warning him about the thick, sour air? Or was it simply impatient, as she was, and ready to move on?

They still had their usual rounds in Kavaklidere, the rich neighborhood where Umit would shine kitchen pots the rest of the afternoon, each one for a few kuruş, the coins with holes. The *gadje*, those who were not Rom, lived there. It was the best neighborhood in town to suit the tastes of the wealthy, who held many parties. They always needed dancers. They needed Meryem. *She* could entertain them. She would, too, but for a higher price than copper work.

The animal fell silent as suddenly as it had started its clamor and returned to grazing. But Meryem wasn't satisfied. Something had gone wrong with Umit's "quick deal."

She rose from her crouch and crept to the backside of the next lion statue. Then, to the stone lion beyond that one. And to the next. Until she found a position at the end of the Lions' Road that gave her a good view ahead without exposing her.

The open concourse of *Anit Kabir* lay empty. Only one tourist stood at the far end, at the Victory Reliefs. A *gadje*, she could tell, because they never allowed the temperature of the day to rule their actions. This was not just any *gadje* but a foreigner. Bright pink flowers, the size of melons, blazed across her dress. Its western style pinched her waist and left her face and shoulders unclothed. But there was no man in sight for her to lure.

Except for the MP, who was above such temptations. Meryem had found out the hard way to leave the military alone.

Then the *eşek* brayed again, startling Meryem enough that she lost her balance and had to reach out to catch the stone wall of her lion protector. The foreign *gadje* suddenly darted up the steps to the tomb. Someone shouted in the distance.

Meryem felt as if ants crawled up and down her legs. She could sense danger in the air as well as the *eşek* could. Straightening, she shook the circulation back to her feet.

What was keeping Umit? She would have to save herself first, before the MPs decided to scour the grounds. The animal's noise would eventually bring them here, to investigate.

Already, the MPs were leaving their stations, sprinting along the concourse, racing to protect the pasha's shrine. Meryem recognized her opportunity, and she never missed an opportunity to escape. She turned to flee back the way she'd come. By the time they backtracked here, she would be gone. She hated leaving her brother behind, but she must. Besides, he would know where to meet her later.

As she rounded the last lion's ass, she saw him waiting for her already, crouching near the *eşek*. "Umit!" she whispered.

The man rose from his crouch, and she realized her mistake. This man was not her brother.

He was too tall, too well-fed, and too poorly dressed. The brim of a peasant's cap pulled down low, dividing his face into shadow and light, like the slash of a wounded soul. But he was no peasant. She could smell the earth on a peasant, even from this far away, but this man did not carry any dirt on him. The lit lower half of his face was clean and shaven free of any hair.

Most of all, there was the gun.

He held the weapon in one hand, and he pointed it straight at her heart. The slash of his face was a gaze like that of the evil eye. Her blood ran cold.

Meryem had faced a living, breathing evil eye once before. Long ago. The Nazi bastard. She sucked in her breath and let her scarf slip.

Before she could bargain her flesh and her gold for her life, the *eşek* lashed out with a hind leg kick and snorted. The man grunted and dropped onto his knees. The gun gave off a dull pop as it fell to the ground. Cursing, the man writhed, digging into the dirt with the toes of his patent leather shoes, shoes that did not match his baggy peasant's shirt and trousers.

By the time his hand left his groin to grope for the gun, she'd already beat him to it. Her foot pinned down the cold metal, the addition on the end that had muffled its sound. She lifted her sing-song voice to cry out, loud enough for the MPs to hear, "Over here!"

The gunman's gaze darted to the hillside where a solitary MP was already running toward her summons. "Whore!" the man whispered, his Turkish as thickly accented as hers. "You'll pay for this!" He cupped his groin and limped away, swishing bushes.

* * * * *

On her knees in the shadow of the tomb's portico, Anna clutched the letter to her breast. Why did the dead man have it? A torrent of Turkish words peppered the air above her head.

22

She looked up. The guard, Priscilla's friend Oscar, stood over her, pointing the bayonet end of his rifle at her.

She drew in a gulping, gasping breath and shifted from her awkward crouch on the floor next to the man's body. The guard shouted again, and the gleaming tip of his bayonet jerked closer to her face.

"He says to drop what you took," Priscilla explained from behind her. "And back away slowly. Don't touch anything."

"But..." It was *hers*.

Anna's chest felt as if it would explode from her bottled-up air. Her heartbeat felt like a runaway train. Here at one of the four corners of the mausoleum, a cool draft swept over her, as if the dead man's spirit touched her, passing from life to death. She shivered.

Another shout. Another impatient flicker of the bayonet. Its razor-sharp point glistened before her eyes.

She dropped the letter and tumbled backwards, scrambled to her feet and wrapped her arms around Priscilla. "Are you okay?" A *bullet* had killed the man in the western business suit instantly, she realized. And it had missed Priscilla only by *inches*. A violent shudder took hold of Anna, and she felt her strength flow out of her, the steel strength that she'd needed to carry her from her safe world to this new and strange place. "They must call for help," she added. "Tell him, honey."

Turkish voices snapped a response, and Anna stiffened from the sound of anger.

"He says don't talk," Priscilla said.

Anna sputtered. "But...this man...and—"

More Turkish words cut her off, and she fell silent, biting her tongue. There's a *sniper* out there, she wanted to add.

23

Maybe even the same person who had been following Anna. How likely was it that it could have been the Turkish peasant she'd seen? She wasn't sure. She blinked at the blinding light where she'd seen him beyond the cool shade of the portico and squeezed Priscilla tighter to her side.

They waited.

Time blurred around them.

Sirens whined a two-toned wail. Voices echoed, bouncing off the stone columns. Men in uniforms ushered them from one waiting spot to another. Others whisked past them, coming and going, clicking their heels on cement. Her mind, numb. Urgent voices spoke at her, and all she could do was shake her head and crush her fingers around Priscilla's hand.

No sounds of a scuffle indicated that they'd caught the sniper.

Every time she closed her eyes, it flashed through her mind: the image of the man in the western business suit, spread out on the floor before her, blood pooling beneath his face. For her niece, it must be far worse. Priscilla had watched him fall. She must've stood only inches away when it happened. Tiny spatters of blood flecked her pretty sundress. Color drained from her cheeks. What exactly had she seen? The killer?

"I just want to know if you're okay," Anna whispered in a shaky voice to her niece.

Unintelligible words snapped at her, freezing her. Priscilla continued to stare dully ahead, ignoring Anna.

Anna's palms grew clammier. She recognized the old, familiar tightening in her chest and throat that signaled rising hysteria. But she'd grown past those nervous attacks. She hadn't felt such uncontrollable anxiety since... Rainer. His

24

death. Twelve years ago.

That was over. She was well now. She'd finally recovered and moved on.

But there was still the matter of the letter.

The letter belonged to *her*. She'd written it. Someone had slit open the envelope. Someone had read her words of love. Private words. Not meant for anyone's eyes but Rainer's. Each time, he'd mailed the letters she'd written back to her for safekeeping. Almost as fast as he received them, he returned them, along with his own letters to her.

Except for the last batch. She'd assumed her last letters had been lost, circling the globe, caught in some backwater bin. Somewhere.

She'd assumed Rainer had never received them. That he'd died first, on whatever secret mission he'd been up to. Somewhere in the Balkans, that's all the government's representative had finally told her. Presumed dead. They'd never found his body.

But now...

Had the man in the western business suit died because of her letter? Maybe he'd known how Rainer had died.

Turkish police busied themselves, trying unsuccessfully to get their flash cameras to flash, and for a moment, Anna and Priscilla were left unattended. Seizing the moment, Anna leaned closer to her niece and whispered, in case any of the officers might be near enough to hear. "What did he *say* to you?"

But Priscilla responded by assessing her with a dull look glazed to her face. She blinked those green eyes of hers as if English were the foreign tongue.

"I wonder who he was?" A chill rippled down Anna's spine. *He'd* followed them, she thought more likely. Not his killer. But why?

To give Anna the letter she'd written Rainer. Because the dead man must've *known* Rainer. He'd known what had happened to Rainer. He'd wanted to tell Anna about it, but his killer had shot him first.

Before Anna could persuade Priscilla to answer, a pair of officers appeared at their side. They led them away from the tomb, down the steps, back across the concourse, filled now with several groups of gesticulating people, buzzing with gossip. Walking rapidly, their escorts pulled them along, skirting the groups. Anna and Priscilla had to run to keep from tripping.

On the perimeter of the grounds, they reached a waiting van, and Anna felt her heart skip a beat when she saw the word "*polis*" painted on its side. Were they being arrested?

What was it Henry—Mitzi's husband—had said about the little red book? Her mind tumbled with incoherence.

"But we have diplomatic immunity!" she said, balking as one of their escorts opened the side door.

He waved away her protest and spoke rapidly in Turkish. Priscilla broke away from Anna's grip and climbed into the vehicle, as if eager to go for a ride. Now, Anna had to follow. She stepped inside and claimed a firm position next to the child on a hard vinyl bench seat.

The interior smelled of baked dust. A chain of blue beads dangled from the driver's rear-view mirror.

The van lurched, or was it her heart? Snapshots of passing scenery flicked by her window. City streets whizzed past, a flash of gray blocks and red flags, ox carts and donkeys and storks.

Oh, God! She'd heard stories about Turkish prisons, stories that chilled her blood. That must be where they were taking her now.

Chapter Three

Questions swirled through Anna's mind like a broken record. *Who was he? Did he die...because of me?*

"Who was he?" said the Turkish detective's voice in a thick accent. They were the same questions, again and again.

The rumbling sound of Priscilla's stomach was like an alarm that detonated around Anna, finally breaking through the surreal fog blanketing her mind up until now. She didn't know how long they'd been at the police station, although she vaguely remembered having been ushered into this office, along with the hammering of questions, in the same muddled way she would remember a dream. No, a nightmare.

She was inside a police station in a foreign country! Her hand flew to her neck. Her throat tightened, and she could hardly breathe.

Keep calm. For Priscilla's sake.

She'd done nothing wrong. The police had nothing against her. They were merely after something, information she didn't have. Well, so was she.

Anna blinked at her surroundings, seeing them through clear eyes as if for the first time. They sat rigidly on metal folding chairs on the visitor's side of a steel gray desk. The furniture suggested that this could've been any office in the States.

Except it clearly wasn't.

A portrait of a balding Atatürk solemnly watched over them from his central position on the cracked plaster wall. A framed diploma from Indiana University hung beside the Father of Turkey. On the desk, a round, copper tray held three demitasse cups, lined with the dregs of Turkish coffee.

Anna didn't remember drinking hers, although the bitter aftertaste lingered on her tongue. She remembered telling what little she knew to Veli Yaziz, the detective with the National Police who now sat across the desk from them.

She sucked air into her lungs and coughed. "I-I've told you all I know," Anna said, forcing her tight, squeaky voice down into a lower, calmer register. "I really must take my niece home immediately. Give her supper." If she couldn't control the events surrounding her, then she could at least return Priscilla to a sense of normalcy. A police station was no place for a child. Above all else, Anna's mission was to protect Priscilla. She reached across the narrow space between their metal chairs to rub her niece's arm.

"Of course, Meess Reeddle. A man from dee embassy will be here soon for you." The detective's English seemed fluent, except for his inability to pronounce "th's" and short "i's."

"And...you'll put a guard on our house?" Anna continued. "Since you haven't found...whoever shot him?" She'd told him about the person in balloon-style peasant pants that she'd glimpsed behind the lion statues, but Yaziz didn't seem too concerned. He didn't seem to think that the peasant could be the same person who'd shot the man holding her letter. Or that she and Priscilla were in any danger from whoever had killed him. What was wrong with this detective? Why couldn't he see that the shooter would come after her and Priscilla next? He had to think they could identify him. And maybe Priscilla could.

Yaziz steepled his fingers beneath a day's growth of salt and pepper whiskers, as if he mentally toyed with her request. A tired sag pulled at the area hidden behind horn-rimmed frames, their lenses tinted gold. "You are certain," he said, "that you do not know who was the dead man?"

She shook her head and dug her nails into the flesh of her palms to stop her trembling. "I've already told you. I've never seen him before." She wished he wouldn't use that word—*dead*—in front of Priscilla. "But you must know by now who he is. Was. Surely you've gone through his pockets and found his identity yourself. Who was he?"

"There is a name sewn into the label inside his suit jacket," Yaziz said, instead of answering.

"Well? What's it say?"

"Perhaps you will tell us."

"How would I know?" The detective infuriated her, which chased away the fading remnants of her anxiety attack. She took a deep breath.

Yaziz picked up her letter, sealed in plastic, and waved it in front of her. "Perhaps you will explain this?"

Her eyes followed its swaying motion. She wanted to snatch it from him. It was hers, after all. Or rather, Rainer's. She remembered writing it to him. Seated on a boulder in the cottonwood grove on her mother's ranch. She tried to remember what else she might've written in the letter besides her words of love. What had she written that would make someone want to kill in order to keep him from giving it to her?

"It is personal, Mr. Yaziz."

"*Efendim*," Priscilla said, reaching over to shake Anna's

29

arm. "You've got to call him *efendim*."

Anna startled from the little girl's insistent shake. "Oh! All right, honey."

Yaziz dropped the letter onto the desk and leaned back in his chair to laugh. He had a soft chuckle that made his thin, shaggy head bob. "I see that young Miss Burkhardt will take good care of you while her parents are away."

He had that backwards, Anna thought, but she *was* grateful for her niece's apparent understanding of the language. Priscilla could bridge the gaps in Anna's knowledge. If only her niece would let Anna love her.

"You admit that you wrote it," Yaziz said. "How do you suppose the dead man came into possession of your letter to Lieutenant Akers?"

"I don't know," Anna said, barely above a whisper. "I was hoping you could tell me that. Do you think he stole it?"

"In London?" Yaziz snatched up the envelope again, and his stained fingernail tapped at the address. "Then he brought it here? To return to you?"

"I told you I don't know," she snapped. "The APO address was supposed to direct the letters to London, where Rainer was headquartered. At least, that was my understanding. I don't know where it went after that." Somewhere in the Balkans, she guessed.

Yaziz tossed the letter onto his desk, then leaned back with a squeak of his chair and aimed his tinted glasses at her. He studied her as if probing her thoughts. She would have to think things through carefully before she revealed too much.

"The Burkhardts left yesterday, is that correct?" he asked, surprising her with his abrupt change of subject. "Is it not unusual for them to leave their daughter here?"

Anna glanced back and forth between Yaziz, whose head tilted to a pensive angle, and Priscilla, whose eyes flew open to wide, green pools of inquiry. Her lower lip protruded again. Both of them leaned forward, anticipating her answer. *Careful,* she told herself.

She cleared her throat and explained. "My sister and her husband believed it would be too disruptive to pull Priscilla out of school since most of their home leave this time falls during the first quarter of the school year."

Priscilla turned sharply away, bouncing her red curls about her shoulders.

Although, who knew what Mitzi really thought? She'd been so remote. So unreachable... Anna was doing it again, protecting her baby sister.

Anna continued, more for her niece's benefit than the detective's. "They have a fine, American school here, you see, and it's growing all the time. This year the American military is taking it over and opening a new facility that will rival any States-side school."

Still, Priscilla aimed her back at Anna.

"Most of our American guests are anxious to return to the U.S. for their home leave," Yaziz said.

Anxious. Yes, Anna thought. That described Henry's state of nerves quite well during the few days between Anna's arrival last week and the Burkhardts' departure yesterday. Henry had brushed off Mitzi's fractured, almost dazed behavior to a desperate need for a vacation.

It was none of the detective's business about her sister's fragile condition.

"My sister and her husband have no home base to return to in the States. Well, there's my folks' ranch, of course. Henry is one of those career diplomats, who moves from country to country. Priscilla was born in West Germany. She knows no home in the States."

Yaziz drummed his long fingers on the metal surface of his desk, and with his other hand, he rubbed his chin, as if it itched. Or else he didn't believe her rambling tale.

She, too, found Henry's story troubling, which was part of the reason why Anna had agreed to come to Turkey in the first place. "Mitzi and Henry would not have left their child behind if I was unable to be here with her," Anna said. "Fortunately I could take a leave of absence from my job during the fall semester. Coming here gives me an opportunity to become better acquainted with my niece."

"How nice. What are they doing that takes them away from their daughter for so long?"

She bristled at the hint of sarcasm to his voice. Perhaps it was only her imagination. Today's extraordinary events had left her emotions raw, and she felt unable to make proper judgments. "See here, are you going to tell me who the fellow was? And why he had my property? I'm afraid I can't be much help to you until I know more about his identity."

"We are investigating that now, Miss Riddle."

"But you said you've got his name. Stitched inside the suit, you said."

"A name, not his name. Now. You were telling me the whereabouts of your sister and why you are here to care for her child?"

Anna shifted impatiently in her seat. "They're traveling

to places that are inappropriate to take a child, that's why I'm here. Their first stop is Kenya, where they'll go on safari. After that, they have not decided yet."

It might sound extreme to average, stateside Americans, but it wasn't so unusual for that adventuring pair. What made Anna uneasy was how inaccessible Mitzi and Henry would be. Should a problem arise. Not that one would, of course. But after today...

"A rapidly changing world, is it not?" Yaziz asked. His attention drifted from Anna to a spot above her head. He was looking at Atatürk, she realized, a man who had changed the Turkish world, yanking it out of its Ottoman past and into its western present. "My parents and their parents never left the home where they were born, but some of us modern Turks have seen places as far away as the United States. And even Korea."

She understood his reference to that war, and she let out a heavy sigh of impatience. "War is a foolish game of men," she said. War had cost Rainer his life.

Yaziz shrugged and wagged his head. The ends of his mouth curled down. "It is as Allah wills."

"That's 'kismet'," Priscilla said, turning to face Anna. "I *told* you about it, but you wouldn't listen."

"*We* control our own destiny," Anna said patiently.

Yaziz sat up straighter in his chair, squeaking it as he wheeled closer to his desk. He picked up the plastic-wrapped envelope. "This Lieutenant Rainer Akers...who is he and where is he now?"

"I wish I could tell you, Detective, really, I do. But I am afraid that's...quite impossible. However, there is still that man at the tomb today. You simply must find out his identity, and also the person who shot him. I told you already, I saw someone—"

Just then, a commotion sounded in the hall outside. She looked up, and through the office door's square window, shadowy shapes of people moved in the hall. The man from the embassy. Thank heavens. She was getting nowhere here. Scooping up her purse, she made a move to rise from her seat.

"Before you go," said Yaziz, "you must tell me more about this Lieutenant Rainer Akers. We need to know why your letter to the lieutenant was in the possession of the dead man."

"They were going to be married," Priscilla blurted out. "But he was killed in the war. Mama says we're not supposed to talk about it."

Yaziz's gaze shifted from Anna to Priscilla, then to Anna again. "This is true?"

Anna sank back into her seat and studied the geometric pattern of the Turkish rug that padded her feet. Until she thought it through, she would let the official story stand. "He died in the war."

"Korea?"

"No. World War II. He was on a special mission, I finally found out, somewhere on the eastern front, where he was ambushed." There. It was out. "Now may we go?"

"I am sorry." His mouth turned down again, and she thought that he truly was sorry.

Why should he care? He hadn't known Rainer. Her last letter from Rainer had arrived only two months before the German surrender. Twelve years and five months ago when she'd last read his words. A long time. An episode in her life that was over. That is, it *should* be over. She'd moved on. Or so she'd thought.

34

A knock sounded, startling Anna from her thoughts. The door of the detective's office creaked open, and a young officer poked his head through the crack. He exchanged a few rapid words in Turkish with Detective Yaziz, then withdrew. No sooner had he left than the office door opened again, wider this time, and another man—tall, lean, and angular—pushed his way inside.

The newcomer murmured something in Turkish and swiftly crossed the room to Yaziz's desk. A badge flapped from a clip against his thin, summer suit as he moved faster than any Turk Anna had seen so far. He radiated the air of a man with a single-minded purpose. Yet, he paused to wink at Priscilla.

Yaziz said something curt, and the door closed. He accepted the newcomer's hand, then turned to Anna. "May I present Hayati Orhon, the man from your embassy."

Anna lifted an eyebrow, and Mr. Orhon chuckled. "You are surprised they send a Turk for you?" he asked. A British accent laced his English.

The mole atop his cheekbone danced as he smiled. A lock of brown hair bounced carelessly over one eye, which reminded her of the color of milk chocolate. She flushed from her frivolous thoughts. Frivolity had no place in these somber circumstances. "Pleased to meet you, Mr. Orhon. Or, that is, uh, *efendim*?" Relief swept through her, and she tingled with warmth. An advocate had finally arrived to help them. She rose from her chair and caught Priscilla's hand. Even though her niece stiffened, Anna pulled her to her feet and hugged her close.

Mr. Orhon laughed again. The neat, narrow line of his mustache suggested meticulous grooming. "Call me Hayati."

Then he turned to Yaziz and said, "I'll take them with me now."

Yaziz shrugged. "All right, Miss Riddle, but I may have some more questions for you later."

Hayati's laughter vanished, replaced by a scowl. His voice dropped to a deeper, no-nonsense register. "We've spoken to your superior, Bay Bulayir. He will handle this matter directly with the embassy from now on."

Yaziz inclined his head, and his tinted glasses shifted atop his high cheekbones. "Very good." He bowed to Anna as if a rod had been inserted beneath his white dress shirt.

"May I have my letter, please?"

Yaziz frowned. "I regret that we must keep it a little longer, until we find out who the dead man was and why he had your lieutenant's letter in his possession. I am sure you understand."

It had been worth a try, she thought, nodding. However, she did not understand. She had never understood the circumstances of Rainer's death.

And today, she understood even less. She couldn't believe that the man who'd been shot before Priscilla's very eyes had "found" her letter and decided to return it to her. How did he know where to find her? No, it seemed more likely that Rainer had *given* the letter to the Turk with instructions to take it to Anna.

But that didn't make sense, either. After all this time, why now? Because Anna had come to Turkey? The man in the western business suit couldn't have known that would ever happen. And then he'd died for his effort, his deathbed promise made to Rainer all those years ago. Unless...

Perhaps Rainer had never died.

Chapter Four

The copper pots strapped to the *eşek's* side clanked and bumped the entire journey, all three kilometers to Kavaklidere from the pasha's shrine. Meryem chose the paths through open fields that riddled the fringes of Ankara rather than follow Atatürk Bulvari, the spine of the city.

She'd had to leave behind one of her gold bracelets in order to escape past the MP's nose without annoying questions. Umit would pay her back, she'd see to that.

Meanwhile, it did not bode well with her that the *eşek* had lost its blue beads in that tussle back there with the gunman at *Anit Kabir*. How would she and Umit ward off the evil eye without the beads? She needed them now more than ever. Already, evil sought her out.

She knew. The high-low cry of sirens pounding through the city center in the distance told her so.

It was too late for her to go back for the beads. Not even *she* could slip unnoticed, once again, past the MPs. By now they would've added reinforcements to plug the holes that had allowed her escape.

Here in the fields she could breathe, at least for now. The fields offered a more direct route to the profitable neighborhoods of settled homes to the south and west. Out here, she could blend amongst peasants. They smelled the Rom in her and gave her room to pass. The city *gadje* with their prying eyes, on the other hand, would never leave her alone.

Meryem would've welcomed the shade from the boulevard's thick line of chestnut trees. Sweat seldom bothered her, except for a ring around her belly, but now she felt the drips of moisture coat her skin like a slick undergarment, binding her. There was no shade out here in the open, and the sun's rays scorched through the heavy folds of her costume that covered her body except for her face and her hands.

Still, *this* was a better route for peasants, not that she was one herself. She was Rom, first and foremost. If it suited her needs to disappear into the background, she could be a peasant.

Except for her hands.

Hers were not the coarse, red hands with crooked, bumpy fingers of peasants who worked the fields, threshing wheat. She prided herself on her hands, the way they could tempt money away from the *gadje*. Hers were a dancer's hands, with smooth, soft flesh and long, graceful fingers that knew how to melt seasoned men into hapless puppies. Her fingers could undulate through the air and read a *gadje's* fortune, all for lira.

Beads of sweat glistened along her fingers that clutched the rope leading the *eşek*. She reminded herself that today, without Umit, the fields were a necessary choice rather than the central boulevard. Atatürk Bulvari housed embassy after embassy, where enough MPs to fill an army observed the comings and goings of passersby. She did not want anyone as observant as they to hear the rhythmic bump of her pots and wonder what out-of-place object might be hidden inside one of them.

Better, not to arouse any questions. Not until she could find a more secure hiding place, one that would not give away the presence of the gun. She must keep it hidden until she found Umit.

And she *would* find Umit.

He owed her.

He would know what to do with the gun, although she thought it would be better to get rid of it. She had no idea how much it would fetch, but at least a few hundred lira, more than a night's work of dance.

She knew of someone, an old, retired *asker*, who worked the black market from the rich neighborhood on the hill ahead. Those military men could never resist weapons, never purge their love of violence from their blood. But he would ask questions. Her mind danced through different stories to explain how she'd acquired the gun.

By the time Meryem crossed her last field and led the *eşek* out onto the pavement of Güven Evler, where the terrain was still flat, she settled on one of the stories. The gun had been a gift to her brother from their grandfather, she would say, a family heirloom that he had to sell in order to feed his children.

"Shine your pots!" she called out in Turkish as she strolled down the middle of the street. Her sing-song voice disguised her Romani accent.

Nothing moved. No cars, not that very many cars ever wandered here to the residential neighborhoods in the first place. Not even other hawkers were out in this blistering heat. She watched for movement at the windows of the few apartments scattered through this scanty neighborhood where there were more fields than cement, but no one moved in them, either. No one seemed interested in her services today.

Just as well. It was Umit's job to handle the pots. She didn't care to ruin her hands, doing his work for him. Besides, shining pots wasn't the real reason they came here. It was a way for them to look for more lucrative jobs requiring her talents.

At the end of this street was a vacant lot with a few trees, a cool place where she and her brother always sat and rested before climbing the first hill into Kavaklidere. He would know to meet her here. "Shine your pots!" she sang again. Her heart was not in the offer, but if she did not cry out her apparent reason for being here, she feared she would be discovered.

No one stirred in response, praises to Allah, not that he was her god. She'd taken the expression as her own. Her skill, after all, was in knowing how to blend in. In truth, she had no god but herself.

She turned off the street and into the dusty weeds of the vacant lot. A small path wound down to a depression in the center, where a ditch cut through, and trees lined a grassy bank. The *eşek* trotted happily around her, brushing past her to lead the way to water, but she grabbed it firmly by its harness and yanked the animal off the path.

"Here, you!" she said, tugging the animal toward a dry corner of the lot. She knew of a hollow stump over there, surrounded by a protective cover of brambles. A perfect hiding place for the gun. Then, she promised the *eşek*, they would settle down by the water, the rest of the afternoon if necessary, to wait for Umit.

* * * * *

Anna felt breathless with hope as Hayati led her and Priscilla out of Yaziz's office, through a maze of gray hallways, and out

40

onto the street. She'd already passed through more phases of grief than she'd ever thought possible, until she'd finally tucked away her mourning for Rainer to a corner of her mind. That was years ago. She'd learned how to shut it off from the rest of her daily functions. Now it seemed as if that door had opened, and the grief poured out once again. If Rainer still lived...

Did it mean...could the letter...could it possibly mean that Rainer still lived? If so, it was a message that the killer hadn't wanted delivered.

It was too impossible. Her hope was futile. She stifled her hope and sucked in a lungful of the peculiar smells that overwhelmed her each time she stepped outside. It seemed that there were more animals pulling carts in the streets than cars, trucks, and buses combined.

However, a car parked in front of the police station. An American car, its dents and checkered trim indicated that it was now used as a taxi. As Hayati steered them towards the taxi, Priscilla broke away from Anna's grip and raced to the back door. The three of them squeezed into the backseat, and Hayati spoke briefly to the driver. A string of blue beads dangled from the rear-view mirror and swayed as the driver put the cab in gear and pulled out into light traffic.

Hayati rested his arm across the top of the backseat, behind Anna's head. How could he appear so relaxed? She tightened, unable to stop replaying the day's events in her mind or to keep her hope stifled for very long.

Rainer...alive? The possibility left her feeling...confused... dazed...delighted. Then her anger flared, smothering out all the rest. If it was true that he was alive, then where in hell had he been all these years? Why hadn't he contacted her?

Rainer was dead, she told herself. She wouldn't let herself believe any other possibility. She wouldn't grieve all over again.

"For a detective, he didn't seem very interested in doing his job," she said to Hayati, trying to shake Rainer from her mind.

"And what do you perceive is his job?" Hayati's eyes twinkled, as if he laughed at her skepticism.

"Why, to investigate, of course." *The murder.* She left that unspoken on account of Priscilla's presence.

"He cannot help himself. He is a Turk. It is not Turkish to admit to not knowing something."

"But that's the point of an investigation." She let out a sigh of frustration. "Finding out what you don't know."

"His methods may be different from what you would expect."

"He thought I knew him, that man who died."

"Did you?"

"No, of course not. And that's another thing. Detective Yaziz said there was a name sewn into the label inside his suit, but he never would tell me what it said. Somehow, he thought I already knew."

The driver glanced at her through the mirror, apparently curious about their conversation. She wondered how much English he understood, if any.

"We'll find out soon enough who he was," Hayati said. "The name in the suit was Henry Burkhardt's. That's why Bay Yaziz thought you'd know."

Anna felt splinters of cold run up and down her spine. The detective had released that information to Hayati—or to the embassy—but not to *her.* "That man at the tomb was wearing *Henry's* suit?" Her brother-in-law. "How on earth did he get it?"

"Fededa knows him," Priscilla said, swinging her leg against the back of the driver's seat. "He came to our house and talked to her."

Silence descended over the car like the aftermath of a bomb. Anna's heart skipped a beat. She took a deep breath, then found her voice. "Fededa." She let the name of the Burkhardts' maid hang in the air. Then, "So you *did* know him. Why didn't you tell us sooner?"

"No one would let me," Priscilla said. "Besides, I don't know his name. That's what you want to know, isn't it?"

Not entirely, Anna thought. The truth, she realized with a stab of dismay, was that she didn't actually care as much about the victim's identity as the information he'd possessed about Rainer.

Is he really alive?

She took a deep breath and turned to Hayati. "Maybe you can help us learn more about that man by speaking to Fededa. She doesn't speak English."

"It's a police matter," Hayati said. "They'll find out how the dead man came into possession of Mr. Burkhardt's suit."

"The suit doesn't matter."

"Oh? And what does matter, if not that?"

Surely he knew about the letter, too, but she wasn't going to inform him in case he didn't. She didn't want to bring up Rainer again. "His identity, of course, as Priscilla said. His family will have to be notified. That's what I meant about your helping us find out who he was. So that we can locate his family."

If he'd had information about Rainer's whereabouts, then someone else in his family might know, too, she thought.

"The police will handle it," Hayati said, "in their own way."

Priscilla tapped Anna on the wrist, poking her again and again. "I can talk to Fededa. She's my friend."

Hayati chuckled. "Oh, you don't need me after all, do you?"

He was still chuckling as the taxi pulled up in front of the American Embassy, a white building that looked as if it belonged among the monuments of Washington D.C., rather than here among the drab brown and gray blocky buildings along the chestnut tree-lined boulevard. Hayati led them inside to the clacking sound of typewriters echoing off what looked like marble walls and floors.

"Wait here," Hayati said, then he strode across the entry hall to the receptionist. He leaned across her half wall and spoke so low that Anna couldn't make out his words. The receptionist's giggles were clear enough, though.

When Hayati returned to Anna, his face beamed with mischief. "She's buzzing him now," he said.

Anna's spine stiffened. This man couldn't seem to respect the somber nature of events that had brought them here.

Before he could say more, a commotion of rapid voices, doors slamming, and tapping footsteps echoed from a corridor behind the reception area. A man and woman emerged from the shadows and paused their conversation long enough to glance Anna's way. He had a thick belly and she was thin as a stick. Both of them sparkled with American high energy and appeared middle-aged in their tailored suits. The man snapped a sheaf of papers into the woman's hand, and she gave him a mocking salute in return. She turned on her high heels and clicked away, down another corridor.

The man carried a briefcase and marched over to them. "Ah, Orhon," he said to Hayati, "very good of you to bring them here for me." Then he turned to Anna. "Miss Riddle, I presume?" He didn't wait for an answer but extended his hand and kept talking, blowing little puffs of onion-laced breath in her face with each word. "Paul Wingate, U.S. State Department. I'll bet you've had enough adventure for one day. Ready to go home? I'll drop you off, as I'm headed up to the neighborhood now. We can talk along the way."

His handshake was firm, and his palm, clammy. The tempo of his baritone voice resonated with efficiency. "Hardly an adventure," Anna said, but she sighed with relief in spite of her quibbles with his word choice. She didn't mind handing off her worries to someone else, and now she felt the tension that had boiled up inside her over the course of the afternoon slowly begin to drain.

He turned away, storming toward the exit, flinging a remark over his shoulder. "I'll expect that report on my desk first thing in the morning, Orhon." Then he stopped, noticing that Anna and Priscilla weren't following him. "Chop, chop," he said with a pointed glance at his wristwatch.

Chapter Five

Long after the American woman left and the reports started coming in from his junior officers, Veli Yaziz brooded alone in his office. Alone except for the ever-present shadow of Atatürk's guiding spirit. The Eternal Leader.

Absently, Yaziz reached into his back pocket and pulled out his *tespih*, as he always did when he had worries to carefully turn over in his mind. His thumb slipped across and around the first bead of jet, feeling the trace of a groove in its cool smoothness.

She was hiding something, obviously. Although she'd witnessed the shock of death, she had not shrieked or wailed or succumbed to hysteria, as he would expect most women to do. As, for instance, her foolish but very attractive sister, whom he had met at numerous embassy receptions, would almost certainly behave. Miss Anna Riddle, he suspected, was not as innocent as she pretended to be.

He slid the bead along its string and fingered the next one. Henry Burkhardt was mixed up in this murder. That diplomat had provided the suit that the dead man had been wearing. Burkhardt's name, although frayed from the bullet's passage, was sewn into an inside pocket.

And Burkhardt had brought the woman here, under the pretext of caring for his daughter. Why? It was abominable to think the man had used his own child for another purpose.

Yaziz had never trusted the diplomat, and with good reason.

Someone was lying, that much he knew for certain. His sergeants had already confirmed through their American embassy friends that the Burkhardts had left the day before from Esenboğa Airport, as Miss Riddle claimed. However, they had left for Frankfurt, with no connection to Nairobi. In fact, the airline had no record of any ticket purchased for departing West Germany at all. Why, then, had they *not* taken their daughter, in keeping with the woman's lame argument of birthplace?

Then, there was the matter of Henry Burkhardt's mission. It was common knowledge, that is, common under the table, that the reason he had been posted to Ankara was to keep an American eye on the Soviets. The Turks gave their unspoken approval to those affairs by not intervening. Turks did not want the Soviets to expand into Turkish territory, a strategic land bridge the Soviets had always coveted for its access to the Mediterranean.

The Americans did not make a public announcement of Burkhardt's mission, but they hardly kept it secret, either. Yaziz couldn't help but wonder what they *did* keep secret. What the Turks did *not* know.

Whatever the diplomat was up to, with perhaps Miss Riddle as his accomplice, Burkhardt had now crossed the line into Yaziz's territory. An unknown man lay in a Turkish mortuary. Unknown, but not for long. Already Yaziz knew that the dead man was no Moslem. His genitals had told him that much.

A knock on his door pulled Yaziz from his thoughts, and he looked up at Suleyman, one of the junior officers with tireless energy.

"This is all we found, *efendim*," Suleyman said, dropping a small bundle wrapped in newspaper onto Yaziz's desk.

Yaziz unfolded the paper. In its crumpled center lay a jumble of blue beads, some of them crushed and slipping off their shredded string. "Where?"

"Behind the north wall of the Lions' Road."

With his *tespih* entwined around his fingers, Yaziz lifted the bundle to his nose and flinched at the faint animal stench. "Any identification yet?"

The ends of Suleyman's mouth turned down. "The beads are coarsely made, like the type that would belong to work animals. Probably came from a source in Ulus. We're showing the victim's photo around there now. We'll find him."

"Good work, Suleyman."

The officer left, and Yaziz returned to his brooding. The angle of the shot that had killed the non-Moslem told Yaziz that the shooter had stood to the north of the victim. Had the beaded animal in question belonged to *him*? Or to the victim? And what had happened to the animal? Perhaps there'd been another witness.

He set the newspaper bundle of beads beside the letter— his other piece of evidence—and resumed stroking his own slick beads of jet.

Whoever the victim was, the American woman hadn't killed him. The shot had come from behind him, not at point-blank range. Furthermore, Miss Riddle was too much of a lady for such bloody business.

Yaziz prided himself on his ability to judge character. His wisdom came from his being *koreli*, a tag that gave him extra respect, all because of his army experience in Korea. The first time that Turks had gone to the aid of another nation had made them national heroes. But there were many things he still did not understand.

For instance, why had Miss Riddle attempted to meet the dead man at *Anit Kabir*? For an exchange of information? The question was, which one of them had intended to give the letter to the other? And, why? She had almost surely known the dead man, since she was anxious to have the letter. Perhaps it was her connection to *him* that she was hiding, rather than any involvement in Burkhardt's plot.

But Yaziz suspected the two of them—perhaps all three— were connected in some way. He'd detected guilt on her as if she'd worn it in the form of a heavy perfume.

With his free hand, Yaziz picked up the plastic encased envelope and held it up against the light from the single bulb dangling above his head from the ceiling. Had she planted her own letter on the dead man? For what purpose?

Already, his sources at JUSMMAT, the Joint United States Military Mission to Turkey, had told him that the U.S. military could not find any records for any Lieutenant Rainer Akers. They were still placing phone calls, but Yaziz suspected that the records did not exist at all. The lieutenant was a fabrication on the woman's part. That's why the little miss was told not to talk about him. Miss Riddle's face had gone white as *Tuz Gölü*—the salt lake—when he'd asked her about him. Fear. Of what was she afraid?

For her life, or for the coded message contained within the letter? Perhaps "Lieutenant Rainer Akers" was the code itself, and already a plan was set into action by the mere drop of this otherwise unimportant letter.

He sensed that some larger plot was brewing. Allah would reveal it when He was ready, but Yaziz could not wait until then.

He had studied in the U.S. and learned too many western ways as a result. He'd learned western impatience.

The mid-afternoon call to prayer warbled in the distance. Automatically, he dropped his *tespih* and the letter next to the broken blue beads on the desk and pulled open his bottom drawer. Within lay his rolled-up rug, but then he remembered his student days in Indiana. He'd learned there that praying was a habit he no longer needed. He slammed the drawer shut.

What he needed now was information. He suspected the American woman was a key instrument in Burkhardt's plot. Yaziz would get that information from her one way or another.

Chapter Six

Traffic was light as they drove under the canopy of chestnut trees in Paul Wingate's green Buick. Anna felt grateful for the ride. She and Priscilla had taken a taxi to Atatürk's Tomb earlier in the day, and now Paul saved them from taxiing back.

He grunted. "I'm afraid today wasn't much of a welcome to Ankara for you, was it?"

If he only knew, she thought. She didn't want to inform him of the full story, especially not in front of Priscilla, who'd found a comic book that someone had left in the backseat. Paul must have children. Instead she said, "Thank you for sending that man to rescue us."

"Just doing our job, keeping our people safe."

"Is he your assistant? Why does he—"

"Orhon? Naw! Good Lord no. He's just one of the Turks who work for us. A bunch of them went stateside to get their education."

"He has a British accent."

Paul shrugged. "By the way, I hope you didn't talk to that detective before Orhon got there."

"Well, of course I talked to him. It wouldn't be polite not to."

"That's not what I mean."

"What *do* you mean?"

"Oh, you know. Stuff. Stuff about our people. They're always after that kind of information."

"I don't have any information."

"Good. Best to keep it that way."

"Frankly," Anna said, "if I knew anything that would help his investigation, I'd tell him." The killer would be after her next, she felt certain. She bit her tongue, refusing to say more. Her fears would only worry Priscilla.

"No need to tell him anything. That's what I'm here for. My office will take it from here."

"I don't know what he's looking for, so I can't help, anyway."

"Coming from your small-town background," Paul said, "you may not realize that we have to be extra cautious these days. The Red Menace is a constant threat."

Goosebumps crawled along her spine at the reminder. Only last spring one of the teachers from her high school had been discharged, all on account of suspicion. It was so unfair! "That detective isn't a communist," she said.

"Do you know that for a fact?"

She didn't. "Anyway, what do the Soviets have to do with a Turkish police matter?"

"We can't be too careful. The Reds try to infiltrate everywhere. They want Turkey for themselves, you see. They've wanted it for millennia—"

"Really. I don't believe they've been in power that long."

He laughed. "Okay, it's an exaggeration, but you get the idea. Turkey could be the Russian gateway to the west. The free world won't let them have it."

"And you think Detective Yaziz is their agent?"

Instead of answering, Paul concentrated on his driving.

He neither confirmed nor denied the suggestion. Anna shifted in her seat, feeling uneasy. She glanced over her shoulder at Priscilla, who appeared engrossed in her comic book.

"What do you know about Yaziz?" she asked, unable to leave it alone.

Paul shrugged. "Not much, really, even though we've crossed paths before, plenty of times. Yaziz spends a lot of time with a fellow over in JUSMMAT. Claims they're buddies."

"But maybe they really *are* friends. What's wrong with that?"

"Nothing. Not really. Mind you, it's no small task keeping the free world free. I'm just saying you can't be too careful, that's all. It raises eyebrows when a guy like Yaziz shows up at our embassy receptions and gets friendly with our people."

"Why shouldn't he? He has a university degree from the States, so why isn't it reasonable to assume he has American friends?"

"Well, that's what Yaziz wants you to think."

"But I saw his diploma hanging on the wall back there in his office. What are you suggesting?"

"Nothing," Paul said, "and neither should you. Here in Turkey, there's the police, and then there's the secret police."

"You think Mr. Yaziz works for the secret police?"

"You'd better keep that to yourself. The secret is who he works for. What his instructions really are."

She hugged herself, not liking his implications. "Your Mr. Orhon said that Yaziz works for a man named Bay Bulayir."

"Ah-ha! And who does Bulayir work for, really?"

"How would I know? I don't understand what you're trying to say."

"Never mind. I'm just telling you to stay out of it. I'll handle that Yaziz fellow for you. You should stay away from him. In case he's putting together dossiers on all of us."

"Why on earth would he do that?"

"You can't understand because Turks don't think the same way we do. They're loyal and ferocious, almost blind with devotion. They make great fighters, as the entire world learned when they went to Korea, but as police investigators... Well, they're not very objective. They're more interested in saving face. It's one of their Turkish concepts. If they don't know something, you'll never get them to admit it. They'll just go on, pretending as if they *do* know whatever. Or they'll make it up. You can't trust anything they say. And another of their concepts that interferes with real police work is that the family unit is more important than the individual, so there's a bit of a hive mentality. All that makes them follow a different set of logic from ours."

"He seems well educated. His English—"

"Oh, he's smart, all right. He just operates differently. Doesn't matter where he went to school. He can't help who he is. Don't you worry about it."

"I'm not exactly worried." At least not about that, Anna thought. "And I *will* speak to the detective again if he needs my help."

"Don't ruffle your feathers," Paul said. "I promised Henry I'd look out for you. It was part of our deal when we pushed through his paperwork post-haste. He got his home leave rather rushed, you see. He wasn't scheduled for leave until June."

"Next summer?" She glanced again at Priscilla, who flipped the page of her comic with a loud snap. If Henry had waited

56

until the following summer, Priscilla could've gone with her parents without missing any school. "I wonder why he didn't wait?"

"Henry gets special treatment as a reward for all his years of loyal service."

"So, he used his seniority to change his schedule?" Anna said. "No wonder Detective Yaziz was suspicious about Henry's home leave. I got the impression Yaziz thinks it's not the real reason why I'm here. Maybe it's only because Henry's leave happened so fast, as you say."

"Right. See what I mean? Yaziz is fishing for information. That's why you need to stay away from him."

"No, I don't see." Anna's jaw clamped, the way it always did when someone tried to tell her what she could or could not do.

"Henry's leave doesn't have anything to do with what happened today at Atatürk's Tomb," Paul added.

"The poor man!" Anna shivered, wondering again who the dead man was and how he'd become involved with Rainer. And with Henry, too. She told Paul what Priscilla had said in the taxi about how the dead man knew the Burkhardts' maid. "Fededa must've given Henry's suit to him."

Paul scoffed. "More likely, he stole it. With your maid's help. He was just one more immigrant from a village no one's heard of."

"You know who he was?" Anna asked. "Did Hayati—that is, Mr. Orhon—tell Yaziz what you know?"

"Call it an educated guess. Villagers are flooding the city, thanks to Ankara's building boom. They've been flocking here ever since Atatürk made this city his capital. Like rats swarming to dry land after fleeing the sinking ship of the dying Ottoman empire." Paul laughed, apparently pleased with his comparison, but Anna's spine prickled.

"Except rats don't flock, do they?" he continued, still chuckling.

Anna thought his rumbling laugh was an ugly, out-of-place sound. She leaned against her door, trying to put more space between herself and this man's tasteless comments. She wondered how he could work here and maintain such a negative attitude toward his host country. She hoped other Americans didn't share his views.

"How about *leyleks*?" Priscilla said, breaking her silence from the backseat with animated interest. "I'll betcha they flock."

"That's 'stork' in English," Paul said. "You and Tommy need to stop getting your languages mixed up."

Anna felt a wave of dismay wash through her, and it wasn't on account of mixed languages. She wondered how much of their conversation Priscilla had overheard, only pretending interest in the comic book.

Paul went on. "We have so many of them here that you could call this the city of storks."

"We have a stork's nest on our roof!" Priscilla slid forward and leaned across the back of the front seat.

"Sit down, honey," Anna said. Her tone of voice came across too harsh, but her niece's safety came first and foremost. Priscilla flounced back in her seat and crossed her arms.

Horrified, Anna stared glumly out her window. What on earth did she know about eight-year-old children? She was a high school teacher, not a babysitter. She'd agreed to this arrangement mainly because family need was far more important than the needs of her classroom. Besides, she regretted that she scarcely knew her only niece.

Priscilla said she'd talk to Fededa, but would she?

They sailed along Atatürk Boulevard, the central street running north-south through the city, and passed an ox cart hauling a load of crusty bread. Splashes of color were painted across the wooden side of the cart and swirled around the design's focal point—a bold, blue eyeball.

Anna drew in her breath with a mixture of wonder, dismay, and delight, then turned back to Paul. "Do you have a translator at the embassy who could help me talk to Fededa and find out what she knows about that man in Henry's suit?"

Priscilla rustled, squirming in the backseat. "But I already said—"

"Your maid doesn't know anything about him," Paul said.

"You don't know that."

"Hawkers come through the neighborhood all the time. Doesn't mean that our maids *know* them just because they talk to them."

Anna sighed with frustration. "There must be a way to find out who that man was."

"They don't carry identification information on them like we do."

They turned off Atatürk Boulevard, and the green Buick was the only car motoring along these side streets. Locust trees graced this residential area of Kavaklidere, a respite of shade and quiet. Sprawling houses, low-rise apartment buildings, and cement foundations of new construction rolled across these gentle hills south of downtown. Vacant lots honeycombed through the neighborhood.

Anna'd had enough. "That man was some woman's son," she said, steeling her voice, "and maybe another woman's husband. Some child's father. They're grieving for him right now. Wherever they are."

"Ulus, no doubt."

"Ulus? What's that?"

"The old city, where most of the poor live. It's back there behind us, all the way across town from our neighborhood. On that cone-shaped hill you've probably noticed." Paul's voice dropped to a lower register. "Stay away from there."

"But why? Is it a dangerous place?"

"It's not a place for ladies."

His curt manner suggested he would tell her no more, but Anna persisted. "Why not?" She intended to go there. She would need to arm herself with as much information as possible.

Priscilla leaned forward again. "Blood runs in the streets."

Anna gasped. "*Blood*? Real blood? Surely not!"

Paul scowled. "Now, young lady—"

"But it's true!" Priscilla said. "Why don't you believe me? I've seen it. It's sheep's blood, Fededa says."

"Did she take you there to show it to you herself?"

Priscilla sighed, letting her opinion of Anna's intelligence show. "Nope. She takes me there because that's where the market is, and besides, that's where she lives."

"She shouldn't take you along," Paul said. "I'll have Ikbol talk to her. Straighten her out."

"But it's fun."

Anna asked, "Ikbol?"

"Our maid," said Paul. "She speaks English, thank God, unlike Fededa. I should've put my foot down when the gals found Fededa for Mitzi, but she's temporary. Mitzi couldn't wait until someone more suitable happened along."

"I like Fededa." Priscilla's voice whined.

Paul scowled and turned the corner onto Yeşilyurt Sokak. The car coasted to a stop in front of the Burkhardts' yellow stucco house, and Priscilla leapt out. Anna apologized for her niece's behavior and thanked Paul for driving them home. When she stepped out and closed the door, the Buick pulled away from the curb, leaving her standing there alone, breathing the car's fumes. The distant warble of a muezzin, calling the local faithful to prayer, echoed her doubt.

Where to begin, she wondered, correcting her niece's manners? She followed Priscilla past Henry's car and across the flagstone driveway. Just as Priscilla bounded up the steps to the porch, ahead of Anna as always, the front door of their house swung open. Anna stopped cold in the middle of the driveway. An American woman with a wide, lipstick-painted smile emerged from the house as if she owned the place.

Chapter Seven

Meryem preferred sitting on her heels instead of the dusty ground. Waiting. That's all she seemed to do. She spent a lifetime waiting for her brother, and she was sick of it. *She* was the one whose deals supported them in finer fashion, and she deserved respect.

A twig snapped, and Meryem startled. "Umit?" she whispered.

When he did not respond, she half-rose from her crouch into a stance that readied her to spring away from trouble. The sudden movement sent blood rushing to her head, and she glanced cautiously around herself. The vacant lot appeared empty, but who could tell who was hiding on his belly, slithering beneath the tassling heads of weeds?

If it was the gunman, she did not smell his presence. She'd never smelled him at *Anit Kabir*, either. She took a wary step backwards.

Nearby, one of the stalks waved in the air, and a turtle crept out of the brambles, aimed in the direction of the water. When it either heard or sensed Meryem and the grazing *eşek*, it stopped, withdrawing its tasty appendages into its shell. It sat still like a rock, hiding in full sight. As she was doing.

She let out a long sigh, plucked one of the weeds, and sank back onto her haunches. She bit off the head and sucked sweet nectar from the stem as she contemplated her brother.

This wasn't the first time Umit had changed his plans without bothering to tell her. The scent of a possibly more lucrative deal sometimes made him veer off their original plans, dress in the western suit their patron had handed down to him, and send him someplace where only Allah knew, without thinking. Such lack of careful thought would get him in trouble one day, she feared. Perhaps the day had come today, if the gunman's interference and the sirens she'd heard were any indication.

Bah! Umit deserved to get locked up by the police. What annoyed Meryem more than worry for her brother, for he could take care of himself, was the prospect of lost income without his half of their partnership. That wouldn't stop her from their scheme. She would find another way.

The melodic chant of the local muezzin drifted to her like the buzz of a meandering insect. It was the signal that her chances for income this afternoon were waning along with the dipping sun. She sighed again. At least the gun was well hidden for now. It would remain hidden until she negotiated with the buyer at the top of the hill. The afternoon wasn't entirely wasted.

She squinted once more at the turtle, who still had not emerged from its shell, and tiptoed to the *eşek*. The animal shook its head as she tugged on the harness, pulling it away from the grasses.

"He thinks he's found something better than you and me," she said. "We will show him. We will find our own fortune." She nudged the *eşek* along the path, in the direction of Yeşilyurt Sokak and the floating song of the muezzin.

"Shine your pots," Meryem sang once they plodded up the smoothly paved street.

The animal balked, clinking the copper pots tied to its sides. Either it was reluctant to climb this small hill or reluctant to go back to work. She didn't blame it, but there were mouths to feed at home and still a few hours of daylight left in which to earn some lira.

The apartment building on her left, straddled by two empty lots, was so new she could still smell its drying cement. No one emerged from the blocky residence. No one scurried down its marble front steps, as someone usually did at the sound of her approach. Only three families—foreigners, all of them—lived in it.

On her right was a row of houses, where wealthy Turks and foreigners lived side by side. Today, their gates remained tightly shut to her calls. When she and Umit did this round together once or twice per week, someone along this street always found a pot in need of repair. Or at least a cleaning. The hired servants were kept too busy to tend to such menial tasks themselves but were in danger of losing their jobs if they allowed the kitchen utensils to fall into disrepair.

Served them right to live in such fine palaces!

Was it because Umit was not with her that they were not answering her call today? If she could not gain entrance to their kitchens, she did not know how to offer her other services. Someone among this wealth always entertained. Would always need her. The question was how to find them. She'd danced only the week before, one street over, but potential clients had no way of contacting her. Telephones were for the wealthy, not for her and Umit. She was solicited only by word of mouth through the servants.

Suddenly the *eşek* broke into a trot and headed for the

empty lot uphill from the apartment building. "Here, you lazy animal," she muttered under her breath. It never wanted to work for her. Only Umit could make the donkey cooperate.

She pulled on its harness, but it was no use. So she let it lead the way, as if she'd planned all along for this diversion. She could take the extra time to readjust its straps. Unlike the open field at the bottom of the hill where they'd waited for Umit, this piece of empty land wedged between the low apartment building on the downhill side and a sprawling yellow house on the uphill side. No stream flowed through here, and once the eşek discovered the lack of water, it wouldn't remain here long. So Meryem thought.

* * * * *

Anna tried to remember the name of the woman standing in the front door of Mitzi's house, waving at Paul's departing car. A cigarette angled between her fingers, manicured red to match her lips. Anna had met so many of Mitzi's friends during the whirlwind of introductions in the space of a few days before her sister left town. This woman, she recognized, was the Burkhardts' closest American neighbor, living on the next street over. Their backyards touched.

"Miss Cora!" Priscilla shouted. She ran to the woman, flung her arms around her, and nestled against her full skirt.

Anna felt a twinge of jealousy flick through her.

"There, there, dear," Cora said, patting her.

"They shot him! That man who comes here for Fededa." Priscilla turned loose and dug into a pocket of her own skirt. "Look what he gave me." She pulled out a chain—some sort of

66

necklace—and handed it over.

Dread pulsed through Anna. With her anxiety about the dead man and questions about Rainer and the letter, she'd forgotten about the way her niece had hidden her hand behind her back at the tomb. The dead man had given Priscilla the necklace, and then she'd said *hayir*. No.

Why hadn't she told anyone about this before now? *No one would let me*, Priscilla had said in the taxi with Hayati, in reference to recognizing the man in Henry's suit.

Priscilla had kept the trinket hidden from *her* all this time—and from the police. Because she shared Paul Wingate's suspicions of that detective? Shuddering, Anna hurried up the steps to the front porch.

"Dear, you know not to take things from strangers," Cora said, holding the chain up, dangling a silver dollar-sized medallion in the sunlight. "Why...my goodness gracious. Is this a *diamond*?"

Anna froze to her spot. Sucked in her breath. It looked familiar, like something Rainer had had. She hadn't thought of his medallion in years.

"*Who* gave this to you, dear?" Cora asked.

"The gypsy at Atatürk's Tomb. What does it mean?"

"I don't know, but Uncle Paul will find out. Now, go dry your eyes and change out of your nice dress and into your play clothes. You want to play with Tommy, don't you? He's waiting for you in the backyard."

This woman—Cora—ignored the shock Priscilla had experienced, as if it never happened. Worst of all, she ignored it at this crucial moment, when Priscilla seemed ready to open up about the tragic events of today.

He was a gypsy, and Fededa knew him.

Anna reached for Priscilla, but her niece darted away, disappearing into the airy interior of the house.

"My dear," Cora said, turning to Anna. She closed her fingers around the medallion and lowered her arm to her side. Her gaze swept Anna up and down, taking in the unfurled strands of hair that had come loose from her bun, and the rumpled cotton of her flowered sundress. Anna could feel the bodice sticking to her with sweat stains and streaks of dirt.

"You look like you could use a martini," Cora said. "Do come inside."

"I'll take that now, thank you." Anna held out her hand.

Cora pocketed the medallion. "First, the martini." Turning sharply, she marched inside, chattering all the way. "Paul phoned me up and said you were in a bit of a jam with the police and needed our help. So here I am."

Anna felt temporarily blinded as she stepped out of the glaring light of the late afternoon and into the shady interior of her sister's house, cooled with cement floors and thick carpets. Gauzy curtains fluttered at the windows, and eucalyptus leaves scented the breeze. In the central room of the house, Fededa knelt on a prayer rug, with her kerchiefed forehead resting on one end of the rug. Cora stepped around her, as if the maid were nothing more than a fixture in the room, and sailed on, chattering all the way about the awful heat and dust.

Anna hesitated, feeling torn between her desire to respect Fededa and the questions that boiled through her mind. The questions could wait until after her prayers. Giving the maid a wide berth, she followed the trail of Cora's cigarette smoke through French doors, and out to a covered verandah overlooking the backyard. Cora headed to a makeshift bar set up on a card table. She laid her cigarette among several stubs in a brass tray the size of her palm, then clinked bottles against each other.

"We all help each other out here," Cora said. "Think of us as your family, dear. We have to rely on each other, you know, in this godforsaken place. I guess you'll have to get used to that from now on, if you're to stay."

Anna didn't think Turkey was godforsaken. It was a rich place, rich with layers upon layers of history, unlike at home. The American west was scarcely touched by its history in comparison to this ancient land.

Cora rattled ice into a shaker and mixed the drinks. "Because in the States, you don't have to rely on community as much as you have to here." She offered Anna a long-stemmed glass.

"No, thank you," Anna said.

Cora laughed, a brassy sound that reverberated with annoying prickles along Anna's spine. "Oh, go on, try it. Mitzi warned me you might be like this."

"Like what?"

"Prim and proper. Comes from being a schoolteacher, and a single gal no less, I suppose." Cora sank gracefully into a wicker chair, sipped the drink Anna had rejected, then looked up. She winked, as if they were conspirators. "You've probably been used to being on your own for a lo-o-o-ong time, haven't you?"

Anna pinched her mouth shut and set down her straw purse.

"I suppose it's for the best," Cora continued, "since everyone knows your kind can't hold your liquor. Oh, go on. Don't look so shocked. Mitzi told me all about it, how you two are really half-sisters with different fathers. Yours was some sort of indian, isn't that right?"

Refusing to let Cora think she'd successfully needled her, Anna crossed the verandah to put distance between them. A little boy, about Priscilla's age, dangled by one arm from a mulberry tree in the yard. Her niece, still wearing her flouncy skirt and petticoat, stood below and eyed the trunk, eager to climb up after her friend.

Movement from next door pulled Anna's attention away from the children. A man, dressed in a khaki uniform similar to Oscar's, patrolled the neighbor's garden instead of tending to prayers as faithful Moslems should right now. He hovered close to his side of their shared wire fence, not doing anything special, except appearing to listen to their conversation. Did he know English? Mitzi had warned her not to bother the people in that house. A Turkish general lived there.

Anna composed herself enough to face Cora. She returned to her side, by the wicker chair, and lowered her voice. "All right, let me see it now."

"See what, dear?"

She knew very well, Anna thought. Why was this woman being so coy? "The necklace Priscilla gave you."

"It's not important." With a fresh cigarette fixed to her fingers, Cora waved her wrist, casting away a serpentine ribbon of smoke. "Paul will take care of it."

Anna held out her hand, palm up. "I wouldn't think of troubling him. It's my responsibility to follow up on this matter."

Cora shrugged, propped the cigarette in an ash tray, and dug into a pocket of her gathered skirt. She produced the silver chain and medallion and dropped them into Anna's open palm.

Anna's little display of defiance crumbled. Her heart skipped a beat as she recognized Rainer's Saint Christopher's medal.

Chapter Eight

The animal's body heat hit Meryem in the face as she bent over its harness where its beads had hung, up until its frenzy at *Anit Kabir*. The sounds of tinkling glass along with a woman's high-pitched voice distracted Meryem from her work, and she glanced up to listen better. It always paid to remain alert.

She sucked in her breath. A dress she recognized, splattered with pink flowers the size of melons, swirled about the backyard of the yellow house uphill. The foreign *gadje* from the pasha's tomb today! Quickly, Meryem bent back over the donkey, so the pair of foreigners wouldn't realize she was listening.

Americans. That much she could make out from their English.

She didn't speak English well, but she had a natural ability to imitate bits and pieces of any language. This was a useful skill, especially now that Ankara was inundated with foreigners—mostly Americans—these days. She strained to listen, but all she could hear were a few words and all the cackles. Once, she caught the word "*polis*." The foreign woman from the tomb had come *here*, to this Kavaklidere hillside, same as Meryem. Their paths of destiny must intertwine.

Meryem slipped around to the downhill side of the donkey, so that she could pretend to work on its harness while watching

71

the American women at the same time. The woman from the tomb held something up, which sparkled as it caught a ray of light from the sun sinking behind Meryem.

It sparkled like...treasure.

Like their treasure. Hers and Umit's.

Was that what Umit's "quick deal" had been about?

The American woman had been there, at the tomb. So had Umit. This *gadje* must be part of the "quick deal" that had involved Umit. He'd given away their treasure to her. And for what?

Why hadn't her brother caught up to her by now?

A shudder rippled through Meryem, and her hands shook as she busied them with the animal's load. Her brother had proven himself clever again and again, she reminded herself. He'd evaded Nazis and Russians, dangers far worse than any Turk. He could take care of himself once more. She must believe that. There was no other possibility.

Movement on the far side of the Americans' backyard pulled Meryem's attention away from the women. A retired, Turkish general lived up there, in a pink palace on the far side of the yellow stucco. Meryem knew from their pots that the general entertained lavishly, usually once per month. The general lived there along with his guard, the old *asker* who worked the black market and was the first one she'd thought of as buyer for the gun. So far he had refused her offers to perform at the general's entertainments, but now that old fool would pay for his refusal. He would pay handsomely for the gun.

Now, she could see the old *asker* on the other side of the Americans' shady yard, on his knees, pretending to work in the dried-up garden of the general's house. There was nothing more that he could do for the garden in this dry heat when not even weeds could grow. Which left only one possibility in Meryem's mind. The *asker* was interested in whatever he was learning from these American women.

This new piece of information tantalized Meryem with possibilities of how she could use it to her advantage.

* * * * *

The instant the cool metal touched her flesh, Anna recognized the relief of Saint Christopher, the patron saint of travelers, and the weary wanderer riding on the saint's back. A white sapphire—it only *looked* like a diamond—was custom embedded over the saint's head. Exactly as Rainer's luck piece had been.

Anna's fingers closed tightly over the piece of jewelry, tightly to still the quiver that ran through her. She whirled around, turning her back to Cora as she struggled to catch her breath. Her entire core felt crushed, as if she'd been punched in the stomach. A stream of protests boiled up from within.

How could *this* medallion possibly be the same one?

But why *not*? The dead man had had her letter to Rainer, too. He must have known Rainer, if Rainer had given him her letter and his medallion. No, not his entirely. It hadn't always been his.

She felt Cora's assessing gaze on her back. "Do you know what it is, dear?"

"No, of course not." The heat of the flush from Anna's lie spread up her throat. She held Rainer's medallion to her breast and closed her eyes. Her mind tumbled with memories of different places. Different times.

Aunt Iris's Victorian house, Anna's house now, flashed before her. It was a place of lilac wallpaper and dark oak woodwork, so unlike this place of copper, brass, and Turkish rugs. Anna remembered Aunt Iris's words that night as she unlocked her jewelry box and dug into its cedar-lined depths.

I am but one old woman, she'd said. *Your young man will need this more than I.*

It was September 1940, the night before Rainer left to join the British in their darkest hours. Aunt Iris—Anna was her companion, not really her niece by blood—pulled out of her jewelry box the silver chain with its dangling medallion. Aunt Iris had made her Saint Christopher unique by having a jeweler custom add a white sapphire, a gem of luck. The stone above the saint's head suggested a halo and imbued the charm with extra powers of safety.

Carry this with you, Aunt Iris had told Rainer, giving it to him, *and it will keep you safe in your travels.*

But it hadn't worked. As Anna had always known it wouldn't. One should never put faith in superstition. That's all faith was, masked under religion.

"I think you *do,*" Cora said, intruding on the memory. "You recognize it."

Anna opened her eyes, feeling momentarily displaced by this Turkish change of scenery. She'd squeezed her fingers closed so tightly that the blood had stopped running to her fingertips. Slowly, she loosened her grip and examined the silver piece, smudged with the oils from her hand. A ray of light from the sun low to the west angled under the verandah's roof and caught the stone, setting it on fire with sparkles.

74

Cora's voice rose in pitch. "You think it's a real diamond? I know a jeweler who could tell us if it is or not."

Anna took a deep breath to still the way her heart thundered and turned back to Cora. The woman's smile might have been innocent, but it didn't feel friendly, not the way her head tilted slightly to one side and her inquisitive eyes, tiny black snake-eye nuggets, probed, always on the lookout for gossip.

"I wouldn't know," Anna said, trying to feign disinterest. She strode across the verandah toward her purse. Quickly, she dropped Rainer's medallion inside and twisted the catch firmly closed.

Cora screeched. "What are you doing? I'll give it to Paul. He'll take care of it." At the sound of her shrill voice, the soldier neighbor looked up from his work by the fence.

Anna anchored her hands beneath her arms to keep them from shaking and to keep Cora from detecting her agitation. She didn't trust Mitzi's friend.

Avoiding her, she fixed her attention on the backyard. Priscilla was slowly inching her way up the trunk of the mulberry tree.

"Priscilla," Anna called, "if you want to climb trees, then you need to change your clothes, as you were told by Mrs..." Anna turned and gave "Miss Cora" a quizzical look.

"Wingate," she said.

Of course, Anna thought. The wife of the rude embassy man who'd driven her home. That's why Paul Wingate had phoned up this particular, nosy neighbor.

"Ah, do I have to?" Priscilla whined.

"Yes, dear," Cora said. "Now scoot. The faster you change, the more time you'll have to play."

Priscilla reluctantly stomped up the steps to the verandah, where she paused to stick out her tongue at Anna. "I wish you'd never come!" Before Anna could find her voice and respond, the child disappeared inside the house.

"Just a minute, young lady," said Anna.

But all that remained of the passage of the little tornado, her niece, was the swish of curtains.

"You mustn't mind Prissy," said Cora. "She doesn't mean what she says."

"I think she does," said Anna. "But now she's stuck with *me*."

Cora laughed. "Aren't you the funny one? Seriously, dear, now that Prissy's gone, I'll just take that little charm of hers, so I can give it to Paul to handle."

"Don't bother yourself. I'll turn it over to the police myself." Anna thought she had enough problems without the resistance of the Americans. They were all supposed to be on the same side.

She took Cora firmly by the arm. "Look, you've been very kind, but I must ask you to leave now. Priscilla and I...need some time alone together. I'm sure you understand."

"But..." Cora protested, shaking her off. "You haven't told me yet about all the fuss, and I'm dying to hear. Paul said that whatever you did to upset the guards today at the tomb was innocent, but really dear, you should be more careful—"

"No, it was nothing like that." Anna realized that Cora didn't know about the murder. Paul must be protecting his wife from ugly news that he deemed unsuitable for a lady.

"Atatürk is their national hero," Cora continued, "and you can't be too careful around icons to him. It's awfully easy for

Turks, especially the *asker*, to interpret disrespect when you're really just going about your business."

"Oscar?" Anna wondered how Cora knew about Priscilla's guard friend.

Cora waved her hand with a delicate, Mitzi-like flick of her wrist. "*Asker*," Cora said. "Not Oscar."

If there was a difference, Anna didn't hear it.

Cora explained. "*Asker* is the Turkish word for 'soldier.' That's something else you have to respect. Their army. I'm surprised that Henry didn't leave you a copy of the orientation memos. Everyone attached to USOM is supposed to read them. Oh dear. Paul will get you a copy. That will save you from further embarrassment."

Embarrassment for whom, Anna wondered. And she did have those documents. Why did everyone speak in acronyms here? It was the United States Overseas Mission. USOM.

Anna had become the unwanted object of scrutiny, first on the part of Turkish police, and now, the nosy, American neighbor, Cora Wingate. Unlike her sister, who thrived under attention, Anna preferred *not* to be noticed. She would rather stay home alone than struggle at social situations with people she didn't know.

Prim and proper. Old maid schoolteacher. Yes. It was all true. Since Rainer, she'd dated a few times, but the right man had simply not come along.

She'd made the decision to come to Ankara. No one had forced her. And now she would have to see her way through the chaos. She had never in her life gone back on her word. This matter was more than a question of giving one's word. She couldn't leave her only niece. Not now, when Priscilla obviously needed Anna more than she realized. No matter how hatefully the child behaved.

Perhaps she should telephone her sister and insist that she return. For what? To show Mitzi that Anna had failed?

Never.

"You're free, aren't you dear?" Cora said, jolting Anna out of her thoughts.

"Excuse me?"

Cora sighed. "I should think a teacher would pay better attention. I was talking about the little party Paul and I are planning tomorrow night. An end-of-the-summer affair. Everyone will be there, including an eligible bachelor I happen to know." She tittered and winked. "And a few of our, shall we say, more *interesting* neighbors?"

After Anna remained silent several seconds too long, Cora went on. "You *do* have cocktail attire, don't you, dear? If not, I'm sure you can find something appropriate in Mitzi's closet."

"I'm sorry, but I can't leave Priscilla—"

"Tish tosh," Cora said, flicking her wrist again. "You're bringing Prissy along. She'll keep Tommy company, and that's settled. Well, I can see that you're tired, so we'll leave you now. Tommy! It's time to go. *Now!* One...two..."

The little boy scampered to Cora's side, and they left, marching across the yard as if all along it had been Cora's idea to go. Anna didn't mind, as long as they *did* leave. But she wasn't looking forward to Priscilla's return, changed and ready to play with her best friend whom Anna had chased away.

Chapter Nine

Veli Yaziz rapped on the open door to the chief's comfortable office of mahogany, leather, and silk. "We've identified him, *efendim*," Yaziz said, feeling proud of his efficiency.

Adem Bulayir waved his fountain pen at a chair that faced the broad desk where he sat. He'd been scribbling on a sheaf of papers. Hastily, he stuffed them into a folder, which he jammed into a drawer as Yaziz crossed the thick carpet.

Yaziz dropped his typed report onto Bulayir's now barren desk, and then stood, waiting for permission to sit while his boss frowned at the document before him.

"Victim's name is Umit Alekci," Yaziz said helpfully, worried by the apparent distraction in the chief. Bulayir flipped through the pages, clearly missing pertinent details.

"What is this?" Bulayir grumbled, not finding whatever it was he looked for in the report.

"About the shooting today, sir. At *Anit Kabir*. My officers have tracked down the victim's identity, and—"

"You waste valuable resources on *this*, Veli Bey?" Bulayir flung down the papers, rose from his desk, and paced to the window.

Yaziz hated being addressed in the antiquated way that

Atatürk had worked so hard to reform, but he wouldn't risk his position by inviting his superior's anger. Bulayir could call him what he would.

"Sir, it is my job to investigate. Because the Alekci family has connections to the copper trade—"

"They're *tshinghiane*, Veli Bey. Gypsies. Nomads. Thieves!"

"Actually, sir, they're not Turkish gypsies. This family survived the Nazi bombing of Bucharest, then years of Soviet persecution, from which they somehow escaped two years ago to Ankara—"

"Enough. We have more important work to do than monitor gypsy squabbles." Bulayir took a deep breath and stared out the window. The boulevard bustled with workers on their way home at the end of the day.

Yaziz watched the chief's back, the way it heaved in and out. Bulayir's hands rested behind his back, the fingers of one hand barely bumping those of the other. A *tespih* dangled from his fingertips, and the fact that its beads hung unused indicated to Yaziz the extent of the chief's preoccupation. Something greater than the aggravation of gypsies surely worried him.

Bulayir turned suddenly from the window and strode back to his desk. His shoes squeaked, echoing the bluster that radiated from the man. Bulayir paused beside the handsomely carved mahogany of his desk and picked up the report on Umit Alekci, the only item occupying space on the glass-topped surface.

"You have no time to waste on this matter," he said, tossing the document back to Yaziz. "There is a plot brewing to take power away from the Grand National Assembly, and you will stop it. You will find the plotters and bring them in before they can do any harm to our lawfully elected Democrat Party."

80

Yaziz frowned. "May I ask what is the evidence?"

The tufts of Bulayir's eyebrows raised up, and at the same time the chief rocketed up on his toes, squealing his patent leather. Yaziz thought the chief would explode. "You have all the evidence you need," Bulayir said, "when the minister's office issues a directive."

"I see." Yaziz's frown deepened.

Bulayir motioned Yaziz to sit in one of the leather chairs facing the desk, and then he sank down into the other one. He templed his *tespih*-entwined fingers beneath his chin. "How long have you been with us, Veli Bey?"

Yaziz tensed. "Four years, sir." Since returning from his duty in Korea. Bulayir knew that.

"And you have been promoted three times already, have you not?"

"That's correct, sir." Promotions came once every three years for officers of the National Police, but Yaziz was *koreli*. He'd been one of the first Turks ever to fight on foreign soil for a foreign cause. The honor sometimes gave him unexpected privileges, and he was gaining steadily on the chief's position. Was *that* what worried Bulayir?

The chief cleared his throat and assumed a solemn tone of voice. "The Minister of the Interior has asked for you personally to handle this matter. You will not embarrass me by failing him. Do you understand?"

"Yes, *efendim*." Yaziz understood more than Bulayir probably wished. His chief didn't think he could do it, *koreli* or no, Yaziz thought, carefully removing a piece of lint from his silk tie. "May I assume, then, that I should start my investigation of this plot in the military?" That's why the Minister wanted *him*, an ex-military man.

Bulayir frowned. "Do not take this lightly, Veli Bey. I trust you will be discreet in this sensitive matter."

"Of course." Yaziz straightened with importance on the lumps of his chair. "I have an informant at one of the newspapers—"

"The newspapers print nothing but lies!" Bulayir shouted. Then, with the speed of a cobra, he snatched up a copy of the *Republic News* lying on the small table between their chairs. "Lies are what fuel the conspiracy." Bulayir smacked the paper against the wooden surface, hard enough to shake the brass table lamp. "But we will break it up."

Yaziz cleared his throat. "Sir, about the murder today—"

"An unimportant matter. Gypsies fight among themselves all the time. Do not bother me with them again."

"I was thinking of the American woman and child who were witnesses."

The chief dropped the paper and leaned back in his chair. His fingers worked at the *tespih*, rattling its beads. "Ah, yes," Bulayir said. "You are correct to be concerned for their safety. You must move with care in that matter. We cannot allow the Americans to become involved in our larger problem. They are valuable to us with their gifts of dollars, and we must not risk offending them, even though..."

"*Efendim*, they are already involved. We found the name 'H. Burkhardt' sewn into the inside jacket pocket that Umit Alekci was wearing. You think the Americans—"

"I think nothing, and neither should you, Veli Bey. You will find the plotters, and you will see that the Americans remain our friends. That is all."

"Yes sir." Yaziz recognized the dismissal and rose. The wound in his leg, a permanent reminder of his Korean experience, throbbed from his sudden movement.

But he didn't mind that pain, not nearly as much as he minded the pain in his heart. He despised what he had to do next. The responsibility did not go away just because he had received new instructions. Someone would still have to speak to the gypsy's mother. Who better for that unpleasant job than Yaziz, a *koreli*?

"And one more thing, Veli Bey. When you bring in the plotters, do not forget to bring in the evidence, too."

* * * * *

Meryem tugged the *eşek's* leather strap, dragging the reluctant beast out of the weeds of the vacant lot and onto the pavement of Yeşilyurt Sokak once again. If her brother had truly escaped the police, she thought, then he should surely have caught up to her by now. That he hadn't filled her with unease. But she banished such worry to the back of her mind. Someone still had to bring home the lira if the family was to eat.

The donkey's resistance pulled her off balance, and she slipped, staggering backwards a few steps on the slick pavement of the hillside street. Perhaps her strength abandoned her while she was distracted with concern for Umit. He was clever, although not as clever as she, and now she worried that a gun could've undone his "quick deal."

She'd seen once before, long ago, back in the hills of Romania another face wearing that same look of desperation, of pure evil, that today's gunman had worn. Evil had permeated

83

that Carpathian foe just as it had scorched her today from the pretend peasant whom Umit's donkey had kicked in the balls.

Had that long-ago horror finally found the Alekci family here in Ankara?

If Umit had also recognized that old evil on the face of today's gunman—and why wouldn't he?—then he would've gone into hiding. That's why he hadn't shown up this afternoon. He couldn't risk leading the evil to Meryem and to the rest of the family. If that old evil found them, they would have to run again.

The anger that had swelled in her breast earlier on account of Umit's absence now converted into anxiety that took her by the throat in a chokehold, cutting off her breath. There was nothing to be done about it at the moment. There was still the matter of feeding the family.

She tied the *eşek's* reins to one of the iron stakes atop the yellow wall that surrounded the Americans' house and left it there to sniff the low-hanging branches of the willow trees. Emerging from their leafy protection, she continued on up the hill, moving swiftly toward the pink wall that enclosed the general's yard next door.

As she crested the hill, rustling sounds reached her, like leaves in a wind. Only, no breeze moved the singed air of this late afternoon. She dropped to a crouch beneath the general's pink wall and held her breath to aid her hearing.

Whispering voices.

She crept to the edge of the wall, where a wrought-iron gate revealed a view into the general's yard. The garden inside was designed like one of the formal parks in Yenişehir, the new business district of the city. Both there and here, gravel paths followed a crisscross design, where planting beds lay between the paths' intersections.

Meryem's gaze followed the source of the whispering to a grove of young trees, protected by a wall of shrubs. The old *asker* knelt on the ground among an assortment of tools for the garden. Hunkered close to him was a civilian whose black jacket-clad back aimed in her direction. A newspaper-tied bundle lay on the ground between them, and the *asker* was ticking his head backwards in the gesture that meant a forceful "no."

Suddenly, the civilian rose and dropped a handful of coins on the ground beneath the old man's nose. He turned with a shrug and strode toward the gate where Meryem spied on them. His step on long, thin legs was brisk, unlike that of the Turks she knew.

She didn't know this man, but she *had* seen him before. Somewhere. Where, she could not remember, but with hair like his, how could she forget? Hair curled in black coils as thick as a lamb's coat, sheared to a point hanging low over his forehead. Hair curled up from the ends of a thick mustache. His nose shaped like a hawk poked out of all that hair, flapping as he walked, no, raced. He closed in on Meryem.

She jerked away from the wrought-iron gate and flattened herself against the rough surface of the pink wall. She nearly gave herself away, crying out when a thorny branch from the general's yard bent over the wall and scratched her face.

And what if she had given herself away? She had every right to stand on this street, even though he might very well accuse her of spying. What was she doing, separated from her donkey that provided her excuse for fouling this fancy neighborhood?

She told herself to avoid it all and run away. Hide, as Umit was hiding. Her heart, thundering in her chest, refused to give in to such cowardice.

The soft sounds of whimpers drifted to her from nearby, echoing the sobs that deep inside her, pricked her heart. No, it wasn't herself crying out, but a child, perhaps. A child cried from the upper floor of the yellow house only a few feet away, over Meryem's right shoulder.

She couldn't be bothered by a child, not when the gate to her left squeaked, and she turned to face the tall, hairy stranger whom the *asker* had sent away. The fabric of his western suit was a shiny black, not on account of expensive threads, but rather its worn thinness. Beneath the jacket, he wore a cream-colored shirt of coarse fabric and no tie. Beneath that, black chest hair curled through the unbuttoned collar.

He was secret police, she realized with a sinking feeling of dread. Now she remembered where she'd seen him, and others like him. In her own neighborhood, patrolling the alleys of Ulus. The secret police were no secret. They wore their identity in the irked lines of their faces as surely as if they displayed a badge.

He recognized her as well, she could tell from the way his flat eyes went dead from under his sheep-like hair. "How convenient," he said, "that you have followed me. Now I don't have to hunt you down."

"Do not flatter yourself. I don't know you. Why should I follow you?"

"Then, what are you doing here?" His brusque tone meant business.

"Nothing," she said.

"Don't lie to me." He stepped forward and squinted past her, in the direction of Umit's donkey tied up down the hill.

"That is yours. You're one of the hawkers from Ulus. Don't you know the other hawkers have all gone home by now?" He inched close, smelling like rotting mutton. "You filthy, gypsy trash have no business on this side of town this late in the day."

He caught her arm in a grip that stopped the blood from flowing. Her arm went numb, then he twisted it in an angle that sent stabs of pain piercing her shoulder. Her eyes rolled back and forth, and she cursed Umit and all men in general.

"Why are you hurting me?" she said, her voice rising to a wail. Pain wracked through her as he ratcheted his grip on her. "I have done nothing wrong."

"Do not become too accustomed to the soft life of our city. You have no business in our affairs."

She refused to protest, and he twisted her arm some more. She swallowed a low cry.

"Go back to where you came from," he said, spitting the words on her cheek. "And take the rest of your gypsy trash with you."

His closeness to her brought him within reach of a thorn, which snagged a coil of his hair. His eyes rolled up and rested on something past her head and beyond the thorns—the source of the stifled sobs issuing from the Americans' house.

The gate squeaked, and just as fast, the *asker* shot into view, jabbing one of his garden tools into the secret policeman's back. "Leave her alone."

Her foe suddenly stiffened. His grip on Meryem slipped enough that she twisted free. Before she backed away from him, she spat on the scuffed, black leather shoe of his nearer foot. He was more peasant trash than she.

"I'll take care of her," the *asker* said, pressing his tool as if it were a gun into the back of the shiny, black suit.

The secret policeman lifted his hands up, showing that he carried no gun. He glanced over his shoulder, and when he saw the old man's harmless weapon, he snarled. He untangled his coiled hair from the limb, snapping the twig in two. By the time his attention turned back to Meryem, she was more than a body length away from him.

"I'm not finished with you, gypsy," he said, pointing a finger at her. "I know where to find you." Then he strode swiftly away, out of sight, toward the mosque on the opposite side of the hill.

Meryem breathed again and rubbed her wrist. "Thanks," she mumbled. She could've taken care of herself. The *asker* did not have to intervene on her behalf. But she was glad he had.

"A man of your strength needs something better than a garden shovel," she continued.

He grunted. "The general provides everything I need."

"But it's not enough. Maybe I could help you find a more suitable weapon. One with real bullets."

His breath rasped on a sharp intake. "How would someone like you find a thing like that?"

"I have my ways."

The *asker's* gaze moved up and down her figure. "The general wouldn't allow it."

Rearranging the heavy folds of her scarf to hide the curves of her body that the tussle with the secret policeman had revealed, she recognized her opportunity. "For only a few lira," she said, her eyelids fluttering, "I will persuade the general for you. At his next party." She took a breath and nodded in the direction of the yellow house. "Or I could tell my friends the Americans of your interest in them. You choose."

The *asker* grunted. "Come back later tonight. You can dance tonight." Then he retreated into the garden, slamming the gate behind him.

Left alone in the street, Meryem glanced first to the east, the direction of the mosque. The secret policeman did not reappear. Then she contemplated the west, where the *eşek* twitched at flies. Finally, she looked up at the yellow house. A small face, framed with curly red hair, watched her from a narrow balcony.

Chapter Ten

From the verandah Anna could see Atatürk's Tomb, miniaturized by distance on one of the swells of the central plateau that rolled along the edge of the city. She wondered if from now on she would always associate the place with murder and death. She wondered if the guard the police had promised to put on her house was somewhere out there now.

"Where'd they go?" Priscilla asked, interrupting Anna's glum thoughts.

Anna turned. Her niece—who hadn't wanted her here only a short while ago—was now obediently wearing her pedal pushers and watching Anna with a look of curious innocence. "They had to go home."

"But why? Tommy and I were going to play."

"I believe they had important business to take care of."

"But we just got home. They wouldn't leave already." Her voice rose to an insistent whine.

"Shhh, lower your voice," Anna said. The Turkish soldier, the *asker* next door, shuffled back into view along the fence.

"Why should I? What are you worried about?" Priscilla followed Anna's flicker of attention to the neighbor. "*Asker*? He just takes care of the general next door!" Whirling around and stomping across the cement floor, she created a small force

91

that shook the verandah as she headed toward the door into the house.

"Stop!" Anna called. Her voice turned to ice. "We're not done talking."

Priscilla's stomping feet stilled, but she didn't turn back to face Anna.

At least she had the child's attention, Anna thought. She'd take whatever small victory came her way. "You said in the car that you knew the man from the tomb today. He's come here to the house. Are you sure those two men are one and the same?"

"Don't you believe me?"

"Of course. I want to know who he was. I'm trying to understand why he came *here*."

"To fix stuff for Fededa, or something. He and his sister go up and down our street every week with their donkey. He fixes stuff, and she tells fortunes, 'cause they're gypsies."

"He has a sister?" Anna's voice rose with interest.

Priscilla nodded.

"What else do you know about them? Do you know where they live? Are there others in their family?" Someone else who might know about Rainer's letter. Someone who might know what happened to Rainer. Someone who could give Anna the closure she'd needed all those years ago.

Priscilla shrugged and turned to give Anna a wary look. Red splotches showed around the child's eyes. She'd been crying.

Anna felt stabs of sympathy and guilt. She hadn't noticed the residue of tears before now. "What did he say to you at the tomb today?"

"He said, 'Come here, little girl'."

"You say he's a gypsy. How can you be sure? He didn't look

like one, not the way he was dressed. Did your daddy give that suit to him?"

"You shouldn't make up your mind about someone just from the way they dress," Priscilla said.

Anna startled, then drew up her posture into a stiff, erect line. Priscilla had accused her of the very prejudice she abhorred. *She* didn't display her mixed blood by the way she dressed.

Priscilla tipped her head to one side, wondering, no doubt, why her aunt had gone silent.

"You're absolutely right," Anna finally said. "And I was wrong. I've been wrong from the beginning."

Priscilla's jaw dropped, parting her puffy lips wide with surprise. Had no adult ever confessed that to her before? An urge to hug her niece overcame Anna, and she took a step closer to her.

"What do you think he wanted today?" Anna asked. "At the tomb?"

"He wanted you."

"Did he say that?"

"No, but he asked me if you were Anna Riddle."

"Is that when you told him 'no'?"

"Of course not. I told him yes."

A sinking feeling weighed through Anna. Then, the man in Henry's suit with her letter to Rainer had known her identity. But even though he'd known where she lived, and even though he'd been here to the house, he'd gone to the tomb, looking for her *there*. Instead of speaking to her here, at home.

Why? Goosebumps tickled her arms.

He'd had something to say to her, but someone had shot him first. To prevent him from speaking with Anna? From telling her...about Rainer?

Anna swallowed hard to summon her voice. "I heard you say 'no.' When did you tell him 'no'?"

"He showed me that necklace," Priscilla said, "like he wanted me to come closer, so he could give it to me, but I wouldn't! Then, he started to fall, and he threw it at me."

Anna looked away. A bird sang from the direction of the apricot tree along the edge of the hill's ridge, where the house perched. She did not share any of the bird's joy. Her niece had so little trust in Anna that she'd felt compelled to hide such important information from her.

"I didn't take it," Priscilla said. "You know what it is, don't you?"

"Why did you hide it from me?"

"The policeman would've taken it away, like he took your letter. You didn't want that, did you?"

"We'll have to give it to him, you know."

"But you don't want to."

"Sometimes we have to do things we don't always want to do. You might've told me about it."

"I'm telling you now."

Yes, and it was a start. She smiled with hope.

"If I can't play with Tommy," Priscilla asked cautiously, "can I play with Gulsen instead?"

"Why, yes, honey, of course." Gulsen was the Turkish name Priscilla had given to her Tiny Tears baby doll. Mitzi had made Priscilla introduce the doll to Anna as if Tiny Tears were real. Now, Anna suspected that her niece would erase today's trauma by escaping to her imaginary world. She felt her heart twist. Tomorrow, they'd find something more fun to do, something exciting to bring a sparkle to Priscilla's eyes.

Ulus.

Priscilla rattled the French doors and skipped into the house. Anna heard her say something in Turkish to Fededa, whose wavering voice rose in a song. She sounded like a bird trilling.

Now that the maid's prayers were done, Anna hurried inside. A sudsy smell filled the air as she entered the narrow kitchen at the back of the house. Fededa still knelt in her balloon pants, but this time she'd rolled up her sleeves past knobby elbows and was scrubbing the floor with a rag.

"*Yok, yok, yok,*" Fededa said, clucking her tongue with each *yok*, a more severe word that meant "no." Her chin jerked up, emphasizing each tick, and Anna sprang backwards.

When Fededa looked up from her pail, dismay shone on her face along with recognition. Anna was the invading culprit, not Priscilla. The maid limped to her feet, bowed, and murmured a stream of apologetic-sounding words. Anna wondered how on earth Mitzi, who didn't know Turkish, communicated with her own maid.

"It's okay," Anna said. "I'm not going to walk on your clean floor. I just wanted to ask you some questions, that's all. About the man who came here to polish the pots a few days ago."

Fededa continued murmuring in Turkish, and Anna felt her chest tighten with frustration. Neither one of them understood the other.

"Priscilla!" Anna called, raising her voice as she turned toward the back stairs leading down to the basement playroom. "Will you come translate for me?"

While Anna waited for Priscilla to appear, she took down

a copper pot from a wall hook and pantomimed the act of polishing it. Fededa watched her, then grinned a toothless grin, imitated Anna's motion, and bobbed with excitement, as if she understood.

"Yes, that's it," Anna said, feeling pleased with herself. "Who was he?" Now she lifted her shoulders in an exaggerated shrug and gestured with her palms up to indicate her question.

Fededa watched her again, then understanding lit her face, and she imitated Anna's shrug. "Uuu-mit," she pronounced carefully.

"Umit? Is that his name?" Anna felt pleased with herself for producing the information without an interpreter's assistance. If Umit was a name, then it was something to go on to start tracking down information about Rainer. But how was she ever going to find a Umit in the labyrinth of Ulus?

Murmuring, Fededa picked up her bucket of sudsy water and disappeared through the back door off the kitchen. Then came a shout and an exchange of angry words. Anna rushed to the window and saw the maid sloshing the contents of the pail onto the grass beside the thin mesh fence that separated the Burkhardts' yard from the general's. Fededa and the *asker* jabbered back and forth, then the maid shook her fist at him and scurried away.

Back in the kitchen, she smiled at Anna as if nothing had happened. She headed for a closet in the back hall, where she pulled out a string bag, crammed full of her things. She flung the pail into the closet, on top of a small package wrapped in newspaper and tied with string. Then she slammed the door shut, told Anna goodbye, and ducked away.

"Wait," Anna said, opening the closet and lifting the pail to reveal the package. "You forgot something. Is this yours?"

"*Yok! Yok!*" Fededa clasped Anna's arm and pulled her away from the closet. Then she reached inside and snatched up the package. With her face drained of color, she tucked the package into her string bag and raced for the back door.

Stunned, Anna watched through the window as the maid darted around the side of the house in the direction of the street. Her lips continued to move in agitation, still muttering "*yok*" as she headed for the *dolmuş*, that sardine can of a Turkish bus Henry had warned her against using. Anna had only tried to help, but clearly the reminder of the package had upset the maid. Perhaps her "*yok*" meant that the package didn't belong to Fededa. Or it might've just meant that Anna wasn't allowed to see it.

Maybe it contained the rest of Rainer's lost batch of letters.

Anna's head spun. Fededa wouldn't have Rainer's letters.

But Fededa had known the dead man, who'd had one of the letters. Maybe the dead man and Fededa were neighbors in Ulus.

Puzzled, Anna collected her purse and headed upstairs to change clothes. She needed to find a hiding place for Rainer's medallion while Priscilla remained absorbed in her healing play. She continued past the landing to the attic bedroom that Mitzi had assigned her. Fresh clothes would help restore a sense of normalcy in a world that had turned upside down, she thought. She peeled out of her cotton dress with the gaily flowered print, now sweaty and dusty.

Then she pulled the medallion from her purse and glanced around the room for a hiding place. A drawer of her writing desk, perhaps? Too bad it didn't lock. There was no place really secure here, and so she decided on her lingerie drawer.

She slid it open and reached inside to lift up one corner of her silken stack. Then stopped short. She was in the habit of keeping her undergarments folded in quarters and layered according to color, but now she noticed the rumpled disarray.

Someone had been in her room while she and Priscilla were out this afternoon, dodging bullets.

Someone had touched her intimate apparel. Picked up her garments, handled them, moved them aside.

Chapter Eleven

Meryem led the *eşek* clip-clopping along the narrow street toward home. They snaked up the hill of Ulus to the two-room apartment she shared with her mother, aunt, brother, sister-in-law, nephew, and two nieces. As she passed the butcher's shop, she saw the butcher standing outside, leaning against the chipped plaster of his doorless doorway. He could relax at the end of the day with the rush of customers gone.

Not Meryem. Coming home without Umit, she had earned no lira today, not even a single kuruş. She had always thought the copper coin with a hole in it was worth next to nothing, but now she realized how wrong she'd been. A purse full of the coins could at least buy the family's supper from the butcher. His eyes narrowed as she approached, as if he could smell the hunger on her. He tugged on one earlobe, the Turkish gesture that showed his appreciation for her beauty. His cheeks puffed out, sucking on the stub of a skinny cigarette, making its tip glow while he filled his lungs with acrid stink. Blood stained his apron, and fly-covered sheep carcasses hung from ceiling hooks in a row behind him. The way he assessed her through his eyes and the earlobe tug made her skin tickle, as if she were nothing more than a slab of meat, a carrier for flies.

Farther up the hill, a flock of sheep, still alive, bleated. A small car was speeding down the hill toward them. The sheep stumbled along, trying to outrun the car, which worked its way into their wooly midst. Honking all the while, the car finally emerged from the sheep. It sped up, scattering cats and stirring other stragglers like herself to oaths.

The *eşek* balked as the little car raced by. Meryem couldn't make out the blue letters blurring across the car's side, and even if she could, she couldn't read. Still, she knew enough to recognize the blue message—"*Polis.*"

The butcher tossed the nubbin of his cigarette at her feet. "Gypsy filth," he muttered. "Nothing but trouble you bring to the neighborhood." Then he turned his back on her and headed into his shop.

She hurried her step, in the direction from which the police car had entered the flock of sheep. That's where her home sat, a crooked, wooden building.

Home, all the same.

Whether or not the roof over her head was crooked, she'd never had a real home before, certainly not for this long. Two years now, since their patron, Ozturk Bey—whose feet she would kiss, even unwashed—had found them in Romania and brought the family here. For whatever reason. She supposed he'd gone to the trouble of stowing them away first by freighter across the Black Sea, then by caravansary across land, to enslave the family.

She did not care.

Life as the great man's slave would've been better than their life of hiding in the Carpathians. Hiding first from the Nazis, then from the Russians. Not everyone had ended up as successful as they. Although, their success had cost the family dearly. Two sisters and a younger brother...gone.

But Ozturk Bey—who could understand what moved such a great man? He'd installed the survivors of Meryem's family in this apartment, brought them clothes and food, started them with their work shining pots. Then he vanished from their lives. She did not know why. She'd learned not to question kismet when it turned a favorable eye on her.

So, even though the upper level of her home tilted like a drunkard in a downhill direction, it looked as beautiful to her as the pink palace must look to the general. Besides, storks lived here, in a jumble of sticks caught in the crook between the chimney and the tile roof. Their nest was a sign of honor, and it corrected for the slant of the roof, too. Meryem's family occupied one corner of the upper floor, directly under the stork nest.

Surely, the police car had business other than the affairs of her home. Still, her heart fluttered in her chest as she raced uphill. The *eşek* didn't resist her tugs, as it could smell its own bed in the weedy patch behind their building. It knew this meant the end of the workday.

Once she released the animal into the dusty yard, she hauled its harness and baskets of copper pots up the narrow stairway to the apartment at the back. She knew something was wrong as soon as she cleared the top step and saw the door of their apartment standing open. Waves of wailing from within rolled out into the hall.

She knew from that moment. She did not have to see her mother in the arms of comforting women to know what the police visit and Umit's failed return and the gunman's sudden appearance behind the lion statues all meant.

She knew. She had always known, although she had not wanted to face it up until now.

She dropped the wicker baskets by the door, ran past the huddle of women, and slapped past the gauzy curtain that served as a door into the sleeping room. To the old chest where they kept the clothes Ozturk Bey had given them. Her scarf slipped from her shoulders as she flung open a drawer and picked through neat folds of worn fabric. The pieces tumbled apart as she clawed through them, digging feverishly among the drawer's contents, ever closer to its bottom. Then she uncovered something she'd never seen before, a tied-up bundle of paper envelopes so thin she could see through the sheets to slanted handwriting. Bah! It was useless to her, and she cast the bundle aside. Finally her fingers touched the soft hide she'd been searching for. She understood now. Umit's "quick deal."

She pulled the small leather pouch from its hiding place of clothes and clutched it to her breast, as if its powers could calm the erratic beat of her heart. Then, with nimble fingers, she tugged at the knots, pulling apart the drawstring. Inside the pouch nestled a few coins, Mustafa's baby teeth, and a gold ring. But the amulet, that circle of silver with the jewel of power, that joint treasure she and Umit had protected ever since those days of fear in the Carpathians... It was gone.

She cursed her brother. For taking their amulet. For making *their* treasure into *his* "quick deal." For losing their treasure, and for allowing himself to be caught. Most of all, she cursed him for dying.

All might not be lost. *She* had the gun. And with it, she could get the amulet back. She knew where it was, with the Americans. Except...she did not know the danger that had taken Umit. His danger would await her as well.

* * * * *

Anna tugged on shorts and a blouse, fumbling with the buttons in her haste. The USOM bulletin Cora thought she didn't have—she *did*—advised that personnel and dependents could wear shorts only in the privacy of their home. Not out in public. No problem. She had no intentions of going out again today.

She fastened Rainer's chain round her neck, tucking the Saint Christopher's medal beneath her collar. Wearing it was the best hiding place she could think of for now.

Her skin prickled with the uneasy feeling that whoever had invaded her bedroom was watching her still. But there was no one in her room. No one in the house except for herself and Priscilla, now that Fededa had gone home. The intruder—or the guard that the police had surely stationed by now—couldn't see her through the windows because leafy trees gave her privacy. She would have to phone the police to report this break-in. If that's what it was. The house was kept unlocked during the day, with Fededa here. Besides, she didn't wish to discuss her underwear with Detective Yaziz.

She sniffed the air, wary. She couldn't smell anyone's presence. Nothing besides the faint stench of dust, heat, and animals, rolled into one, the scent of Turkey.

A scratching sound rose from the yard, and she rushed to the window. It stood open. Had she left it open? Was this how he'd gotten in? Did she hear him fleeing now?

All she saw outside was the *asker* next door, digging with

his trowel in the parched soil of the general's garden.

He looked up just then, and she lifted her hand in greeting. He scowled back.

"Did you see anyone climbing through my window a little while ago?" she called out to him with the impossible hope that he understood English.

He grumbled a few words in Turkish and returned to his work, handling his trowel with renewed ferocity. His strength surprised her, considering that his grizzled face suggested he was an older man.

"Thank you, never mind," she called again, then turned back to her room. Goosebumps ran across her spine at the thought of someone riffling through her underwear. Searching for something?

Rainer's medallion.

Her fingers went to her throat and tightened round the medal beneath her shirt collar.

What if her intruder had been the killer at Atatürk's Tomb? Had he come here to finish the job that was interrupted today at the tomb?

Maybe he'd followed her home.

"Priscilla!" Anna called, springing to her feet. She'd left her niece alone.

Anna ran down the half flight of stairs from her attic. Priscilla hadn't returned to her room on the second floor. Anna clattered down the main staircase to the central room that they used for dining. "Where are you?"

She darted towards the kitchen, where narrow, cement steps led down to a walk-out basement. Mitzi stored boxes of unknown things down there, and Priscilla kept a playhouse for her dolls. "Are you down here?" Anna called, running down the steps. Still, there was no answer.

The Tiny Tears doll lay forgotten on the floor of the playroom.

Anna's pulse thundered. Where was Priscilla?

Chapter Twelve

Yaziz could've asked his driver to drop him off at his apartment near Ulus, but he preferred not to make it easy for the department to know his whereabouts. Bulayir was not a man one should turn his back to.

So, after delivering the news of Umit Alekci's death to the victim's mother, Yaziz instructed his driver to return him to headquarters in Yenişehir. It was the end of his shift, but he still had work to do and no family at home to return to.

He could not shake from his mind the stricken look on Umit Alekci's mother's face. Yaziz thought his own mother would wear such a look if she were brought similar news, and given his profession and the uncertain times, that possibility seemed more likely each day.

Alone in his office, he removed his tie, rolled it into a ball, and stuffed it into his coat pocket along with the clinking beads of his *tespih*. Ignoring the papers stacked neatly atop his desk, he nodded at the photograph of Atatürk on the wall, then left, locking the door behind him.

He avoided the boulevard and wound through narrow side streets, where he ducked into crowds to make sure he would lose anyone who followed him from headquarters. Not that anyone should. Until he learned the truth behind Bulayir's preoccupation, he would stay out of the chief's way as much as possible.

Even with his limp, Yaziz reached the nargile salon in only fifteen minutes, a walk that would've taken most Turks almost twice that amount of time. But he was *koreli*, a man like any other Turk, yet unlike most Turks.

By the time he reached the inconspicuous doorway, a hole in the chipped plaster wall beside a coffee bar, he felt certain he'd shaken the junior officer Bulayir would've assigned to tail him.

Who would it be this time? Resnelioğlu? Çinkay?

The sounds of burbling water and soft conversation mingled with the smell of sweet tobacco and floated down the narrow steps, promising to clear the worries of the day from Yaziz's mind. At least, for now. Coming here was similar to fondling his *tespih*. Both his worry beads and his addiction to the water pipe were habits that his personal hero, Mustafa Kemal Atatürk, would've frowned upon as idle practices typical of Ottoman decadence. But Yaziz, despite his worldly experiences, and despite his Kemalist leanings—although he was openly a member of the Democrat Party—was unable to shake either of these habits.

He paused at the landing to survey the men gathered here. Most of them were on their way home after a day of work and eager to share a bit of gossip and camaraderie. Yaziz, however, was more interested in listening than sharing. His workday never ended.

Low sofas angled this way and that, filled with men of all ages and all levels of wealth and poverty. Yaziz searched for the familiar cascade of snowy white hair that distinguished one old man. If his friend was in town, instead of away at his horse farm, Yaziz knew he would be here at this hour.

Then he spied him. Murat, a long-time family acquaintance and now a retired judge, lazed on one of the cushions beside an open window. He had nothing better to do with his time in town but monitor the lives of his sons and the prospective marriages of his daughters. Yaziz made his way across the room and stood before Murat's sofa, then waited patiently. The judge had clearly seen him coming, yet he continued to puff on his pipe, whose bowl sat on the thick carpet before him.

Finally, Murat removed his meerschaum mouthpiece. A smoke ring drifted out of his mouth as he offered the back of his hand, which Yaziz kissed to show his respect to his elder. Yaziz sank down to the empty space on the sofa beside Murat, and his movement gave him a glimpse through the window of the sidewalk below.

Erkmen!

Yaziz blinked and looked again. Erkmen, the man out there leaning against a lamppost, was certainly no junior officer. He was Bulayir's lieutenant, the one who'd tracked down the identity of today's victim wearing the American's suit. Erkmen was making no attempt at discretion. His black hair of tangled curls formed a V-shaped mat that made him stand out in any crowd. Perhaps he was meeting someone. Not really tracking Yaziz's movements to report to the chief.

Murat began the ritual inquiries about the wellness of their families, diverting the detective from the problem outside. That someone as careful as Yaziz had *not* shaken a tail gave rise to a gnawing sensation of doubt. Perhaps the distraction of the gypsies had clouded his effectiveness.

An attendant appeared beside their sofa just then with a pipe and a tray of tobacco. Yaziz startled, jerking at the interruption.

"Relax, Veli," said Murat.

Yaziz shrugged in an attempt to regain his composure and selected his usual blend, cultivated on a plantation near Adana. While the attendant fueled the bowl with tobacco and burning coals, Yaziz stole another glance out the window. Erkmen studied his wristwatch.

Yaziz drew in his first drag, then nodded his approval. He would wait until the attendant left before he spoke again, but when the time came, speech escaped him.

Murat coughed, rattling loose phlegm. "There is no need for you to hide behind those movie-star glasses of yours when you are with me, my boy."

"I'm sorry, *efendim*." Yaziz removed the heavy frames with the tinted lenses that he always wore, outside or in. He felt Murat's curiosity penetrate him, as it usually did when someone—even someone as familiar as Murat—saw him like this, exposed. Yaziz's one blue eye and one brown eye presented a flaw that compromised his authority.

"That's better," Murat said. "Now we are more comfortable, eh Veli?"

"Yes, *efendim*."

The comfort Yaziz felt, however, was not from his naked head but from the rich smoke that he drew deep into his lungs. Its warmth spread through his body, and slowly, he felt the tightness in his muscles drain away. The image of the gypsy's sorrow faded. The nuisance of losing the witness he'd wished for all along—a young veiled woman, the MPs at *Anit Kabir* had reported to his assistant, Suleyman—no longer mattered. The urgency of Burkhardt's plot, Miss Riddle's suspicious behavior, Erkmen's surveillance, and Bulayir's preoccupation mellowed.

Time slowed, and *this* became most important, this communion with one's soul.

"Now, perhaps you will tell me what makes you buck today like one of my proudest stallions?" Murat said.

Yaziz's right shoulder lifted to his ear and the curve of his mouth turned down, rather than confess the limitations of what he knew. The old man could be tiresome, but he was a friend of his parents, who'd insisted Yaziz renew his acquaintance with the judge when he returned from Korea and settled in Ankara. Now, he found Murat useful with his many contacts in this city Yaziz had learned to love for its rawness and explosive progressivism.

"A gypsy was murdered today, and my boss thinks it's too unimportant to deserve an investigation."

"But you disagree?"

"I'm sure it's more important than Bay Bulayir believes," Yaziz said, gazing thoughtfully at the window. Or, at least it was more important than Bulayir *claimed* to believe.

Yaziz couldn't toss off the gypsy's murder as the result of a squabble. After visiting the mother, he was certain there was no such conflict, not of the warring nature. The Alekcis were a family on their own, trying to make an honest living.

He didn't believe that Bulayir really believed his own story of a gypsy squabble. No, Bulayir was trying to sidetrack Yaziz. He wondered what his boss did *not* want him to find out.

Murat chuckled. "I see that your father has not yet convinced you to give up police work."

"God willing," Yaziz said with a shrug, "I will have as long and lucrative a career as you have had."

The two men sucked on their pipes, producing clouds of

smoke to accompany the heavy silence that weighed on their heads.

Murat finally spit out his mouthpiece and shrugged. "Mine was nothing special." Then he resumed his smoke.

Yaziz regretted his choice of words, even though it was his duty to praise a friend. Turks would not praise themselves. But Yaziz had evoked a memory that threatened to dampen the warmth of their company.

Murat had started his career in a lower court of Istanbul in the early days of the Republic, but he soon moved to Ankara, following Atatürk to the seat of his new government. After a life's service interpreting the Eternal Leader's laws, Murat had been rewarded only the year before with a forced retirement imposed by the Democrats. The Democrat Party had won control from Atatürk's Republican People's Party.

"It is always necessary," Yaziz said, trying to explain his poor judgment, "for a policeman to stay informed of troubles on the streets."

"What you need," Murat said, "is a wife to keep you *off* the streets."

Allah had favored Murat with an industrious wife, three sons and two daughters.

"Are you offering me one of your daughters?" Yaziz grinned. Even if the pleasing, younger one were offered, he wasn't interested.

Murat jerked his head back and ticked his tongue. "My daughters will have someone worthier than you. Already I am negotiating with Ahmet Aydenli for one of their hands."

"The assistant minister of the Interior? But *efendim*..." In spite of the light-hearted tone of banter, Yaziz felt wounded. He was destined for the top one day, perhaps as high as the minister of the Interior, who headed the entire police force.

But not if he failed Bulayir in this assignment.

Yaziz sucked again on his pipe, and the mix of tobaccos relaxed the knots that riddled his clouded mind. How could Murat consider such a match after the way he himself had lost his job? "I will consider myself a lucky man if I do my job as honorably as you have done yours."

Murat sighed. "What is it that you are asking of me, Veli?"

Yaziz frowned. "The Americans are somehow involved in this business of the gypsy."

"Ah. That's why you come to me. You want to know if their involvement means some responsibility. But your chief does not wish to upset our American friends—*my* American friends—by including them in a messy investigation."

Perhaps Murat was right, Yaziz thought. Bulayir was not a stupid man. He would've seen the connection for himself in the report before tossing it aside. Umit Alekci had fled from Romania—part of the larger Balkan area, where Miss Anna Riddle claimed her young lieutenant had been working undercover. Whether or not the lieutenant existed beyond Miss Riddle's imagination, geography alone tied her to the murdered gypsy.

Yes, that must be it. Bulayir wished not to pursue the gypsy's murder because he only wanted to steer Yaziz away from involving the Americans. But Yaziz could not help but wonder what the Americans were up to. Why Burkhardt had given his suit to Umit Alekci.

"This murder is another example of the increasing spread of discontent throughout the city," Yaziz said, certain at least of this one thing.

"Really? And how is a gypsy important to such issues as the trade-gap? Or rising inflation?"

Yaziz shrugged, implying that the question of relevance was an unimportant matter. He would never admit that he did not know. He did not know *yet*.

"It is all part of the national unrest," Yaziz said. "Demonstrations are no secret."

Murat spit out his mouthpiece. "They protest the Press Law, Veli, you know that."

"No. There is more to it than that. Besides, Menderes promises to reform the law."

"The prime minister's promise is as good as the newspapers' reporting of the news."

"Shhh," Yaziz said, glancing around, almost expecting Erkmen to have come up the stairs from the streets below and to now lurk on the next sofa within hearing distance. Not seeing Bulayir's lieutenant, Yaziz turned back to Murat. "It is troubling, the stories that are suppressed by the newspapers." He studied the wrinkled face of his friend for a flicker of recognition.

Instead of complying with the suggestion of a lead, Murat went back to puffing on his pipe.

"Your eldest son works at the *Republic News*, does he not?" Yaziz asked.

Murat's head, swathed with white hair as fine as silk, dipped briefly in a nod. Not only did Yaziz know that he was correct, he knew that Murat also knew what Yaziz knew. The question was merely a signal that their business finally drew to the heart of the matter.

"I have heard it said that *Republic News* prints lies." Yaziz waited while Murat slowly withdrew the meerschaum from his mouth.

"My son, Nizamettin, only writes the truth," Murat said, shooting puffs of smoke with each word. "It is the government that does not wish to see the truth of our economy printed for all to see. For this, they arrest journalists? Outsiders call us Yokistan, 'the land of not,' but is this the fault of those within who wish to convey the news?"

Yaziz's gut twisted in sympathy. He inhaled calming smoke, drawing it deep inside.

Spittle formed on Murat's lips as he grew more agitated. "God forgive me," he continued. "As a judge, I could never convict any of them for printing the truth. When I lost my job for that small defiance, it was as Allah wills. But one day the Democrat Party will find that it cannot dictate the truth that newspapers must print, not if we are to keep up with the modern world. Not if we follow Atatürk's vision."

Like Murat, Yaziz also was a man of principle. But could he go as far as Murat had gone? His own job answered to the very government that had retired Murat for acquitting the accused journalists who'd printed the truth. What would they do to Yaziz if he defied Bulayir's order to drop the gypsy affairs?

Yaziz glanced out the window. Erkmen was gone. Yaziz turned back to Murat and lowered his voice. "There is much discontent with the Democrats in power. There are rumors of a revolution," he said. "I am searching for the source of it." He waited for the offer of help, as it was not Turkish to ask for it himself.

"You have no farther to go than to the banks," Murat said, "where there is no money."

Western impatience twisted through Yaziz. "Your son must've learned something. He's told you, hasn't he? I must talk to him."

"You wish for him to lose his job, too?"

"Then, tell me what you know."

"I know that we are going bankrupt as a nation and cannot survive much longer without finding another answer. Most of the income we have so far, we owe to the Americans, but where that came from, there is no more. Their courtship of us is already over, and they grow weary of us. Perhaps we will have to listen to the Soviets from now on."

"You don't mean that."

Murat lifted his thick eyebrows and sniffed. "It is no longer up to me to pass judgment. We will see what the people have to say in the elections next May. We will see if the DP remains in power that long."

"Then you *do* think a revolution is imminent?"

"I say nothing."

"It's Atatürk's generals who plan it, isn't it?"

"I know nothing."

"*Efendim*, give me a name, a place where I can start to track them down."

Murat remained silent. His head tipped farther back.

"Don't you understand?" Yaziz said, foolishly disrespectful. "It's not up to them to determine the law. No one is above the government when it has been voted in by the people. It is my job to uphold the law. It is your duty to cooperate."

"My duty is to Atatürk and his dream, as should be yours."

"Atatürk's dream was to have a democracy."

"And so we have one."

Yaziz, who had other duties as well, thrust aside his pipe. He jabbed his glasses back in place, and sprang to his feet. "Western democracies don't have revolutions when the people are displeased with the ruling party."

"My boy, your trouble is that you have spent too much time outside our borders. You have forgotten what it is like to be a Turk. Why don't you ever wear your veteran's badge and let the world know you for who you are?"

Murat, his elder, was wrong. That badge earned Yaziz false respect, only for the killing he'd done in Korea. But Murat didn't deserve that answer any more than Yaziz had deserved such a blow—the suggestion that his Turkish core was tarnished! Yaziz wheeled around and strode away. His step pounded the wood, but his heart felt heavier than usual.

Chapter Thirteen

"Priscilla!" Anna called, swaying on her feet as a rising wave of panic threatened to overcome her. She felt light-headed, and her head rang.

She took a deep breath. It was more likely that Priscilla had gone outside to play, that's all. If she'd used the basement door, then Anna wouldn't have heard her leave.

Then she realized it wasn't her head ringing but the doorbell. She stepped over the doll to glance out the window and across the driveway. A wave of relief rushed through her. Her niece stood on the stoop and pressed her thumb against the ringer. With her was another little girl about her size, although dressed in flowered balloon pants and a scarf wrapped about her head in the same fashion as Fededa. Behind the girls stood a short, sleight man in a western business suit.

Anna turned and ran back through the playroom. She stumbled up the half-flight of steps and across the central room to answer the front door.

"Priscilla!" Anna scooped her niece into her arms. "Where have you been?"

"Playing with Gulsen. You said I could." Priscilla squirmed free of Anna's hug.

"But Gulsen is a doll. I didn't know you meant to leave the house. Honey, you must never leave without checking with me first."

"This is Gulsen." Priscilla squeezed the hand of her Turkish friend and pulled her forward. "I named my doll after my friend. Gulsen and her dad walked me home."

Anna smiled at the little girl, and then at the man who had been standing quietly behind them. "*Merhaba*," she said, using the Turkish greeting, one of the few words she knew.

"Good afternoon," Gulsen's father replied in excellent English. His gaze skimmed Anna's bare legs, exposed beneath her shorts, then flitted back to her face before he smiled in return. "I am Ahmet Aydenli, at your service."

He squared his shoulders with a confidence greater than his size. He appeared to be a man accustomed to having his way. His importance reflected in his business suit, which gleamed with a silken sheen and the look of a custom fit.

"Pleased to meet you. And I'm—"

"Yes. You're Anna Riddle." He did not step forward from his position on the top step. His eyes rolled up toward Anna, who was not a tall woman at five feet five inches but taller than he by a couple of inches. A blood vessel had burst in the white of his eyes, so striking next to the dark iris.

Anna's lips moved, but no sound came out. She cleared her throat, then said, "You know my name." She chided herself silently for the inadequate response.

"Of course. The Americans are well known in our neighborhood."

Mitzi and Henry were well known, perhaps, but not *her*, Anna thought.

"Won't you come in?" she asked.

"I am sorry. We must return home immediately. We live just around the corner."

Priscilla had overstayed her welcome, Anna thought with dismay. Her cheeks flushed. "I'm so sorry. She went to your house without my permission."

"Another day both of you must return," he said, glancing down at the Keds she'd changed into after her trip to the tomb. "And I will serve you some tea. My house is your house."

An awkward moment passed between them, and she realized it had something to do with shoes. "Thank you," she said. He lingered, waiting while the girls chattered in Turkish. Then Priscilla burst past Anna, dragging Gulsen across the threshold with her.

"I have to show her my game," Priscilla said as Gulsen removed her shoes.

Anna bent down to catch her niece by the arm and whisper. "Honey, they're in a hurry to go home."

"You don't understand," Priscilla said, pulling away. As she tugged, Rainer's medallion swung out from under Anna's shirt collar. Priscilla paused her struggle long enough to glare at Anna. "Why are you wearing the gypsy's necklace? You *said* you have to give it to the police." Then she twisted free of Anna's grip, and said, "C'mon, Gulsen."

The two girls bounded inside, and Anna glanced back at Gulsen's father with dismay.

"Never mind," he said. "They will only be a minute. I can wait that long."

"I'm sorry that we're interrupting your schedule, Mr. uh..." She struggled, trying to remember the various forms of address.

"Please. Call me Ahmet."

She smiled with relief. "Won't you come in for a moment, then?"

He ticked his head back, meaning no. "I would've asked you to come for tea today, but you see, I'm expecting visitors soon."

"We mustn't keep you." She glanced over her shoulder, but the girls hadn't returned yet.

"Gulsen has enjoyed becoming friends with your niece," Ahmet said. "Ever since her mother died, she has been very lonely."

His personal tragedy no doubt explained some of their social awkwardness, Anna thought. "I'm sorry about your wife."

He sighed. "Thank you. It has been lonely for me, as well. I stay busy with my work, and Bahar, our servant who lives in, takes good care of Gulsen for me. But there is an empty spot in the house now, you know?"

Oh, yes, Anna knew.

"It has been three years," Ahmet continued, "since my wife died. Already they are arranging another marriage for me."

"They?"

"My aunt and uncle. It is tradition for the family to take care of such matters."

"But I thought... I mean, with Atatürk's reforms, and all..."

"Not everyone wishes to break with tradition."

"Oh. I see."

"My aunt and uncle will arrive at any moment with the woman of their choice. And with her father, of course, who is a respected judge. Before the final arrangements are made, my aunt and uncle wish to see how Gulsen gets along with her new *anne*, that is to say, 'mother'."

"Congratulations," Anna said. "Priscilla and I must not detain you. Shall I go hurry them along?" Anna made a move to follow the girls to the playroom, but Ahmet caught her by the arm.

"The children enjoy their time together, no?" he said. "While we wait, you must tell me what you have seen so far of my country?"

"Not much. The airport. The commissary. Atatürk's Tomb."

"Ah! Our latest architectural monument. What do you think of it?"

"Um, very impressive, but..."

"But?"

"Well, unfortunately there was an accident while we were there today."

"An accident?" He frowned. "Tell me about it."

And so she did, standing there in the open doorway of her house. She told him about how Priscilla had run off from her, and how the gypsy had already been shot by the time Anna caught up to her niece. How easily it could've been Priscilla who'd been shot, instead of the—

"Gypsy?" Ahmet interrupted. "How do you know the man was a gypsy?"

"I don't. Priscilla told me. She recognized him. Apparently, he's one of the hawkers who come up and down these streets regularly."

Ahmet drummed his fingertips along his bare upper lip, where most of the Turks she'd seen so far wore mustaches. "And this gypsy's necklace she said you wear—it belonged to him?"

Anna felt her heart race as her fingers clumsily re-inserted the necklace beneath her collar. "No, I'm afraid she's mistaken. It belongs to me."

"Ah. Children. They often do not understand."

"Yes."

They stared in silence at each other, and Anna felt her jaw

clamp. She had no intentions of telling him any more, nor about her letter.

"Well," he finally said, "we must not allow you to have a bad first impression of Turkey."

"Oh, I don't. I realize that what happened at Atatürk's Tomb has nothing at all to do with Turkey. It's a terrible thing, but it might've happened anywhere. Now it's over. Detective Yaziz is handling it."

"Yes. Well, we shall see. I'll have my office check into matters first thing tomorrow."

"Your...office?"

"My office controls all police matters. I am assistant minister to the Interior."

"Oh. You mean, the police department reports to you? Then, I'm surprised you didn't already know of the incident."

He made a noise that was a cross between a grunt and a laugh. "My role is administrative. A government appointment. More of a favor than anything else. I really can't be aware of all the details of what goes on every day on the street. Perhaps I can use my influence to encourage them to speed up their investigative process. What else can I do to be of service?"

"Letting Priscilla play with other children is probably the best thing for her." She wondered why he was rewarded with a favor from the Turkish government.

Ahmet nodded. "Has she talked about her experience?"

"She's not very communicative with me."

"Then you don't know to what extent she interacted with the...gypsy, did you say it was who died?"

He had such an odd way of putting things, Anna thought. Language was still a barrier in spite of his excellent grasp of

English. "No, I don't know entirely. Apparently our maid, Fededa, hired the poor man to repair some of our kitchen pots. Isn't that a remarkable coincidence?" Not as remarkable as possessing Rainer's medal and her letter, she thought.

"Yes, quite. Has Priscilla...shown you anything else?"

It was all Anna could do to keep her voice steady. Her heart pounded, a drummer gone wild. Surely he could hear it. "I don't understand what you mean."

"Something that she found at the crime scene, perhaps. Something that would help the police solve the crime. Something she might not recognize as evidence."

"She didn't take anything," Anna said, tensing. "Besides, the police have everything under control."

"Yes, of course. I ask because you must report to the authorities exactly what either of you saw or heard, you understand?"

"Naturally. I always do my duty, Mr. Aydenli. That's why I'm here."

"Ahmet, don't forget."

"I shan't."

"Please. I am only concerned for your safety. Gypsies are known to cause trouble."

Children's voices bubbled out from the interior of the house just then. The gleam of Ahmet's face switched from concern to relief. His gaze shifted to the collar of her shirt. "I can take that along with me," he said, holding out his hand. "If it is true what she said. This is something that belonged to the dead man?"

"That's not true."

"Nonetheless, you must turn over evidence from a crime scene. You may think Turkey is a backwards country, but even here, we must follow correct procedure."

"I don't think that!" Anna's pulse accelerated. "You said yourself that your role is only administrative. Besides, I told you, the necklace is mine."

Silence chilled the air between them. They waited while Gulsen slipped on her shoes. "As you wish," he finally said.

Anna breathed again, then said goodbye and ushered them out the door. Through the closed door she could hear Ahmet's rapid voice, speaking Turkish with Gulsen. Anna didn't have to understand the language to hear Ahmet's anxiety.

She swallowed a lump in her throat and wondered if she'd made a big mistake. Ahmet Aydenli wasn't just an anxious, prospective bridegroom. He was the authority behind Yaziz's superior. The man Paul Wingate had hinted about. Although, Ahmet had offered her no proof other than his word. She wondered if she could trust that word of his.

And how many other police might be involved with one gypsy's death.

* * * * *

After much wailing and breast-beating, after running feet and stray cats wandering in and out, after many baby squalls and soiled pants fouling the air, Meryem pieced together the news the police had brought her family.

Her mother finally exhausted herself and drained down her wellspring of tears low enough that she was able to speak without having a sob catch at her voice. "You will have to accept the butcher's offer now."

"No, *an-ne*, never," Meryem said, using the Turkish word

for mother, as she always did, much to her sister-in-law's annoyance. Meryem had rejected the Romani way of life the minute she and her immediate family became sedentary here in Ankara, and now Meryem rejected the clan's language as well.

"How are we to live without Umit's income?" her mother wailed.

"There are other ways." It was true that Umit had brought home the kuruş from shining pots, but what her mother didn't know, nor did the rest of the family, was that Meryem was the one responsible for bringing home the lira, each one worth a hundred kuruş. She would go on without Umit, as she was doing later tonight for the general. But after that... Without Umit's cover of shining pots, it would be harder for her to gain access to the *gadje* who hired her to entertain at their parties. She would have to take over his business. If that's what it would require to stay out of the butcher's clutches, then she would do it gladly.

After more wails, her mother finally cried herself to sleep. Meryem slipped away as her sister-in-law prepared the children for bed. The storks clacked overhead, also settling down for the night, a time when she could think. A time when the nightmares would come back if she didn't keep her mind otherwise busy.

Out in the street, she scurried amongst the gathering shadows, reliving the day in her mind. She figured out more or less the sequence of events from that day. The man under the peasant's cap at Anit Kabir had flashed his gun at her *after* he'd shot Umit. Only, he was no peasant if he didn't know enough not to stand within kicking reach of the *eşek*. She wondered if he was the one with whom Umit had arranged his "quick deal."

Now she understood why Umit had made her wait for

him out of sight. She had thought at first that it was because whatever he was up to, he hadn't wanted her to share the profits with him. Then, when he failed to show up at the drinking hole in Kavaklidere, she suspected there was more to it than that. Danger. He hadn't trusted the pretend peasant any more than she had.

At the bottom of the hill, she awaited the *dolmuş* and thought some more. Spending a few more kuruş would be well worth the speed of riding the bus across town.

Her first instincts were always right. Umit had sold their amulet without her approval, and he'd intended to keep the money all for himself. But the police had found nothing on him, no amulet, no money. So they claimed. Either the police were the thieves, or Umit's buyer had double-crossed him.

If she'd been with him, he wouldn't be dead now, shot in the back of the head by the clean-shaven man pretending to be a peasant.

Or would she be dead, too?

The police did not know what business Umit had at Anit Kabir, or if they did, they were not telling the likes of gypsies. Umit had nothing on him, yet *something* had brought the police to the family's home on their no-name street, to their tilting, unnumbered apartment. The police did not know who had shot him or why, but they knew it was with a German gun, something they called a Luger, and they vowed to find the dangerous man. That's what they had called the pretend peasant. Not a gunman nor killer, as killing a gypsy did not count for much.

The "dangerous man" had already done it, had already left Umit to die, when the *eşek* kicked him in the balls. The sirens Meryem had heard on her way to Kavaklidere had been the police hunting for the "dangerous man," dangerous because of the weapon and his potential for harming a real person.

Bah! She spit on the blue-lettered men. Their blue letters, handed out like sugar treats from the government, were all that made them legitimate.

She did not believe them. Umit had guarded the silver piece of jewelry with his life, from the time they were children, from the desperate days when their other sisters and little brother died and the family wandered from hiding place to hiding place in dusty, wild mountains. Umit wouldn't barter away the amulet now, not after all the lengths they'd gone to in order to protect it. No matter how much rent they owed.

So, the pretend peasant had *taken* the amulet. Yes, that was it. And he'd killed Umit for his trouble.

The *gadje* foreigner in the pink flowered dress had been there, too. Racing up the steps to the pasha's tomb. Racing because she'd seen what happened?

Then Meryem remembered... The sparkling thing she'd seen the foreigner holding today. In the backyard of the very house where Umit had worked on pots only the week before.

She was the reason Umit had gone to Anit Kabir in the first place, only to die.

Meryem fought against the memories, but they kept returning, flashing through her like a sour belch. Before she could suppress them, she saw again the Nazi bastard grinning with blood against a Carpathian backdrop of mountains as vicious as he. He lost a tooth in their battle, but in the end, he captured her, Umit, their two sisters, and their younger brother. An evil incarnate that she'd loathed but not feared. Such worthless creatures would never deserve her fear, not even when he tried to have his way with each of them. Meryem was the youngest, only a child then, but the scrappiest of all.

She shoved the memory-nightmares to the back of her mind as she climbed onto the *dolmuş* headed for Kavaklidere.

Chapter Fourteen

After supper, Anna tried to settle down for an evening of reading Senator Kennedy's Pulitzer-prize-winning book, but her thoughts still distracted her. Then the doorbell rang, sounding like an electric current jolting through the tranquility of the house.

"I'll get it," Priscilla said. She jumped up from the dining room table, where she'd laid out a hand of solitaire after dinner was done and the dishes put away.

"Wait." Anna sprang up from the sofa in the adjoining living room and rushed to stop her niece. Not wanting to alarm Priscilla further, on top of the murder today, she explained her skittishness. "We must see who it is first, before opening the door to just anyone. Especially at night."

"But it's not dark yet."

"Still, we have to be careful." Through the glass block beside the front door, she recognized the Turkish detective, Yaziz, and his assistant standing on the stoop. Her heart fluttered.

She opened the door a crack. "Why, Detective. Is everything all right?"

"Please forgive us. It is a matter that cannot wait. May we come in?"

She grasped the knob to keep her hand from shaking and pulled the door open wider. "Of course. May I offer you a beverage? We have...let me think...mineral water."

"Mama gives guests raki," Priscilla said, "and I know where she keeps it."

Anna frowned. "I believe *that* is all gone." Then she turned to Yaziz. "Shall I make some coffee?"

"Thank you, no. You remember my assistant, Suleyman Bey?" He nodded to the man beside him, the one who'd tried to keep Hayati Orhon from barging into Yaziz's office. At least Suleyman didn't wear dark glasses indoors as Yaziz did.

"Pleased to meet you, Mr. Bey," Anna said, extending her hand.

Yaziz grinned. "No. 'Bey' is a term of respect, not his name. Never mind. He doesn't speak English, anyway."

"Oh. Well. Come and sit down, won't you?" She led the way, but the men lingered in the foyer, fumbling with their shoes. She paused beside the phone and turned to Priscilla. "Honey, it's time for you to get ready for bed."

"But it's still light out."

"Let her stay," Yaziz called from the foyer. "My questions are for her, too."

Anna's breath tightened in her throat. She didn't want to involve her niece in more police questioning. She wondered if she should phone up Paul Wingate, who'd told her to call anytime during the day or night. Anytime that she needed anything at all, he'd come right over. But she didn't agree with his assessment of Yaziz as a threat.

"All right," Anna said once they were seated, "what is so important that it cannot wait until morning?"

The men perched stiffly side by side on the government-issue sofa, sleek and plain as a vanilla wafer, while their stockinged feet twisted into the colorful pile of Mitzi's Turkish rugs. Yaziz nodded at Suleyman, who then pulled a paper-wrapped bundle from his jacket pocket. It was smaller than the package she'd seen in the closet, before Fededa had snatched it away, and this one was wrapped in tissue paper, not newspaper. Suleyman passed the wadded lump to Anna, and the paper crinkled as it unfolded, revealing a coil of blue beads strung together on a frayed piece of twine. Some of the beads were crushed.

"Do you recognize that?" Yaziz asked.

"No. Should I?"

"They don't belong to you or to little Miss Burkhardt?"

Priscilla leaned shyly over Anna's shoulder to look at the beads. They both shook their heads.

"They're not mine," Anna said. "I've never seen them before. Well, wait a minute... They're similar to what the taxi driver had dangling from his rear-view mirror. What are they? Worry beads?"

"No, no," Yaziz said, ticking his tongue. "Blue beads such as these ward off the evil eye. They are often worn by children and by animals. It is tradition. Children and animals are especially vulnerable to evil and must be protected."

"Since we have no pets, you must think these beads are Priscilla's?"

"They're not mine," Priscilla said, "but I *have* seen *eşeks* wear them. Donkeys," she explained to Anna.

Yaziz leaned forward. "These very beads?"

"Maybe not *these* ones. They all look alike."

"And the donkey, where was it?"

"Well, I dunno, they're all over the place."

"Think of the donkeys you've seen and who they were with."

Priscilla crooked her finger and tapped her upper lip while she thought. "Well, there's the milkman's *eşek*. And—"

"Just a minute," Anna said, cutting her off. "What's the meaning of this?"

Yaziz and Suleyman exchanged more words in Turkish. Finally, Yaziz aimed his gold-tinted lenses at her and smiled. She wished she could see his eyes, to see a hint of his thoughts.

"Forgive me," he said. "My assistant thinks it's not necessary to bother you with this matter, but I cannot help myself. When I was a student in your great country, I learned to be—how you say?—thorough. Very thorough. I had to be sure. If the beads aren't yours, then they belong to someone else who visited the tomb. Now we begin a new search first thing tomorrow morning. Perhaps they belong to the shooter, or even the victim himself."

"So that's where you found them? At Atatürk's Tomb today?" She wondered what other information they were withholding from her. She handed back the bundle and then patted Priscilla's arm. "Okay, honey, I think they're done with you. You can scoot off to bed now."

"But—"

"Don't argue. Do as I say."

Priscilla stomped her feet, stuck out her lower lip, then marched out of the room and up the steps, testing each one for durability along the way. "You're just like the rest. I won't tell you now."

"I'll be up in a little while to tuck you in." *Tell me what?* Anna thought. When she heard Priscilla's bedroom door slam shut, she turned back to Yaziz and lowered her voice. "I believe I may have some information for you. The name of the victim may have been something that sounds like 'Umit'."

"His name was Umit Alekci."

"Oh. So you already know?" How long had he known that, she wondered. "Our maid says that he was a hawker who came through this neighborhood fixing copper pots. Perhaps the donkey with the broken beads was his."

Yaziz turned to Suleyman and spoke sharply to him. Suleyman pocketed the beads and withdrew a worn notepad and chewed-off pencil. He flipped open the pad and scribbled a note.

Anna continued. "You've talked to his family? He had a sister, I'm told."

"Meryem," Yaziz said.

"A lovely name. Please extend my deepest condolences to the family the next time you see them. Or, perhaps I could do that myself, if you'll tell me where I might find them?"

Yaziz smiled, not taking her bait, and flicked his head backwards in the no gesture. "It is not your concern."

"Oh, but it is, Detective. That man had my letter, and I want to know why."

"Me too, Miss Riddle. The Burkhardts will tell me, once I find them."

"Mitzi? What makes you think my sister and brother-in-law would know anything? They're gone. Umit Alekci had nothing to do with them."

"He was wearing Henry Burkhardt's suit. You knew that already, did you not?"

"Only because Mr. Orhon told me. Why did you tell him but not me? Did you really think I could recognize Henry's *suit*? Look, are you playing games with me?" She sighed, remembering Paul Wingate's admonishment. *They don't think the same way we do*, he'd said. Okay, she'd try another tactic. "Have you come here tonight to return my letter? That's it, isn't it? You *said* you would once you learned the victim's name. And now you know it."

"I regret that I no longer have it. Someone removed it from my office."

"Someone...? You mean, it was stolen?" Panic rose within her. It was only a letter, for goodness sake. "Someone broke into your office? Do you think it was the murderer? Then you can narrow down your suspects to those who have access to your office."

"Very good, Miss Riddle. We will recover it. Have no fears."

"I'm not worried."

"Aren't you? Tell me, what's in the letter that makes someone kill for it?"

"You tell me. It's only a letter."

"Is it? Is that all it is?"

"What else could it be? You think it's some sort of code? Even if it were, the war's over."

He shrugged, cocking his head to one side to meet his rising shoulder. "Perhaps for you it is."

"What's that supposed to mean?"

Yaziz glanced over at his assistant and silently evaluated him. Suleyman didn't know English. Was Yaziz sure of that?

"War leaves behind troubling times," Yaziz finally said.

"Peace is not troubling, Mr. Yaziz."

"At least in war you know who your enemy is."

"You would find in my letter that I'm not your enemy. What are you doing to locate it?"

"I've had to check out a few things first with my sources."

The buddy at JUSMMAT, she thought. "Such as?"

"There is no record of Lieutenant Rainer Akers in your military."

"Well, of course not. He signed on with the British."

"And used an APO address, which is American?"

"He had contacts. It was called 'Allies,' Mr. Yaziz. Is there anything else? It's getting late."

"I regret to keep you up, but yes, there is one more thing I wish to know. The Burkhardts' travel plans."

"I've already told you they're in Nairobi, headed for a safari. They can't be reached."

"That is exactly the problem. We can't locate them. One thing is certain—they are not in Nairobi. They left on a plane for Frankfurt, yes, but there was no connecting flight. You will tell me where I can find them."

"That's not true! They wrote out an itinerary for me. Just a minute, and I'll show you." Anna ran to the phone stand in the dining room and rummaged through papers until she found the slip that Henry had penned with the names of the places where they planned to stay for the next several weeks. In case of emergency. She ran back to Yaziz, waving the paper. "See? Here it is." She dropped it in his lap and stood over him, breathing heavily with her outrage.

He scanned the paper, then folded it up and slipped it into his pocket. "We will check out these places, but I am afraid we will find that this list is false."

"Whatever do you mean?" Alarm pounded through Anna's veins.

"What I mean, Miss Riddle, is that the Burkhardts have vanished. They were last seen on a plane to Frankfurt. The plane arrived, but there is no record of them anywhere, not in any of the hotels there. Nor leaving Frankfurt on a connecting flight. Not even on a train. They have simply vanished. You must tell me where they are. As guardian of their child, you must know."

"Noooo..." Anna felt her legs give out, and she sank into the nearest chair. "You must've missed something. My sister wouldn't just disappear. She's in Nairobi, I tell you. That's why you can't find her in Frankfurt."

"Are you sure you cannot think of anything else that would help us find the Burkhardts? Something that is, perhaps, connected to the activity at the tomb today? Something, perhaps, that you are not telling us?"

Anna's spine stiffened. Rainer's medallion burned in her mind. "Now that you mention it, there is something. But it's another matter. Not about Mitzi and Henry. It's not related to what happened at the tomb today, either." She took a deep breath.

"Go on."

"I didn't wish to speak about it in front of Priscilla and alarm her unnecessarily. It's only a feeling, you see. I have no proof. And there's been no damage."

"What is it, Miss Riddle?" The gold lenses studied her.

Then the story poured out. She was only reporting her suspicions to gold lenses, after all. She told them about her belief that someone had entered her room, touched her things, and no, she had no proof. There was no damage. Nothing missing.

"May we have a look?" he asked.

"Really, Detective, I don't think that's necessary."

138

Yaziz spoke rapidly to his assistant, then turned back to Anna. "Is there something of interest that someone might have been searching for? Something, perhaps, of your lieutenant's? Another letter?"

"No, Detective." Anna tightened her jaw muscles. Her fingers fluttered to her collar, but she'd removed the Saint Christopher's medal and hidden it safely away in her purse. Now, her purse was upstairs in her room. Still, Yaziz was presenting her with an opportunity to hand over the medallion to the police, as she'd promised her nosy neighbor Cora she would do. It was really none of Cora's concern, was it? Anyway, the medallion had originally belonged to Aunt Iris, which made it Anna's now, on account of her inheritance. Aunt Iris had only loaned the medal to Rainer. To keep him safe. As Anna was continuing to do.

"There is nothing of Rainer's," she said, feeling heat rise to her face. "But maybe something else of interest. Our maid carried off a package from her broom closet. She was in quite a rush. I'm quite sure it was something she didn't want me to see."

Yaziz lifted an eyebrow, instructed his assistant to write a note, then rose. "Thank you, Miss Riddle. If you will be kind enough to show us the closet and your bedroom, then I will speak to the man who is assigned to watch your house. Have no worry. You will sleep safe and sound tonight."

She wasn't so sure about that, but she rose, too, and led them to the closet first. They could look if they wanted. They could even keep Henry's itinerary, since she'd had the foresight to write out a backup copy that she kept in her purse. Anything, to divert their interest from the medal. She had a right to keep a trinket in honor of Rainer's memory. She had a right to her own privacy.

* * * * *

Meryem shook her hips, and the gauzy fabric she'd tied low around tawny flesh rippled, along with the muscles of her bare belly. Her arms ringed in gold bracelets lifted above her head, and her long, tapered fingers caressed the air, keeping time with the beat of the music that throbbed repetitively in the general's sitting room. She laughed behind her veil, knowing that her laughter would bring a sparkle to her eyes.

Old, fat men sat on rugs and carefully tracked her movements with their eyes, trying hard not to turn their heads to follow her prances across the room. They wore looks on their faces as if the breath had been squeezed out of them. Except for one of them, the general, who was hard in all of the wrong places.

Meryem laughed again, thinking of the promised lira, and only wished that Umit were sitting downstairs in the kitchen, waiting to escort her safely home. But he wasn't, and she had to go on without him.

For now, she pushed the worry of Umit from her mind and wiggled closer to the general. She bent over his bald pate, ringed with steel hair like a crown of olive leaves. Her breasts were even with the mole on his face, and her upper body undulated. Bangles shimmied and jingled from the silk cloth that outlined her nipples.

Gasps filled the air. One old man with hair as white and feathery as a stork's and as long as a horse's mane turned loose of his glass of raki, spilling drops of its clear liquid. The general's guests reached for their pockets and rattled coins. Then, groping hands tucked silvery lira pieces and worn bills into the wedges between her body's curves and the fabric stretched tautly across them. Fingers lingered against her flesh, brushed across her breasts, but she didn't mind as long as they left behind their tips.

Their breath surrounded her with a taste of licorice, and then the general suddenly shot up from his cushion to his feet. He lifted his chin and puffed out his chest military style. His medals and ribbons, earned while in service to Atatürk, sparkled under the glow of crystal lamps. Bits of brass decorated his uniform as thickly as the bangles on Meryem's costume. His guests, always aware of their host above all, fell away from Meryem as the general clapped his hands at a servant, dressed in a white coat and waiting patiently by the phonograph. The servant whirled around faster than a dervish, and the music came to a scratching halt.

"That's enough for tonight," the general said. His stern gaze swept down his hawk nose at his guests. "It is time for the nargiles, *efendi*."

The men pulled handkerchiefs from their pockets and mopped their brows as the servant bent low over a table of equipment to spin dials and adjust this and that. Now would come the part of the evening where Meryem entered new territory. Without Umit, she would have to create her own rules.

She lingered as a new band of servants entered the room with hookahs and began setting them up. A filthy habit, she thought, but a necessary one for men who needed a little help loosening up their thought process.

Men! Let them think they could control anything!

Just then, the servant in charge of the phonograph pounced on her, grabbing her by the arm. He pushed her to the door of the grand hall, and his grip pinched her in a familiar way. She scowled up at him in protest, then sucked in her breath, as she recognized his hairy face and the firm clamp of his fingers on her arm. The dull glaze of his all-knowing eyes. The tight coils of his black hair, thick as a lamb's.

But he was no lamb. He was the secret police, the same one who'd caught her earlier that day. Outside the general's gate. What was he doing here *inside*, dressed as a servant? Then she remembered the coins he'd thrown down at the feet of the *asker*, the old guard who patrolled the grounds. And the cloth bundle. Bribes? That's how he'd entered the general's house tonight.

This was information Meryem could use.

The policeman in disguise shoved her through the doorway into the hall. He slammed the door of the meeting room behind them, shutting the two of them alone together under the crystal chandelier of the grand hall. "You waste your time spying here," he said. Irritation rolled off his forehead in the form of sweat beads.

"What business do they discuss while they smoke those silly water pipes?" she asked.

He jerked his head back and clicked his tongue, giving a sharp, smacking sound that meant "no" in the highest degree of negativity. The general's business, and his business with the general, were none of her business. All the same, it could be profitable for her as well as for the secret police.

"Get out," he said, pointing to a narrow staircase at the back of the mansion. Then he waited, trying not to eye her as she plucked bills from the tucks of her scarves and shook out coins that rattled to the marble floor.

She felt his eyes ogle her as she gathered up her money and stuffed it into the pouch she kept hidden inside her underwear. Her tongue ticked against the roof of her mouth to express her disapproval, and she whirled away in a flutter of scarves to clatter down the steps.

Meryem's step slowed as she descended the stairs. The secret police had let her go too easily. He'd promised her only that very afternoon that he was not done with her. And now he dismissed her, just like that.

Why did he no longer need her?

She puzzled over this, for surely it meant something she could turn to her profit. Deep in thought at the bottom of the stairs, she reached up to the wooden peg by the outside door where she'd left her *tsharchaf*.

The wrap was gone.

Her arm fell to her side, and she glanced between the empty peg and the door. A glass panel showed a square of deep night from the gardens behind the general's palace. She couldn't leave the house without her *tsharchaf*. The black robe covered her from her head to her toes, hiding her near nakedness and allowing her to slip across the city with minimum stir.

Meryem, the family's only hope now without Umit, had an idea.

She turned a corner and tiptoed down a narrow hall that ran alongside the stairs. At the end of the hall shone a light bulb hanging loose from the ceiling of the kitchen.

Spread across the wooden table in the center of the room was a puddle of black cotton—her *tsharchaf*. The *asker*, a grizzle-whiskered old man, sat there, pawing through the folds. Years beyond his official service, he still wore the undecorated khaki uniform of an ordinary Turkish soldier, not that any soldier was ever ordinary. He looked up from his work and his glass of raki as she entered the room, and his eyes settled slowly from their swimming circles into a tight focus on her.

"Where is it?" he said, his voice a snarling slur.

She snatched her garment out from under his grasping clutches and wrapped it around her like a cloak. "We had a deal," she said, then marched around the table to where he sat. She rubbed her fingers together under his nose and wished Umit were here. He had handled the business end of their partnership.

The old soldier jerked his head back. "You already got your money. You lied about the weapon."

You old fool! "I softened the general for you, as I said I would."

"The general does not bargain with gypsy trash."

"You promised me lira."

"You promised to dance tomorrow night, too. That's when you'll get your money. And do not come back empty-handed."

Chapter Fifteen

Wood creaked. Soft cries floated through the night.

Anna jerked upright in bed. Hot, dark air pressed against her.

The air smelled wrong...like used shoes...instead of the cedar that usually permeated her bedroom at home.

She wasn't at home anymore.

The events of the day tumbled through her mind. She closed her eyes against the image of the dead gypsy with his arm outreached to her.

To Priscilla.

Anna held her breath and listened to the silence. Something scratched and chittered overhead—the storks! That's what she'd heard and thought was a cry.

Rainer used to write to her about the storks where he was on his last mission, somewhere in the Balkans. Birds went about with their lives, not knowing there was a war on. Anna would have to find a way to have them chased off her roof.

Then she heard something more. A breath. And a muffled sob. Anna swung her legs out of bed and groped with her feet for the spot on the rug where she'd left her slippers.

Armed with the flashlight she always kept beside her bed, she opened her door to a dark hallway and switched on the flash.

She stepped carefully down the stairs from her attic bedroom and followed its lurching beam as it drilled into the darkness.

Priscilla's door stood ajar. Anna nudged it gently, and a hinge creaked.

Sheets rustled like a whip through sagebrush. "Who's there?" Priscilla said, her voice high-pitched and thin.

"It's me. Aunt Anna." She brought her hand holding the flashlight slowly around the doorframe, illuminating one corner of the bedroom.

"Turn it off," Priscilla whispered.

"What, this?" A light, she thought, would soothe a child. She was wrong.

She clicked off the flash and stepped into the room. "I thought I heard you." Beyond the doll-laden dresser, a balcony door stood open, admitting light that shone from the general's house next door. "Are you all right?"

"Hnuh."

Anna couldn't tell from the choking gasp exactly what Priscilla's answer meant to be, but the sound of fear came through clearly enough. She crossed the room in three strides and bent over Priscilla's bed. "You had a bad dream," she said, putting her face close to Priscilla's.

Priscilla rolled over, turning her back to Anna.

"Sometimes talking about bad dreams will make them seem less real."

The child lay still.

"Would you like anything?" Anna asked, wondering *what*. Warm milk? Mitzi had instructed her that milk had to be made from a powdered mix and boiled water. Anna thought it only produced a disgusting pitcher of cloudy water with white residue at the bottom. "Mineral water, perhaps?" No. The bubbles would only unsettle her more, instead of soothe her.

Priscilla still didn't respond, except for a swish of her sheets.

Anna sighed, not liking the way she felt helpless. These night terrors were surely caused by the man at the tomb today and exacerbated by the detective's appearance shortly before bedtime. *I won't tell you now*, Priscilla had threatened. Priscilla was holding in a worry all to herself, and Anna couldn't help her.

She straightened and stared down at her niece, curled up in the fetal position. Then she turned away and tiptoed across the room, this time heading toward the balcony. Through the filter of leaves hanging over the balcony railing, she could make out the source of the light from the general's house, a crystal chandelier in a central room of the upper floor. Anna reached for the handle of the balcony door.

Sounds of thrashing erupted from the bed behind her. "Don't close it!"

Anna's fingers hesitated on the cool brass of the handle. Over in the general's house, people—all men—milled about under the chandelier and one by one disappeared from sight, as if they filed through a receiving line into an adjoining, dark room.

Lowering her hand, Anna left the door open and tried to keep her voice calm in spite of the urgency in Priscilla's. "You're right. It's such a hot night, you need a little air."

The air wasn't moving. The fragrance of something sweet thickened the air from the garden next door, and she imagined something exotic. Night blooming jasmine?

"Are you sure you don't want a light?"

"No! Then he'll see in!"

"Who?" Anna felt her heart thud in her chest.

"The man who's chasing me."

"But it was only a dream." Anna tensed and peered out at the night, like a dark tarn between her and the party next door. A spark of light pulled her attention to the street lamp on the corner where she glimpsed a shadowy figure holding a glowing cigarette—Yaziz's watchman, she supposed. It was too dark to make out any details about him other than the outline of a fedora pulled down low over his head. "There's no one chasing you," she said with perhaps too much emphasis.

"Not me. Someone's chasing Daddy, though."

"How do you know that?"

"I saw him."

"Where?"

"Here."

"I'm sure you misunderstood," Anna said, then bit her tongue. She didn't want to patronize Priscilla, but her niece *did* have an active imagination. If Anna could convince her that her fears were groundless, then perhaps she could allay them.

"Why would anyone chase your father?" Anna said, trying again.

"Because of what he does."

Anna tried to laugh, but her voice cracked. "Your daddy's an important man who works at the embassy. He must have lots of meetings with different people."

"I don't care if you don't believe me."

"But dear, it's not that I don't believe you—"

"Because of *him*, Mama and Daddy went away. They're not coming back."

"Nonsense! Of course they'll be back." Anna's duty was

to maintain a sense of normalcy for her niece. She mustn't let Priscilla's fears or the detective's disturbing news interfere with that duty. In the morning, she would locate Mitzi and Henry herself, since Yaziz was apparently too incompetent to do so. Of course they were in Nairobi. Why had the detective fixated on Frankfurt, instead?

When Priscilla didn't respond, Anna probed further. "Was this the thing you said you wouldn't tell me?"

Still, no response.

"Would you like for me to stay with you, just until you fall asleep?"

"If you want."

Priscilla fidgeted again in her bed, and Anna hurried back to her side. She sat down on the edge of the bed and listened to Priscilla's uneven breathing and thrashing movement.

The still air stirred, carrying with it the exotic fragrance from next door. "Would you like to hear a story?" Anna asked after a while.

"About what?"

"About a princess who had to tell a different story for one thousand and one nights in order to stay alive."

"Was someone chasing her?"

"No, dear. No one's chasing anybody."

Priscilla flipped onto her back, then lay still. Attentive. Anna retold one of the tales in the dark, lowering her voice to a soothing level.

Midway through the story, Priscilla relaxed into a curl edging closer to Anna. "What does it mean?" she asked all of a sudden, interrupting Anna's story. "That necklace the gypsy gave me at Atatürk's Tomb?"

Anna sat in the quiet aftermath of the story's spell, stunned for a moment by Priscilla's change of thought. "It's a type of charm, called a Saint Christopher's medal. Some people believe charms of that sort will keep them safe when they travel."

"Do they?"

"I'm afraid not. That is, not if a charm is the only precaution people take."

"Can Saint Christopher hurt you?"

"No, of course not, honey."

"But that charm made you feel afraid."

"No. Surprised, perhaps."

"Well, you *looked* afraid. I think it's an evil charm."

"It can't be evil if you don't believe in those powers."

"But it can be evil if it makes people do bad things. Like the way the gypsy was killed. I think he died because he had the charm, and now I'm going to die because he threw it to me. You're going to die, too, because now you've got it."

"No, honey. We have to take control of our own lives. That's the best way to stay safe. The princess in the story knew it, too. Want to hear the rest of the story now?"

Priscilla yawned. "I guess so."

She wiggled closer, and Anna resumed the tale in her lulling voice. By the end of the story, red ringlets nestled in the crook of Anna's arm. Finally, Priscilla's steady breathing and silent form told Anna that the child had fallen asleep.

Carefully, so as not to squeak the box springs beneath the mattress, she disengaged herself from Priscilla. She tiptoed toward the hall, then stopped. The sweet scent of whatever the soldier next door was growing lured her to the open door of the balcony. One quick breath of fresh air, she thought, then she'd settle down for what was left of the night in her stuffy attic.

She stepped outside onto the wooden planks of the narrow balcony, half hidden under a canopy of leaves along the eastern side of the house. She leaned against the splintery rail and inhaled the night air. Leaves whispered overhead, and the fragrance of the garden intoxicated her.

The chandelier still blazed across the way, but no one remained in the central hall where it hung. Soft light glowed from an upper window at the far end of the mansion, where Anna could see the tops of heads. A room full of men sat on the floor.

She wondered about a gathering of all men—what they did, what they talked about.

Then a crunching sound from the general's garden pulled her attention away from the goings on inside his mansion. It was the sound of a footstep on pebbles, and it came from the same area where the *asker* had been toiling that afternoon, near the wire fence that separated their two yards. From the dim light of stars and the chandelier, she could see the paths that outlined planting beds of non-flowering rose bushes, leggy and sparse from thirst. One of their slim branches waved as a shadow skimmed past, stepping carefully on gravel.

Wood scraped against wood. A hinge creaked, and the door to the *asker's* shed opened partway. *Asker* stood there in the slit of the open doorway, leaking out light into the dark garden. Through the slice of the door, Anna could see in a flash the inside of the shed: a lantern sat atop a wooden table, and behind the table, a narrow cot.

Outside, in the general's garden, the newcomer was striding toward the light in *asker's* shed. He moved with swift, impatient steps, turning his—or her?—back towards Anna. She assumed that he was a he, for he wore trousers and a hat pulled low over his face. But she couldn't be sure. There was something familiar to his stride on long, lean legs as he darted into the circle of light. Anna dropped into a crouch, ducking low behind the railing of Priscilla's balcony. Her shifting weight caused a board to squeak just then under her fuzzy house slippers.

The newcomer stopped and whirled around, scanning the balcony where Anna hid. Between the slats of the railing, she glimpsed him long enough to recognize his profile and the distinctive outline of his crooked nose.

Rainer!

Chapter Sixteen

Long after Meryem returned home, she lay sleepless on her pallet, listening to the dark as the narcotic of the evening slowly drained away. Through the open window she heard the whump of a hoof stomping on packed earth below. Each time one of the work animals shifted in the yard, it raised up a puff of dust to their window, making Meryem's nephew, a sensitive child, roll over and cough.

She stiffened. Something clinked below, beads rattling softly against each other. One of the animals was shaking its head. Not Umit's donkey, who'd lost its beads. She hoped the animal would not awaken the children with its brays. None of them would sleep the rest of the night.

Suddenly, she shot up from her pallet and raced into the other room, the all-purpose room of the apartment. She leaned out the window, but before she could tick her tongue against the roof of her mouth, she saw the outline of a man moving beside one of the three *eşeks* that shared the yard with an ox.

"Hey!" she cried, before considering fully the wisdom of alerting the thief.

For that's what he surely was. A thief. Umit wasn't even buried, and already someone was trying to steal what little remained to them of their livelihood.

Except, this thief wasn't running away. Her cry should've scared him off, but he remained standing still beside the *eşek*. His chin, lit by moonlight, tipped up in her direction. The skinny brim of his peasant's cap pulled down low over his brow, concealing details of his face except for the moon-bathed chin. The way his pale flesh gleamed, Meryem thought at first that a jinn had come to her aid. Or Umit in the form of a ghost. Then she realized the smooth glow of his face appeared so because a beard did not speckle his jaw.

Surely, he was the clean-shaven pretend peasant who'd lost his gun. He had found her. Slowly, he lifted his gun arm up the side of his black peasant's coat, and Meryem gasped.

Remembering her near miss with the gun before, she shrank back. Far enough into the apartment that she hid herself from his view. Not so far that she lost sight of him down there.

She glanced over her shoulder at the apartment's door, so thin that by day one could see light shining from the hall through the wooden slats. All was dark now, but if the gunman wanted her badly enough, that door wouldn't stop him.

Because he knew where she lived.

Who had betrayed her, giving him that information? The butcher? The secret police? He and his kind were nothing more than a band of police thugs who scoured her streets until they knew who was who and who belonged where.

She turned back to watch the man by the *eşek*. His arm continued to rise, slowly, until it stretched above his head. As if he aimed at her.

No. He had nothing to aim, since he'd lost his gun.

In the thin light of the moon, she could see something small glitter, something held tightly between his fingers. Coins! It wasn't a gun. He offered her coins!

He was waiting for something.

Waiting for her. He'd come for his gun.

"Auntie?" little Mustafa said from behind her.

She whirled around. "Go back to bed."

Aside from rubbing his eyes, he stood still. Much as the visitor downstairs.

At first she felt her heart jump in her chest, from fear, she supposed. Two men today, first the pretend peasant and then the secret police, had tried to fill her with fear. It had almost worked, but she'd outsmarted them both, taking the first one's gun and taking away the second one's identity. Now that the first throb of fear faded, she felt the pull of interest. Who knew what profits awaited her this time? She wondered how many coins the man downstairs held for her.

She took Mustafa by the hand and pulled him to the curtain separating the two rooms.

"But...auntie?"

"Shhhh." She pushed him through the door of gauze, then sped back across the room to the wicker baskets she'd unloaded earlier from the *eşek*. She lifted the lid of one. Her hand dipped inside, skimmed amongst the smooth pieces of copper, explored the shapes as a blind person might test them. Then her fingers recognized the curved handle of the dipper. She pulled it out carefully, trying not to scrape it against the other pots and pitchers.

Tucking the dipper under one arm, she hurried to the wooden door that led out into the hall.

The apartment door creaked when Meryem opened it. Sucking in her breath, she flattened herself against the cool plaster of the wall and waited. Nothing stirred on the second floor landing, so she closed the door, giving off another creak, and paused again.

Not even cats prowled the stairwell.

She tiptoed down the steps, one by one, avoiding the boards that she knew from experience would always squeak. She lowered herself into the dark, into the usual smells of urine and dust and nearby animals. Nothing out of the ordinary.

Three steps from the end of the stairs, she stopped. Below her lay a cobbled passageway, a narrow tunnel between the street and the animals' yard. He would be waiting for her in one of the shadows down there, she realized. Her own foolishness flirted with her mind, but she chased it away as quickly as it had appeared. She'd outwitted danger many times before. She was a survivor, too.

Umit hadn't survived this time.

The offer of coins was too great a lure. For a profit, she would risk her safety. And if she lost? In truth, there was nothing to lose, not with a life like hers.

From three steps up, she leapt the rest of the way, as far into the middle of the passageway that her jump would carry her. She did not want to land in the thicker shadows along the perimeter of the passage walls. The cobbles felt cool on her bare feet, and she curled her toes around the uneven edges of the stone to give her better footing.

The passageway was so narrow that the moon could not reach here. Which suited her purpose fine. She tucked the brass dipper beneath her arm so that the end of the handle protruded in front of her. With just the right amount of moonlight, it might be mistaken for the barrel of a gun.

She crept forward, knowing that he awaited her, had already heard the soft thud of her landing, could probably see her outline slipping through the shadows even now. She did not like the idea that he knew her path while she could not see him. He might even stalk her from behind, having slipped through the passageway to the street while she'd tiptoed down the stairs. She did not know, and not knowing was a condition unfamiliar to her. She did not like the way her heart raced, either, or the sour taste in her mouth as if something wicked rose from her gut, a memory that filled her essence with instinctive hatred.

Resolve steeled through her, as it had before, long ago in the Carpathians. Her hatred for the Nazi bastards drove her forward through the cobbled passage. Ahead, moonlight washed over her dead-end, the weedy patch shared by three *eşeks* and an ox. The animals, a silvery gray, stood silently, sleeping on their feet. The man she'd seen bothering Umit's donkey was no longer in sight.

But he was here. She could feel his presence the way the air shifted about her, as if it was his breath that moved the air. In. Out. Goosebumps tickled her neck.

Pausing, she curled her fingers around the brass handle and scanned the dark lining of the passageway. A bulky shape thickened the shadows where nothing bulky should exist. It was he, hunkered against the wall. Beyond the edge of moonlight.

She took a step backwards, toward the street. "Stay where you are, or I will shoot." She clicked her nails along the brass handle of her dipper.

He swore. "You wouldn't."

"I would as soon shoot you as breathe the same air with the killer of my brother."

"Your...brother?" He laughed, a snort of laughter that resonated evil.

"You killed my brother, and now I will kill you." Meryem cursed herself for having hidden the gun across town when she needed it *here*, with her now. Instead of having to pretend with this dipper.

She would've used the gun if she'd had it. There was never any doubt about that. Even though she didn't really know how to use a gun and would probably only succeed in shooting herself. She did not care. What did she have to lose? Her life was nothing. Worthless.

"Whore!" he said in his thick, non-peasant accent of superiority. A tendril of a shadow lashed out at her, but she sidestepped it with one of her deft dancing steps. His cap pulled down low over his face, but there was something familiar about the way he moved, lunging like a cobra. "Give me my gun!"

"How much will you give me for it?"

After a heavy pause, he said, "One hundred lira."

She spat on the cobbles in his direction. "You insult me."

"Five hundred, then."

"Bah! I can get twice that much on the black market."

"All right, one thousand."

She had no idea how much the gun was worth, but with the ease of his agreement, she suspected it was worth far more than that. She tried to imagine how far one thousand lira would go, and she couldn't.

"Hand it over," he said.

"Let's see your money first."

She heard the sliding sounds of fingers searching pockets, clinking coins, thumbing through bills. Then, coins sprayed her feet, rattling across the cobbles. There weren't enough rattles to add up to the full amount, but it was a start.

"Hand it over *now*," he said.

"Okay, I'll get it for you."

"You'll what?"

"You think I'd risk hiding it *here*? Where any thief could help himself to it, or worse yet, let the children find it?"

He lurched at her, and this time he connected. His fingers wrapped around her throat, choking off her breath. "Where is it?"

"If you want it that badly, I'll give it to you. But I have one more condition—"

His fingers tightened on her throat. "Where. Is. It."

"In...in..." The fingernails of her hand not holding the dipper dug into the flesh of his fingers that squeezed her throat. "Please..." She gasped.

"Where?" He shook her by the throat, and what little breath she had left in her, shifted.

"Kavaklidere," she managed to say. Although the hollow stump where she'd left the gun was actually in the neighborhood of Güven Evler, one street over from Kavaklidere's boundary.

"You were on Yeşilyurt today. That's where you hid it." He gave her another impatient shake.

"No!" If he knew that, then he'd followed her from the pasha's tomb. Impossible! More likely, the secret police or the *asker* had reported to him.

Or perhaps the red-haired American child.

"You have it here tomorrow night," he said, growling like one of the pitiful stray cats, "or else the kid upstairs is dead."

He gave her one more shake, then tossed her away like a

piece of garbage to the ground.

Massaging her neck, she scuttled away from his reach. "There's one more thing I want in exchange for your gun. The amulet you stole from my brother."

"You're in no position to bargain, whore. Remember this: you and your family cannot escape me." He stormed away, striding along the passage.

His shape bobbed against the circle of gray at the end of the passageway. The moonlight of the street finally swallowed him. She turned back to the cobbles and scrabbled amongst them in the dark. She picked coins out of the cracks and plucked clammy bills from the grit. She didn't care who the pretend peasant was. She didn't care who ended up with his gun, either. As long as she got the rest of the money. And the amulet.

Chapter Seventeen

Distant roosters crowed, awakening Anna. Memories of the night washed over her.

It hadn't been Rainer. It *couldn't* have been. He was dead. The shadowy man in the general's garden had only been someone who'd reminded her of Rainer. Or else it was his ghost.

It was a trick of the mind.

Rainer had been heavily on her mind since the events at the tomb the day before.

She hadn't left Priscilla's balcony and returned to her bed until convincing herself this was true. And even after she'd fallen asleep, dreams of Rainer continued to plague her. She wasn't so sure that she cared for such reminders. She'd come to Turkey hoping to move forward with her life. Not slip backwards.

She washed and dressed for the day, trying to scrub away her exhaustion, then went downstairs to stir up pancakes for breakfast. Pancakes could fix anything. Their sweet taste could banish the residue of nightmares and nighttime prowlers under their bedroom windows. Most of all, pancakes offered a sense of normalcy and reminded Anna of home in Colorado.

She wasn't home.

She wasn't Rainer's fiancée anymore, either. Their engagement had long been over. She needed to stop thinking about him. That's why his Saint Christopher's medal had felt heavy round her neck after Ahmet's visit, and that's why she'd taken it off. She'd been right to hide it in her purse but wrong not to hand it over to Yaziz last night when she'd had the opportunity. She would correct that today. Or soon.

The pancakes did their job of chasing the sulkiness out of Priscilla and warming the air between them. They laid out plans for a fun day of exploring.

When the taxi arrived after breakfast, she told the driver in the broken remnants of her college French to take them to the American Embassy. Henry had told her that French was widely understood here, and to her surprise, the driver understood.

"Are we going to Daddy's office?" Priscilla said as they pulled up in front of the embassy.

"No, honey."

"They won't let you in. Daddy always keeps his door locked."

"Then it wouldn't do any good if I'd wanted to go there, now would it?"

"But why are we here? You said we're going to the covered bazaar."

"We will, as soon as I ask about another matter. This shouldn't take long."

Anna told the driver to wait for them, and then she grabbed Priscilla's hand and marched up the sidewalk. She stepped firmly in spite of the confusion that washed over her. She had no plan, really, but she had to do something. She couldn't sit idly by, awash in memories of Rainer that were so strong she even imagined she'd seen him the night before in shadows. She didn't know who had visited the *asker's* shed, but it couldn't have been Rainer.

The heat had never abated during the night. Electric fans cooled the shade and marble interior of the reception hall. Anna wondered if she was doing the right thing. Rainer was dead. *Let him go.*

Voices echoed across the stone chamber as the receptionist greeted Priscilla by name. Then she turned to Anna. "You must be Miss Riddle. Welcome to Turkey. Sorry you had to go through that dreadful incident yesterday, so soon after your arrival."

Anna shifted on her feet, uneasy that strangers were talking about her behind her back. She squeezed Priscilla's hand. "Thanks. I'd like to speak to the person who handled those events. Mr. Wingate, I believe?"

The receptionist nodded and led them down a hall to a small office, similar in size to the Turkish detective's office but softer with colorful cushions propped against vinyl guest chairs. A brass vase held yellow and red zinnias. Framed photos of laughing faces lined the top of a credenza, and a Turkish rug warmed the floor. The cheery touches contrasted to the stark chill of marble, and Anna thought it strange that a man like Paul Wingate, all business, would be attentive to such detail.

The receptionist brought them tea, then left them alone to sip the sweet taste of apple. Moments later, the efficient-looking woman who'd received Paul's sheaf of papers the day before appeared in the open doorway and leaned against its frame to study Anna.

"So you're Anna Riddle," she said, sweeping into the room with her hand outstretched. Heavy charms on her gold bracelet jingled. Tiny and slim in a tight-fitting suit snug against her curves, she managed to fill the room with her energy. "Welcome.

I'm Fran Lafferty. What can I do for you?"

"We were waiting to see Paul Wingate."

Fran laughed, a throaty, tired sound. The gentle sag at the corners of her eyes suggested an overworked woman, around forty, only a few years older than Anna. "Then you'll have a long wait. He's in meetings. But never mind him. I'm his assistant. I do most of his legwork for him behind the scenes. Maybe I can help you."

"I hope so," Anna said, encouraged by the sincerity that radiated from Fran. "I need an update on what the police are doing about it. Mr. Orhon said the embassy is handling the matter."

Fran coughed on her laughter and leaned against one corner of her desk. "Why on earth do you want to know? You don't need to get involved. That's why we're here, to take care of problems for you."

"I want to extend my condolences to Umit Alekci's family, and I was hoping you'd give me their address."

Fran shook her head. "Uh-uh. No can do."

The direct approach hadn't worked, Anna thought, disappointed. Then a flicker of irritation rose within her. "Very well, I shall have to find them without your help. Come along, Priscilla. Our taxi is waiting."

Fran sighed and smiled. "Look, I can't help you not because I won't but because I don't have their address. They live in a place of no addresses, okay? Sit down, and let's start over. I have an idea there's more on your mind than merely extending condolences. Now, how may I help you?"

Anna sank back into her chair and stifled her irritation. Fran was right about having more on her mind. "I also need to make some inquiries. About a person who may be missing. I'm not sure where to start."

One of Fran's eyebrows arched. "You don't know if this person is actually missing?"

Priscilla piped in, "Mama says—"

Anna raised her voice over Priscilla's. "You see, I thought all along that this...missing person...died in the war, but now I wonder if... I don't know. Maybe there's a file about him or about any unusual incidents that might've involved him. Any records, perhaps leftover from the war?"

Fran's lip drooped. Either her facial muscles didn't work properly or she smirked with indifference. "I see. Have you thought of going to the police?"

"No, I can't do that." Anna stiffened, confused by Fran's mixed reactions, first of welcome, then of withdrawal. "Don't you have access to some records? I mean...I've tried before, in the States, and got nowhere. But a request coming from the embassy..."

"Would have more clout? Maybe. But the police specialize in that sort of thing, you know."

"They don't believe he ever existed in the first place."

Fran reached across her desk for a cigarette case, leather with intricate carvings, and held it out as an offer to Anna.

"No, thanks, I don't smoke."

Fran shrugged and shook out a cigarette. "Does this person have a name?"

"Yes, of course," Anna said, irritated again. "Rainer Akers. Although he might be using an alias now."

Fran winked. "An old flame?"

Priscilla swung her feet that didn't quite reach the floor and started to speak. "He—"

Anna cut her off. "He was just a friend of the family's."

Fran narrowed her eyes as she lit her cigarette. "Why don't you tell me the whole story? From the beginning? I assure you, you can trust me."

Anna glanced first at Priscilla. Then back to Fran. It wasn't a question of trust. She'd always repressed her true feelings, always been a prisoner to society's dictum of proper decorum. If she and Priscilla were going to get along over the next few months, however, Anna would have to be more forthright.

"You're right." Anna let out a long sigh. "We were engaged to be married." Selected pieces of the story tumbled out, and she told Fran how she'd met Rainer at the university, had helped persuade him of the need to stamp out the oppression running rampant through Europe. Anna despised persecution of any kind, and no one was standing up to Hitler's perverse form of it. Rainer was graced—or cursed—with German fluency, thanks to his immigrant grandparents, and so Anna had convinced him in those days before Pearl Harbor that he was in a special position to contribute to the cause. She hadn't meant that he should actually *go* in the field and become a spy. He knew nothing of being a spy.

Anna kept her guilt to herself. If not for her, things would've turned out differently for Rainer. She'd never seen him again, and after the war, when she followed up with a visit to Ohio to speak to his family, she found that the last of the Akers had died the year before she'd gotten there.

"I thought he died in the war," Anna said, summing up. "I hadn't thought of him again for a long time, not until yesterday... er, afternoon."

"The incident at Atatürk's Tomb," Fran murmured, eyeing a smoke ring that drifted above their heads. "You took up a rather sizable chunk of our afternoon yesterday, getting you through all the paperwork generated by the local police."

"I'm sorry."

"Don't be. That's what we're here for. Okay, I'll check with our military attachés and see if they have anything on Akers."

Priscilla remained quietly attentive throughout the story. Thank goodness, Anna thought, that Priscilla didn't interject anything embarrassing she might've overheard from Mitzi. Not that Anna had anything illicit to hide. She simply didn't welcome Mitzi's pity over her single status. Didn't want to become the object of a matchmaker. Anna had the right to keep some things private, for heaven's sake.

Fran rose from her desk and glanced at the papers stacked in her in-basket. "Anything else I can do for you?" Apparently, their time was up.

"Yes, actually. I want to phone my sister in Nairobi before she leaves on safari, but when I tried this morning..." Anna broke off, overwhelmed by her failure to place a simple telephone call.

Fran chuckled. "Nothing to be embarrassed about. I can start that process for you, too. It usually takes a long time, sometimes all day, to get through long-distance. Make sure you're home tonight, and I'll have it put through to that number."

"Okay, we will."

Priscilla kicked the metal legs of her chair with an anxious thump. "But we're going to Tommy's house tonight! You promised!"

"No, this is more important, honey. We'll have to cancel."

"She's right," Fran said, smiling at Priscilla. "We'll *all* be there tonight. There's no reason why we can't have the call ring through to the Wingates' house instead."

Anna felt as if she'd swallowed something disagreeable. She didn't want the entire American community to listen in to her conversation with her sister, but she felt boxed in between Fran's offer and Priscilla's anticipation. She nodded glumly and dug into her purse for her backup copy of telephone numbers she'd hastily scribbled. "Did Henry leave a copy of his itinerary with someone here at the embassy? When Mr. Yaziz visited me last night, he took mine."

"He came to your house? Why'd he do that? He shouldn't have bothered you."

"It's okay. He had to show me some beads he'd found. He thought they might've belonged to us."

"No, it's not okay." Fran reached around to her telephone and spoke into it. "I need Mr. Orhon in here on the double." Then, to Anna she said, "You were right to tell me this. Only, you should've phoned up Paul last night, the minute Yaziz showed up on your doorstep."

The air chilled between them as they waited for Hayati Orhon to arrive. Anna wondered why the people in the embassy were so intent on buffering her from Yaziz.

Fran drummed her fingernails against the metal surface of her desk, smiled at Anna, glanced at her watch, then at the door. Finally, she sprang to her feet. "What's keeping him?"

"Why do you need Hayati?" Anna asked. "Do you think he knows something about that detective?"

Instead of answering, Fran muttered her displeasure in general about the difficulties of getting work done. She stubbed out her cigarette in a brass ashtray and said, "I'll go find him.

Wait here. I'll be back in a jiff."

Anna shifted in her seat, uneasy, as Fran left the room. Her clicking footsteps faded away into the distance. One thing was sure: Anna didn't want to risk having her thoughts and fears exposed to Hayati, who seemed able to read the discomfort on her mind.

"Come on," Anna said to Priscilla, taking her by the hand. "Let's get out of here."

Chapter Eighteen

Yaziz waited on the street outside the offices for the *Republic News* as roosters greeted the day. A *dolmuş* rolled to a stop, screeching its brakes. A few passengers spilled from the sides of the bus, where they'd hung on for the ride to the city center. A few more squeezed out from the stuffed interior.

Yaziz scanned the faces of the new arrivals while they lingered on the street, either dazed or reluctant to start a day of business. This was the day of the week that used to be set aside for prayers. Before Atatürk forced Turks to join the west.

Not spotting Murat's son among them, Yaziz dug his fists into his pockets and waited some more.

Murat had been useless the night before, and now Yaziz had to forge his own way. Not only had Murat given him no leads but he'd also insulted him. What was wrong with his old friend?

It was true that in the years since he'd first traveled abroad, Yaziz had found his country smaller than he'd once thought, and at times embarrassingly backward. Those observations, however, hadn't really changed him. Not so much, anyway, that he deserved insults from a loyal friend. Loyalty counted for more than that.

Murat's son tumbled off the next *dolmuş* that arrived.

"Excuse me, Nizamettin?" Yaziz said, hardly recognizing the

young man whose light brown hair had grown a bit too shaggy. He hurried his pace, which only pronounced his limp.

Nizamettin turned and squinted, chewing gum with an air of insolence. "Do I know you?" Away from his father's house, he was a boy who thought he was a man.

Yaziz sighed and reached for the inner pocket of his western suit jacket. For field work, he preferred a suit to his official uniform of blue and grey. As *koreli*, he'd earned the freedom to choose the way he worked on an assignment. Of course he had to answer to Bulayir for those assignments, but as long as he solved the case, no one cared how he did it.

He'd only met Nizamettin a couple of times at family feasts, where boys were less interested in remembering their father's friends than the friends were curious about the sons. Yaziz pulled out his badge from the inside of his jacket pocket. Nizamettin's eyes widened, and his jaw stilled. He stepped back, into the shade of the office building, and loosened the stiff collar of his white shirt.

"I have done nothing wrong," Nizamettin said.

It should be enough that Yaziz was Murat's friend. Yaziz shouldn't have to show his official identity. But Nizamettin was a modern Turk, which was both a good thing and a bad thing. "I am a friend of your father's, and I bring you his greetings. Is there somewhere we can talk?"

Nizamettin frowned, a scowl that only looked petulant on a face still plump with baby fat. He glanced at his wristwatch, then placed his hands defiantly on his hips. "I can give you a moment or two. Here, or nowhere."

Yaziz shrugged. "Suit yourself. What I want to know is what you have learned on the streets about a possible revolution."

He was not happy about being so direct, but he knew how to summon western directness when necessary.

Nizamettin tipped his head back and laughed. Yaziz shifted his weight from one foot to the other, but he couldn't find a comfortable position while he waited for the laughter to subside. Finally, Nizamettin led Yaziz around the corner, into a side street. The roar of traffic fell away behind them.

An outdoor café offered a wooden table, alone and untended beside an ox cart. Thin, dusty leaflets of a locust tree draped overhead. Nizamettin claimed the table, and Yaziz ordered breakfast—crusty bread, olives, goat's cheese, and coffee. Once they were served and alone again, Nizamettin leaned low across his plate. "What's this about a revolution?"

"That's what I hoped you could tell me. The people are unhappy with the way the prime minister is undoing all of Atatürk's good work, clamping down on them, and making a mess of our economy. You, a journalist, of all people, should know about unrest."

"I know nothing." Nizamettin's glance lifted over Yaziz's shoulder. "My father is a dangerous fool to have sent you here to me."

"Don't lie to me. You can either tell *me* what you know, or you can let the secret police persuade you to talk to them. Your choice."

"You, a friend of my father's, would turn me over to them? Of course. You must be the one who set them onto my father in the first place. And you call yourself a friend."

Yaziz, grateful for the cover of his tinted lenses, returned the hard stare. He would never confess to not knowing what the young man referred to.

Then he remembered Erkmen, lounging below the nargile salon the day before. Erkmen was a young lieutenant who made himself available at the office for a wide range of duties. He'd had ties to the secret police before Bulayir recruited him with a promotion almost as big as Yaziz's last promotion. And all along, Yaziz thought Erkmen had been trailing *him*. Erkmen had been following Murat, instead.

"No, that is not my doing," Yaziz said. "Tell me, why are they interested in your father? Is there something more of interest than merely his sympathies for your colleagues in journalism?"

Nizamettin sucked on an olive, then paused to turn down the ends of his mouth. "I suppose it has to do with the marriage my father is arranging for my sister. I have told her not to go along with the old ways, but she won't listen."

"Ah, yes, your father mentioned such an arrangement. The assistant minister of the Interior, I believe he said, will be the happy groom."

"Your boss."

"Well, not directly, but he is one of those in charge of my department."

Nizamettin licked his fingers. "Very well. You call off your secret police, and then I might talk to you. Not before."

Yaziz shrugged. "You give me more power than I actually have."

"I don't believe you." Nizamettin scraped his chair back against the cement of the sidewalk.

"Believe what you will. But believe this: I am a paid servant of our lawfully elected government, and I will do what I have to do in order to protect the Republic. A lesson you could well learn."

"Even if I had the information you seek, I would not betray my friends as you are betraying yours."

Beneath the table Yaziz clenched one fist so tightly that a knuckle popped. Better that than Nizamettin's nose, he thought. "Not even for your country?"

Again Nizamettin laughed. "A revolution would be the best thing that could happen to this country right now. If I knew of such plans, I would not betray them, either."

"Then you would be a traitor."

"Not if I chose to do nothing."

"Doing nothing, while knowing of something, is the same as doing something."

"Then I am a hero for my country." Nizamettin stood and grinned down at Yaziz with triumph while he stuffed his pockets with bread.

"If you won't give me a name," Yaziz said, "then at least give me a time and date. How long do we have before the plans are carried out?"

The young journalist jerked his head back, disgracing his father. "You are clever, as wise as a *hoça*. I'm sure you already know more than I know." He stormed away, disappearing into the morning crowds as he rounded the corner.

Deep in thought, Yaziz wondered if that was true. But what did he know? The order to investigate the threat of revolution had come from the minister's office itself. Yaziz slowly sipped his coffee, turning over in his mind the connections among the various divisions of the National Police, all of them branching from the office of the Minister of the Interior.

That's where Bulayir's directive had come from. Yaziz wondered, as the rich brew warmed him, lubricating his thought processes, if Aydenli—one of the assistant ministers of the Interior and groom of Murat's daughter—was the reason behind Bulayir's preoccupation and Murat's silence.

Interesting, that the directive had come specifically to Yaziz, interrupting him from the investigation of a murder that no one wanted investigated. Why him? Because he was *koreli*?

Or did they want to hush up something bigger? Like evidence they thought Yaziz was already working with.

But he had nothing of importance, not yet. So far, only a love letter for someone who didn't exist, a Luger's bullet, some broken beads, and Burkhardt's name sewn into the suit—which suggested nothing more than the probable fact that Umit Alekci was a thief.

Besides, Aydenli and Bulayir would not work that way. Nor would they cover up evidence that would expose a revolution, since exposing it was exactly what they wanted Yaziz to do.

There was another answer. And Yaziz suspected the American woman could provide it.

Chapter Nineteen

Fifteen minutes later, Anna paid the taxi driver and climbed out behind Priscilla into one of the dusty streets of Ulus, the old city. She could hear a voice warbling an off-key melody somewhere in the distance, as if the singer were slipping along the cobbled street that rose at a sharp angle before them.

If you could call it a street, Anna thought. Somewhere up there in that labyrinth lived the Alekci family. They'd known Rainer.

She gazed up at the winding way, where the taxi driver had refused to go. Their mutual knowledge of French had only gone so far, and then Priscilla had had to take over with Turkish. Anna hadn't understood their exchange, but the refusal was clear enough. The passage was no wider than an alley, and wooden buildings stacked on either side of it in the fashion of precariously perched tinker toys.

The museum was somewhere in this maze of streets, and her guidebook indicated that it contained historical artifacts from the Hittites, that mysterious people referenced briefly in the *Bible*. She yearned to go.

Instead, she had other, more pressing matters. Rainer. Before she could let that matter go, she had to learn what Umit's connection to Rainer had been. So far, her only lead was Fededa.

"Where is this shop you mentioned?" Anna asked. "The one

that Fededa's husband owns?"

"This way." Priscilla tugged on her arm and pranced with impatience as she led Anna through jabbering crowds. Men wore baggy pants and narrow-brimmed caps. Women also wore baggy pants, but instead of caps, they draped scarves, some white some flowered, around their heads and shoulders.

Anna felt the eyes of the crowd follow them as they wound their way up the street. She and Priscilla stood out in their summery gingham dresses with full skirts. Several small boys, bare-headed and barefoot, raced after them, shouting something.

"What do they want?" Anna asked, keeping a firm grip on Priscilla's hand. Despite their western dress, a short person could easily disappear beneath the shoulder height of a crowd this dense, and Anna wasn't going to risk another incident today.

"They want to carry our bags for us," Priscilla said.

Anna paused to smile at the boys and shake her head. She held out her free arm to show them she hadn't bought anything. All she carried was a straw purse, and she wasn't going to give that up.

"*Hayir*," she remembered to say.

She must learn Turkish. Her pathetic French wasn't enough. Even if she knew a small amount of Turkish, she wouldn't have to always ask Priscilla to translate for her. With language, it would've been a simple thing—well, maybe not *simple*, but surely easier—for Anna herself to place the call to Mitzi in Nairobi instead of asking for help and feeling like an idiot as a result. Without language, Anna felt stymied.

"Come on." Priscilla yanked her through the congestion,

showing an amazing strength for someone half Anna's size.

At a slim opening in a wall of shops, a short flight of stone steps disappeared down into a dark tunnel. Anna hesitated. Today she'd worn her sensible Keds, rather than Mitzi's slick sandals.

"Fededa brings me through here when we go to Ozturk Bey's store." Priscilla spoke with an impatient edge to her voice.

For now, Anna put her frustrations aside and gave herself up to the place. Earthy smells pervaded the air, the result of all the donkeys and oxen and sheep and feral cats that roamed the streets. Anna followed Priscilla down into the subterranean passageways and felt as if she left all the dirt and filth of the real world behind and entered a magic kingdom. She wouldn't have been surprised had one of the carpets drifted up from its stack and floated away.

She blinked, allowing her eyes time to adjust to the dim light inside the partially buried market. Thin streams of outdoor light trickled in through occasional openings that reminded her of portholes with jelly-glass thick windows. Against the weak rays of light, dust motes spiraled into the darkness overhead, yet the air inside the bazaar was cool and damp and heavy with fresh smells of leather, wool, and a medley of spice.

Filtered light streaked across bins and stacks and shelves of multi-colored clutter. Anna relaxed her grip on Priscilla, and they wandered companionably past narrow shops that squeezed side by side in the covered alleyway. Priscilla moved with purpose, tugging at Anna past copper and brass that gleamed with lustrous shades of amber. There were leather bags, plush rugs and towels, slippery silk fabrics and filmy gauze, ceramics painted with intricate designs, jewelry, meerschaum, glass baubles, and a thousand other things that Anna couldn't absorb.

She wanted to stop and inspect everything closer, but Priscilla pulled her on, reminding her of their mission. Merchants, wearing resigned grimaces on their faces, watched them pass without trying to tempt them inside their stalls. Anna was grateful for their placid nature.

Finally, Priscilla stopped before a low wall, which displayed leather slippers across its rim. Pairs of tied-together slippers were all of one style, having a single strap across the arch and curled-up toes with a tassel at the tip. Where each pair differed was in its size and the design of beads or sequins sewn onto the slippers' velvety straps.

"My friend Gulsen wears funny shoes like these inside her house," Priscilla said. "You're not supposed to wear outside shoes inside, did you know that? She lets me borrow a pair of hers when I go play with her."

Anna ran her fingers along the smooth leather sole and traced the curve of the toe. Something about this shape charmed her.

Priscilla squinted up at her. "Why aren't we supposed to wear slippers like these in our house, too?"

"It's a Turkish custom, and inside the privacy of our homes we don't have to follow their customs."

"But our house is Turkish. It even has a *leylek* nest on top."

"That means stork in English, right? Honey, we're Americans, and as long as we live in that house, it becomes... sort of an extension of the States."

"But I don't feel very much like an American. If I'm an American, how come I don't live in America?"

Anna set down the slipper she'd been holding and turned her

full attention onto her niece. "Haven't your parents discussed this with you?"

"They're not here." Priscilla shrugged. The way the ends of her mouth curled down reminded Anna of the facial expressions she'd seen already on some Turks—a sad look, as if they regretted having to admit "no." In this case, Priscilla probably *was* sad about her parents' absence. And resentful to have Anna, a poor substitute for Mitzi and Henry.

Anna couldn't be sure what her niece was thinking. She didn't know her, not really. "Your mom and dad will be back, honey, later this fall. Meanwhile, maybe you could invite Gulsen over to our house to play."

"She isn't allowed to come to my house because it's too different."

"Then we have to make her feel more comfortable. Perhaps we need some of these slippers. We could make a rule to wear them in our house, too."

"But, Mama says—"

"Your mother's not here, is she?" Anna had never known her sister to adhere to anyone's customs but her own.

A smile flickered about Priscilla's lips, and her eyes glittered. "You mean, we should *buy* some to wear at home while Mama and Daddy are gone?"

Anna nodded. "We'll each need a pair. And one for your friend, too, when she comes to visit. What do you think of this flower design?"

Priscilla flitted from one pair to the next, gathering samples of different sizes to bring to Anna. She held them up against her shoes for size, and the merchant encouraged her to try them on. Priscilla unlaced her saddle shoes and pranced around the cramped space in curled-up slippers, shaking the tassels and giggling.

Anna felt drawn to the rounded outline of the toes. This was a country of curves, she thought, as if the ancient clock of its history had eroded away any sharp edges, leaving behind a land of worn hills and domed roofs and rounded minarets. Even the people reflected curves, the way their baggy pants ballooned out, their soft caps rounded against their heads like berets with narrow brims, and the way the tips of their shoes curled up.

Instead of trying on the slippers, as Priscilla was doing, Anna only wanted to touch them, hold them, and run her fingers along their outline. There was something familiar about this shape...

Then, a memory of special evenings long ago...flowed through her like a warm elixir. She glimpsed flashes of herself sitting with Rainer on his porch. It was summer, before he left for war. They'd watched the oranges and reds of sunset seep into purple shadows of the foothills. They sipped German wine from his family's heirloom stemware, brought over from Germany when Rainer's grandparents immigrated in the 1880's. Anna used to trace her fingers along the stem and across the slick surface of the glass where a strange orange design was painted of a stoop-shouldered dwarf with curled-up feet.

Curled toes, much like the ones on these slippers.

"I said, how do you like *these*?" Priscilla's insistent voice penetrated the fog that numbed Anna's mind.

"What?" Anna blinked away the memory. "Yes. Let's take all of them."

"What's wrong?" Priscilla asked, squinting up at her.

"Nothing." Twelve years after Rainer's disappearance,

nostalgia hardly overcame her anymore.

The slipper merchant said something to her and motioned her to a chair, but she shook her head.

"You're crying," said Priscilla.

"No, I don't think so. Something in my eye. That's all. Can you pay for me?" Before Priscilla could question her further, Anna handed over some of her limp bills displaying Atatürk's face and turned her back on the rows upon rows of curled-up slippers to gaze out at the main thoroughfare of the bazaar. She just needed a minute to compose herself. She didn't like the idea of appearing weak before Priscilla. After all, she was here to care for her niece, not the other way around.

By the time Priscilla reappeared, holding a package wrapped up in newspaper and tied with string, the wave of nostalgia had passed. Anna smiled. "All right, then. Where is this shop we came here to see?"

"Oh, it's not in the bazaar."

"It's not? Then why did you bring me here?"

Priscilla giggled. "'Cause Fededa always brings me through here. There's a candy man on the way, and he sells Turkish Delight. You want some, don't you?" When Anna hesitated, Priscilla continued, "There's enough money left over for some candy."

"Okay...but honey, I *must* speak to Fededa's husband."

"This way." Priscilla set off past cluttered rows of stalls, and three young boys ran after her, holding out their hands in a gesture offering to carry the bulky bundle of slippers. A man looked up from behind the newspaper he was reading to watch the disturbance. His mat of thick, black hair bobbed, like a V-shaped bird's nest spilling over his forehead.

Anna's heart fluttered for an instant. She was certain she'd seen him somewhere before. Where? She scanned her memory of all the rushing faces she'd seen in the last day but wasn't sure. He was one of the police, she thought. She *hoped*. He'd been watching her house. Now he snapped the newspaper back into place before his face, and she turned back to Priscilla.

But her niece had disappeared from sight. All the surrounding people had swallowed the little girl from view.

"Priscilla, wait!" She glanced back at the policeman with the bird's nest hair as if he could lead her to Priscilla, but he had disappeared, too.

Chapter Twenty

Yaziz didn't have to work hard to keep the American woman in sight. The design of her dress, he remembered from his days in the States, they called "checked"—a disagreeable pattern that made her stand out in the bazaar like a neon sign from downtown Bloomington.

He thought it fit the boldness of the woman, however. If her western dress weren't enough, then she had her western height that kept her in view above the bobbing heads of Turks, who were, in general, a shorter people.

Because she was easy enough to keep within his sights, and because she was occupied inspecting every slipper in *efendim's* store, Yaziz took the time to order a coffee from one of the boys that worked the area. Who knew how long it would be before he'd have the opportunity to enjoy another sweet shot?

Yaziz's *koreli* nose had told him from the beginning that the American woman held the key. He'd survived Korea thanks to those instincts. They were instincts he'd learned to trust.

Miss Riddle was the key to the gypsy's murder, which was the key to whatever was bothering Bulayir, and yes, even to the general unrest on the streets of Ankara. Solve the puzzle of the Americans, and the rest would fall into place.

Which was why he was following her now. That, and the fact that he'd been unable to find Suleyman or one of his other junior officers available for this routine surveillance duty. Yaziz was keeping all of his boys too busy, running background checks on Miss Riddle. And pestering the lab, which still hadn't decoded the message that the phony letter surely contained.

Was it possible that the letter to the questionable Lieutenant Rainer Akers was nothing more than a *love* letter?

No.

Yaziz supposed that in the end, it was better for him to do his own tedious field work. He didn't know exactly what he was looking for, and if he didn't know, then how could he instruct someone else to find out what he would end up wanting?

Then, understanding hit him. The *letter* had been the American woman's role in this affair all along. The letter itself wasn't evidence. Its delivery was the *signal* for the start of the revolution! Its code was in the address, not the flowery message within. The address contained a number—109—that supposedly directed the letter to England.

Now he realized the number itself was the code. Such a simple answer, and he'd overlooked it.

He would have his boys track it down, but for now, he bet that no such address existed. It was a date. September 1. A date for when the revolution was set to begin... Day after tomorrow.

Aydenli already knew. That's why he'd pulled Yaziz from the gypsy's case. He wanted to suppress the so-called evidence, and therefore the signal that would put into motion the very event Yaziz must stop.

He wondered to whom the letter should've been delivered. The generals planning the revolution would ultimately need to receive that go-ahead signal.

Very handy that one of them lived next door to the Burkhardts.

The warm froth had just touched his upper lip when Miss Riddle emerged from the shop. Yaziz kept his head lowered over his brass cup, but his eyes rolled up in her direction. Two shops beyond the slipper shop, a man in a suit rattled an opened newspaper that otherwise hid him from view.

And why not? The American woman made herself into a spectacle much more interesting than any newspaper account that had been approved by the government for publication.

But now Yaziz wondered about the man. He must be one of Miss Riddle's own people, reading the *Republic News*. Only U.S. intelligence would hide behind such an inconsequential barrier as censored newspaper print.

He wondered why they would become interested in a woman who had the bad taste to wear checks and the bad luck to always find herself in the wrong place at the wrong time.

Unless, it was as Yaziz had suspected all along, and the woman was involved in a scheme far bigger than her innocence protested. She was working for Burkhardt—probably about to pass information—and she was using an innocent *child* as her cover to do her business. Abominable!

The child appeared at Miss Riddle's side, and her contact folded his newspaper, exposing himself to Yaziz's view. Erkmen! How could Yaziz have guessed so wrong?

Suddenly, the child darted away into the crowd, as if she intended to run straight into the arms of Bulayir's lieutenant. The woman lurched after her. Yaziz slammed down his brass cup on the nearest tray and followed.

* * * * *

Anna shoved her way through the crowds and finally caught up to Priscilla at an exit from the covered bazaar. Her niece had stopped to examine a display of candy. Anna paused to glance over her shoulder, searching for the man with the bird nest hair, but if he was there, she didn't see him. Shadowy outlines of people moved behind her in the bazaar, hiding any stalker from view.

Was that what he was? She wondered in a brief flare of anxiety if he'd also been the person following them the day before at Atatürk's Tomb.

He worked for Yaziz, she reminded herself.

No. She *assumed* he worked for Yaziz.

Her heart pounded in her chest. If he'd meant them harm, he could've easily grabbed Anna by now. She'd given him the opportunity back there with her momentary lapse of confusion. He hadn't. She took a few deep breaths to steady her nerves.

Priscilla spoke in Turkish, and Anna turned back to watch the vendor peel several cubes of sugared, gummy candy from a tray. Priscilla traded her money for the sweet treats, then skipped along a ray of sunshine that stabbed into a side street. She paused long enough to hold out a piece of candy for Anna.

"But honey," Anna said, taking the thumb-sized block. It was both soft and firm like a gumdrop. "Is it safe to eat?"

Make sure you don't eat anything from a street vendor, Mitzi had warned her.

Priscilla bit into her piece and munched happily. "I'll have yours if you don't want it."

Anna didn't hesitate long. She nibbled a corner of her Turkish Delight and followed Priscilla.

They weaved through the crowds up the street and around

a corner. They must've lost the man with the bird nest hair, and so she relaxed enough to savor the rosewater and almond flavors of her candy. As they continued up the hillside streets, the crowds thinned. Each alleyway grew narrower than the one before. Shade cast into the tight space, lowered the temperature several degrees, and eased the strain on her eyes from the glare of the outdoors. The last drop of powdered sugar from the candy melted away, and she was breathing deeply by the time they reached a cramped row of shops.

Priscilla stopped before one of the open doorways, festooned with tiny trinkets of silver and glass. "Ozturk Bey?" she called, stepping inside.

No one responded. Anna lingered in the doorway, where her attention fell instead to the copper shop next door. A shelf beside the open doorway displayed copper and brass items—pots and vases and trays and candleholders and ashtrays...

Brass ashtrays were shaped like miniature shoes. Their toes curled up like the slippers they'd just bought. Like the design on Rainer's wine glasses.

Priscilla returned to her side. "He's not here."

Just then, a young, lanky man sauntered out of the back of the copper shop and smiled at them with a grin that split his thin face from one prominently pointed ear to the other. "May I help you?" he said in hesitant but hopeful English.

"Where's Ozturk Bey?" Priscilla asked.

The man's grin slid off his face, and he shrugged. "In back."

Priscilla darted inside, calling out in her sing-song voice, "Ozturk Be-ey!"

The man with the pointy ears turned to Anna and brightened, nodding at the ashtray shoes. "These pieces are little. Come inside my shop, and I show you big samovar instead."

"Very nice," Anna said, "but we've come to speak to Ozturk Bey."

Furrowing his brow, the man placed one hand over his heart and gestured into the gleaming interior of his shop with the other. "He is my uncle. I am Emin Kirpat. Come in. You wait. You want me to show you trays, maybe? You like copper or brass?"

"I'm afraid I didn't come to buy anything, but I *do* find these items rather interesting."

"Please," he said, sweeping his arm along a path into the shop. "You look. We have the best copper and brass of all Turkey. Because of Ozturk Bey, we have the best shops for Americans."

"I expect it helps that you speak English."

Emin laughed, a joyous sound that came from his heart and infected Anna with its warmth. Sugar danced in her veins. "You like?" he asked.

Anna glanced up from the brass slippers, whose curved shape she'd been tracing with her fingers. "I've noticed these curious curled toes in more than one place."

"Hittite."

"I beg your pardon?"

"Very, very old. They are people who lived here long ago."

"Yes, I know who the Hittites were, but what do curled toes have to do with them?"

"They are Hittite. You like I show you our museum? Is not far from here."

"Thank you, that's kind, but today I need to talk to Ozturk Bey. Or, rather, Priscilla will talk to him for me. I need to ask about a young man named Umit Alekci. Maybe you knew him as well?"

Emin's face darkened with a scowl. His ears pulled back and his head snapped backwards in the "no" gesture. He ticked his tongue. "He *tschingaine*. Gypsy. No good. Better that he is dead." Emin shuffled away from her, no longer the helpful clerk wanting to sell her his merchandise.

"Wait," she called after him. "So you knew him? And you know about...what happened to him?"

"Nobody knows gypsies. They lie."

"You mean he lied to you?"

"Not him," he said with another tick. "*Her*."

There was a sister, Yaziz had said. Was that who he meant? "Look, maybe you *could* help me. I only have a few questions about him."

Emin slowly turned around, keeping his distance from her. "You must not ask."

"But why not?"

"He is dead now. You no want same for you."

A chill worked its way down her spine in spite of the heat of the day. "Have the police been here already to talk to you?"

"Yes. They come for pictures."

"*Pictures*? What pictures? I thought the police might've shown you something, instead. Something that Umit might've had. Something Umit might've told you about, like where he'd found it." Her letter.

Emin cocked his head and frowned, and she realized he didn't understand her. He wasn't following the way she danced around her letter to Rainer, the letter that Detective Yaziz had stubbornly kept.

"I am also photographer," Emin said. "But not always. I am student, you see. My uncle finds work for me sometimes. Ozturk Bey knows many people. Some, from police. They called me to *Anit Kabir* yesterday, where you were. I saw you there. Later, I developed pictures and police came here for them."

"You were the photographer for the police?"

He shrugged.

"And you knew Umit." She was trying to understand. This man had been the photographer with the flash the day before. And he'd known the victim, his subject. How awful for him, even if he had feared the gypsies.

As if he could read the despair on her mind, he said, "They no good."

She wondered how well he'd known Umit. If he knew about the letter, or maybe about Rainer's medallion. "He was trying to give me something, and I want to know why. Maybe he was trying to tell me something." *Why did he die for it*, she thought.

"Who knows why?" Emin shrugged again.

"Did *you* see anything?" The killer, maybe.

The ends of his mouth turned down, and he took a few steps backwards into the shadows of his shop. "I see nothing. You see nothing."

"Wait." She followed him into the shop. "If you knew him, then maybe you know where he lived. Did he live with his family? I'd like to speak with them. That's really what I've come to find out from Ozturk Bey. Where Umit lived."

Emin's gaze rolled in the direction up the hill from the shop.

"Did he live nearby?" Anna said, thinking *yes, just up the hill from here.*

"Too close. My uncle, he help *tschingaine*. I tell him no,

they are no good, but he never listens to me. Thinks I will marry her." Emin snorted.

Marry whom, she wondered. The *sister*? "Since you speak English, maybe you can tell me how to find his family."

"They live under...how you say? *Leylek.*"

Stork, she remembered. That's what Paul had said the word meant, only the day before in his car. The Alekcis lived under a stork's nest, up the hill from here.

Emin ticked his tongue and snapped his head backwards. "You stay away from them. They are... danger."

Anna's pulse raced. Danger to her because of what they knew?

Chapter Twenty-One

Yaziz lost the Americans in the crowd, something he'd never thought would happen. They were faster than he'd supposed. But he wasn't worried, as he caught glimpses of Erkmen's bouncing mat of black hair in the distance. Not Miss Riddle's contact after all, Bulayir's man was weaving around shoppers—following the woman. And keeping her path evident for Yaziz.

Suddenly, Erkmen slipped out onto a side street. Yaziz hurried his pace so as not to miss the transaction he felt certain the woman would make somewhere among the shops that lined the maze of alleys surrounding the bazaar. She seemed to like working in the middle of the day, under the public eye.

He bumped past a few shoppers, mostly Turkish women in the latest fashions of Paris, who scolded him for his disturbance. Men in silk suits, emboldened by their western enterprise, swore at Yaziz's aggression. Adolescents, on break from one of Ankara's many technical institutions, huddled together, forming an obstacle as they whispered and giggled at Yaziz's frustrated attempts to pass them politely. They would all treat him with greater respect if he'd worn either his veteran's badge or his National Police badge.

When he again spied the woman clad in checks, she was inside one of the shops of Ozturk Bey, who was one of the men

Yaziz's office routinely kept under surveillance. It was common knowledge that the old merchant smuggled opium in a thriving trade, but so far the National Police had been unable to prove it. Judging from the sharp tang in the air that hung over these narrow streets, Yaziz thought someone must be smoking a blend of it in his pipe just now. But Yaziz had to let that go if he was to see what Miss Riddle did.

He had not expected her contact to be Ozturk Bey. He had not figured that drugs would be involved in the Burkhardt-Riddle plot. But why not? A smuggling ring of illicit drugs would be far more profitable than the political problems of the struggling Turkish nation. Besides, he'd learned from his education in Indiana that Americans were more concerned with the profit in their pockets rather than who controlled the Dardanelles.

If what Murat had said was true about the Americans no longer courting Turkey, then the Americans wouldn't care if the Soviets controlled Turkish access to the Mediterranean or not. Why should foreigners care about the outcome of this nation?

Suddenly, an outburst disturbed the placid flow of traffic along the lane. The crowd came to life, shouting, pushing. Movement streaked past, and Yaziz caught sight of a young boy darting around shoppers, producing a ripple of cries and flailing arms and shaking fists in the wake of his flight.

A thief, surely. Yaziz took pursuit, cursing the boy who would cause him to miss the woman's transaction.

* * * * *

Following Emin, the clerk, into the cave-like interior of his copper shop, Anna heard rustling sounds coming from the back.

She squinted her eyes in the shadows and saw Priscilla emerge through a curtain of stringed beads at the back of the narrow store about thirty feet away.

She shouted. "Come on, Aunt Anna! I found him!" The glass beads of the curtain clicked against each other, settling back into place after the disturbance of her passage.

Anna hurried her pace past gleaming brass tubs. She felt Emin's gaze burning her back. She would have to find a way to uncover what he knew about Umit, what he wasn't willing to tell or didn't have the ability to tell.

She stopped before the beaded curtain and peered through. The clicking beads covered a doorway to a workroom, twice as wide as the narrow width of the copper shop. This back room appeared to service the trinket shop next door, as well. Priscilla stood in the center of the workroom with her back to Anna and spoke to an older man. Gray hair grizzled his thick beard and straggled out from beneath his cap. Dressed in the baggy black pants and white shirt of a traditional Turk, he sat cross-legged on a cushion on the cement floor and paid no attention to Priscilla. His attention focused instead on the gurgling water pipe before him. He puffed steadily away at his nargile. It looked like smoking a vacuum sweeper, Anna thought, the way its glass bowl, wrapped in silvery tubes, also sat on the floor and connected to his mouth with a hose.

"This is Ozturk Bey," Priscilla said, glancing over her shoulder at her. "Fededa's husband." Then she spoke again to the man, and her gestures suggested that she was introducing Anna to him.

Anna nodded and smiled. For all of Atatürk's efforts to build a modern capital, Ankara was still rather a small town.

Why else would the wife of an enterprising merchant work as a maid in one of the American homes? Unless Ozturk Bey had a hidden agenda. She guessed him to be in his fifties, judging from the creases that lined his weathered face and the amount of his gray. He pulled the pipe from his mouth, and slips of smoke leaked into the air, scenting it with spicy tobacco.

"How do you do?" she said through the curtain. "We are so pleased that your wife works in our home, and I was wondering if—"

"He doesn't speak English," Priscilla said.

Ozturk Bey laid his pipe aside and climbed slowly to his feet to bow at Anna.

Before Anna could ask Priscilla to translate for her, the child darted away again, through a second doorway of beads, leading into the trinket shop.

Anna followed and found herself in a room filled with delicate baubles of glass and ceramic, sparkling and glittering. Little bangles of silver and blue suspended from the ceiling, looped around pegs, and stacked on shelves. They tinkled as Priscilla breezed through the store.

Ozturk Bey followed them, his shoes squeaking as he unfolded a canvas chair and plopped it down beside Anna. He smiled and nodded first at her, then smoothed away a speck of dust from the canvas surface.

Anna sat down, and he beamed with pleasure, exposing several missing teeth. Then he scurried to the doorway to the street. "Coffee," he said, holding up three fingers at one of the boys who hovered outside. About Priscilla's size, several of the bag boys waited with their attention fixed on the new customers. Anna wondered if they were the same boys from the bazaar, hustling for a wage.

The chosen boy, whose hair was shaved close to his head, scampered away. Then, Ozturk Bey disappeared around the corner, in the direction of the copper shop.

"When can we get around to talking about Umit?" Anna asked Priscilla.

"You have to let him do all this first. Mama says it's not like shopping in the States."

"But I'm not shopping."

The sound of angry words suddenly rose above background noises, piercing the medley of bleating animals, rhythmic music, and laughing voices.

"Is that Ozturk Bey?" Anna whispered to Priscilla. "Yelling at Emin from the copper shop? What's he saying?"

"Something about not remembering to do something the right way," she said with an indifferent shrug. "Everything has to be right. That's why he sells so many evil eyes here. Look at all of them!"

"Evil eyes?" Superstition was always the same, Anna thought, trying to keep her voice merely inquisitive and not derisive. This was a universal superstition in a Turkish manifestation.

From her chair, Anna glanced at countless strings dangling from ceiling hooks. There must be hundreds of round, blue eyeballs staring at her from every vertical inch of space.

Butterflies rippled through her. She had to remind herself that these eyeballs were glass. Ceramic. Plastic. Whatever they were, they weren't real. Still, she couldn't shake the uneasy feeling that they watched her.

That someone watched her, even now.

Why not? Someone had watched her yesterday at Atatürk's Tomb, and then Umit was shot. Someone watched her at home and knew when to invade her bedroom to search her underwear. The man with the bird nest hair watched her, too. Yaziz's man, she hoped.

"Fededa says I'm supposed to wear an evil eye because I'm a kid," said Priscilla, "but Mama won't let me because she says that's silly."

For once, Anna agreed with her sister. "I don't understand," Anna said. "If you're trying to avoid the evil eye, why would you wear one?"

Priscilla gave a weak laugh, as if she wasn't sure whether or not she believed the superstition. "These are good evil eyes. They look the bad evil straight in the eye and scare it off."

"Deflecting evil away, in other words?"

Anna remembered from her university days, before the war interrupted her life, learning about the concept of an evil force that most cultures believed threatened life in one way or another. The Saint Christopher's medal was really just a Christian version of the same concept of doom.

Ozturk Bey clicked through the beaded curtain, having apparently circled back through the copper shop. He carried a wooden tray that he set on top of a footstool by Anna's side. Laid out in the tray were bundles of cloth that he unwrapped to reveal stacks of bracelets and rings and earrings of gold, decorated with amber and jet and sparkling gems.

"You like?" he said in English, perhaps the only two words that he knew.

Anna drew in her breath, then managed to say, "Very pretty. But I'm afraid I didn't come here to buy anything." Then she turned to Priscilla. "Go on, honey, you tell him why we're here."

"Mama says you have to let him show you the new stuff first. That's how you find out what you want to know."

"His jewelry certainly is beautiful, but..."

He nudged the tray closer to Anna, urging her to examine the gleaming gold. Her glance swept across the unwrapped contents, and she admired the jeweled bands and dangly pieces of jet shaped like crescent moons. Gold stars dangled in the center of the moons, little replicas of the star and crescent symbol of the Turkish flag. Hesitant to touch the treasures, she had no intentions of falling in love with anything that would require her to spend as much as these expensive items would surely cost.

Ozturk Bey seemed to read her mind. Holding up one finger, he said something in Turkish. Then he moved away, his shoes squeaking as he headed toward a stack of boxes. He bent down to examine them.

"Mama buys most of her jewelry here," Priscilla said. "Ozturk Bey knows someone who makes it. Ozturk Bey knows everyone."

"I hope he'll be more helpful about Umit's family than Emin was." Anna sighed. "He's gone to so much trouble that now I feel I have to buy something from him."

"You're funny," Priscilla said, narrowing her green eyes at Anna. "You're not like Mama."

Thank goodness. Anna bit her tongue to keep from voicing her thought aloud.

Ozturk Bey chose one of the boxes from his stack and returned to Anna's chair with it. He moved aside the tray of expensive jewelry and set his new box on the footstool. He pulled off the lid, revealing wrapped-up pieces of tissue paper. He grabbed one, unwrapped it, and held up a shiny ring of intertwined, silvery bands. With a flick of his wrist, it fell apart into four linked bands. Then his fingers worked it back into a single puzzle ring.

"You like more?" he said, presenting the ring to her.

"It's charming." She took the ring and tried it on with a laugh. "I wouldn't want to let it drop and fall apart."

Just then, the boy with the shaved head reappeared, carrying a round brass tray by its hook, like a balancing scale. On the tray were three demitasse cups of brass, and not a drop of the steaming coffee they contained had spilled.

The little boy passed the coffee around. Anna was about to protest his serving the adult drink to Priscilla, of all things, but a commotion erupted outside in the street. Someone was shouting above a babble of excited voices, and Anna heard the tapping sound of running feet.

"Hey!" Priscilla shouted suddenly, then sprang toward the door.

Anna twisted around in her chair in time to glimpse a piece of brass swinging through the air above her head.

Then pain.

Pain thudded into her head and sparked through her body, all the way down to her toes and fingers. The last thing Anna remembered was a smell of wool as her vision faded into a sparkly golden aura, then blacked out.

Chapter Twenty-Two

Yaziz sprinted after the boy thief, ignoring the splinters of pain from his wounded leg. Where was Erkmen now, when his assistance was needed? Yaziz had no other choice but to chase the thief himself. He was police, and it was always his job to uphold the law. He followed, not by sight of the boy, but from the part knifing through the crowd. The boy was fast, faster than Yaziz, in spite of the hours he spent training at the gymnasium.

This open-air labyrinth of shops was nothing compared to Istanbul, where Yaziz had grown up, but it was still complex enough. Especially when chasing a small boy. Yaziz had to be fast because the disruption settled down almost as quickly as it had occurred. As if the crowd absorbed the disturbance within their throngs.

The boy could be hiding anywhere, Yaziz thought, his gaze sweeping the innumerable bins and walls and stacks of merchandise and hanging ropes of merchandise. He elbowed his way past doors and smaller passageways and dead-ends and bridges and tunnels. Yaziz—not the boy—became the target of oaths and shaking fists.

"Excuse me," he mumbled, pushing his way in a direction he thought to be forward. The boy could be anywhere by now.

Yaziz stopped. He studied the shops. And their displays. Leather. Copper. Carcasses of mutton. Oranges from the coast. Business as usual.

Not only had he missed whatever the woman was up to, he'd lost the thief as well.

Perhaps Miss Riddle had hired the boy to cause the disruption and intentionally shake Yaziz from her trail. Indeed. She was more clever than he gave her credit.

He wheeled around, heading back to Ozturk Bey's shop.

Then stopped again.

Kneeling beside a stack of kilim rugs, out of view of where Yaziz had swept by only moments ago, were Erkmen and the boy thief. The police officer was rummaging into a straw bag, while the boy waited, holding out his hand, palm up.

Yaziz took off toward them.

"Hey!" shouted a shopper that he bumped against.

Erkmen and the boy looked up, then scattered in opposite directions.

By the time Yaziz worked his way to the spot behind the rugs, the suspects had disappeared. For that's what Erkmen had become, by virtue of his flight just now. Erkmen—what was he up to?—slipped through a back door of the rug shop, and the boy melted into the crowds. On the cement floor before Yaziz lay the straw bag.

Yaziz snatched it up and started after Bulayir's lieutenant. Two rug merchants blocked his way, ticking their tongues at him.

"Police," Yaziz muttered back at them. "Let me through."

"I don't see your uniform," said one of the merchants, thrusting back his head.

"We are a peaceful shop," said the other. "No one else is here but us. You have no right to harass us."

Yaziz wrenched his arm free of the merchants and pulled his badge from a pocket. The two vendors bowed, begging his pardon, and Yaziz stalked to the back of the shop.

The door led up a half flight of stone steps to an alley where an ox stood patiently, harnessed to a painted wagon. No one was about. Erkmen could've disappeared in any direction. He could be hiding in any doorway, watching him, knowing now that Yaziz was on to whatever betrayal he had planned.

Or he could be a block away. In either case, Yaziz had lost his cover of stealth. Never mind, he'd eventually catch up to Erkmen.

The detective cursed under his breath and stomped back down the steps into the rug shop. At least Erkmen had prevented the boy thief from stealing the bag. Yaziz opened up the bag while the merchants watched and pulled out an identity card. "Anna Riddle," it read.

* * * * *

Anna opened her eyes to a gaze that simmered with chocolate warmth. A strand of hair irritated her eyes, making them blink with fury that pounded through her head. A finger, light as her mother's touch, skimmed across her forehead and smoothed away the irritant. Tension melted from her muscles.

A man's voice murmured soft as a summer breeze whispering through cottonwoods. Except, his voice sounded crisp and

British, nothing like the slow twang of a western rancher's... "Welcome back. How do you feel?"

She tried to sit up, but pain hammered at her head and pushed her back onto the plush fibers of a Turkish rug. Someone had deliberately attacked her! With that realization, she pushed herself up onto her elbows despite the throb in her head.

The room spun around her. Evil eyes danced in the air above her. Voices whispered around her at the pitch of a roar. It hurt to breathe.

"Priscilla?" Her heart lurched in her chest, and her voice rose with it. She pushed herself up onto her feet, wobbling. "Where's Priscilla?"

The man with the cottonwood voice offered his arm for support, and she saw for the first time that he was Hayati Orhon, the Turk from the American Embassy. Where had *he* come from? Confusion sent another stab of pain to her head.

"Don't worry," Hayati said. "Your niece is with Ozturk Bey."

Anna leaned on Hayati's arm. His gentle touch warmed her, easing the pain. Her breathing settled back to a constant rhythm.

Hayati continued in a soft, murmuring voice. "Ozturk Bey sent Emin the photographer from next door to chase the thief and get your purse back for you, before he gets away."

"My..." Anna glanced down at the floor beside her chair where she'd set her straw bag. The bag wasn't there. Instead, a brass candelabrum lay on its side. Her temple throbbed, protesting her movement.

"In a public place like this, you cannot be too careful, Miss Riddle. Can you walk outside? Where we can find a taxi?"

"But where's Priscilla?"

"Just outside, not far."

Alarm pounded along with her pain. "By herself?"

"No, I told you. She's with Ozturk Bey. Do not worry. Come. Shall I help you to the doctor?"

"That's not necessary." She took a step, trying hard not to sway on her feet from the pain pounding her head.

"The doctor I know is not far from here. He is very good. He studied in London, one of the chaps I met there in my student days."

"What are *you* doing here, anyway?"

"Miss Lafferty sent me after you."

Anna's mind swam in circles. "But...how did you know where to find me?" She tried to remember the conversation back at the embassy, tried to remember what she had revealed to that woman...Fran... But it hurt to think.

He shrugged. "She thought you should not come here alone. Are you ready to go now to the doctor?"

"No, no, not now. I'm okay, really. I can't go anywhere without Priscilla." She took another step, wavering closer to the door. She saw milling people through the open doorway, but not her niece.

"Did you have anything valuable in your purse? A passport, perhaps?"

She massaged her temple, but it didn't help with the pain or her memory. "No, I'm sure I left my passport and most of my money at home."

Home? This wasn't her home. Home lay on the opposite side of the world. Home was where she felt safe from assassins and shadows in the night. Shadows, who followed her in broad daylight, who invaded her bedroom and pawed through her underwear.

Random events? She thought not. Her heartbeat sped up.

"I should've gone after the thief myself," Hayati said. "When I arrived, I saw a boy run away. I didn't know then what had happened. I could've caught him if I hadn't waited for Ozturk Bey to explain it all. Because of my English, he wished me to stay here with you while he assesses the situation with his various shops."

Hayati's gentle manner made Anna glad that he'd stayed with her, although she wished he'd insisted that Priscilla stay, too. "He has other stores besides these two? Why isn't he back by now? Surely he wouldn't leave his shops unattended."

The street filled with people stirring in every direction and gossiping voices that echoed throughout. From what she'd seen so far of this shopping area, she suspected that such chaos was the norm and not the result of a stolen purse.

"Do not worry," Hayati said. "They will be back soon. Then we can go to the doctor."

"But you said Priscilla is right here, just outside, and clearly she's not." Then alarm caught hold of her once more, and she reached for the doorframe to steady herself. *Priscilla!* she called out into the street.

Thieves, she thought, didn't usually hit their victims over the head before stealing their purses.

This had not been a casual purse-snatcher. Out there on the street was where purse thieves would more likely work. They wouldn't charge into one of the shops.

No, someone had targeted her. Someone had sent the boy in with coffee to distract her while someone else hit her over the head and stole her purse. She didn't think the boy could've done it. He was too little to wield the heavy brass. Besides, he was busy with his coffee tray. No, someone had hired the boy. The man with the bird nest hair whom she'd thought worked for Yaziz?

Whoever it was had been looking for something—the letter that Umit had tried to pass to her at Atatürk's Tomb.

Or... Maybe it was the medallion that he wanted.

Her heart raced and her mind spun as she stood there in the doorway scanning the busy crowd, waiting for Priscilla to return.

Finally, the crowds parted as someone short rippled through them.

"Priscilla?" Anna called hopefully.

It wasn't a child, but a man. A short man, dressed in a western business suit, emerged from the crowd. Grinning behind his gold-tinted lenses, he carried her straw bag and headed straight toward her, as if he'd known all along to find her here in Ozturk Bey's shops.

"Miss Riddle," Yaziz said, holding out her purse, "does trouble always follow you wherever you go?"

Chapter Twenty-Three

Yaziz offered the straw bag to the American, but she did not take it. She did not even seem to see it, her own missing bag.

Her voice rose to a shriek. "Oh, detective! It's you! Did you find her? Where is she?"

He shrugged off the spectacle of her disturbance. "It was just a boy. He was hiding behind some rugs when I found him, going through your bag. But he ran off, the little thief. You should be more careful." He nudged her with the bag, and this time she noticed it.

"You found my purse?" She grabbed it from his hands, flung open its lid, and dug into its basket shape. "How fortunate for me that you happened to be passing by at the right moment."

"Yes. Fortunate." Yaziz watched her claw faster through her bag, rattling items one by one. The hairs rose at the nape of his neck as he realized he was standing next to the embassy man, Hayati Orhon, a sorry example of a Turk. "Tell me what happened," Yaziz said to Miss Riddle.

Her face, a chalky bronze through his lenses, paled another degree as she shook her bag, searching for something that was not there. Perhaps the white of the salt lake of *Tuz Gölü* was her natural skin color. The woman was full of surprises. He intended to uncover every one of them.

"What are you doing here?" she asked, instead of assisting him in his investigation.

"Doing my duty, Miss Riddle."

Orhon the embassy man moved closer to her, as if his allegiance lay more with the Americans.

Miss Riddle did not appear to notice. "You and also the man you assigned to watch my house," she said. "Did you know that he followed me to the bazaar today? Yes, of course you know. That's why you're here, because he phoned you to report where I am."

Yaziz frowned, careful not to betray his inability to soothe her rising hysteria. "It is a police matter. Someone will please explain what happened here."

Orhon spoke up. "The embassy sent me along to accompany Miss Riddle, and—"

She dropped the bag with a yelp and examined her trembling hand. A puzzle ring decorated one finger, and she twisted it off. "I only tried it on," she said, swooping down to place it in one of the opened trays of jewelry that littered the carpeted floor. Yaziz also recognized her bundled-up purchases from the slipper shop.

Nearby, a brass candelabrum lay on its side.

"Ozturk Bey was showing me these rings," she continued, even though he was not interested in the rings, "when someone suddenly ran into the shop and hit me over the head. It must've happened while the boy distracted us with coffee. Or maybe it was the boy himself. I don't know."

"Where did this come from?" Yaziz pulled his handkerchief from a pocket and used it to pick up the ornate piece of brass, heavy enough to damage anyone's head. "Does Ozturk Bey sell brass items in this shop?" He looked around at the glass evil eyes, dangling from the rafters on strings, at the stacks of jewelry trays, and a glass counter displaying meerschaum pipes and cigarette holders.

"Not here," Orhon said, "but he does sell brass only next door."

"You are familiar with this merchant's set-up?" Yaziz already knew it too, but he had his routine.

"We at the embassy refer the Americans here, to these shops."

"A convenient arrangement for Ozturk Bey," Yaziz said. "Surely he cannot manage both shops by himself."

"It is true," said Orhon. "There are helpers that he employs. Ozturk Bey is a wealthy man, thanks to his increasing popularity with the Americans. They like to buy their copper and brass from him."

Yaziz carried the weapon to a spot under the single electric light bulb illuminating the shop. He thought he saw a smudge of blood along the carved side of one of the three shafts designed for holding a pair of candles each. Perhaps the lab could lift fingerprints, although he was fairly sure there would be no records to match their owner.

"How is your head after that blow?" Yaziz asked, laying down the weapon on a piece of tissue paper. Then he glanced up at the woman, who still frowned. She rubbed the crown of her head. Hair coiled there in a thick, black rope the Americans called a "braid," and a wet cloth balanced atop the whole thing. The overall effect was that of a turban, and he couldn't help smiling.

"It hurts."

"You need to see the doctor," Orhon said.

Miss Riddle turned to the embassy man and said, "You were starting to tell the detective what you saw, when I interrupted."

"You saw what happened?" Yaziz asked Orhon.

"No. I was just arriving when Ozturk Bey suddenly cried out for help."

"You saw nothing unusual on the street?"

"Someone running. It must've been the boy, but I didn't know then that she'd been attacked." He smiled shyly at Miss Riddle, and Yaziz felt his skin prickle again at the back of his neck.

"What about the copper and brass shop?" Yaziz said with a cough. "Did you see anything unusual there?"

Orhon's downturned face told Yaziz that he had noticed nothing.

"You'll have to ask that nice young man who minds that store," Miss Riddle said, interrupting the interview. "But you already know about him, don't you? He works for the police sometimes as your photographer. He told me his name is Emin Kirpat."

Yaziz covered his embarrassment from the assault of the American's forthrightness by pulling out a small notebook from his pocket. He flipped through its pages until he found the notes that his assistant, Suleyman, had given him. They confirmed Miss Riddle's information.

"And where is he now?" Yaziz said.

"Ozturk Bey sent him out to chase the thief. He should have returned by now." Orhon glanced at Miss Riddle's stolen bag, returned now.

"Detective," Miss Riddle said, "didn't you find my niece on your way here?"

"The little miss is here?"

"Well...not *here*, as you can see. She's out there. With Ozturk Bey. They must be looking for the thief, too. You must've seen Priscilla, since you found my purse. Where is she?"

Yaziz shrugged rather than admit that he'd lost them all. Even if he wanted to tell her the truth, he couldn't, since that would reveal that he'd been following the woman and child ever since they'd climbed into the taxi at the Burkhardt house on Yeşilyurt Sokak earlier that day.

"Don't worry," said Orhon, stepping closer to Miss Riddle. "She is safe with Ozturk Bey, I promise."

But the American woman's face twisted in consternation.

"Is something missing?" Yaziz asked, nodding at the bag at her feet.

She hesitated a moment too long for such a simple question. "My money is still here, and so is my identification card that Henry's office gave me. How did you know...where to find me?"

"What do you think the thief wanted in your bag?" Yaziz asked, instead of confessing.

"Why don't you tell me? You probably have a much better idea of these things."

He shrugged again. "It's usually money they want. Are you in the habit of carrying something else, something valuable, perhaps?" The *thing*, Yaziz thought, that she was going to pass to Umit Alekci before he'd inconveniently been murdered. He'd been wrong about Erkmen, and he could just as easily be wrong about the letter serving as a signal.

"Of course not."

The theft of the bag was a ruse, Yaziz decided, for passing the information he'd known all along that she would pass to her contact. He hadn't found anything suspicious when he examined the contents of the bag back in the rug shop. He'd missed the transaction after all. Thanks to the incident of the woman's purse.

But the wound to the head puzzled him. He didn't think she would have gone so far as to arrange an injury to herself.

"I'll tell you something that would have interested a thief," Orhon said, rippling his fingers through the unwrapped bundles of jewelry scattered on the floor. "Harem rings. I know Ozturk Bey sells them because the Americans from the embassy always want them. Those rings are worth a lot of money with their rubies, sapphires, and emeralds."

"Who are some of the American customers?"

"Miss Fran Lafferty has recently placed an order."

Yaziz lifted his notepad, but his pencil remained poised in mid-air. His attention had been caught by the movement of red curly hair, a flicker he'd glimpsed beyond the wall of hanging evil eyes, out on the street. He was about to tell the woman, whose back was turned toward the street, that she could stop worrying. Her niece was returning. Then the red-haired one stopped before the display of brass and copper pots and trays next door.

Ozturk Bey stepped out of the crowds and ducked beside Priscilla. He lifted the lid of a brass brazier and withdrew a small bundle about the size of his hand. It was wrapped in newspaper and tied by string. While Yaziz watched, the old Turk passed the package to the American child.

The detective glanced at Miss Riddle. Perhaps he'd been

wrong about her. It wasn't Miss Riddle who worked with Henry Burkhardt but the Burkhardt child herself.

But Yaziz refused to believe such abomination was possible. He would find the explanation, for surely another one existed.

Chapter Twenty-Four

"Priscilla!" **Anna's** head pounded, keeping time with the pain that throbbed through every cell of her body. "There you are! You had me worried."

Priscilla whirled around, bouncing her red curls. She dropped a package wrapped in newspaper and tied up with string into a copper pot and then stepped away from it. "I was only helping Ozturk Bey."

"I can see that now." Anna decided to back down. She didn't want to jeopardize the feelings of warmth that had started to grow between them the night before. Besides, all was well now, except for Anna's head.

And the Saint Christopher's medal. She hadn't found it in her purse after Yaziz had returned it to her. That's where she'd put it.

The purse thief—only a boy, the detective had said—hadn't touched her money or her little red book, her official document giving her diplomatic immunity. Both items were worth more than the necklace. Perhaps the boy thought the jewelry valuable. He was wrong. Its value was more sentimental than anything else.

Rainer... If only...

Confusion in her heart matched the agitation surrounding

her. Yaziz shuffled over to Ozturk Bey's side and asked a series of questions in curt-sounding Turkish, while Ozturk Bey raised his voice to answer, flailing his arms as if to better illustrate his tale. Hayati stood off to one side with his hands in his pockets, quietly listening. Priscilla flitted through the shop, touching the evil eyes one by one. Anna would deal with her niece later.

For now, she slipped next to Hayati and whispered, "What are they saying?"

"Ozturk Bey confirms that one of the coffee boys is your culprit. He says the boy must be new here in the city, recently arrived from the country, because he doesn't remember ever seeing him before with the other boys. Or else he is protecting him."

"Accusing him is not a very effective means of protecting him."

"He's just a child. What is more important is his name. *That* is what Ozturk Bey is protecting. His identity."

"Why does he protect him?"

Hayati shrugged. "Ozturk Bey is well known around here for his connections. He finds work for people who need it, and they give him their loyalty in return. The boy is probably the son of one of them."

A ripple of anxiety washed over Anna as she wondered about Priscilla's loyalty. The package her niece had tossed inside Ozturk Bey's copper pot looked like the package that Fededa hadn't wanted Anna to see in the Burkhardts' broom closet.

"Are you ready to go to the doctor," Hayati said, "now that Priscilla has returned? I will take you. I believe the detective is done with you for now."

"I don't need a doctor. I'll be fine. Besides, I already took an aspirin from the tin I keep in my purse. Luckily, Detective Yaziz returned it to me. What I mean to do, since I've come this far, is to find the Alekci family. I need to ask Ozturk Bey how to find them." That's why she'd come here in the first place, and she wasn't going to be led astray from her purpose. "How much longer is he going to be tied up with the detective? I'll have to wait."

She glanced at her wristwatch. The day was slipping away, and she hadn't given Priscilla any lunch yet. "I don't suppose... Since you've been handling all the paperwork... Do you know where the Alekcis live?"

Hayati grinned. "You never give up, do you?"

She couldn't afford to, not with all the questions on her mind. She must settle the question of Rainer before his ghostly reminder drove her mad. But she couldn't tell Hayati any of that, so she smiled as winningly as she knew how. "You *do* know. Would you take me there, please? Miss Lafferty says there's no address, but you know where they live, don't you? If you don't have enough time, perhaps you could just point out the way to me, and I'll find the family myself."

He smoothed the narrow lines of his mustache and rolled his eyes. "Well...if I were to take you... You would owe me a favor."

She frowned. "Is there something you'd like for me to pick up for you at the PX?"

"No. But I would like the honor of taking you to dinner some night."

Anna gasped, letting out the sound before her sense of decorum could cover up her initial shock. "Oh, no, Mr. Orhon, that's quite impossible."

"Not at all. We have a few decent restaurants, even here in Ankara, in some of the modern hotels."

"No. That's not what I meant. I'm sorry. You don't understand." Heat flushed up her throat and cheeks.

"Never mind. You're not ready now, I can see that. But when you are ready, the invitation is still open."

"Thank you. I mean... Really, I appreciate the invitation, I really do. But you see... That is—"

"It's all right," he said in a soothing tone of voice, like the one Anna had used the night before to calm Priscilla from her night terrors.

She realized, from her shaky knees and furious patter of her heartbeat, that she felt terrified, more terrified by his invitation than the blow on her head.

"Orhon!" said a woman's voice, scolding through the fog of doubts that threatened Anna. "Get back to the office *toute suite*. Mr. Wingate needs you. I'll take over here."

Anna looked up and saw Fran's pencil-thin figure outlined in the doorway, her hands planted on her hips and a smug grin on her face.

* * * * *

They were all bastards, Meryem thought, glaring at the general's pink palace. She tugged on the *eşek's* reins, hauling the donkey up the hill with its load of clinking pots. The midday sun scorched her skin, and the dust in the air dried the insides of her nostrils and throat. A mirage flickered before her.

She blinked and for a moment the jagged cliffs of the Carpathians rose from her past, replacing these worn-down

Turkish hills of the present. In a flash, she thought she was seeing that other palace, not the general's, but the Romanian palace with its skinny towers of wooden spindles and its overgrown gardens that the Nazis had captured for their own. The memory still lived fresh in her mind, smothering her.

She could still see it now, as clearly in her mind as if those Carpathian mountains rose before her. Each mountainous hump jutted with a bold thrust to the sky. At their base lay a slanting meadow, and for the rest of Meryem's life, she would always see Tereza, Elena, and Andrei in her mind, stumble-running toward the safety of the forested hillside. The peaks appeared near enough to reach out and touch.

But they could not.

Meryem watched her siblings go. She was the youngest, only a child in the nightmare that haunted her, but even then, she was the wisest.

Even as the gap between her and her siblings widened, she heard the desperation of sobs that caught in their throats. Sobs wasted good breath, breath they would need if they were to make it away from their captors. Into the shelter of firs.

Her distraction with the Nazi bought her siblings time. Not enough time.

Beside her, he suddenly stiffened. His eyes widened with... (Surprised, are you, Nazi? To see gypsies escape?) *His pants, down. Round his ankles.*

Meryem seized the opportunity. She lingered long enough to spit on the Nazi. To scratch his face. She bit his chapped hands that tasted of chicken feathers and blood. Or was it her sisters' blood? She did not know.

Blood splatted onto the rumpled heap of the bastard's

pants. He collapsed to his knees, his bare butt flashing in the gray gloom that saturated the air before the dawn.

From somewhere behind Meryem's shoulder came the garlic-breath smell of someone new. Not Umit, who was busy pawing through the pockets of a dead guard beside the open gate. Then came a voice, along with the breath, and it snapped out a terse order in Meryem's ear: "Run!"

Not "stop," as she would've expected, but "run!" An offer of freedom.

The offer came first in German, then in Romanian. But Meryem could not move. Umit, neither. Fury overwhelmed her—Umit, too—left her immobile in the fire-ice of her hatred.

Meryem did not know the newcomer with the garlic breath, nor why he wanted to help the gypsy prisoners of war. That he did was enough for her. He sounded German but appeared more Greek with his thick, black hair. Desperation wrinkled his face, and his broken-nose profile told her of his fearlessness.

Once again she looked down at her Nazi torturer, who writhed in the pile of his clothes. A knife handle protruded from his back. The newcomer-savior had put it there, and he whispered again, "Hurry! There's not much time!"

The Nazi clawed at the ground, groped through his clothes, then pushed himself up, swinging a pistol, firing again and again at Meryem's fleeing siblings. They cried out and fell. One by one.

"Tereza! Elena! Andrei!" Meryem wailed.

Grief exploded, bursting like the flame that ignited their grandmother's campfire. Blood and air circulating through Meryem's body became a tidal wave of surging rapids, sweeping her over the cliff of no return. She lunged at the *bastard, fell on his arm of pure evil. One more shot fired as his arm resisted her, and the newcomer, their rescuer-savior-liberator, grunted. Stumbled to the dirt beside her. He was bleeding, too.*

She was a rabid animal, a feral nomad of the mountains, and she leeched onto the bastard's arm. Ripped his flesh for the gun. Twisted it from the Nazi's dying fingers. Turned it on the bastard. Fired.

Again and again.

Tears sluiced down her cheeks. Each time she closed her eyes, her strength slipped away, and she saw it again. That ugly dawn in the Carpathians, that last day of the person she once was.

It was dawn no longer, but the middle of the day. And she was alone. The Black Sea lay between her and those distant memories. Trudging on up this Turkish hill, she thought that her revenge was not yet done.

Chapter Twenty-Five

Anna felt relief at Fran's interruption. The woman had saved her from the embarrassment of stumbling through an inadequate explanation for turning down Hayati's invitation. She couldn't accept a dinner date with him.

Hayati grinned at Anna, as if amused by her discomfort. She felt ill. Mere moments ago he had appeared concerned about her physical pain, receiving that blow to the head, and now he was making matters worse. The pain in her head thumped even harder.

Before she could find an acceptable excuse, he slipped past Fran, standing in the doorway of the trinket shop. Fran turned her head, her gaze following him as he disappeared, blending into the stream of people on the street. Ozturk Bey, gesturing with his hands at Detective Yaziz, seemed too immersed in that interview to notice anything else happening, and certainly not the women. Emin, the young photographer who helped next door in the copper shop, still had not returned. Anna wondered briefly if his absence was due to the police presence. She felt certain he'd had something to hide when he'd expressed his dislike for gypsies in general and Umit in particular.

"Let's go," Fran said with a nod of her head at Anna. "I'll take you and the kid home."

"That's very kind," Anna said with a shiver of annoyance,

"but we can take a cab home when we're ready to go." She wasn't done here. She still had to find a stork's nest.

"Suit yourself." Fran surveyed the disturbed interior of the shop. "I'll be here shopping for a while, in case you change your mind and want a ride."

Anna didn't have to ask Priscilla twice. Her niece seemed as eager to escape the shop as Anna. She gathered up her purse, and Priscilla carried the string bag, which held the wrapped package of slippers. Outside, they mingled with everyone else walking in the street. Very few cars came through here, and besides, there were no sidewalks.

"Where do you want to go now?" Priscilla asked.

Anna pointed up the hill. "I'm looking for a stork's nest. Want to help me find it?"

"Sure! There's one," Priscilla said, pointing. "And there's another."

"I think the one I'm looking for is actually farther up the hill from here."

"You don't know?"

"Not for sure, but we'll find it. Maybe along the way you can tell me about that package back there. The one that Ozturk Bey tried to give you. What was inside it, and why did you throw it into that copper pot?"

"It's just some stuff he wanted me to take to Fededa. It's supposed to be a surprise, but you spoiled it."

"Shall we collect it on our way back? I'll act as if I didn't see it."

"If you want," Priscilla said with a shrug. She fell silent, and Anna marveled at the sights along the way.

There were donkeys carrying baskets of wares across their

backs and clip-clopping behind their owners along this narrow lane of cobbles. Women balanced baskets on their heads, and men stooped over, hauling bundles of sticks on their backs. Music, with rhythms as sinuous as this alley, floated through the open doorway of a butcher's shop. Carcasses the size of sheep hung from ceiling hooks in the doorway, releasing their pungent odors.

"Maybe we can ask inside for directions," Anna said. Flies lifted into the air as she stepped inside, and she waved their buzzing circles away from her face. A man with a bloodied apron was busy slicing a slab of meat on a table.

"*Merhaba*," she called out over the music. "Do you speak English?"

He laid down his knife, wiped his hands on his apron, and grinned at her. He turned down the radio and responded in French.

She smiled, relieved that just this once she didn't need to ask Priscilla for help. In faulty French she asked if he knew of an Alekci family and where she might find their apartment.

He waved and pointed and fired off words she didn't understand. Then he held up a finger in the universal signal to wait. Shuffling behind his counter, he rummaged for a pencil and scribbled a map in the margins of a newspaper. Newspaper sheets stacked up beside bundles of twine, apparently used to wrap up a side of mutton. He ripped off the map and handed it to her.

"This is where I can find the Alekcis?" she asked.

"*Oui*." He beamed with pleasure.

Back out in the street, she took Priscilla's hand and followed the butcher's directions. After winding through the shadowy labyrinth of wooden buildings, she thought she finally found the place. A stork's nest tucked against a tilting chimney above. Women's agitated voices streamed through open windows.

Anna ducked into a passageway leading off the street. It was a stone tunnel with a floor of packed dirt, where a stairway led to the upper levels. The passageway emptied into an enclosed courtyard, a square of sun-drenched weeds, but Anna took the stairs. They creaked as she and Priscilla climbed to the top floor. The door of an apartment stood open, and waves of wailing rolled out into the hall.

Inside the barren room stood a huddle of women. Behind them, a gauzy curtain served as a door into another room, and through its sheerness, Anna glimpsed other faces peering at them.

A withered woman with no teeth broke away from the huddle and approached Anna. She dropped to her knees before her and murmured anxious streams of words between bursts of tears. A forgotten head scarf fell around her shoulders.

"Do you speak French?" Anna asked hopefully, but she got no answer.

She stood helplessly by, despairing that she might not find out what Umit's family knew about Rainer. Priscilla, meanwhile, murmured with the children of the family. Anna recognized *hayir*. *No.* A boy with a buzzed head who was almost the same size as the boy who'd brought coffee to them in the shop a short while ago, drifted closer to Priscilla. The children eyed each other. Anna rubbed the sore spot on her head and wondered if this boy was Umit's son. Had he been here all along, with his widowed mother and grandmothers and aunts and neighbors? Or had he been out on the streets serving coffee and conspiring with purse thieves?

Priscilla finally translated. "The little boy saw the bad man, just last night. He thinks the bad man is going to come back for the rest of them. Isn't there anything we can do?"

Anna's heart wrenched. What *could* she do? Her resources were so limited here. "I'll talk to that detective again. Tell them, honey. Maybe he can send one of his officers here to protect them."

"The police aren't doing anything, he said. They were here not long ago."

The gauze curtain separating the other room swooshed aside just then. A young woman with a baby on her hip emerged from the second room. The curtain fell back into place behind her. "Mustafa!" she said to the boy. She said something else and ticked her head backwards. The boy—Mustafa, Umit's son—slunk away from Priscilla's side and retreated into the other room.

The woman with the baby must be Umit Alekci's widow, Anna guessed. Her eyes were red, and her face splotchy from dried tears.

"I am so sorry for your loss," Anna said.

Mrs. Alekci was far too young to be a widow. And now she had two children, maybe more behind the curtain or out on the streets. It was up to her alone to raise the children and care for her elderly mothers and aunts. Alone, without her husband.

"Ask her about the letter," Anna said to Priscilla. "Why did her husband have the letter I wrote? And where did he get it?" She searched her memory for the few Turkish words she'd learned. "*Nerede?*" Where, she remembered.

Mrs. Alekci stared at her as if Anna had sprouted a second head.

She said it again, louder. "*Nerede*?" She looked Mrs. Alekci in the eye and pantomimed writing.

The huddle of women wailed in the background, but Mrs. Alekci remained silent. Numb.

Anna shook Priscilla's arm. "Ask her again about the letter Umit had." Then she pointed to herself and spoke slowly, willing the woman to understand her. "I wrote that letter. Where did your husband get it? Did Rainer give it to him?"

Mrs. Alekci's eyes widened, and one hand flew up to cover her mouth. "Rainer?" she whispered.

"Yes, that's right," Anna said. "*Evet*. Yes. Rainer. Did you know him?"

"Rainer," Mrs. Alekci said again. Her face lit with recognition. She turned to Priscilla and spoke a stream of unintelligible words.

"What's she saying?" Anna finally asked.

"She says we've done enough."

"But I haven't done anything."

"Not you. My daddy. It's kismet that we gave Fededa a job."

"What?" Anna startled, and her head throbbed, trying to follow the change of subject. She felt twisted inside, yanked in different directions. "What's Fededa got to do with this? Does she have a connection to this family?"

"Because of my daddy's old suit. Remember?"

"Ah." Henry had given his old suit to Fededa, who then gave it to Umit. "What can she tell me about Rainer? I'll pay—"

"Rainer!" Mrs. Alekci said again, then ran from the room and swished past the gauze curtain.

Sounds of running feet came from the other side of the curtain, and then children darted out and pressed against the huddle of women. Behind the curtain, wood scraped against wood and hinges creaked and objects thudded against walls and dropped to the floor. Finally, Mrs. Alekci reappeared, flinging aside the curtain. Ignoring the screams of the baby on her hip, she marched toward the huddle of women while spitting out angry-sounding words and shaking a wooden box in her baby-free hand.

"What's going on?" Anna whispered. Hysteria mounted around her, punctuated by glances of hatred aimed her way. "What does she know about Rainer?"

"She says they're gone."

"What's gone?"

"I don't know. Something they must've kept inside the box."

The woman's face twisted with anger, and tears streamed down her cheeks. She hissed and spat in Anna's direction.

Anna reeled, edging backwards, toward the door. She grasped Priscilla by the hand.

Then the box came hurtling through the air, striking the wall beside the door, only inches away from Anna's head. Anna watched it fall and break open, empty. Using her last reserve of strength, she yanked Priscilla by the arm and darted out into the hall.

Chapter Twenty-Six

At the top of the hill, Meryem turned the corner from Yeşilyurt onto Guneş. Shade trees spilled out over the pink wall surrounding the general's palace. The sun slipped farther to the west, sinking as did her spirits. Military men thought they could live like kings, did they? She would use her wiles to fool them all.

Blood had already spilled.

And there would be more.

She could never cleanse her mind of that memory, of the blood dribbling from the Nazi's mouth. A sweet revenge, but not enough. That bastard had deserved more than a mere death spasm crossing his face.

Since that blood-filled day, Meryem had never moved so fast again.

"Tereza! Elena! Andrei!" She'd cried that day, sprinting to the meadow. In her memory, she fell again and again where her siblings had fallen. She threw herself across their still bodies. Finally, at rest. Never, at peace. Frightened dreams carved horror in their unseeing eyes. Meryem heaved with sobs.

"Help me," Umit had cried from behind her. "This one is still alive."

Meryem lifted her head from her sisters' blood, looked past the bleeding hulk of the Nazi to her older brother. With forever new eyes. Umit knelt beside their liberator. "We can do something for this one," he urged.

And so it began. Their bond. Their destiny.

Together, they helped the wounded man, their savior, stand. In those bloody days when she still had one brother left, she would have done anything, short of giving her life, for that newcomer who had freed her.

It had not been easy.

Go back!

They could not go back for the bodies of their sisters and brother.

By the time Meryem and Umit and the wounded man— the man who freed them—had staggered to the shelter of the firs, it was too late. They heard the first cries of alarm from the Nazi camp they'd left behind. Other Nazis, roused from sleep. Alerted to the trouble the newcomer, their liberator, had stirred up. The unknown man had risked his life to save theirs. An angel, come to their rescue.

Now Meryem was the last of her brothers and sisters. At times along their difficult path of survival she wished their liberator had never appeared out of the Romanian hills. Look where fate had brought her. To this pitiful fortune. Her fingers, destined for ruin. The little ones at home, and the old ones, too, starving.

But without him, she and the rest of her family would have been dead by now, many times over. Dead, along with Tereza, Elena, and Andrei.

And now her last brother, Umit, was gone. The revenge would begin again.

Perhaps tonight... It was up to her to use her cleverness

to feed the family. But she could not stop thinking of revenge. Revenge, in the form of a gun.

* * * * *

Anna clattered down the steps. Clutching Priscilla's hand, she stepped out into the narrow street. Downhill was easier going, and they tripped and slid along the cobbles, dodging people and startling animals.

She wondered what had once filled Mrs. Alekci's now empty box. Mention of Rainer had led the woman to seek the thing she'd apparently kept inside that box, the thing that was now missing. Rainer's medallion.

Her head pounded with each footfall. That woman had wanted to hurt her. Perhaps her aim, hurling the box, was deliberately off target, so as not to actually hurt anyone, but the truth remained that she *wanted* to hurt Anna. Was it just because of grief, or was there something more? Somehow, Mrs. Alekci blamed Anna for the loss of her husband. Anna had seen the blame in her eyes as clearly as if it had been her language.

Had Mrs. Alekci blamed Anna enough that she sent her son, Mustafa, to Ozturk Bey's shop to hit her over the head and steal her purse? If Mustafa had been the boy who'd done that, then he'd now recovered Rainer's Saint Christopher's medal. Perhaps that's what had been kept in the box. Anna slowed her pace, turned, and looked over her shoulder, hesitating. Wondering. No, she wouldn't go back there, not now.

Since Anna didn't have language on her side, she would have to come up with a new plan. One thing was sure, there was a connection between the Alekcis and Rainer.

A woman's voice called to them from the crowd, bringing Anna's attention back to the present moment. "Fancy finding you here." It was Fran. She sauntered closer, and then apparently read the consternation on Anna's face. She said, "Everything okay?"

"I'm staaaarving," said Priscilla.

Anna glanced at her wristwatch. "It's late, and we've missed lunch. We must find a cab right away."

"It's never too late." Fran grinned. "I know a place nearby that's good. I could use a bite to eat, too. Come on, I'll take you."

Anna had to admit that she felt grateful to find a familiar face in the midst of her recent turmoil. Mrs. Alekci had a right to her anger, on account of her grief, but still, Anna was glad to escape its reach. This made twice in one day that Fran had rescued her.

Fran led the way to her car, parked a block away, and several minutes later, they pulled up in front of a downtown hotel. A flush rose to Anna's cheeks, reminded of Hayati's invitation to dinner in one of Ankara's modern, new hotels. Maybe this one.

They chose a lunch table outside in the closed-off area of a sidewalk. Waiters moved in and out, bringing bottled mineral water, crusty rolls, balls of butter, and olives the size of walnuts. Animal smells wafted on the air, and wooden wheels of a cart creaked nearby. In the distance, a horn honked. Nothing made sense.

Priscilla tore into her bread, and Anna crunched hers more delicately. She hadn't realized how hungry she'd been.

Fran narrowed her eyes and watched them eat. "Why'd you run off like that this morning when I told you to wait?"

"You mean from the embassy? We had things to do. Places to go. Promises to keep." Anna smiled at Priscilla and her chipmunk cheeks.

"And you thought you could get it done by yourself?"

"Is that why you sent Hayati after me? To help me?" Or not. Anna wondered if his real purpose had been to prevent Anna from fulfilling hers. If so, it hadn't worked. She'd found the Alekci family on her own, without his help.

"I didn't send him after you," Fran said.

"He said you did."

Fran leaned back in her seat and pursed her lips. Then she dug in her bag and pulled out her leather cigarette case. "You want one?" She slid out a cigarette and tossed the case across the table.

"I still don't smoke."

Fran laughed.

But Anna noticed that Fran avoided her counter claim of what Hayati had said. One of them was covering up. Lying. Hayati? Or Fran?

Fran slowly lit her cigarette, as if the action gave her time to think. "So," she said, finally blowing out a smoke ring, "did you? Did you get your tasks done that you wanted to do?"

"Indeed. In spite of the accident."

"What accident?"

Anna told her, describing the events that led up to being hit on the head with a brass candelabrum. As she went on with the story, Fran's cigarette burned down to a stub.

Anna finished her tale, and the waiter placed a plate in front of her. Lemony lamb smells made her mouth water.

"Yum!" Priscilla said, bouncing in her seat.

Fran jabbed the stub of her cigarette into a brass ashtray. "Why didn't you tell me sooner? I'll take you to the embassy doctor as soon as we finish eating."

"As I told Hayati, I'm fine. Really."

"Nonetheless, that's where we are going next. Eat up."

Anna sighed and gave in to the savory flavors. She suspected no one argued with Fran. "Lucky for us you showed up when you did," she said between bites. "What made you come to Ozturk Bey's store today? Don't you have to work?"

"I *am* working," Fran said. "Does he scare you that much?"

Anna felt a flush rise. What on earth did she mean? It didn't look as if this efficient woman, Paul Wingate's assistant, was working. Unless... Her job was to follow Anna.

Anna took a sip of water. "So you heard?"

"Heard what?" Priscilla asked, suddenly more interested in their conversation than her lunch.

"Mr. Orhon wants to take your aunt out to dinner," Fran said with a chuckle.

"Oh, *that.*" Priscilla's attention shifted from her plate to a nearby donkey standing asleep under a tree.

"Why don't you go with him?" Fran asked.

"Oh, I couldn't."

"Why not?"

"I don't know him."

"Isn't that the point of going out with someone? To get to know him better?"

"It's been such a long time since I've done that sort of thing. I guess I've forgotten how."

"Not much to it. Maybe you don't want to remember. Maybe on account of Akers?"

"Have you found anything about him yet?" Anna didn't think it very likely that Fran had tracked her to Ozturk Bey's shop just to volunteer information about Rainer, but she held out hope anyway.

"Nothing, really," Fran said. "But it's curious. Matheson, over at JUSMAT, said that if they have anything on him it would've been in one certain file. And it seems that file has gone missing."

"Someone stole it?"

Fran shrugged. "He didn't say that. Only that it's missing. Misfiled, probably. They're looking."

"Well, thanks for checking." Anna felt her hopes sink. But then, there would be no reason for a file to exist on Rainer in an American military office. Rainer had volunteered with the Brits. And died before he'd ever had a chance to don an American uniform.

"Want some advice?" Fran said.

Anna looked up, unsure of how long she'd been lost in her gloomy thoughts. Apparently, Fran took that as an affirmative, as she went on.

"Talk to Hayati," Fran said. "He might know a thing or two about our files. After all, he's worked with Henry."

Anna tipped her head sideways, trying to understand. "What does Henry have to do with it?"

"We're a community. We all work together." Fran motioned the waiter for the check, and then pulled crumpled lira notes from her purse. "And besides, it will help you from becoming homesick."

"I'm not homesick."

"Not *yet*. You might feel differently after you've been here long enough. It's not easy to give up what's familiar." Fran scraped her chair back and watched Priscilla lead the way, winding past tables. "The children adapt better. Life around them, right here, today, *this* is what's familiar to them. The world of their parents is as unfamiliar to the kids as this place is to their parents."

That helped explain Priscilla, Anna thought. She was worried about her parents, traumatized about all that she'd seen that a child shouldn't even have to know about, and worst of all, she didn't think she could talk to Anna about any of it. "I'm a stranger to her," she murmured to Fran.

They followed Priscilla out to the sidewalk. "My advice?" Fran said. "Find someone to talk to, someone who will make things feel familiar here for you. Then again, maybe I'm wrong."

Anna doubted that Fran was ever wrong. Even so, she felt drawn to Fran, in spite of her suspicions. Or maybe because of them. They shared a bond of secrets.

Chapter Twenty-Seven

Anna was grateful for the ride, even if it meant a detour to the embassy doctor. An hour later, when Fran's car stopped in front of the yellow stucco house, Anna thanked her and assured her that she would indeed take it easy. At least until the party later that night at the Wingates'.

Priscilla skipped away to her playroom off the kitchen. She needed to assemble gear, she'd told Anna, for the spaceship game she and Tommy liked to play. They were planning to blast off to an unknown planet, and tonight was their chance to continue the game. It was their last chance before school started next week, heralding the end of summer.

Anna smiled at her niece's imagination and climbed the stairs to her attic bedroom. She hoped to get rid of her headache before her gossipy neighbor Cora could stimulate brand new levels of pain for her at the party tonight. She wanted nothing more than to change into shorts and stay in her room to rest and brood over the day's events. She hardly knew who or where she was anymore.

Only the week before, she would never have imagined that someone could target *her* in an attack. And now she saw several possible explanations. Perhaps Umit's killer thought she could identify him. Or maybe he thought she had the letter, and for some unknown reason, he wanted it, too. After all, he'd killed to get it—or to keep *her* from getting it.

But those explanations assumed that it had been Umit's killer who'd attacked her today. And if that was true, then he'd hired Umit's son to distract her with coffee while he somehow, sight unseen, had slipped into Ozturk Bey's trinket shop with a brass candelabrum...

No, she didn't think any of that was very likely.

Her head throbbed.

She needed facts to help her sort it out. The fact was that the Saint Christopher's medal was missing from her purse after today's attack. Perhaps that's all her attacker was after. He'd known she had it, and he wanted it.

Or maybe he was a she.

Cora Wingate was the only person who'd known where the medal was. No, maybe not the only one. The soldier next door might've seen Anna drop the medallion in her purse. He'd been spying on them from the fence.

Anna moved swiftly to her bedroom window that looked out over the general's yard. The old puttering soldier wasn't there now. Nor Rainer. She'd imagined him the night before, but here was another fact: *some*one had been down there in the middle of the night, looking up at her. Someone who'd reminded her of Rainer.

But they weren't the only ones who'd seen the necklace. Her neighbor Ahmet, that Turkish widower about to remarry, had seen it when he came to the door with Priscilla and Gulsen. Although, he hadn't known she'd put it in her purse. Or did he? Truth was, anyone could've been spying on her during that martini episode with Cora. Yaziz's man, supposedly to protect her. The smoker by the lamppost on the street corner the night before. Erkmen, Yaziz had called him. Erkmen had followed her to the bazaar today. As Yaziz had.

They were all suspects in her mind, but she would've seen any of them enter Ozturk Bey's shop before hitting her.

Fact: the only ones who were there besides herself, Priscilla, and the two shopkeepers were Yaziz... And Hayati.

She started at the beginning and rehashed all that she knew. Although, where was the beginning? When Umit was murdered, holding her letter to Rainer? Or much earlier... When Rainer went away to war, causing her to write the letter. Perhaps when Mitzi ran away from home and ended up joining the USO... Which led to her meeting Henry... And Anna's being here...

She wasn't sure if it was a fact, but one thing was certain: that Turkish detective—Yaziz—seemed utterly incompetent. He would never unravel this mystery, and even if he did, she suspected he wouldn't share the information with her.

She would have to find the answers herself.

She would also have to find some suitable cocktail attire. Cora had been right to suspect that Anna didn't own any. Anna had attended a few receptions before, but never a real cocktail party. She didn't think her Sunday dresses would be appropriate for tonight, and she remembered that Mitzi had invited her to borrow what she might need.

She was getting nowhere with her reasoning abililties, and so she pushed her questions to the back of her mind and headed down the hall to Mitzi's bedroom. Her hand hesitated on the cool brass of the doorknob. Everything she'd ever thought before was now wrong. Turned upside down, inside out. Her mind spun, and she couldn't sort out truth from lies, fact from fiction.

Rainer.

She turned the knob and stepped inside her sister's bedroom. Drawn blinds darkened the room and lowered the temperature several degrees from the rest of the stuffy house. She shivered, but it wasn't *that* cool in here. Something about this room gave her an uncertain feeling, echoing and defining a hollow spot inside her. The room felt so...empty. As if it had once been alive but now had gone dormant in the absence of its owners.

But Mitzi and Henry were coming back!

Anna gave herself a shake and stepped with resolve across the throw rugs toward the closet, situated on the opposite side of the room beside the balcony door.

Inside, clothes filled the narrow space. Mitzi's dresses occupied more than half the length of the closet, while Henry's suits took up the rest. Anna wondered how it was possible that they owned this much clothing, and more. Besides these clothes, they'd taken enough with them for a three-month trip.

Anna riffled through the dresses, sliding them apart to examine them better. They were much too flamboyant in their bright colors, or too frivolous with lace and ruffles, for her taste. She was about to give up her search and choose one of her own sensible Sunday linens when she found a possibility. Tucked between two frilly taffeta dresses was a simple, black chiffon.

She pulled it out of the closet, brushing at some lint, and managed to knock one of Henry's suits off its hanger. Reaching for the gray pinstripe jacket, she noticed a tiny scrap of paper on the floor. It must've fallen from a pocket.

She picked it up. It was one of Mitzi's calling cards. Beneath her printed name, *Mrs. Henry Burkhardt*, a note was scrawled by hand. Anna recognized Henry's chicken scratch scribbling.

Saturday @ 10

An appointment. Last Saturday? If so, it was the day before Anna had arrived.

Although, it could've been any Saturday in the past. She wondered why Henry had used *Mitzi's* card instead of one of his own. Was it an appointment for him, or for Mitzi?

It probably didn't matter.

And it was none of her concern.

Anna tucked Mitzi's card back into Henry's jacket pocket and hung the suit in the closet. Mitzi must own a clothes brush that would take care of the lint on the black chiffon. Anna's gaze wandered to the shelf above the hangers, but there were no small items like a brush. Round hatboxes in bold, blue and white stripes, tied up with ribbons, lined the shelf.

Borrow what you want, Mitzi had said. *Except...*

Except, what?

I don't care. It doesn't matter anymore.

Anna assumed her sister was being overly dramatic. Having been a USO entertainer, Mitzi had always had a flair for drama. Still, Anna couldn't get the calling card with Henry's appointment out of her head.

If what Yaziz suggested was true—that the Burkhardts' itinerary was fake—then Mitzi and Henry were deceiving her about something. Intentionally? What were they up to? Not that Anna necessarily believed the Turkish detective, but what *was* true was that nothing in her life was normal anymore.

Anna reached for one of the hatboxes, but her hand jerked back. They were closed. Tied up. And that made them private. They could be the "except" that Mitzi had mentioned. Privacy was something Anna valued above all.

Anyway, she didn't need a hat with a cocktail dress. Looking in Mitzi's firmly closed hatboxes would constitute snooping. Her sister was entitled to privacy.

No, Anna couldn't, *wouldn't* touch them.

* * * * *

The Wingates' backyard later that night looked like a fairyland of Chinese lanterns hanging from the treetops. Turkish servers moved about the lawn in their crisp, white jackets. Crystal and china tinkled together, and the smell of grilling shish kebab filled the air.

Anna didn't feel much in the mood for a party.

Someone bumped her elbow. "Here you are!" It was Cora, singing the words in a slurred fashion. "I saw Prissy running off to Tommy's clubhouse, and I knew you had to be here somewhere." She pushed a martini glass into Anna's hand, then nodded at the children's slip-shod assortment of plywood sheets that pretended to be a rocketship tonight.

"What're you doing over here by yourself?" Waving her drink hand, Cora seemed oblivious to the way she sprayed both of them. "C'mon and join the party. I'll introduce you around."

So this was how Mitzi passed her time abroad, Anna thought, following Cora back across the lawn. They approached a small cluster of guests, and she only recognized two of them. Their host, Paul Wingate, looked deep in thought, and his assistant at the embassy, Fran Lafferty, looked bored. A cigarette in a meerschaum holder drooped from her mouth. Neither of them paid attention to the conversation of the group.

"Everyone," Cora said, "I want you to meet our new arrival, Anna Riddle."

The woman who'd apparently bored Paul and Fran paused her chatter and waggled white gloves, clutched in her fingers. A strand of hair curled around a beauty spot at the side of her mouth.

Then someone shifted from his hidden position behind Fran's shoulder, a man dressed in a white suit. Hayati!

Amusement sparkled from his carefree manner as he stepped out from behind Fran. His face beamed and his gaze ran appreciatively up and down Anna's length, leaving shivers along her spine. She drew her shawl tighter about the low cut of Mitzi's black chiffon.

"Of course you already know Paul," Cora continued, "and here we have Eve Matheson, Fran Lafferty, Hayati Something-or-Other, and Major Matheson. He's from JUSMAT, not the embassy. I know, it's confusing."

"Pleased to meet you," Anna said.

"And over there," Cora said, pointing out a nearby group with heads lowered over someone on a chaise longue, "we have Viktor Baliko and his wife Tonya, who're here recently from Hungary. That redheaded man with them is Don Davis, the kids' teacher this year. A bachelor." Cora rolled her eyes and elbowed Anna. "Yoo-hoo, Donnnnie! Oh dear, he's not paying a bit of attention to me. Well, don't worry, dear, I'll find a way to fix you two up. I'm sure you'll have plenty to talk about."

Eve Matheson flicked her gloves and said, "Did y'all cross by ship or air?"

"I came alone, and I didn't have enough advanced warning for anything besides a plane."

Fran tutted, then spoke in a husky voice. "Too bad you had to rush. Ships are much more civilized."

"You're quite right, Fran, but..." Eve blathered on about the speed and efficiency of modern prop planes in general and Pan American specifically.

Cora cut into Eve's rambling praise. "Anna's come here all the way from Colorado to take care of little Prissy while Mitzi and Henry are on their safari. It was all very last-minute, rush-rush, you know."

The soft undercurrent of nearby conversation suddenly died. Ice cubes clinked over a low hum of ahhhs. Unknown faces peered at Anna, watching her. Always watching. She shivered, despite the warm breeze that rustled through leaves.

Cora leaned close. Her breath carried the sharp smell of alcohol as she whispered loudly enough for all to hear. "Miss Lafferty is here on her own, too. Single, like you."

"Divorcee, she means," said Fran, whisking the cigarette from her mouth.

Anna felt a charge ripple through the group from Fran's bold pronouncement. Times were changing fast, but divorces were still not discussed openly. No more than Anna had been accustomed to talking about her lost fiancé.

Now all that was changing. Like the times.

"I've never been married," Anna said softly, taking a sip of her drink. She nearly spat the liquid fire back into her glass. It was all she could do to keep from choking.

"A technicality." Fran's lips twitched with amusement in what might be a smile.

Major Matheson, a hefty man in a crisp military uniform, looked ill at ease as he spoke up. "How are you getting along so far, here in Ankara?"

Anna started to answer, but Fran beat her to it. "She's already required the use of our diplomatic services." The cigarette holder dangled from Fran's lips and gave her words a tired sound.

"We heard they arrested you," Eve said. The lock of hair kept bothering her mouth.

Heat rose to Anna's neck. "No, they didn't—"

"Everything's fixed," Cora said. "We have Paul to thank for that."

"Thank Hayati, you mean," said Fran, smirking at the quiet man beside her. "He's the one who made most of the arrangements. Paul is just the one who gets the credit."

Hayati stepped forward and took Anna's hand. "It was a pleasure." His chocolate eyes glittered under the light from the lanterns.

Surprise charged through Anna, as he continued holding her hand longer than felt comfortable. Not more than an hour ago, in her room, she'd put his name on her short list of suspects. Just because he'd been there. But she didn't believe it. He was too caring to be guilty of such violence. She slipped her hand from his grasp.

Eve and Cora tittered together.

Fran chuckled. "Aren't you just fed up with how stuffy our conventions can be? We don't have to act like twits."

Silence fell over the group. Then Cora let out a shrill cry. "Oh, that Fran! What a joker she is!"

Everyone's attention turned to Anna with expectancy. Anna cleared her throat and summoned the steady voice she'd had to use in the classroom when a few ornery students tried to rile her.

"What I mean to do," Anna said softly, smoothly, "is to take Turkish lessons. Perhaps you could advise me on finding a place?" She returned Hayati's gaze with equal intensity.

"Turkish lessons?" Eve shrieked. "What on earth for?"

"I suppose she wants to learn the language," Fran said, blowing a smoke ring.

Cora scoffed. "You don't have to do *that*. Everyone you'll ever want to talk to speaks English, anyway."

Hayati beamed with pleasure. "Yes, I know a place where they help you learn."

"That language is way too hard for us to learn," said Eve. "For us adults, that is. The children pick up anything and everything."

"Let the Turks learn English," Cora said. "Viktor did, and he's not even Turkish. He picked it up real fast. They have to, you know. Besides, we have interpreters."

Fran rolled her eyes toward Paul. "Who are available for our personnel, not our dependents."

Cora waved her wrist, fortunately not the one that controlled her martini. "Oh, la-dee-da. I'm sure special arrangements can be made for certain dependents in times of need."

"I intend to learn it myself," Anna said. They could stunt their minds if they wished, but not her. "If I start with language, then perhaps I'll pick up bits of information from the local newspapers."

Paul snorted. "You won't find anything there. They don't use newspapers for news the way we do. The Press Law has made reporters too afraid to print anything but propaganda. They only print what the party wants the public to know."

Hayati shifted his stance and glanced around at the other

partiers, as if looking for escape. Fran's gaze darted back and forth between Paul and Anna, and her eyes glinted with amusement. Cora tottered away to her other guests.

"This country is a democracy," Anna said, "thanks to Atatürk. How can the people allow suppression of information to happen?"

"Technically, we're a republic," Hayati said, then coughed. "The Democrat Party is in office, that's all. They're not the party of Atatürk, and they're not democratic as you know it in the States."

"It happens," Paul said, "because you don't say anything negative here. Atatürk himself set that law in place. So for instance, you can't even report news about the worsening economy. They call this place Yokistan, the land of not. It'll be interesting to see what happens in the upcoming elections next spring. We'll see if the Democrats remain in power or not."

Eve wagged her finger at Paul and gave a dramatic yawn. "Blah, blah, blah. Politics are so boring." She turned to Anna. "You must come to our bridge club, dear, that's much more interesting. I'll bet you didn't know about the woman who was giving us belly-dancing lessons. A schoolteacher, can you imagine that? Anyway, she stopped coming to our group, so that's why we have a hole to fill. We think she had a tête-à-tête with her paramour in the Bolu Mountains, but she hasn't come back yet. And school starts next week! Now, don't you think that's more amusing than politics?"

Speculation about a colleague must've drawn the redheaded schoolteacher—Don Davis—closer to Anna's circle. His shift away from the Hungarians on the chaise left a clear view of the man identified as Viktor. Viktor lifted his head, and his gaze locked with Anna's. Only...he wasn't a Hungarian at all. Anna gasped. He was Rainer.

Chapter Twenty-Eight

The tang of tobacco stained the air, lingering from meetings that held no end. *Bah!* Meryem thought, dancing before the general's men. They lounged on their woolen rugs beneath the foul cloud that intoxicated this upstairs meeting hall, glowing with crystal.

This second night of dancing at the general's pink palace would finally earn her payment, and she would get it, too. Even without the aid of Umit's bartering skills.

She danced on, rippling her flesh, carefully exposed in all the right places. Naked between layers of gauze and rows of tinkling bangles, she danced closer. The general's men twisted with desperate desire and rising anticipation. She swooped closer, jiggling and shimmying long enough to tease them with her offerings and entice them to collect their offerings of coins.

She danced on, until the general finally stood and clapped his hands and called his men to their nargiles. On, until the secret police, disguised as a server, ushered her out. On, until she faced the *asker* in the kitchen below. With his glass of raki, he would surely try to cheat her again.

"I promised you nothing," he said as predicted.

"Then you are a thief. Shall I tell the general how you cheat him? How you take bribes that bring men to spy on him and invade his privacy?"

The *asker* rose so fast that the wooden legs of his chair scraped the stone floor, and the whole thing crashed over backwards. "Lies! That's all you gypsies are good for!"

"We'll see who lies." She wheeled around, kicking up her skirts as she left the kitchen. Clearly, the *asker* did not intend to pay her anything additional beyond the tips she'd gathered upstairs. They would have to do, for now.

"Wait!" His fist slammed against the table.

She did not stop. She fled down the hall toward the staircase to the grand hall above.

"Let's talk!" More wood screeched against the floor. Then the thud of heavy boots, stomping out an erratic beat.

She was halfway to the second floor when he called up to her. "Hey, you can't go up there."

"The general will want to know how you cheat him." She slowed her step, feeling caught between the *asker* below and the secret police above.

Neither the policeman in disguise nor one of the general's servants appeared ahead, under the crystal chandelier. Her hesitation had given the old soldier enough time to lumber up the stairs.

"Come back here!" he called after her.

The sound of the *asker's* heavy movement reminded Meryem of his physical strength, despite his age and his drunken stupor, and she ran on. She must hurry, since she had an appointment to keep.

Speed was in her favor, and she quickly reached the landing of the upper hall. Empty. No servants. She felt certain that the secret police lurked somewhere nearby, probably already aware of her presence. The double doors into the sitting room remained closed, sealing the general and his guests inside the place where she'd entertained them only a short while ago.

The old soldier thudded up the steps. She glanced first at the closed doors, then behind her. The general's man meant to corner her in the manner of a guard dog. Feeling a flash of regret for perhaps the second mistake she'd made tonight, she darted down the grand hall. Beyond the double doors. To a glass door leading outside to a balcony that overlooked the garden behind the mansion. Another way out. Before the *asker* rounded the top step and could spot her, she slipped out, into the night. The night swallowed her, covered by the black of her garment.

Laughter floated on a current of air from the house next door. Americans. She should've danced for them, instead, but she'd been blinded by greed because of the gun that had killed her brother.

She'd known her path intertwined with the Americans'. She *hadn't* known it would only lead her to trouble. She should've left kismet alone.

She crept along the balcony, looking for a way into the garden below, when another sound reached her. The soft murmur of voices. They lured her on to the far end of the balcony, graced by overhanging branches of a tree. A window stood open, brushing into leaves and releasing men's voices along with soft bursts of their laughter. Meryem ducked beneath the branches and caught a whiff of tobacco from the open window above her head.

"Bring the girl back," said one of the men inside the general's sitting room.

"Patience, Murat, in the name of Atatürk," said the general. Authority resonated through the deep registers of his voice, making him easy for Meryem to recognize by voice alone.

Water gurgled—they were smoking their nargiles. Men, and their filthy vices, she thought. How she hated the games they had to play, when everyone knew it was always the women who held the real power, unrecognized as it may be.

"But Atatürk was the least patient of us all," said a third man.

"It is in honor of his memory that I have asked you here for our evening discussions," the general said.

"You risk all of our lives, pasha, by inviting us here. It is against the law to hold political—"

"This is *not* such a gathering, you fool, and I remind you not to use that word again. Spies are everywhere these days."

"Surely not in your employ?"

"To the best of my knowledge, but no one is ever completely certain. That is why I brought the girl here, so that outside eyes would think she provides pleasure for nothing more than casual entertainment among friends."

"Where conversation naturally turns to ways to unseat the Prime Minister and his party," said one of the guests, amidst throaty chuckles and gurgles.

"One must learn caution," the general said, "when the assistant minister of the Interior lives only across the street."

"Perhaps we take unnecessary risks by meeting here," said another. "This rich neighborhood is where the men in power live."

Another voice spoke up. "This is the last place where they would expect us to meet, right under their very noses."

"'Where makes no difference," said the first man who'd spoken. "These are troubled times for all of us. Nowhere is safe because the Press Law has everyone stirred up."

"Especially for you, Murat."

"Murat is correct to see the depth of our concern," the general said. "Our Prime Minister has failed to keep his promise to amend the Press Law, and that is one more example of the promises he breaks. Promises he never intended to keep."

A restless murmur rumbled among the guests.

"Worse than that," the general continued, "the current government is undoing all of Atatürk's reforms, one by one. Now the fez is back, even though Atatürk banished it. Religious instruction is back in our schools, after Atatürk correctly gave us a secular Republic."

Murmurs grew to outcries.

"Gentlemen!" The general's voice rose above the unrest in his parlor. "Our greatest fears are coming to pass. The men we have entrusted with our government are wringing the secular out of our state, and no one will know it until after the deed is done. Now they've banned reports of what goes on within the Grand National Assembly. Each day they move us farther away from the Eternal Leader's vision for us. It is time for us to bring it back. It is time for us to act. Remember Atatürk's words when he said, 'Resistance to the flood-tide of civilization is in vain'...ah! But my memory is not so great as it once was."

"'...nations which try to function with medieval minds'," continued another voice, "'are doomed to annihilation—'"

A tapping sound suddenly interrupted the buzz of excitement that the general had incited. A door clicked.

"What do you want, old man?" The general's voice rumbled with impatience.

"A thousand pardons, pasha, but I must warn you that the girl is a thief."

"A thief? Explain yourself."

"I told her not to disturb you. I paid her, as you instructed. I did! But she demanded more, the greedy slut, and she came up here to bother you for the money."

"You are the only one who is bothering me. Why are you bringing your problems to me? What have you done with the girl?"

"But...she is not here?"

* * * * *

Anna felt the world stop around her. The moment froze in time, as she stared, no, *gaped* at Rainer... His nose, just slightly crooked from that time long ago when his horse unseated him. His fearless jaw, defining the defiance that gave him the strength to leave her. The coarse black hair that allowed him to blend with Mediterranean people... He was Rainer, *not* someone who merely reminded her of Rainer. Yet, he was the man who called himself Viktor. Their gazes locked together, and the other partiers surrounding them in the Wingates' backyard ceased to exist.

"Oh!" Cora said with a little titter that broke the spell. "I see the two of you have already met?"

"No," Rainer quickly said from the chaise where he sat. "I no yet have the pleasure." Using an accent—a fake accent—Rainer aka Viktor sprang to his feet. His long, lean legs and his familiar, swift stride carried him closer to her.

Anna got the message, although she did not know why. Why didn't matter. Their relationship was over. She'd thought him dead these last twelve years, but her love for him had never died. Still, it was over.

If he'd deliberately kept his survival hidden from her all these years, then there was no hope that their relationship could be resurrected.

It really was over.

In a supreme effort to keep her voice steady, she held out her hand and managed to say, "Pleased to meet you. *Viktor*, is it?" Later, he would explain to her why she had to lie for him.

"Yes, Viktor," he murmured, taking her hand and bringing her fingers to his lips. Her hand burned in his grip, or perhaps it was *his* hand that felt like fire.

"Oh my," Cora said again, giggling. She narrowed her eyes, and her gaze darted back and forth like worry beads sliding along on a strand.

Hayati stepped into the circle and chuckled. "Don't tell me you two forgot, already. The taxi, remember?"

"The taxi?" Anna repeated.

"Yes, the taxi, of course," Rainer said in his heavy accent, an accent that pretended to be heavier than Hayati's. He laughed.

Cora laughed, too, a shrill sound. "You met in a taxi?"

Anna frowned, not wanting to be pulled into their silly cover story. There had been no meeting in any taxi. What was this all about?

Hayati shrugged and laughed.

Everyone seemed awfully damned merry, Anna thought. As their merriment increased, her initial shock faded. Anger took its place. This charade now—the *need* for such a charade— reminded her of the questions circling through her mind, and she frowned with a mixture of confusion and impatience. She glared first at Hayati and then at Rainer. Were they in league together? And then she remembered her own suspicions of danger. Rainer was involved in some dangerous game. Somehow, Hayati knew.

Anna tried to laugh too, but now doubts replaced her anger.

Rainer smiled, his teasing, tiny smile that Anna remembered, and memories came flooding back of other times he'd teased her with that smile, the smile that no one else realized was a smile because the corners of his lips barely flickered, and she could see by the sparkle from the depths of his hazel eyes, yes she could see now under the distorted light of the Chinese lanterns that his eyes were hazel (changeable, that's why she hadn't remembered before in Yaziz's office), and she knew now that he actually meant to smile at her.

"Viktor?" said the woman from the chaise next to Rainer's.

Anna remembered Cora's introductions—*Mrs.* Viktor Baliko. Tonya. The soaring song that filled her being crashed rudely back to the ground. His wife. Viktor's wife. *She* would explain Rainer's absence all these years. His silence.

"Darling?" said Tonya, Mrs. Viktor Baliko, as she pointed to her wristwatch.

Rainer bowed his head to his hosts, Cora and Paul Wingate. "Please, I beg you forgive us. My wife..." Rainer's gaze avoided Anna. "She is...not well."

Anna raised her glass to her lips, hiding her cheeks that flamed with the heat of her anger and hurt and fear and more. Confusion. Next to her, murmurs of concern rippled through the guests.

"No, no," Rainer continued, "please, it is nothing. A little rest and she is good as new."

Giggles and snatches of whispers arose as the guests parted for Rainer and the woman he called his wife. Tonya.

Anna watched, stunned, as Rainer walked away, swallowed bit by bit by a sea of partiers. Snatches of gossip snapped around her. "Indisposed," and "poor dear," and "the family way."

None of that mattered. Anna didn't care about anything. Nothing mattered except one single fact: Rainer was alive. She didn't even care that he seemed to be married. There was a logical explanation, there *had* to be, and she would get her answers. The party was simply not the best setting in which to get those answers. She and Rainer would have to have a private discussion, and it would happen. Later. She'd waited twelve years for word of what had happened to him, and she could wait a little longer.

"Dear," Cora said, shaking Anna's elbow. "You schoolteachers are off in a world of your own. Wool-gathering? I do believe you haven't heard a word I said."

"I'm sorry," Anna said. "Do go on."

"Don't you think it's interesting? Our belly dancer *and* the Balikos? They all live in that apartment building down the hill from us, on the other side of the vacant lot. Isn't that just so handy? We'll get to spend lots of time with them."

Anna stiffened with attention as Cora continued.

"Mitzi and Henry have included them in their Saturday afternoon barbecues," Cora said, "and I expect you will continue the tradition, too. That's why you need to know about them, dear. About how they managed to escape through the Iron Curtain. They came here after that trouble in Hungary last fall."

"My, but isn't he handsome?" said Eve, leading a round of oohs that rippled through the group. "Weren't they in the middle of all that trouble in Bucharest?"

"Budapest, you mean," said Fran. "Bucharest is in Romania."

"But I'm quite sure there was some problem in Bucharest, too," Eve said with a pudgy frown.

"There's trouble wherever the Soviets go." Paul scowled and cast his gaze down.

"I declare," said Eve. "Isn't it dreadful the way those commies think they can just march into whatever country they want and do whatever they want?"

Cora wobbled from Anna to her husband and clung to his arm. "What the Reds did in Hungary won't happen here, will it, dear?"

Paul shook his head. "Not if we can help it."

"Why else do you think Uncle Sam is spending so much money on this mission?" asked Fran, fitting a fresh cigarette into her meerschaum holder. Hayati glided forward, snapping a lighter to life.

Eve fanned herself with her gloves. "Thank goodness. I can sleep at night with Ike in the White House."

"Although, he wasn't much help in Cyprus," said the major. "Anyway, Mr. Khrushchev is geographically closer to us than the White House is."

"Oh dear," said Eve, fanning herself faster. "Now I'm sure I won't sleep a wink after all."

"Phooey." Cora leaned against her husband. "They'd evacuate us before anything could happen to *us*."

Paul's scowl went deeper. "It won't come to that. We'll keep the trouble in our backyard from exploding into violence."

"Like the gypsies," Cora said. "They stir up trouble, too."

"I wasn't talking about gypsies."

"But I *am*, dear," said Cora. "You see, a funny thing happened to me today regarding one of them. A gypsy woman came to the door and spoke to my maid. Turns out she was offering up something rather interesting for sale, some old love letters to a soldier during the war."

Fran arched her eyebrow. "Where'd she get them?"

"She didn't say. They weren't doing her any good. Their kind can't read, you know. So she thought she'd make a little money from them."

"What'd you do?" Eve asked, breathless.

"Bought them, of course."

"Oh, good lord," said Paul, digging through his coins again. "What'd you go and do that for?"

"I thought it'd be amusing," Cora said with a laugh. Then she turned to Anna. "Anything wrong, dear? You're white as a ghost."

Chapter Twenty-Nine

Meryem perched on the balcony, swallowed by night. Tipsy from the sound of laughter that floated through treetops, she did not wait for the general and the old *asker* to discuss her whereabouts any further. Without a moment's hesitation, she reached for one of the limbs that sprawled over the balcony's railing, and she used it to balance herself as she swung across to the tree. Its trunk was sturdy enough to support her as she climbed slowly down, pausing on each branch to pull her garment loose from its twiggy snags. By the time she dropped to the ground, a commotion stirred behind her. Doors of the general's palace slammed, lights blazed, feet ran, voices raised in questions.

Meryem landed on a garden path of gravel, bathed in a ring of light that now surrounded the mansion. The old man must have switched on every light in the place as a show of his employer's power and wealth. *Bah!* With a few brisk steps, she moved out of its blazing circle, into the shadows that enveloped most of the garden.

The men's words that she'd overheard played through her mind. They'd used her, like a nargile, as their cover, while they met illicitly, at risk to their lives, so they'd said, to plan the overthrow of the government.

They would not allow her to escape with that information.

Her slow, careful steps—careful, to minimize the crunch of gravel—made her want to scream her impatience. There was no choice but to stay on the gravel paths, since they boxed in little plots of shrubs and flowers that someone cultivated. *Asker.* She'd seen his garden tools. None of his plots would provide enough cover for her escape now.

It was only a matter of minutes before the general's men would realize she'd overheard their plans. They would join the old soldier in his inspection of the grounds now that every light in the house had been turned on, doing its best to illuminate the entire hill of Kavaklidere.

But the old *asker* was not fast enough in his drunken stupor, nor as smart as she. Shadows skirted the perimeter of the blazing mansion, and she moved deeper into them. Both cautiously and swiftly, she fled to the gate at the back of the garden. Only a few more feet away.

All she had to do was escape to the street, then run the short distance to the bottom of the hill where the vacant lot with the hollow stump awaited her. That's also where the fields began, where she could disappear into the peasant fold. Her *tsharchaf* concealed the dancer's costume, which would have given her away, even among peasants.

By the time she made it to the gate, she was breathing deeply. Her hand stopped in mid-air, reaching for the latch. A footstep scuffed the pavement of the street. She ducked against the wall to one side of the gate and craned her neck to see through the wrought-iron grillwork. Something moved out there, on the street.

Someone stood just beyond the puddle of light coming from the lamppost on the corner. A man. Now she saw him, leaning against a low wall. The end of a cigarette glowed in her direction, as if he watched her. No, not her, but the *gate*. Her very means of escape. As if he waited for her to leave the general's palace.

That was impossible! He couldn't be her enemy. The gunman didn't know where she was.

Even so, she jerked back against the rough surface of the stucco wall, sucked in her breath, and studied the dark for an alternate escape.

If she couldn't use the street, she'd have to slip through backyards. Over fences.

She turned away from the gate and crept on, groping her way along the wall. The Americans' yellow house, which she could not see, lay ahead. She paused long enough to release her *tsharchaf* from thorny snags and branches. From somewhere off to her right came the sounds of muted laughter. Here, the dark that engulfed her was so dark that she had to hold her arms in front of her, feeling her way past branches and stems and dried flower pods.

Her fingers brushed the thin wire of the fence before she saw it. This, her first fence on her way down the hill, strung from the end of the general's pink wall at the street and ran along the side of the Americans' yellow stucco house. Only wire separated the general's garden from the Americans' side yard.

She paused, breathing hard, frowning over her planned escape. The thinly woven wire, not as sturdy as the tree, would never support her weight if she attempted to climb over it. It would snare her flowing skirts and slash her flesh. Anyway, whether she climbed the wire fence or the pink wall in this corner where the two of them met, she'd end up on the street where the man with the cigarette could see her.

The back door of the mansion opened, and the hulking shape of a man stepped out into the ring of light. "I know you're out there, gypsy!" The old soldier bellowed. "There is no way out."

Meryem clutched her robe tighter around her, pulling the fabric over her face in case the moon attempted to betray her. Using the wire fence to guide her, she ran along its length, away from the street and toward the interior of the city block. But this direction wasn't promising, for now she closed in on the sounds of laughter, American voices and their clinking glassware. The backyard party where she *should've* danced.

If the Americans caught her, she thought her chances of escape would be greater. So she kept going. The wire fence that she followed suddenly disappeared into the side of a small hill. A cement wall as high as Meryem's waist skirted the base of the hill, retaining dirt the way a belt held in a fat belly. She scrambled up onto the wall, now that she saw it was conveniently placed here for her. No way out, was there?

From her position on the rim of the wall, she spied a shack in the neighboring yard. Its roof butted up against the general's hill. It would be an easy matter to lift up her skirts and step across the top of the fence, onto the roof of that shack. But she hesitated, running through her mind a few stories to explain her presence, in case the Americans caught her. It was dark enough that probably none of the party guests would notice her, anyway. They huddled under paper lanterns dangling from trees that formed a natural barrier between them and the shack. If they noticed anything at all, it would be the blazing lights at the general's house and the commotion of the *asker*.

Not her.

Men's anxious voices stirred from the dark behind her, rousing a scent of anger onto a current of hot air. Apparently the *asker* had recruited help in his search for her. Meryem hesitated only a moment before leaping across to the roof.

* * * * *

The party dragged on, but Anna couldn't leave yet. She had to wait for her call to go through to Nairobi, but the longer she waited, the more suffocating and close the air felt. It was almost too thick to breathe. Blades of cool grass poked through her open-toed sandals and sent tickling shivers up the seams of her nylons.

Cora, her nosy hostess, had her letters to Rainer! It was bad enough that the Turkish police had one of them. And subsequently lost it. Far worse that Cora had more.

Anna bit her tongue to stifle her simmering rage and nodded politely at the conversation around her. She laughed when prompted. She smiled until her face ached. She sampled whatever the servers passed around on trays: kebobs of grilled lamb, eggplant, and succulent bits of unidentifiable delicacies that she couldn't identify.

How was it possible that Rainer was alive? Any minute now, she would surely wake up from this impossible nightmare.

A burst of light flashed in their faces just then, blinding Anna. The dark outline of a man aimed his bulky camera with its cone-shaped flash for another photo.

"No, please," said Hayati. He stepped in to grab the photographer by his arm and push him away.

Paul charged at the photographer in a reawakening of

yesterday's high energy. "Blast it, man! Haven't you learned to ask before you shoot that thing off?"

Fran, always the assistant, stepped between Paul, the boss, and the photographer. "I'll take care of this."

Paul took a deep breath, then turned back to Anna's group. "Sorry about that. Those flashes are a bit of a nuisance, is all."

"Everyone has a photographer," one of the guests said. "That way, we can always have a souvenir to remind us of these special get-togethers."

"The man's a clumsy idiot." Paul's voice rumbled with a growl. "He's not one of ours, otherwise he would've asked permission before using that damned flash."

Cora waved off his question. "Fran found him somewhere. It was all last-minute. Ask her."

In a quiet corner of the yard, Fran planted her hands firmly on her hips and spoke under her breath to the photographer, who looked vaguely familiar to Anna. He pulled a handkerchief from his pocket, lowered his head, and mopped his brow.

Anna marched to a bar set up on a sidewalk beside the house. "Ice water, please," she said to an attendant in a crisp, white jacket.

While he prepared the drink, she set down her martini glass and conveniently forgot it. Then she carried the tumbler of water back across the lawn, straight up to Fran and the photographer. A peal of laughter sounded from Cora's circle as they watched.

"Oh!" Anna said. "I remember you now. You're the man from the copper shop today."

"Emin Kirpat," he said with a friendly smile.

The part-time student photographer, Anna remembered. "You're the one who told me about the Hittites."

Fran harrumphed. "All our regular photographers were booked for tonight. I was pretty sure Ozturk Bey had someone else we could try. That's why Paul sent me down there today. I can see it was a mistake."

"Have some water," Anna said, handing the glass to Emin. "Go on. There's no point passing out from the heat. You look like you could use a drink."

Emin gaped first at the glass, then at Fran.

"You'd better do as she says." Fran folded her arms across her chest and smirked.

He took the glass, murmured his thanks, and downed the water.

"For once, he listens," Fran said with a huff. "But it's not going to help him now."

Anna's eyebrows rose. "What's the problem?"

Fran shrugged. "It's not the flash. It's the pictures he chose to take that are wrong. Why don't you run along, honey? This really doesn't concern you."

Anna sucked in her breath with surprise. Fran had been kind taking her to lunch today, but here, tonight, she was behaving downright rude. "In that case, I'll leave you alone. I need to check on the children, anyway, before my call comes through. Someone will let me know, I presume?"

"Of course. The servants have been alerted." Fran glared again at the photographer as Anna turned away.

Beyond the light of the lanterns, Anna felt the night air slide over her. Once darkness fell here on the Anatolian plateau, it fell fast.

Unease rippled the edge of her mind as she replayed the day's events in the old city. Fran had gone to Ozturk Bey's shop specifically to book Emin for tonight. It had nothing to do with tracking Anna. The coincidence of their connections sent a shiver through her. Emin... Umit... The killer...

Anna hurried her step to the playhouse. Muffled voices murmured from within the tumbledown heap of plywood. She bent down to an opening and called inside, "How are you children doing?"

"Another alien!" Priscilla squealed. "Gimme that ray gun! I'll get him!"

Anna sighed, satisfied that all seemed well with the children. She didn't want to alert them to her concerns. Glancing back at the thick gathering of partiers under the lanterns, she saw the flash of a camera spark the night. She thought about slipping away from the party, but it would be difficult to persuade Priscilla to abandon her friend.

Besides, leaving was out of the question until after the call to Nairobi came through.

Still, she'd had enough of the party. She would sit out the rest of it inside, waiting by the phone. There must be another way inside the house, other than using the back door where busy servers whisked in and out. Skirting the area of the lanterns, she slipped around to the side of house that faced the pink mansion. Their neighbor the general lived there, on the corner of Yeşilyurt and Guneş. The Burkhardts, to his west on Yeşilyurt; and the Wingates, to his north on Guneş.

Tonight, lights blazed again at the general's house, and through the windows she could see men moving about. The general certainly entertained often, Anna thought, but then he was an important man. Henry had told her that this general, their neighbor, had served under Atatürk during the wars of independence from the Ottomans. Not that long ago, as far as history went. It was only thirty-five years ago that they fought for their independence, giving this part of the world a complete reversal of their way of life.

Or had it been so thoroughly complete? She remembered all the veils she'd seen, especially in Ulus, yet Atatürk had banned the veil.

On her way through the shadows at the side of the house, she passed through a small garden, pungent with petunias. A bench offered respite beneath an open window. She could sit there quietly a few moments. Unnoticed.

The bubbling noise of the lawn party made the bump on her head throb. Cora's outrageous behavior hadn't helped. The very idea! That she could purchase someone else's private letters...

Thank goodness Anna had had the good sense not to include her name on the return address. And even if Cora opened up the envelopes and read the letters, heaven forbid, it wouldn't be obvious right away that it was Anna who'd written them. She'd signed herself "Annie."

All the same, Anna intended to get those letters back. Before Cora had the opportunity to read them and figure out by context just who Annie really was.

Anna inhaled the fragrant air. The soothing dark offered a sense of peace that bit by bit absorbed the pain pulsing through her body. The solitude gave her breathing room to form her plans for what she would tell Mitzi once the call came through.

Gradually, her eyes adjusted to the dark, and the garden hardly seemed dark at all. She could make out the shadowy shapes of a birdbath to her right, a flowerbed to her left. Rose bushes straight ahead.

A tall and gangly *objet d'art* stood just beyond the rose bushes. It seemed an odd place to arrange statuary. Perhaps it belonged to the general's house.

She rose and moved across the garden for a closer look. There were no stepping stones through the rose bed. If it was meant to be garden art, it wasn't easily accessible.

Carefully pushing aside one of the branches, she stepped across the mulched bed into a patch of weeds on the far side of the roses. The gangly thing rising up from tall weeds was a tripod. With a camera and a long, high-powered lens fixed to the top. Perhaps it belonged to Emin.

Except...

The lens aimed at the general's house, not at the Wingates' party.

A twig snapped, and Anna's attention jerked away from the tripod to follow the sound. A shadow split away from a nearby tree trunk, and a man moved slowly toward her. Every muscle inside her tensed in the split second before she would dart away. And then he stepped close enough for her to recognize him. Rainer!

"It's not what you think," he whispered, reaching out with the swiftness of a rattler to grab her arm.

Anna stiffened, appalled by the image her mind had conjured. "How would you know what I think?"

"Shhhhh."

How dare he attempt to quiet her when twelve years worth of questions festered in her heart and soul? She would not be silenced, but she hardly knew where to begin. Just then, a light flicked on behind them.

Chapter Thirty

Meryem landed with a thunk onto the roof of the shack and held her breath. The wood beneath her creaked, resisting her weight. The shack was a sloppy building of loose walls, and it would surely collapse in the next earthquake.

Hissing sounds came from the darkness, no more than an arm's length away. She crouched, melting into the shadows, assessing her escape. From here, she would have to jump down into the Americans' yard. It was a farther jump than the one she'd just made from the lowest branch of the tree by the general's balcony.

If she twisted her ankle, she had no hope of income for a while. The pain might even delay her return to the appointment with the gunman who'd killed her brother.

"Over here," a child's voice whispered in Turkish that was worse than Meryem's. "It's lower over here."

Meryem hesitated. This was a trick, but what was to gain? And for whom?

"Hurry!" said another child, a dark shadow against the faint glow of light from the Americans' party a stone's throw away.

Relief swept through her. It was only children, not the *asker*. Why they had come to her aid, she did not know. She did not question her good fortune but jumped where they showed her, and then followed them into the shack, through a hole.

Once inside, one of the children slid a board across the opening, sealing them into darkness.

Meryem wrinkled her nose from the dry stench of soiled sand. "Who are you?" she whispered. "Why should you help me?"

The little girl clicked on a small light no bigger than a coin and held it up to her cheek. The dim light gave her freckled face a red, transparent glow. Red curly hair framed her distorted face. "I'm Priscilla, and that's Tommy." She pointed the light at the boy, who had yellow hair and missing teeth. They were small enough to be about seven or eight years old, Meryem decided, judging them against the size of seven-year-old Mustafa, who was Umit's oldest.

Rattling sounds indicated lumbering steps on loose gravel in the general's garden. Closer now. Then the sounds settled.

"I was only teasing you," the old soldier called from the other side of the fence. He stood close enough that Meryem could easily make out his words as he spoke. "I have your money. You can come out now."

Meryem grabbed the little coin of light from the girl and buried it in her skirts, not knowing another way to douse the light.

"It's okay, he can't—"

"Shhhh." Meryem's heartbeat quickened, and she pressed into the deeper shadows of one corner.

* * * * *

Anna felt a shove that sent her sprawling into darkness. She landed face-down in dirt and scratchy weeds, just beyond the pool of new light that spilled from the Wingates' house and seeped into the garden. Rainer fell on top of her, pinning her down. His warm gasps tickled the back of her neck, and a woody branch dug into her breast, into the part of her flesh that the low cut of the black chiffon had exposed.

She spit dirt from her mouth and struggled for breath. "Let. Me. Up. You're hurting me." A sharp pain throbbed in her chest.

"Shhhh." His breath blew in her ear as the pressure of his hold on her eased. "We can't let them see us." His words scarcely rose louder than a whisper of air.

"Is that why you stayed away all these years? Or was it because of your *wife*?" As a concession, she kept her voice low.

"She's not my wife. Is that why you're fighting me?"

"You're the one who tackled me."

He rolled off her and slithered away farther into the dark, away from the light that leaked out of the room. From her position on the ground, she could see bookcases through the lit window. The room was a den of some sort. Voices murmured from inside. She lifted herself into a low crouch, despite a tweak of pain in her knee, and darted after Rainer. Weeds scratched her legs, but she didn't care. Relief surged through her. His words reverberated in her mind. *Not my wife.*

He caught her by the wrist and pulled her out of the weeds, across a soft strip of grass and into a bed of overgrown lilacs standing tall beside the stucco exterior of the house. "We have to talk," he whispered, squeezing tightly. "But not here. Not now. Go back to the party and pretend you never saw me." He released her, put his fingers to his lips, and then crept through the lilacs, closer to the circle of light spilling out the open window of the den.

She followed him.

When he stopped long enough to glance over his shoulder, she nearly bumped into him. "Go on," he whispered. "Do as I say."

"Who is she, then," Anna said, "if she's not your wife?"

"No one. Never mind about her."

"No one? So you're telling me the Balikos aren't real, either? And she's not pregnant?"

"Hush. We'll talk later. I promise."

"Because now," she said, "you intend to spy on those people inside, don't you?"

"Of course not. Why should they matter?"

An interesting response, she thought. He hadn't denied spying, only the target. *They.* She didn't know if they mattered or not. In fact, she didn't even know to whom the voices belonged. All she knew was that she didn't care for the hard edge behind Rainer's voice. Had the war done this to him? Or had it been the intervening years?

Rainer gripped both her shoulders and gave her a little shake. "You've got to trust me."

"Why should I? You didn't come home."

"I'll make it up to you, I swear."

"How is that possible? After all these years?"

"I will, you'll see. But first, there's something I have to finish." He patted her, the way he used to do, lovingly, but now it only felt like a pat he would reserve for a faithful dog.

"I don't even know who you really are anymore," she said. "The war's been over twelve years."

"It's not over for everyone."

"You don't have to spy anymore."

"Go on. Back to the party. Wait for me just a little longer, like a good girl."

"Forget it. I'm done waiting. I'll find out *now* what this is all about." She charged ahead of him, stepping away from the lilacs, and she didn't stop until she came even to the window's ledge.

"Shit," said a man from within the room. "I can't believe he actually used us for his set-up." The deep voice sounded like Paul Wingate's, but Anna couldn't be sure without risking peeking inside, and she wasn't that daring. Rainer crept up beside her. Enough light shone through the window for her to see the frown on his face.

"He denies knowing anything about it," said a woman's voice from inside. Fran Lafferty.

"Of course he would," Paul snapped. "We can't be any part to this. You've got to get rid of it."

Anna furrowed her brow and glanced at Rainer, but his attention focused on the conversation inside. Get rid of what? The tripod?

"Me?" Fran said. "What do you want me to do with it?"

"Get him to get it out of here. I don't want it on the property or your prints on anything."

"I don't think he's in deep—"

"I don't want to know about it. The less we know, the better it'll look for us, if there's a coup."

Anna sucked in her breath. A coup? She looked again at Rainer, whose lower lip twitched, as if he struggled to remain silent. Was that why Rainer was involved? As a *spy*?

"It may be too late for that," said Fran, "now that *she's*

stumbled into the middle."

"You'll think of something. Just get rid of him, understand? And don't let *her* get in the way."

Paul's slow, heavy footsteps and Fran's rapid clicks crossed the room. Then their footsteps faded away, but the light stayed on in the den. Now Rainer studied Anna, his gaze burning into her. His frown deepened from an unhappy discomfort to undisguised worry.

Her? Did Paul and Fran mean *Anna*?

No, it couldn't be. Anna didn't feel that she was in the way of anything. Well, perhaps she'd crossed paths with the murder investigation of the gypsy, but only because she didn't really think that the investigation was proceeding as it should.

Rainer grabbed Anna by the arm and yanked her back the way they'd come, along the row of lilacs.

"You know what they were talking about, don't you?" she said, gasping to keep up with his pace.

"Quiet." He pulled her across the stretch of grass toward the area of weeds that served as a boundary between the Wingates' and the general's properties. They were moving in a direction away from the backyard party, and out toward the street. She resisted, and finally he stopped, crouching behind a tangle of bushes that protected him from the streetlamp.

"I'm not going with you," Anna said. "And I can't leave the party yet. I'm expecting a call from Mitzi any minute."

"No, you're not."

"Yes, I am."

"The call was never placed."

"How do you know that?"

He grunted. "Trust me."

"Oh, there you go again."

"Look, I'm sorry."

"I'll bet you are. What are we doing here? Where are you going?"

But he was gone already, darting across the street. Over there was the house where Gulsen lived—Priscilla's friend. The house looked dark now, deserted, and Rainer disappeared from her sight as he slipped into shadows. She felt torn. Should she follow him? Or go back to the party?

Perhaps he didn't *want* her to take the call from Mitzi. But that didn't make sense. Neither did any of the events so far tonight. Or today. Or yesterday, for that matter.

The episode of the purse thief made no sense, either. She'd thought she'd been hit on the head with Ozturk Bey's candelabrum so that the culprit could steal her purse. But maybe it was because she'd gotten in the way of whatever Paul and Fran thought she was in the middle of. She wondered how long Fran had been there, before revealing her presence.

If it wasn't Anna they'd referred to, then she wondered who else they could've meant. Maybe Cora. That woman certainly had a talent for inserting herself into the middle of affairs she had no business knowing. And she was a gossipmonger. Yes, perhaps they meant Cora. They didn't want word to spread about...

A coup?

Feeling a little dizzy, Anna realized that she couldn't stay here, hiding in the bushes. Fran and Paul would surely find her. They'd return soon with the photographer, no doubt, to disassemble the tripod, and...

Did they mean that the general next door was planning

a *coup*? Perhaps that's what his men-only "parties" were all about. She shivered. Coups meant violence. And she and Priscilla lived next door to the mastermind of violence.

She'd have to get Priscilla out of the way, maybe out of the country.

Meanwhile, she had to get out of *here*. Unseen. She had to return to the backyard party without being noticed. She couldn't go back along the side of the house and risk getting caught near the incriminating tripod, so she'd use the front door. Enter the house through the front door and exit through the back, returning to the party under the watchful eyes of the servants.

She stood up from the bushes, brushed off some dirt, and swished past branches. No one was around, thankfully, to hear her rustling movement. The front lawn appeared like a smooth sea, and she darted across it to the sidewalk that led up to a porch.

She ran up the steps and stopped abruptly. On the middle step. With a gasp. A man sat atop the low wall that lined the perimeter of the porch.

Chapter Thirty-One

Only a thin panel of wood separated Meryem from the *asker*. She could not see anything but the blackness of the interior of the children's shack, but she could smell the drink on him as he stood outside. For an instant she considered charging out there like a wild cat, leaping onto his back and scratching out his eyes.

But she did not know who partnered with him. She'd heard other, arguing voices pursuing her along with the *asker*. Her chances against more than one, in times of desperation, were too uncertain. She shrank back into a dark corner and listened to his slurred words. He spoke as if he knew the exact spot where she hid. And why not? He'd surely seen this shack before on his regular patrols. He'd guess that she would've found it by now. He was playing with her. She could play, too.

But not with children present.

Meryem's skin crawled with her eagerness to escape these foul-smelling quarters. Something lived here besides children. Snakes? Her heart lurched in her chest, and she sprang up, ready to take her chances with the *asker* and flee. Her head smacked against the ceiling.

"Why is he chasing you?" Priscilla asked.

"Shhh." The children were about to betray her with their noise.

"Don't worry," said Tommy. "He's deaf and blind. He can't hurt us here. We're safe in our spaceship."

The *asker's* footsteps scuffled farther away. "Come out, come out!"

Meryem realized from his fading movements that he didn't know where she was, not exactly. He was fishing for her. She inched closer to the hole that served as her exit from the shack.

"It doesn't matter," Priscilla said. "He doesn't need a reason to chase anyone. That old *asker* is mean. He killed my kitten."

"Oh," Meryem said. "I'm sorry. You can find another kitten. Take your pick, in this city of stray cats."

"No. There was only one Muffin."

"I suppose you're right." Meryem shifted on her haunches. Now was her chance to escape while the *asker* had turned his back. She scrabbled around in the dark for the piece of wood that had sealed them inside the shack.

"You can stay here, if you want," said Priscilla. "My turtle won't mind."

"Your turtle?"

"I hunt turtles, and when I find them, I bring them here. Mama won't let me keep them more than two days, but she's not here."

"Where is she?" The child's *an-ne*, the foreign *gadje*, was surely at the party. She would be looking for her child and discover Meryem in a matter of moments.

"Gone away," Priscilla said.

The sadness in the girl's voice tugged at Meryem's heart. "Well, it's very nice of you to offer me a place to stay, but I have someplace else where I have to go."

Then the footsteps crunched outside once again, louder. The

asker's voice floated through the night, nearer. "I'm coming!"

* * * * *

The man rose, and Anna stepped backwards, down to the next lower step of the porch. His white suit gave him a ghostly appearance in the dark, and she took another step backwards.

"Don't go," he said, sauntering toward the top step. One hand in his trouser pocket. The other, holding a cocktail. Hayati.

She let out her breath, not realizing she'd been holding it. He must've watched her furtive movements just now with Rainer in the bushes. "Oh! I didn't see you."

"A pleasant evening," he said. "Your head is better now?"

She touched her temple where pain still throbbed, freshly exacerbated by Rainer's rough handling in the bushes. "I'm fine, thank you. I didn't expect to see you here."

"Nor I, you." He chuckled.

"Isn't it odd? It seems to be your job to rescue me. First from the police station, and then from Ozturk Bey's shop." *And now, from Rainer.* She fanned herself with her hand and went on. "That is, what I mean to say is that I keep running into you everywhere I turn. Did Henry put you up to this?" Finally, she bit her lip to stop her blathering.

He tipped his head to one side and studied her, as if trying to read her thoughts. "You are not happy," he finally said as a statement, not a question.

She gripped the railing beside the porch steps to keep from stumbling as her thoughts switched directions again. Regaining her balance, she climbed the steps the rest of the way and stood tall, facing him. "You astonish me with such an observation.

I'm quite content, thank you."

But, *happy?*

"You are...how do they call it? Homesick?"

"If I were homesick after only one week away from home, then I'd be in serious trouble." She laughed off his question, and he laughed with her, but her laughter caught in her throat with an uncertain edge.

"Forgive me," he said. "I often see this sadness in the people at the embassy, especially when things don't turn out as they expect."

"I have no expectations, so I can't be disappointed. Although, I certainly didn't expect all that's happened." *Rainer, alive!* She wasn't sure how she felt about that—joy or betrayal?

Hayati watched her silently, as if waiting while she decided. Did he know about Rainer?

She rushed on with her questions. "Why did you say what you said back there? About that man... Viktor. You seemed to think that I'd met him before. In a taxi."

"But you did. At the police station. The first time I came to help you. Don't you remember?" He grinned, and his white teeth gleamed in the dark.

"I'm sure I would've remembered. No, it's not so. That man wasn't there. You lied about that, and I want to know why."

He chuckled and nodded towards the weeds where she had just tussled with Rainer. "You said it yourself. It is my duty to rescue you, is that not true? Would you prefer to be the subject of Mrs. Wingate's gossip?"

"So you only *thought* that man, Viktor, meant something to me. He doesn't."

"Okay, I believe you." His teeth flashed again. "Come sit

with me for a while, and allow me to tell you about the places we might choose for our dinner."

"Really, Mr. Orhon. I don't see how I could abandon Priscilla."

"No doubt she has a friend she can stay with."

"I don't mean to sound ungracious. It's just that..."

"Yes?"

"It might...appear frivolous. In these somber times, you see."

"You do not strike me as the sort of woman who cares much for the games society plays. I wonder who you really are, Miss Anna Riddle?"

"Sometimes I wonder that, too." She blurted it out before thinking. She knew who she'd *been*, up until now, but she didn't care to explain her personal history to strangers, how she'd come to this moment and this uncustomary state of uncertainty.

She turned away from his scrutiny of her. A solitary streetlamp flickered on the corner, where Yeşilyurt intersected Güneş. Where Erkmen had stood watching her house the night before, after Yaziz's visit. Rainer was out there now, somewhere in the dark between the pools of light from the streetlamps.

She wasn't going to let Hayati distract her. "I'm sorry," she said, "will you excuse me?"

"No, actually, I won't." Ice rattled in his glass as he set it down and stepped closer, taking her wrist gently in his hands.

"I beg your pardon?" Her voice rose, matching the rising hammer of her heart.

"Shhh," he said. "Stay with me another moment. Would you like a cigarette?"

"I have to get back."

"Why? Are you afraid someone will see us together? An American woman alone with a Turkish man?"

"Of course not. Please turn loose of me this instant." She could step away from him any time she chose, since his light touch on her wrist wasn't restraining her, not the way Rainer's grip had squeezed her with force.

He released her, but she did not step away. "Did you really want to learn Turkish?" he said.

"Yes. Of course."

"Why? They don't encourage learning our language."

"You learned English."

"That's different. I was in London for a while, in school."

"And now I'm in your country. Why should it be any different?"

He laughed. "Some people think the Americans don't actually live in my country but in a little America within my country."

His soft laughter infected her with his good humor and gentle nature, easing her anxiety, encouraging her to stay. "Paul said that you sometimes work in Henry's office," she said. "What do you do there?"

"Translate, mostly."

"Was that what Paul wanted from you? That report he wanted by this morning. Was it a translation of the police report?"

Hayati shrugged, rummaging into his jacket pocket. He pulled out a small pack of cigarettes. "If you won't have one, may I?"

"As you wish. They're your lungs, not mine." She felt a prickle of annoyance from his indirect way of answering her direct question.

He took his time lighting up and exhaling the bitter smell of tobacco. "Did you find them?" he finally said.

"Find what?" Her pulse sped up. How did he know that she was intent on recovering her letters from Cora?

"The Alekci family. You wanted me to take you there today, remember?"

"Oh!" The heat of a flush crept up to her cheeks. To cover the embarrassment of her misunderstanding, she told him all about it. She described how she'd found the family's place and how her visit had ended with Mrs. Alekci's hysterics. How Anna had nearly sustained another bump to her head when the woman had thrown a small, wooden box at her.

"What do you think she kept in the box?" Anna said, thankful that it had been empty.

"The letter, probably."

"But how did she get my letter in the first place?"

"From your Rainer, I imagine."

Anna gulped, trying to swallow her rising confusion. Was she supposed to claim that Rainer was dead? "He's not 'my Rainer'."

"As you wish."

"What I *wish* is that I could have talked to her myself."

"You were asking about Turkish lessons, and I will teach you."

"Oh, no, I didn't mean—"

"It is no trouble. I sometimes teach English downtown. Why not my own language?"

"I had in mind something more formal."

"You can pay me if that will make you feel better."

The more he insisted, the more reluctant she felt. He was

being both helpful and evasive, and she wondered why.

"It's not that I'm not. Comfortable, that is."

"Then what is it? I assure you that I am qualified."

"Yes, of course you are," she said. "All right, when do we start?" The words flowed out before she could think through the arrangement.

Besides, she wanted to know why he'd lied to her about meeting Rainer in a taxi. He'd practically admitted lying. Because, she felt certain, he was covering up something.

Why else had he been here on the front porch, conveniently waiting to intercept her? If he was working with Rainer... He'd been watching Rainer's back just now.

Chapter Thirty-Two

Anna finally escaped from Hayati with an excuse no one could argue. She had to powder her nose.

He offered to escort her to the powder room, but she insisted she would find her own way.

The powder room on the ground floor, however, turned out to be a Turkish toilet—a hole in the floor, straddled by two cement footprints. Anna smiled. This would work to her advantage. If the Wingates' house was anything like the Burkhardts', then there would be a western toilet on the floor above. If someone caught her upstairs in Cora's bedroom, she would claim to be searching for the western facilities.

She ran up wooden stairs to a darkened hall. At the end of the hall, a light shone in a bedroom, drawing her to it, the moth to flame. A small lamp sat atop a vanity table, cluttered with a disarray of boxes and spilled cosmetics and sprinkled with a fine dusting of perfumed powder.

Anna's heart soared. This would be easier than she'd thought.

She hesitated only an instant, distracted by a display of miniature photos in silver frames, and then bent down to the narrow drawers beneath the cluttered tabletop. A place to hide stolen letters.

Her fingers shaking, she went to work, pulling out drawers

one by one, sifting through beads and feathered clip-ons and rhinestone pins. Halfway through her search, the letters still hadn't turned up. She dug on, certain that the very next drawer would be the hiding place.

"Looking for something?" a husky voice said from the doorway.

Anna lurched, straightening upright. Beads slipped from her fingers, clattering back into the drawer she'd been searching.

Fran!

Anna squared her shoulders and stepped away from Cora's vanity table. What could she say? She'd been caught red-handed. The heat of a flush crept up her neck. Her ears must be red flags.

Fran Lafferty smirked while leaning one shoulder against the doorframe. Her cigarette holder, even though it was empty, cocked between two fingers. She arched one penciled eyebrow high as she studied Anna and waited for an explanation.

"Um, yes," Anna said. "Cora has something of mine, and I was looking for it."

"I see. And you took it upon yourself to reclaim the presumably borrowed item? I wonder what that could be?"

"Never mind, it doesn't matter. Look, I know what you must be thinking, but you're wrong. I didn't take anything. Search me if you want. You must believe me."

"Why should I?"

"I can see this looks bad. I would prefer that you not say anything about this to anyone."

"No doubt." Fran switched her meerschaum holder to her other hand. Her eyebrow arched even higher, and frowns lined her forehead.

Anna's head throbbed as her indignation flared. "I was on my way to the powder room, you see, and when I saw the light on in here, I became distracted."

"You don't seem like the sort of woman who distracts very easily."

"Oh, I am. Really."

"No. That's Mitzi. Not you. You don't strike me as anything like Mitzi. In fact, it's hard to believe you're sisters."

"Oh, we are. Half-sisters, actually. Our fathers are different."

"It's okay," Fran said. "You don't have to pretend with me. I know all about it."

"You do?" Anna took another step back. "That is, what do you know?"

"I know what you're looking for. And I know why you don't want me to tell anyone."

Great. Anna had been caught, and she couldn't deny it. As bad as her position appeared, however, Fran's was worse. She steeled herself and pressed on. "What you think you know...is that also why you think I'm in the middle of some coup that may be brewing?"

Fran tipped her head sideways. "Where on earth did you come up with that?"

"I heard you and Paul talking. I was waiting for my phone call, and you two came in and—"

"Forget it," Fran said. "It's nothing."

Anna didn't believe her. The scrapes and bruises on her knees and wrists still stung, as a result of Rainer's tackling her. He certainly hadn't thought the conversation they'd overheard was nothing. It was important enough that he hadn't wanted to be caught.

"I don't understand," she said.

"Don't worry," Fran said. "I won't say anything. Why should I? I'd lose my job if I told."

"Is that why you want to bury whatever information you have on Rainer?"

"Rainer? Ah, yes. Your 'friend.' Look, you and Henry are going to great lengths to cover up Mitzi's addiction, and if I blew the whistle, he'd have me fired. But you don't have to hide it from *me*."

Anna's heart skipped a beat. *Addiction?* What was this woman talking about? She opened her mouth to say something, anything to deny Fran's outrageous suggestion, but only a choking sound came out.

Fran continued. "What we don't know is where the opium came from. You think Cora supplied her, but you won't find it here. That's what you're looking for. I know. I'm sorry. Look, it didn't come from Cora, that much we know."

Opium? Anna swayed on her feet, feeling the same waves of pain she'd felt earlier from the brass blow to her head. "W-what do you mean 'we'?"

"Paul's the one who found the treatment center in Switzerland. Maybe you didn't realize that."

"Uh...no, I didn't." They'd gone to Switzerland, instead. That's why Yaziz couldn't find Mitzi and Henry in Nairobi. There would be no call from there. Rainer was right. But how had he known?

The call could still come from Switzerland.

Fran sighed. "It's always a danger in places like this for the wives. They have nothing to do but get into trouble."

The initial shock slowly eased its chokehold on Anna.

296

She lifted her chin, steeling herself against this woman's preposterous claims. "I wouldn't say they have *nothing* to do. There are the children to raise."

She shuddered. Priscilla *knew*. That would explain her difficult behavior.

Fran went on. "They have enough help from the servants and the entire community that the children don't notice their mothers' absence from time to time. Mitzi was clever, I'll give her that much credit."

"She'll be back!"

"I hope so. For Henry's sake."

Anna collapsed onto the velvet cushion of the stool before Cora's dressing table. The ghost of her face reflected back at her in the mirror, where photos of family and everyday life tucked into the frame.

"In that way," Fran said, "being clever, I suppose she was like you."

Anna didn't care for the reference to her sister in the past.

"But as for you," Fran said, "you're too clever for your own good. You can forget about that little conversation you thought you overheard between Paul and me. We're not here to interfere. We let underlying sentiments run their course. You understand?"

Anna stared into the mirror, understanding one thing too well. The woman who stared back at her was not the woman Anna thought she was.

Several heartbeats later, Fran broke the silence. "I'm sorry," she said. Her deep voice broke through the fog that clouded Anna's mind. "This is clearly a difficult subject for you. Has Mitzi suffered...other addictions in the past?"

It took all of Anna's strength to turn her head, to lift her focus from Cora's mirror to Fran Lafferty, who'd moved from the doorway to stand by Anna's side. Anna felt as if a lead blanket weighed her down and strapped her to the dressing table's stool. The cry for help from Henry about Mitzi...

Please come stop we need you

Anna's instincts had been correct to drop her own life and come to their aid, to be here with Priscilla while Henry found the proper care for Mitzi. Teaching history to Boulder teenagers was not as important as her own family's needs.

It wasn't just Priscilla and Henry who needed her help.

Anna wished that her sister had felt she could confide in her. What were sisters for, but to help one another in times of need?

"No," Anna said, her voice a whisper. She closed her eyes, squeezing back moisture that she would not allow to form into tears.

Anna felt an arm slip around her shoulders, and her eyes flew open. Fran knelt beside her. "She'll be okay," Fran said. "She's stubborn. Like you."

"Don't I know it. And trouble, too." Anna made a choking sound, a failed laugh. "I remember one of our more serious arguments, back on the ranch, during the war. Mitzi was in such a rush one morning that she wouldn't do her chores, and she had the nerve to beg me for a ride to town. *Not* to school, where she was supposed to go. I wouldn't give her a simple ride, even though..."

Heat rose to Anna's cheeks as she realized with a shock what was happening. She was confiding personal information to a stranger. And not just to any stranger, but to this hard-edged

298

woman whose temperament changed from moment to moment. Fran knew more than she let on, and Anna wasn't certain she could even trust her. This was what the threat of tears could do. This inappropriate confessional must be the result of receiving the shocking news of Mitzi's addiction to opium, of all things. She'd always known Mitzi was at risk for serious trouble one day, but she'd assumed that Henry would protect her from it, not lead her into the opium den, so to speak.

"Even though what?" Fran asked.

Anna shrugged. "Oh, nothing. We argued some, and then it was all over."

"Well, did Mitzi end up getting her ride?"

"She ran to the neighbors and got a ride with one of them."

"Did you ever find out where Mitzi was going that was so important to skip school that day?"

"She was auditioning as a dancer somewhere, and that eventually led her to performing with USO. If she'd only told me how important that day was, I would've driven her. But I thought I knew what was best for her. I ended up letting her down." Anna lowered her chin, embarrassed that she'd confessed the long-held guilt.

"She found her own way, didn't she?" Fran squeezed her shoulder and rose.

"She sure did. That job got her out of Boulder. And led to her meeting Henry. He came to one of her performances. Somewhere in Europe."

"I knew she'd been a dancer," Fran said, "but I never realized it was anything professional. She gave up her career to become a diplomat's wife. Funny how things work out. As if it was orchestrated from the beginning."

"What do you mean?" Anna watched Fran pull a fresh cigarette from a silver case on Cora's dressing table.

"Probably nothing." Fran moved restlessly across the room to an open window, where she fixed the cigarette in her holder and lit it. "I heard a different story, that's all. I heard that Henry and Mitzi were introduced through an old boyfriend of *yours*."

"*Mine?*" Anna felt the erratic beat of her heart. "Who told you that?"

"Henry. Maybe I misunderstood."

Anna stood up so fast that she knocked over the stool.

Fran's eyebrow arched again. "Rainer Akers, right?"

Anna tried to keep her voice even, but it cracked anyway. "What'd Henry say? About Rainer?"

"You knew they worked together during the war, didn't you? Some sort of secret mission, although he wouldn't say."

Anna wanted to scream her protests. *Henry and Rainer?* It wasn't true! Her mind swirled with contradictions. She'd known Rainer *before* the war. Her sister hadn't met Henry until *after* the war. After Rainer was gone. Rainer and Henry couldn't have known each other. Unless...

They'd known each other *first*.

On a secret mission.

Which was apparently still secret.

Anna managed to push back her distress and compose herself. She was good at hiding her feelings.

"Why, yes, of course," she said, flushing. She wasn't good at lying. "What else did Henry tell you?"

It was a mistake. It *must* be. What right did any of them have to keep such a secret from her?

Fran shrugged and flicked ash out the window. "Nothing."

Anna marched across the room to Fran's side. She wanted to shake the woman, the "gal from the embassy" who'd worked with Henry and probably knew more than she had any business knowing. She wanted to take her by the arms and shake the information out of her.

Henry and Rainer had known each other. *Worked* together.

Quivering inside with disbelief, she lowered her voice to a soft level of innocence. "How long have you known Henry?"

"We go back to India, where we were stationed together before this assignment. Priscilla was just a baby. So you see, we share history."

History. As if that gave Fran the right to private information.

"That's why I'm concerned about Mitzi," Fran said, "and I wanted to make sure you were the answer to her needs. I think you are."

"I don't feel like much of an answer to anything." *Damn!* She hadn't wanted to voice her self-doubt. It had just slipped out before she could control it. Anna sighed. She might as well see it through, now. "If I could face the truth, I would've been more forthright about my fiancé from the beginning. I wouldn't have to be up here, searching, behind Cora's back."

Fran puffed thoughtfully on her cigarette, narrowing her eyes. Finally, she stubbed it out in a brass ashtray in the windowsill. "Ah. I think I see the picture now." From her pocket she withdrew a paper bundle, tied with a crushed ribbon. "This is what you were looking for, isn't it?"

Anna gasped. Then nodded. "What are *you* doing with my...that is, with those letters?"

"Paul beat you to them. He got them from Cora and asked me to hand them over to the police, since they seem to go along

301

with some evidence they already have. Maybe that's the right thing to do, but I don't think this is evidence, do you? Well? Are you going to take them or not?"

Anna hesitated only a moment, then snatched the letters and stuffed them into her own pocket.

"You see?" Fran said, smiling. "We have to trust each other. I have no intention of saying anything about any of this."

"Thanks. Although, I don't know why you've—"

Just then, a scream pierced the night air. A woman's shrill scream rose above the hum of voices from the party in the backyard below.

Chapter Thirty-Three

Meryem's heart thudded as the *asker* sang. He surely knew where she hid, inside the children's shack. Even so, he finally turned away. His voice and footsteps faded into the distance. Now was her chance. Or was it a trick?

She slid the piece of wood aside that served as a door, stared out into the night, then turned to hand the flashlight back to the little girl. She said goodbye to the children and escaped through the hole, out onto cool grass of the Americans' yard. She darted from tree to tree, headed for the fence on the opposite side of the yard, and had barely made it there when she heard the scream.

The scream, a woman's piercing voice, curdled Meryem's blood. What had the *asker* done now? Killed one of his American neighbors? He'd practiced on kittens, after all.

What's done was done. She picked up her skirts and sped faster, no longer taking care to cross in the shadows of trees that filled the Americans' yard.

It was a waist-high wrought-iron fence on the far side of this yard, separating it from the vacant lot on the downhill side. Umit's *eşek* had balked, pulling her into this very same vacant lot only the day before. Where Meryem had first put herself into this mess. Only yesterday. When she'd noticed the *asker* spying on the cackling, American women.

Bah! She had better things to do now than to become

embroiled in their affairs.

She swung first one leg then the other over the top of the fence and dropped into the empty lot. She ran, slipping and snaring her *tsharchaf* on prickly weeds. She had to cross this open terrain as quickly as possible. No one had cultivated trees or shrubs here that would protect her from watching eyes. Not that anyone should be watching her, anyway, not after that blood-curdling scream from the American party she'd left behind.

By now, she was probably safe from the watching man on the street, but she wouldn't take that chance. She posed too great of a risk for the general and his men. She could trust no one.

The conversation she'd overheard among the general's men... They were plotting revolution while outside eyes thought they were merely old men, partying. Did the *asker* know what his pasha was really up to? Was that why he'd attacked the American woman to make her scream just now? He'd taken out his wrath on the foreign *gadje* because he hadn't been able to lure Meryem out of the children's shack.

The children. She might be able to trust Priscilla and Tommy. The girl had seen Meryem's tussle with the secret police the day before. What else had she seen?

Meryem slid the last few feet in the dust. At the bottom of the slope, a cement retaining wall stopped her. She jumped down onto a narrow strip of ground behind the neighboring apartment building and crept along its wall to the far end. She glanced around the corner of the building at the street, Yeşilyurt Sokak. Nothing moved.

Now, a tomb-like quiet fell over the place, and she wondered if she'd imagined the scream. People should be running, alerted to trouble. Windows should be thrown open and lights should blaze.

But nothing happened. Meryem felt a cool shiver, a premonition of disaster.

Avoiding the street, she followed a path behind this building, and then behind the next one. Finally, Güven Evler lay directly ahead. She came out from behind the buildings even with the ditch that streamed through the vacant lot where she and Umit liked to rest by their water hole. Where a hollow tree surrounded by a thicket of brush made a good hiding place for valuable things.

She darted across the street and dove into the brush. A pulsing siren wailed in the distance. It hammered its route along the boulevard and whined around sweeping curves. Grew louder as it screeched closer to Kavaklidere.

Perhaps she hadn't imagined the scream after all, she thought, falling to a crouch. Thick brush swallowed her.

She crept along, low in the brush, listening to the sirens gaining on her.

The sound of sirens always caused her heart to flutter.

Not now, she told herself, feeling as good as blind. Panic filled her breast, and the wailing siren echoed in her head. She felt dizzy and in danger of being physically ill.

Just a few more feet. The siren bleated through the air, sailing closer. Ever closer to her.

She followed the ditch through this empty field. Staying clear of the trickle of water. Then up a small rise, climbing away from the ditch. She was making far too much noise, that's what panic did to her. She crashed through the dried stems and branches, stumbling the last of the way to the hollow stump.

She didn't know how to handle a gun. No. She didn't. But she *did* have experience. With a gun like the one she'd hidden in the hollow stump. A gun like the Luger. Or maybe that one had been a Luger, too.

She didn't know anymore.

Hadn't seen the other one slip up on her before.

Didn't see this one slip up on her now. As she hunkered down to the hole in the stump. Groped around inside. Felt nothing.

Disappointment raged through her. Kept her from seeing the shadows move in the night. As they did that time before. She'd never thought it could happen again.

It did.

The stink of his body hit her first. Then one arm grappled round her breasts. His other hand pulled her head back at an angle that made her bones ache and her scalp tear. His breath tinted with licorice breathed hot and damp on her neck.

"Gypsy filth," the *asker* snarled in her ear.

* * * * *

Silence descended in the aftermath of the scream, as if the party's plug had been pulled, draining its bubble of merry voices.

"Oh, my God," Anna mumbled, lunging to the window of Cora's bedroom where she scanned the backyard below. Guests surged from the central lawn, strung with lanterns, to the dark perimeter of the yard. To the area where the children played in their clubhouse.

"Priscilla!" Anna turned and ran. She didn't know if Fran followed or not.

The woman's scream outside echoed the tumult of Anna's mind. Danger had followed her everywhere, stalking her from Atatürk's Tomb to Ozturk Bey's shop to here.

Danger had finally caught up to Priscilla. Why ever had Anna left her precious niece unattended, even for a moment, even in the company of her friend? This was a strange land, she reminded herself. Where anything could happen.

Coups.

Anna raced through the hall. Clattered down the steps. Flung open the back door.

A lull had fallen over the party. Some guests, women mostly, milled under the lanterns and stared into the dark beyond the periphery of the tree-lit glow. Anna had stood with them only a short while ago, listening to their innocent gossip.

Nothing was innocent anymore.

Farther away, a cluster of men huddled in the shadows of the untamed areas beyond the edge of grass. Somewhere in that tangled mess of weeds and wild brush was where Anna had found the tripod, and Rainer had found her.

Anna plunged past the servers and their bar tables. She shoved her way into the crowd of women. "What is it? What's happened?"

Soft voices rippled under the lanterns. Someone cried. The ripple grew to a buzz. Then to a roar.

One of the women Anna had bumped said, "It sounded like Eve screaming."

"Remember how she screamed at the bridge party that time?" another said.

"She'd seen a mouse."

This was no mouse, Anna thought. Judging from the shrill

index in her scream, Eve had seen something far worse.

Anna followed the direction of their stunned gazes, aimed at the edge of the yard, where the children had set up their playhouse as a spaceship tonight.

Oh God.

The playhouse barely held together. Had it finally crumbled? With the children *inside*? Her pulse hammered, and she pressed on, past the gossiping women, onward through the lantern light.

"Priscilla?" she called.

A man in a white suit separated from the group of men who gathered near the boundary between this yard and the general's. It was Hayati, and he trotted toward Anna.

She turned her back on him and called, louder this time. "Priscilla!"

"She's okay," he said, breathing heavily as he reached Anna's side. He laid his hand on her arm, a gentle move to prevent her from investigating any further.

She shook it off and kept marching toward the children's playhouse. "Priscilla! Come out of there this minute."

"She's not in there."

Anna stopped in her tracks. Wheeled around to face him. "How do you know? Where is she, then?"

"With the lady of the house, Mrs. Wingate."

Anna breathed again. Priscilla was safe.

Then jealousy flared through her in a flash. Her niece had sought out someone else for comfort. *Not* Anna. She pushed aside her unfair thought and focused on Hayati's words: *She's okay.*

"You're cold," Hayati said, stepping closer.

"On a night this warm? Of course not." Yet, she trembled and spoke in breathless spurts. "What's happened?" she asked, trying to keep her teeth from clattering.

"There's been an accident." He took her by the arm and forcibly steered her away from the murmuring voices in the tangle of weeds. "The men will take care of it. You should go back with the other women."

Anna flung off his restraint and dug her heels into the grass. "I won't hear such nonsense. If someone's hurt, why are we wasting time when we can—"

"It's too late. If anyone needs help, it is Mrs. Matheson, who is in a state of shock. She found him."

"Found *who*?"

Hayati gave her a sad look. "The photographer for this evening. He's...dead."

Anna gasped. Emin! Ozturk Bey's employee. He'd known Umit.

Her trembles grew to a shudder. Remembering. The scolding. The hidden tripod and camera. The talk of a coup. Paul Wingate had told Fran to get rid of the photographer.

But surely not this way.

Rainer, whom she no longer knew, had overheard their discussion, too. And now he was gone. But perhaps he'd never been here in the first place. Had she imagined him?

Swaying on her feet, she took a deep breath to steady herself and asked, "How did it happen?"

Hayati shrugged. "It's not apparent yet. Someone from the medical dispensary is here tonight, fortunately, and he's looking at him now."

"So he wasn't shot?" As the gypsy at the tomb had been shot.

"No, no. He went into convulsions, and then collapsed. Maybe he had a massive heart attack."

"I doubt it," Anna said.

Hayati narrowed his eyes at her, evaluating her, probing her mind. She wouldn't let him in. She clamped her hands together to still the trembling.

Just because the man was dead didn't mean he was murdered, she reminded herself. "Someone had better call the police," she said.

"Mr. Wingate is handling everything."

"Did anyone see the photographer collapse?" She was willing to bet it wasn't a heart attack.

Hayati's mouth drew itself into a tight line, making his voice terse. "The children, I believe."

Dear God, Anna thought. How much more could her niece take?

Just then, a commotion erupted at the table set up as a bar. Two Turkish servers raised their voices at a third man, short and tired-looking in a rumpled, gray suit with no tie. He wore sunglasses, even though it was night.

That Turkish detective. Yaziz. How had he gotten here so fast?

Chapter Thirty-Four

Tears wet the corners of Meryem's eyes. He dragged her to her feet by her hair, but she refused to cry out. How dare the old man treat her like this!

"So this is where you hid it," he said. "I let you go free from those brats so you could lead me to it."

"You're a thief and now a liar," she said, stomping on his foot.

He swore and loosened his grip on her, but not enough for her to slip completely free. Even in his drunken state, his size overwhelmed her. His arm circled around her chest and her arms, and a leg wrapped around her legs. His strength surprised her.

With his other hand in the frizzy tangles of her hair, she felt immobile with her head tilted back. But she still managed to jerk her chin to one side and chomp down on his inner arm. It stank and was too solid for her teeth to penetrate.

He swore again and threw her to the ground. Pain pricked her back, and then he sat atop her. His weight cut off her breath.

"You can't get away, so you might as well stop fighting me," he said.

She responded with a scream, although who would come to the aid of a gypsy?

He grabbed one corner of her *tsharchaf* and stuffed it in

her mouth, down her throat until she heaved with gags. By the time she'd coughed the cotton out of her throat and her choking spasm settled to mere discomfort, he was tying her wrists together with rope, and then her ankles. He pulled so tightly that she thought her flesh would peel away.

He wrapped the rope around and around, binding her arms to her body, her legs to each other. Finally, the struggle in her died, and her body felt limp. Still, he did not lessen his hold on her until she remained limp for what felt like forever.

He climbed off her, and she took in a deep sigh of air.

"All right," he said, watching her as he reached inside the hollow stump. "Let's see what you have."

His hand scraped the inside of the stump. "There's nothing there. You lied."

"Let me go."

"You've lied all along." He drew his arm back, as if he meant to hit her.

"Yes."

"You're still lying."

"No. There's no gun." Too bad it was gone. She could've used it to bargain for her freedom.

Without the gun...what would happen to Mustafa? And to the rest of the family?

The *asker's* eyes rolled up in his head, and he contemplated her in silence while her mind replayed the mystery of the gun's disappearance. Someone must've followed her. Here, to the water hole. Yesterday. Someone had known where she'd hidden the gun.

Not the gunman from Anit Kabir. He hadn't known.

"Where'd you get a thing like that?" the *asker* finally said, suddenly sounding sober.

"Let me go! I've done you no harm."

"Oh, but you have. And now you pay. The general wants to have a little talk with you." The old soldier plucked her from the ground and tossed her across one shoulder as easily as if she weighed nothing more than Priscilla's kitten.

Thinking of the kitten, she felt the flutter of her heart as he bounced her along the path, toward the street. Her life was worthless to him. She was no more important than one more stray from an unwanted litter. When the general was done with her, the *asker* would probably bring her back here.

To the stream.

Head tied in a sack. To drown her. No one would ever notice if she disappeared forever.

* * * * *

Anna moved swiftly across the lawn toward Detective Yaziz. She wanted to intercept him before the others discovered who he was.

Paul beat her to it. Emerging from the house, he paused in the light of the back door for only a moment before striding across the verandah, catching up to the detective. "Ah. We meet so soon, *efendim*. I only just now got off the phone from summoning the authorities."

"What is the problem?" Yaziz asked, stepping away from the servers who'd detained him.

"They didn't send you? But of course not. You couldn't have arrived that fast."

"Nothing moves so fast in my country," Yaziz said with a soft chuckle. "But you are right. I was already in the neighborhood when I heard a cry for help. How may I be of assistance?"

In the neighborhood, Anna thought. Doing *what*? Something underhanded with Rainer? He had not reappeared yet from whatever task had drawn him across the street.

"This way, *efendim*." Paul cupped the detective's elbow in his palm and led the way across the lawn.

Anna matched the speed of their step. "Detective Yaziz, are you always on duty?"

He paused, aiming his face in her direction. Through the dark lenses of his glasses, she couldn't tell if he saw her or not. If his eyes registered recognition or not.

"I regret that it seems that way," he said.

"How fortunate for us. Once again."

He shrugged and continued along with a limp behind Paul, toward the darkened area of death. A place, Hayati had said, that was not suitable for women's eyes.

Anna hurried after them. "How fortunate that you respond so quickly to a call."

"Miss Riddle." Paul stopped and turned around, stepping close to her. "The detective happened by at the right moment. Perhaps you and the other women should wait inside with Cora and the kids."

She moved away from his face and tried again. "Detective, is it a purse thief that brings you to this neighborhood?"

"If you like."

"What purse thief?" asked Paul.

Anna smiled. "Hadn't you better attend to more pressing matters now?"

"Yes. Of course. Well, come along, *efendim*."

Moving on toward the group of men, they hurried their step, as if anxious to put distance between them and Anna.

Anna picked up her pace and trailed along behind them.

"Miss Riddle!" Paul shouted, stopping again. "This isn't a pretty sight. Go on inside with the other women."

"I'll decide for myself what I happen to look at and where I go, thank you. Unless Detective Yaziz doesn't want anyone around to disturb his investigation." She glanced significantly at the huddle of men by the fence. Still, no Rainer. "They'll have to go, too."

Yaziz's sunglasses looked at her, then to the men, then back to her again. He shrugged. "One eye is as good as another," he said.

It was a small victory for Anna, but an important one. It had been impossible for her to establish her authority, either with Priscilla or with gossipy Cora and her friends. This was one way to do that. Not that it mattered so much to her whether or not she was admitted to some sort of male club, but just that she had the freedom to make her own choices.

Two deaths in two days. Death asphyxiated the air. Followed her. Tormented her with its nearness. Rainer's gypsy, first, and now the photographer. They were both connected, somehow. Along with the purse thief and her very own sister, who teased death with an opium addiction. The common denominator was...Anna. Not Rainer, after all.

Perhaps *she* needed an evil eye.

The photographer's body lay in broken weeds beyond the reach of grassy lawn. At first she thought he was only asleep. She thought that the men who hovered over him had made a dreadful mistake. There was no blood, not as there'd been the day before at the tomb.

It wasn't until she saw his camera lying smashed to one side of his still body that Anna felt her own desire to scream boil from within. Even with her knees thus weakened, she would not allow herself to succumb to hysteria, not as Paul expected from her. She jerked her head to one side and stifled a sob. Yaziz turned away from the body and gave her a gentle push toward the house.

"Please do me the favor of seeing that no one leaves the premises."

She started to protest, but then a wave of nausea stirred, and her hand jerked to her mouth. She couldn't lose it now. Couldn't lose everything that she'd gained by tromping out here with the men. She'd made her point. So she nodded, then scuttled away to organize everyone, guests and servants.

Trapped. Hours passed, unfolding the night. Teams of police and medical personnel arrived.

The phone call placed to Nairobi never came through. Naturally. It had never been placed because Mitzi and Henry were in Switzerland. No calls arrived from Switzerland, either.

Why had Henry lied to her?

Fran had lied, too. She'd known all along that Mitzi wasn't in Nairobi, yet she'd pretended—no, *lied*—about helping Anna with the call. As if there was an urgent, a hidden reason to make sure that Anna came here tonight. And stayed.

Well, she was staying, all right, whether or not she wanted to. Thanks to Yaziz.

* * * * *

Bound, Meryem rode across the *asker's* shoulder as he carried her upside down up the hill. After many bruising bounces and several squeaking gates and doors, she was dropped like a shovel full of manure.

Meryem landed on her face in the toilet. The rough cement edge of the footprint cut her cheek. Blood streamed down the side of her nose and sopped into the kerchief, fastened tightly round her mouth. The *asker* was done with her for now, but he'd be back.

She felt... She felt...

Nothing.

The sting of her cuts, the bruises against her hips, were nothing compared to the empty shell from which her soul had been ripped. Anger, hatred, humiliation—none of them fueled her anymore. Least of all, fear.

She was a body waiting for the release of death.

She wished he would've killed her. But it wasn't time yet. The general hadn't arrived. To speak with her. To learn what she didn't know. About revolution.

And so she waited for the release of death or the arrival of the general. Whichever came first. She didn't care. As long as it wasn't the *asker*.

She closed her eyes, but she could not blot out the memories of evil.

* * * * *

Gossip raged like wildfire among the partiers held captive in the Wingates' stuffy living room.

The photographer was a student by night. That much

Anna thought was true.

A communist, some of her fellow detainees whispered.

By day, he polished copper.

And worked to support his ailing mother.

He was a red journalist.

Anna strained to listen, not to the surge of anxiety spreading in the snatch of stories around her, but to the sounds of police moving about outside. Beams of light swept through the night out there, occasionally striking the living room's picture window, a dark rectangle against the blaze of interior lamplight. Anna twisted a handkerchief in her lap and sat silently, feeling Fran's watchful gaze on her.

Fran had given Emin Kirpat a chance at being a real photographer. Fran wouldn't have killed him.

Get rid of him, Paul had told her.

No matter what her instructions, Fran wouldn't have done it. She'd taken a risk by giving Anna the letters—Anna's own letters. She felt their lump resting against her thigh, hidden inside the pocket of Mitzi's black chiffon cocktail dress. Paul would not be happy once he found out that Fran hadn't obeyed him. With that single gesture of friendship and trust, Fran had awakened a warmth inside Anna that had been lost to her too many years. No, Fran simply wasn't capable of murder. Besides, she'd been upstairs with Anna at the time.

When the body was discovered. But, even so...

Anna remembered Emin's bias against gypsies in general and Umit in particular. He'd been outraged that his uncle, Ozturk Bey, helped the gypsy family, and outraged further that his uncle thought Emin should marry the sister. Emin hadn't been sorry at all about Umit's death. In fact, he'd been so emphatic that Anna wondered if he could've had a role in Umit's death. She didn't think that anymore.

Now she wondered if Emin had died for what he knew about Umit's death. Maybe for the photos he'd taken. The photos at the tomb, or even the photos taken here tonight.

Get rid of him.

Maybe Emin had photographed the general's party, where a coup brewed. Was that why he had to die?

Rainer, not the Rainer she'd once loved, but the new Rainer, Rainer the Spy, had been interested in that coup.

Oh, God, had Rainer and Emin and Umit all worked together? Did that mean Rainer was next to die? She'd just begun to accept the fact that he hadn't died all those years ago, and now she didn't know how she felt about him. Even so, she didn't want him to die this time for real.

Finally, Yaziz entered the room, releasing her from her whirling thoughts. He held his notepad and thumbed through pages as he scribbled names and phone numbers of the guests.

Anna marched over to him while he wrote the red-headed teacher's information. "Detective Yaziz, how did that man die?"

"Thank you, Mr. Davis, you may go now." Yaziz turned from the teacher to Major Matheson. "I already know where to reach you, so you may go, too."

"Detective," Anna said, "shouldn't you excuse those with children first? It's well past their bedtimes."

Yaziz looked up from his pad and finally aimed his gold-tinted sunglasses at her. "Why are you still here, Miss Riddle? We have your information."

She gave a short sigh of frustration. "And we have none. No one has told us anything. We deserve to know what happened.

For our peace of mind."

"That is what we are trying to find out."

She glared at him. "When are you going to start asking questions, then? You should find out what people might have seen, rather than send them home."

"I will remember that." He shuffled over to the next cluster of people.

Don Davis, the schoolteacher Cora had tried to pair up with Anna, lingered by Anna's side. He tapped her elbow. "C'mon, I'll walk you and Priscilla home."

"Thank you, Mr. Davis, but—" She stopped herself short of taking out her frustration on him. It would be better, she decided, to return home via the sidewalk, around the block, rather than take Priscilla back through the darkened lawn, past the crime scene. "That's very kind of you," she said, forcing a smile.

Chapter Thirty-Five

The smell of urine reminded Meryem of other days long ago. She'd been trapped, the hunted prey of the Nazi dogs. She did not like to remember that time. And so she hadn't. But now, bound and gagged in a toilet, there was little else to do. Memories crawled through her mind like lice in her hair. Those other times had been similar to this, except now she knew the sweet release of liberation.

The memories of their escape washed through her mind. She waited, expecting another liberator. What else could she do but wait, hungering for her liberator?

There had been more than one.

Their angel-savior had not worked alone against the Nazis. His partner, a man called "Stork," had waited for them that day with packhorses in the shelter of firs on the other side of the meadow. They rode all day and into the night through mountains that grew wilder as the sun coursed through the sky.

The gunshot wound to their savior's shoulder festered, and infection set in. When all looked lost, Stork—the coward partner—left them. Meryem and Umit and their savior hid in a cave with a few supplies from one of Stork's saddlebags. She knew he wouldn't return, even though he promised he would. His was a hollow promise to bring back more help. She could not rely on his promises, but turned instead to her grandmother's teachings about making poultices from certain roots and leaves. She gathered what she needed from the wilds near to their cave, mixed them up, and packed the shoulder. She couldn't let their rescuer die.

He did not die.

And then when he recovered his strength, their liberator vanished into the night.

Perhaps he did not know that certain treasures were missing from his saddlebag. They were joint treasures for Meryem and Umit, repaying the kindness of their care. One was the amulet, a silver piece with a lucky jewel, humming with power. The other, a bundle of folded paper with unknown markings, tied up with string. Worthless, no doubt, but the amulet would keep them safe.

From then on, they carried their few treasures with them in their journeys, running from hiding place to hiding place while the Nazis and Russians fought their own battles. And over the years, their savior's amulet *did* keep them safe. Safe, when they finally reunited with their clan near Bucharest, eked out a living, and waited for their next benefactor to appear in their lives—Ozturk Bey.

Safe, until Umit tried to sell the amulet. Now it was gone, into American hands. Gone, along with Umit.

How long would she have to wait this time for rescue?

* * * * *

Anna held Priscilla's hand, and they followed Don Davis out the front door. She paused for a minute on the porch where she'd spoken to Hayati such a short while ago. Yet, it felt like a lifetime ago. Before hearing Fran's story about Mitzi's addiction.

Anna's gaze fixed on the globe of yellow light piercing the darkness—the streetlight on the corner. Rainer had darted away in that direction. Yaziz's man had lurked there the night before.

She felt overwhelmed by the questions running through her mind. Events beyond her control had caught her in some unknown whirlpool. She wasn't altogether certain that she and Priscilla could emerge safely into a normal world again. Nothing would ever be normal again.

Priscilla clung tightly to her hand, and the gesture gave Anna the strength she needed to walk down the steps. Now she was grateful for the teacher's company and his idle chatter about next week's start of school.

Her thoughts felt distant to her as they walked briskly down the sidewalk, toward the corner. Where Rainer had run. Did he still lurk in the shadows? If so, he might have watched the events unfold in the backyard. She hoped he hadn't been involved in that man's death.

She really didn't know him anymore. Didn't know what the new Rainer, Rainer the Spy, was capable of doing.

She would have to confess to Yaziz about Rainer's presence here tonight. That is, if the detective ever got around to interviewing the witnesses.

"Their process isn't like ours," Don said, as if reading her mind. "They're still trying to learn western ways."

"He studied in the States," Anna said. "He should know what to do."

"It may not be him, but his department that he has to answer to."

Yaziz answered to one of her neighbors, Anna thought, the father of Priscilla's friend. Ahmet, he'd wanted her to call him. Ahmet and his daughter Gulsen lived in one of those houses across the street. Where Rainer had run. "They've had time to westernize," she said. "It's been...what? Twenty-some years since Atatürk?"

"Nineteen, since his death. And not all Turks wanted to adopt western ways when he forced them to. Their old ways are still out there, alive and well, and little by little they're eating away at the westernization that Atatürk accomplished."

"So you think there's a struggle of ideology within the police department?"

Don shrugged. "All I'm saying is that those opposing forces cancel each other out and make it difficult to accomplish anything. There's the law, and then there's the unwritten code. Which do you choose? Your duty or your loyalty?"

"Why can't you choose both?" Anna squeezed Priscilla's hand. Both duty and loyalty to her family had brought her here.

"You're lucky if you can," Don said. "In the modern Turks' case, their duty may be following Atatürk's westernization policies, but their loyalty may still be to the old ways that the new has forced them to abandon."

Like Ahmet, Anna thought. He was about to be remarried in a traditional arrangement made by his aunt and uncle. She wondered, as they walked the rest of the way, what was Rainer's interest in Ahmet.

* * * * *

Later, after tucking Priscilla into bed, Anna climbed the last of the steps to her attic bedroom. Weariness wrapped around her shoulders, yet her heart still raced. She flicked on the overhead light and leaned against the door to shut it behind her. Light filled the room, spilling down atop a dark-haired man. He sat at her writing desk, his hand in one of the desk drawers. His head jerked up, and he blinked at her. In the same instant, she swallowed her scream. It was Rainer!

"What are you doing here?" she whispered. "How did you get in? How did you even know—" She remembered the intruder who'd been in her bedroom the day before, subtly rearranging the layers of her lingerie. It had been *him*.

He slid the drawer shut, sprang to his feet, and crossed the room in three strides. "Oh, God, I've missed you. I just...had to find a way to get closer to you. I thought...seeing where you sleep, touching your things... Oh, Annie... My Annie... I'm sorry. I'm so sorry." He held out his arms to her, but Anna took a step backwards, instead. Away from him. Her jaw muscles tightened.

"You didn't come back," she said.

"I'm here now."

"I don't mean just tonight. Rainer, it's been twelve years. Where have you been all that time? What happened?"

"Annie, please understand. I couldn't let you know anything. After the war, there were still...problems."

She remembered Yaziz's statement about enemies being unclear after a state of war, and she wondered now if that was true, if that had contributed to Rainer's absence. "What could possibly be that big of a problem that you couldn't have gotten a message to me that you were still alive?" The coldness in her voice surprised her.

"It was too dangerous. You saw what happened to the man at Atatürk's Tomb."

"Is that why Umit died? Because of you?"

Rainer shrugged and looked away. His careless body language said it didn't matter. One man's life didn't matter.

Anna shivered. "He had one of the letters I wrote to you towards the end of the war. How did he get it?"

"Who knows? He probably stole it."

"I want to know the truth. I want to know why you made me lie for you tonight."

"To keep you out of it. I can't risk letting you get involved."

"It's not up to you. I already *am* involved." She turned away from him to glance at the window, holding the dark of night at bay. The killer could be out there now, unseen. Waiting. Watching *Anna*. Because Rainer was mixed up in some sort of dangerous game. Rainer had put her through hell, grieving for him.

"Swear to me, Annie," he said from behind her. "Say nothing about this. Swear that you'll stay out of it."

"How dare you!" She whirled back around to face Rainer. "Twelve years, you let me think you were dead."

"I know. I know. I'm sorry."

He'd said nothing about love, Anna thought. It really was over between them.

"All I had were your letters," he said. "When I lost them, I thought I'd lost you all over again."

He'd lost them. Not one, but all of the letters. However Umit had come into possession of that single letter he'd tried to show her back at the tomb, he must've had the other letters, too. That's what had been kept inside the empty box his wife had hurled at Anna. Hayati's guess was right. Hearing Rainer's name must've triggered Mrs. Alekci to look inside her box and find it empty. Empty, because Umit's sister had taken the letters to sell to Cora Wingate. His sister was the gypsy woman Cora had mentioned.

Anna swallowed hard and took another step backwards, away from Rainer. "Why now? Why after all these years? Why did you come in disguise to the party tonight? Viktor Baliko! How could you? Why are you pretending to be a Hungarian with a pregnant wife?"

"I can't tell you why."

"That woman is pretending to be your wife."

"It's just a job."

"You're a spy, aren't you?"

"Do you think I could tell you that, even if I were?"

"So it's true."

"I didn't say that."

"But it is. It's true. The war's over, didn't you know? Why are you still fighting the war? Are they using you to spy against the communists? Why did you agree to do that, instead of coming home?"

"Home. Where is home? I have no home anymore."

"You *had* a home. Why didn't you come home?"

"You're saying you want me to come home?"

She started to answer, and then bit off her retort. The truth was, she *didn't* want him to come home anymore. Too many years had gone by, and she no longer knew him. "Why did you ask me to pretend I never saw you?" she said, avoiding the truth.

"Please, Annie..."

"Because it would destroy your cover, if I revealed your true identity? You were there at the Wingates' party for another purpose, weren't you? You had to find out whatever it is that Fran and Paul are up to."

"No, Annie..."

"Why didn't you want me to hear what they had to say? They were talking about a coup and something else. Getting rid of something. Was it the photographer they meant?"

"Good Lord, no."

Her pulse pounded in her ears, and she swayed from the impact of her questions. "What are Fran and Paul doing that's so wrong? And why did Hayati make up that story about meeting you in the taxi? How's he involved in your little masquerade?"

"He's not. I don't know why he said that. Who can tell with the Turks?"

"You had to meet someone after the party, didn't you?"

"I can't tell you."

She let out a strangled laugh that was more of a cry. "I should've guessed you'd say that."

"Annie, let me—"

"Who are you?" she whispered. "I don't know you anymore. What have you become? Why can't the world know that you exist?"

"I wish I could answer all your questions," he said. "I can't. Trust me, Annie."

"Trust?" She felt hysteria creep to the edge of her voice, and he rushed to her, covering her mouth with one hand and holding her tight against him with the other.

She struggled at first, and then she remembered that this man was Rainer, a man she'd once loved. Her body went limp against his, and when his arms loosened their hold on her, she stiffened and pulled away.

"Why are you *here*?" she said. "In Turkey? Why are you here, after all these years, in the same city, on the same street where I am?"

"Because I sent for you. Annie, it was me."

"No, you're wrong. Henry asked me to come. To take care of Priscilla. While they had to go away."

"And I arranged it."

"You...and Henry..." They'd worked together in the war, Fran had claimed.

Rainer grunted. "We were somewhere in the mountains, and we came across this German camp. We freed some prisoners so they could come over to our side. But it all went wrong. There was an accident, and Henry left me for dead, and I had to survive, you see? The gypsies knew better than anyone how to survive. I would've died, if not for—"

Anna's eyes widened with understanding. "The Alekcis."

"What matters now is that you're here because of me." He reached for her again, and she sidestepped him again. But not fast enough. He caught her by the arm and pulled her toward him.

The door creaked open. "Aunt Anna, I'm afraid—" Priscilla's shaky voice ended in a whimper.

"Oh, shit," Rainer murmured in Anna's ear, shaking her arm loose from his grip. "I'll be back. Wait for me." Then he swept past Priscilla, standing in the open doorway, crying.

Anna rushed to Priscilla and scooped her in her arms. She hugged her close and listened to Rainer's footsteps pound away, down the stairs. A door slammed.

"Hush, honey, it's okay. He didn't mean to frighten you. He's a good guy. He's Rainer, honey."

"No!" Priscilla kept sobbing. "It's him! The man who's chasing Daddy!"

Chapter Thirty-Six

Using translation help from Hayati Orhon, officers from the National Police spoke to the Wingates' guests late into the night. Yaziz stayed until the unhappy end. He'd arrived in the fancy neighborhood, Kavaklidere, earlier that day, on a lead from a butcher in Ulus about his missing witness from Anit Kabir—she was a gypsy girl, hawking copper pots up and down these streets. Yaziz eventually tailed her to the big house, owned by one of Atatürk's generals and conveniently located between the Wingates' and Burkhardts' houses. Now, hours later, Yaziz found himself at the far end of the city without transportation in the middle of the night. One of the sergeants gave him a ride home.

The city block where he lived in Yenişehir, the new downtown, was a cement wall of joined apartment buildings that all looked alike. Even to Yaziz. Especially when he was so weary that he mistakenly identified his own building. He ended up walking the last block, rather than confess his mistake to the sergeant. The walk, at least, cleared the fuzz from his mind, and he would be good for another hour or two.

He limped slowly up the stairs to his apartment on the top floor. There was an elevator, which sometimes ran, but that wire cage more often than not entrapped him. Even this exhausted, he preferred the security of the stairs.

With each step of the first two flights, he breathed deeper. He puzzled over the mysteries that disturbed his life. Only yesterday he'd received the summons about trouble at Anit Kabir. Who had wanted to kill a gypsy? Now, he wondered, who would want to kill a student photographer?

Unrelated deaths, perhaps, except for the presence of Miss Anna Riddle at both crime scenes. Although he'd changed his mind about her guilt after today's incident in Ulus, she was not entirely free from his suspicion.

It could be weeks before the autopsy was done. But Yaziz needed no report. Tonight's victim was surely the result of murder. As the first one so clearly was.

The camera had been smashed. Yaziz had led the Americans to believe that the damage was the result of the man's falling on it. Yaziz knew better. The camera had been destroyed deliberately. The film it contained had been removed.

What was on that missing film?

Perhaps there'd never been any film in the camera in the first place. Still, *some*one hadn't wanted *some*thing seen. Plans for the revolution that frightened Bulayir? Such plans—had they been in progress next door in the big house?—could easily be seen from the spot where the photographer had fallen.

What did the Americans, they who had their finger in every pot, have to do with this latest development?

Yaziz rounded the third flight of steps. Paused while his laboring breath settled a fraction. Trudged on.

Then there was the mystery of what Erkmen was up to. Yaziz had never trusted his curly-headed colleague. Theirs was a friendly rivalry, long underway before yesterday, when Erkmen appeared under the lamppost outside the nargile salon.

Why had he wanted Miss Riddle's purse?

It wasn't that Erkmen was so incompetent. No. His greatest fault was that he was a little harsh in his treatment of the public. Which, in itself was only a nuisance and not a problem.

The problem Yaziz had with Erkmen was that both of them vied for the top. Both of them moved swiftly through the ranks, swifter than the norm. But Erkmen wasn't *koreli*. Yaziz did not know what had generated the favors being showered on Erkmen. He'd always thought his rival's success was on account of some distant family connections with the police.

After tonight, Yaziz was no longer sure. He'd seen Erkmen dressed in a servant's uniform at the general's house. What was he up to?

But the biggest surprise development during tonight's surveillance, discounting the complication of the murder next door, was when he saw Murat show up. Apparently the old judge was on the general's guest list. Yaziz felt betrayed. Why hadn't his old friend told him he was on such familiar terms with one of Atatürk's men? Close enough to be invited to dinner? Clearly, Murat had some information Yaziz did not know and could have used.

Yaziz staggered a bit on the last flight of stairs.

He was in better shape than this. His weakness was the result of festering problems. Erkmen, with the newspaper. Erkmen, caught examining Miss Riddle's purse. Erkmen, prowling the neighborhood tonight, too.

Left Yaziz with a sense of foreboding.

Which only doubled when Yaziz saw Erkmen leave the general's house and cross the street. Enter the house that belonged to the assistant minister, Ahmet Aydenli.

Instead of going home. Most people would go home. After leaving a party.

Then, his apprehension was realized. Like a bad dream come to life. With the scream.

Yaziz shouldn't have been surprised. To find the troubling Miss Anna Riddle at the American party.

All the same. He was. Trouble followed that woman. Like stray cats after a piece of meat. During the days of sacrifice.

With a deep sigh, Yaziz took the last step. Onto the fifth floor landing. He stumbled into darkness. The light bulb had apparently burned out again. He groped for the lock, rattling his keys, stabbing at the dark. Finally his door creaked open and Yaziz tripped inside to the sour smell of unwashed dishes.

"Nasreddin!" he called, throwing his key ring with a clatter onto a small table by the door.

The Angora cat didn't respond. He usually sulked when Yaziz left him this long—twenty hours, this time. The storks, in their nest overhead, reminded him of their presence with a clap of their bills and a rustling of sticks.

Yaziz stepped closer to the table and reached for the lamp. Something crinkled and squished underfoot, which made his fingers hesitate over the lamp's switch. He flicked it on.

Dim light cast about the disaster of the room. Books and papers and dirty cups and plates spilled across table tops. Pillows and soiled shirts tossed across the sofa. His open gym bag by the door reeked of sweaty underwear.

The place was just as he had left it.

He never thought of himself as being untidy. As long as the floor remained free of clutter, then he was content. Sometimes Nasreddin bounced things onto the floor and chased them around. A cat toy. That's what Yaziz had stepped on.

But he didn't recognize the bundle on the floor, wrapped in newspaper and tied with string. Similar to the package he'd seen Ozturk Bey attempt to hand over to the red-haired Burkhardt child in his copper shop today.

He bent down and picked it up. Carried it to the table and brushed aside bread crumbs from his breakfast. The string that tied this package was the thin, green kind that shopkeepers often used to tie up their customers' purchases. The knots were too tight and tiny for his thick fingers, and he had to rummage in a drawer for a knife.

With a snip, the string fell aside, and the newspaper wrapping unfolded. It was a sheet of that day's *Republic News*. He unwrapped the bundle the rest of the way and stared at a note, handwritten in a crude pencil scrawl: "More of this if you drop the matter of the gypsy."

He lifted the note, and underneath lay a cube of raw opium.

Chapter Thirty-Seven

A cock crowed somewhere in the distance, then crowed again. And again. Until Meryem finally opened her eyes. To the dark. She was still alive.

Although, the afterlife would surely be a better choice than *this* place.

This was not the Carpathians, but a prison all the same.

A narrow stall encircled her with no windows and a cold, hard floor was her bed. Cement? A sewer stench hung in the air. Arching her back, she scrunched away from the hole in the center of the floor and pressed herself against a wall of wood that enclosed her. Imprisoned her.

The dream, not really a dream, haunted her sleep, such as it was, dozing in fitful bursts throughout the hours. She was the *asker's* prisoner now. Not the Nazi's. It was all the same.

Bindings chafed against her wrists and feet. Pain sliced through her flesh like a knife. She banged her head against the wall.

When no one responded to her thudding noise, she sucked air from her lungs, summoning a scream that burned in her chest. "Let me out, you bastard!"

But her words came out a gargled muffle. A wad of cotton plugged her mouth. Spit dribbled down her chin. A knot full of her hair tore from her scalp each time she twisted.

She could do nothing.

She, who had escaped impossible odds before, would end her days now, bound up in a toilet.

She wouldn't have come to the general's house in the first place, bartering away the gun that had killed Umit, if not for Umit. She wouldn't have been unlucky enough to overhear plans of revolution. Not on her own.

Bah! Let the men do as they would with their government. It was all the same to her. As long as they did not disrupt her life again with their wars.

Their plans of revolution did not concern her, and for a few lira, she would never speak of it. Would never even know what she'd once known, having the misfortune to overhear such talk.

But the gun. She *needed* that gun. For Mustafa's life. She hadn't saved her sisters and brothers, but she could still save her nephew.

She banged her head against the wood and yelled again. "Let me out! OUT!" The words, however, existed nowhere but inside her throat and head. Not in the actual sounds she voiced, which resembled more the howls of a wounded animal.

Something crunched. Footsteps slugged through gravel. A clink...keys. Rattling around inside a lock. Then the creak of a door opening. Footsteps thudded across a cement floor, coming closer to her prison.

"All right, all right," said the *asker* from the other side of her wooden wall. "Keep it down in there."

The wall she'd leaned against—a door—suddenly whisked away from her, spilling her onto the floor of a light-filled room. The light hurt her eyes, and she blinked several times.

The room she fell into was the same cramped size as one

of the rooms of her apartment. Narrow windows framed leafy branches on four walls and suggested that this was a detached building in someone's garden.

The general's.

But the general didn't live *here*, not among such simple furnishings. A narrow bed with rumpled covers that smelled of dung pushed up against one wall, next to a brazier and a collapsed hookah. A wooden table with three chairs stood against the opposite wall. In its center, a crusty loaf of bread.

Her stomach growled.

The *asker* filled the middle of the room with his brawn and towered to the wooden ceiling. He held a scythe in one hand, and he scraped its cutting edge against the floor.

"I will have to untie you, if you want to eat," he said. "But I warn you. One sound out of you, one attempt to run, and I slice your pretty flesh." He demonstrated with a sweep of his scythe. "Understand?"

She nodded, saliva clogging her gag and smearing her chin.

He pulled some of her hair loose when he undid the gag, but she refused to give him the pleasure of a flinch. He stared deep into her eyes, his own, bloodshot. As if he waited for a reaction before proceeding with the knots round her wrists.

But she was not stupid enough to give away her reaction. Instead, she returned his stare with her own seething stare of permanent hatred. Her jaw muscles quivered as she resisted crying out.

Anything, for bread.

"I won't say anything," she said, testing her voice. The song was flushed from her soul, but the words still formed.

"Save it for the general when he returns later today. You

will tell him what he wants to hear."

"What does he want to hear?"

"That you weren't listening at his window. That you have nothing to give the Americans next door."

"Why do the Americans worry you so much?" She usually wasn't that direct, but she'd had a rough time, all the hours she'd spent in the toilet, and her thoughts moved sluggishly.

The *asker* made an evil sound. Then she realized it was his attempt at a laugh. "The Americans are in bed with the government in power. They want to stomp all over any ideas that the general and his friends might have about unseating the prime minister."

She was not so sluggish that she missed the implications. Or the error of her previous threat of going to the Americans with her information. The *asker*, she realized, would never let her go anywhere ever again if he suspected her claims of friendship with the Americans were true. The prospect of forceful escape from that toilet seemed bleak considering her aching weariness.

"I lied about the Americans," she said.

The scythe clicked as he laid it down on the floor and reached for her bound wrists. "Gypsies always lie."

"For a price, I will have nothing to say, not to the Americans or to anyone."

He backhanded her across one cheek. Slivers of pain needled through her neck and head. "Do not dare to bargain with me! The only price you should be bartering is your life."

"Then, what do you want?"

His gaze roved her body. The tip of his tongue wet his lips as they curved, although it could not be said to be a smile. "I have an idea," he said, reaching once again for her.

* * * * *

Yaziz hunkered low, shifting his weight carefully so as not to crack the tiles of the roof of his own apartment building where he squatted. He'd come up here to search for answers, but so far he'd found only storks. Aside from their jumble of twigs where they slept, and aside from a few broken tiles and a gritty layer of dust, he found no clues that his visitor had dropped, nor footprints crossing from one rooftop to the next. The storks knew nothing about the writer of the note who had accessed Yaziz's locked apartment, leaving him a bribe of opium. One bribe led to another, he guessed.

And no, he would not drop the case of the gypsy.

From the murky gray distance came the pre-dawn warbling of the muezzin, who'd climbed minarets to call the faithful to prayer. These days the call was delivered in Arabic, rather than Turkish, as decreed by Atatürk.

But that was another matter.

Yaziz felt impatient for the sun to rise. With the muezzin and the faithful out of their beds for the day, he decided it was not too early to start. He crawled across the tile ridges to the open window and the ladder, leading down to the hallway before his apartment. He hesitated before reaching for his phone, but his mind was made up.

He rousted several other residences from sleep.

First, his landlord denied having unlocked Yaziz's apartment, but then he would, with the offering of an opium bribe.

Then, a house servant informed him that Murat was away

at his horse farm today. No, he would not attend the nargile salon at their usual time.

Erkmen could not (or would not) see Yaziz for lunch later today. But Yaziz suspected that even if he did gain an audience, Bulayir's man would refuse to divulge what he might have learned from his hours of surveillance.

Mr. Wingate already supervised his team, who searched his grounds for the missing film from the broken camera the night before, thank you very much, but he welcomed the Turks to go over it again. If they insisted.

Yes, Yaziz insisted.

And finally, Doctor Vardarli suppressed his anger at being hauled out of bed. He promised to do what he could in the police lab, although he was in no rush to track down the source of the opium. He would not even begin until the day after tomorrow. Never mind. Yaziz was fairly certain that the opium had come from Ozturk Bey, who claimed he was no longer a poppy farmer. The question remained, what interest was it of the old smuggler-turned-merchant to see that the police drop the investigation of a gypsy?

Yaziz did not know, but he would find out.

* * * * *

Anna tossed and turned the rest of the night with one thought dominating her mind. *Rainer had come here, into her bedroom, searching for something.*

It had taken some time to settle Priscilla, but even after the child slept, Anna still could not. She replayed the scene with Rainer over and over. She reviewed the sound of his voice, the scent of his skin oils, the feel of his arms around her. The way his breath tickled her ear.

What had he been looking for in her desk drawer?

After he left, she tucked her letters there, the packet of letters Fran had given to Anna. They had still been in her pocket when he'd been searching. Tossing through the night, she felt tempted to get up and re-read those old letters, but her doubts surfaced again. Joy—the revelation that he lived—*should* tingle through her.

She felt no joy. Only shivers, from the coldness of his words. And from his actions.

Rainer had been searching her desk, not to touch her things but to *search* her things when she interrupted him. He hadn't been waiting for her at all, not as he claimed. Hadn't missed her at all.

He'd lied. All those years, a lie.

He was a spy. What did he think he would find in Anna's bedroom except for Anna?

The Saint Christopher's medal.

Which was gone.

Stolen, by the purse thief in the market.

But this was Henry's house, and Fran claimed that Henry and Rainer had worked together during the war. Was it something of Henry's that Rainer had searched for? He'd spoken of Henry with a hard edge to his voice. Henry had left Rainer for dead...

Then she remembered what she'd found while looking for a cocktail dress in Mitzi's closet. Mitzi's calling card with the note of an appointment had fallen out of the jacket pocket of Henry's suit. A meeting, perhaps, between Henry and Rainer.

It seemed that no time at all had passed with her thoughts

of Rainer spinning through her mind when the distant roosters crowed. Their pre-dawn call startled Anna from her thoughts, and finally her weariness won out and she slept.

She awoke to Priscilla's tugging on her arm. "C'mon, Aunt Anna, wake up."

Light flooded her attic bedroom, and Anna flung one arm across her face. "What time is it?"

"I dunno," Priscilla said. "You've been sleeping forever. C'mon, you've got to get up. He wants us to come for tea!"

"He?" Anna's voice caught. Rainer. Had Rainer really been here in the night, or had it been a dream? "Who?"

"Gulsen's father. He just phoned and said so himself. If me and Gulsen want to play. We can go over there. He says it's okay. So can we?"

Anna yawned and smiled. "Can I get dressed first?" It was good to see Priscilla act with such child-like enthusiasm now, after the frightening way last evening had ended. Anna didn't have to consider the request very long.

She shooed Priscilla away and climbed out of bed, heading for the bathroom and a long, soaking bath. Water gurgled through the pipes and thundered into the tub. She wondered what she should wear to tea with an important Turkish neighbor. He'd said he was Assistant Minister of the Interior, she thought, not sure what that meant exactly, but it sounded important. Perhaps she should borrow a daytime dress of Mitzi's, complete with hat.

She'd seen hatboxes in her sister's closet.

Still in her pajamas, Anna moved swiftly into Mitzi's bedroom, crossed to the closet, and pushed aside the folding doors. There on the top shelf was a row of blue and white striped hatboxes. With an addiction to opium, her sister had lost her right to privacy.

Anna pulled down the largest of the boxes. It felt heavier than a hat should make it, and something clunked within. Her curiosity aroused, she undid the ties and lifted the lid, exposing the flowered brim of a yellow, straw hat with velvet ribbons. Priscilla's Easter bonnet, no doubt. Something lay underneath, separated by a layer of white tissue paper. The paper crinkled as she dug down, her fingers touching something cold and metallic. She pulled out a high-powered lens for a camera.

She gasped and glanced up at the two remaining boxes on the shelf. She grabbed the next one and yanked off its lid. Inside, a white fur pillbox sat on top of another bundle of tissue paper. Flinging the hat to the floor, she tore at the paper. With her fingers, she could feel the hard edges of the heavy object wrapped within. She fumbled and clawed and ripped the paper away from...a camera. Old equipment, she could tell from the nicks and scratches. But hidden, all the same.

Her sister had hidden photographic equipment.

Anna pulled down the last hatbox from the closet shelf. This one felt lighter, but something jingled inside. Lifting the lid, she found a black hat with a wide brim. A glimmer of orange fabric tucked out from underneath the hat. Anna yanked the hat away and discovered a pile of silk and chiffon.

She pulled it out, and coin-sized bangles clinked from an orange bra. The rest of the costume unfolded into frothy swirls of veils and fully gathered pants. It looked like a belly dancer costume.

Mitzi's?

"Aunt Anna, your bath is running over!"

Chapter Thirty-Eight

It was a short walk to Gulsen's house. Priscilla tried to persuade Anna to take the shortcut through the backyards, but Anna preferred the respectable approach, via the street. Besides, she didn't want to pass the crime scene again, nor risk arousing curiosity from Cora.

What in the world had Mitzi been up to?

They followed the same route in reverse that they'd taken with Don Davis the night before. They passed the general's pink mansion and turned the corner. Across the street was Gulsen and her father's modest house. Off-white with curtained windows, it faced both the general's and the Wingates' houses.

Had Mitzi's secret something to do with her opium addiction?

Gulsen's father, dressed in a navy blue suit shimmering with silken threads, met them at the front door with a smile as wide as his face. His chin glistened, recently shaved, and his forehead shone, where his hairline receded. Behind that line, long, wispy hairs slicked back from his face.

Anna and Priscilla traded their shoes for slippers and followed him across thick carpets to a room of reds. Shades of crimson, maroon, and purple swirled across the rugs, low sofas, and heavy tapestries hanging on the walls. A sweet fragrance filled the air, reminding Anna of orange blossoms.

He waved them to a pair of sofas. "Gulsen will bring the tea momentarily."

Anna sat down. "How nice of you, Mr. Aydenli, to ask us here."

"Ahmet, please."

"Ah, yes, Ahmet. Where did you learn English? It's very good."

"In an English-speaking university in Istanbul. It's quite popular among Turks who admire the west."

"Such as yourself?"

He hesitated, and a moment of awkwardness touched the air. She smoothed a pleat in her skirt, and finally he said, "It's a complicated issue. My school was a better choice than the War College." His smile revealed more amusement than happiness. "That is where my father wanted me to go."

"But you resisted."

"Yes. I did not wish to become another military man like my father. He served the last Sultan, you know, as military attaché to Berlin."

"He must've been disappointed that you did not follow in his footsteps."

"He never knew. He died several years earlier, fighting Mustafa Kemal."

Priscilla piped up. "That's Atatürk."

He nodded. "Kemal didn't take the name of Atatürk until later, not until its meaning came true: 'Father of Turks'."

Some Turks hadn't wanted to be rid of the Sultan, Anna realized, and apparently Ahmet's father was one of them. Just as she was wondering what kind of response to make that would sound neutral, maybe something about her impending Turkish lessons, Ahmet's attention switched to a doorway.

"Here is Gulsen now," he said, springing to his feet with an alacrity that made Anna wonder if she'd brought up painful memories for him.

The USOM bulletins warned against saying anything negative about Atatürk, and now Anna had practically made Ahmet confess that his own family opposed the Father of Turks.

While Anna worried about her blunder, Ahmet supervised Gulsen and her pouring of the tea into two glass cups. Smiling shyly at Anna, she passed the cups to the adults and then sat down in her puffy pants next to Priscilla. The two girls giggled and looked as if they were about to pop with excitement.

"Well, go on," Ahmet said with a laugh at the girls. "Run along and play. I know you're more anxious to play than you are to have tea."

Linking arms, they skipped out of the room.

Anna felt grateful that Gulsen distracted Priscilla from her recent glimpses of death. No child should have to witness such a trauma. She wondered about Gulsen's loss of her mother and how difficult it would be to accept a new one, a woman forced on her. Not willing to risk another blunder, she said nothing and took a sip of her tea, flavored with jasmine.

Ahmet finally spoke, breaking the comfortable silence. "It is a new world we face, is it not?"

She agreed, remembering that Yaziz had said something similar in his office. "How is the investigation going? You said you'd have your office check into it. Have they found anything yet?"

Ahmet flicked his head backwards in the no gesture, then set his cup down and rose slowly. He looked tired. Fingering his worry beads behind his back, he crossed the room to the heavy drapes covering a window. "It will have to wait until Monday, thanks to Atatürk."

"Monday? Why Monday?"

"Kemal gave us the western weekend, even though not everyone wishes to observe the days he chose for us. Still, my office follows the Eternal Leader's dictum. By now, we Turks have grown accustomed to the imposition of western ways on our lives."

Was there a note of sarcasm to his tone of voice, Anna wondered, or was it her own disorientation that was affecting her? "Anyway, I thought Detective Yaziz was already working on the case. Only last night, he—"

"Veli Bey is too valuable a resource to waste on such a case of *tshinghiane*."

"*Tshinghiane*?" She stumbled over imitating his pronunciation.

"Turkish gypsies. They are not important enough to deserve the talents of a man like Veli Yaziz. He is *koreli*, a veteran of Korea." Ahmet lifted one end of the drapes and peered through the crack. "But I did not invite you here today to hear myself talk." He stood at the window several long minutes contemplating the scene outside. "There was quite a lot of activity last night. I suppose you attended the party across the street?"

Anna nodded. "You mean at the Wingates?" He probably didn't mean the general's gathering of men. "Do you know the Wingates?"

"Yes, but they don't often invite anyone outside their circle to one of their parties. I couldn't help but notice the arrival of many police last night. I gather the party did not end happily?"

"You don't know what happened?"

"I am nothing more than an administrator, as I told you, and my office is closed. You will have to tell me the gossip."

Anna shifted in her seat. Well then, she had been summoned here, *not* invited to a neighborly tea. Still, she always cooperated, and so she told him the story of the photographer's death, and how they supposed it was a sudden heart attack. She left out her opinion: *murder*. And of course she left out the parts about Rainer.

His face paled throughout her tale of the night before, and he thumbed his worry beads. When she was finally done, he said, "But I know him. Young Emin is the brother to one of my employees in the rug shop that I own." He dropped his string of beads into his trouser pocket, strode across the room, and glanced at his wristwatch. "No, I can't believe it. A fine, young man in excellent health. It's just not possible that he would fall dead like that. I shall have to go to the shop. You understand?"

"Yes, of course." She stood. "The girls will be disappointed to interrupt their play. Perhaps Gulsen could come home with Priscilla and me?"

"No, no, no." More finger drumming on his upper lip. "I've got a better idea. Our maid Bahar will stay with them. Here. Why don't you come along with me? I would be honored to show you my rug shop."

* * * * *

Yaziz palmed the broken blue beads as he stood in the shade of the covered passageway. Above him rose the crooked building where the Alekci family lived. Before him, the lone *eşek* slept on its feet, twitching in the sun. Already the sun scorched the air, and the day had hardly begun.

From the sound of women's agitated voices streaming through the open windows above his head, Yaziz thought the Alekcis had been up a while, too. With one last glance at the *eşek* that wore no blue beads round its neck, Yaziz pocketed the broken ones he held in his palm and headed for the wooden stairs.

A withered woman with no teeth let Yaziz in through the broken front door of the second-floor apartment. She wore fear in her eyes and a forgotten head scarf falling around her shoulders.

"You have news of my niece?" she asked.

He lifted an eyebrow and shrugged. Something else he did not know.

"Meryem hasn't come home all night," she said in a wavering voice, on the verge of tears.

Yaziz pulled out his notebook. Flipped it open. Meryem, missing when the gypsy died, had led Yaziz to Kavaklidere last night, where Emin had died. Now, she was missing again.

"What happened to your door?" He nodded at the splintered hole beside the doorknob.

The old woman wailed instead of answering.

"The *eşek* in the yard below," he said, faltering, "does it belong to Meryem?"

The wailer sniffled, quivering her knobby jaw. "T-to her," she managed to say. "And to Umit, too. One of them has never owned anything that the other does not share." Then, overcome, she fled the room, leaving Yaziz standing there, staring at a small boy with inquisitive eyes. He was tall enough to be five or six years old but skinny enough to be much younger.

"A bad man came and broke the door," the boy said.

"Did you see him?" Yaziz asked.

The boy nodded. "But auntie was already gone. I think he was looking for her."

"What's your name?"

"Mustafa."

"What did the bad man look like?" Yaziz asked, his pencil poised over a fresh sheet of paper in his notebook.

"Rich."

"He looked rich? How could you tell?"

"From his coins." Yaziz supposed that everyone would look rich from the perspective of this boy.

"Mustafa!" said a woman—another one—from the doorway into the second room of the apartment. She held a bald baby in her arms. "Go play with your sister."

The boy gave Yaziz one more bashful look, then slunk away, past his mother, into the other room. The woman with the baby stepped closer.

"You have found my husband's killer?" she said.

Yaziz jerked his head back. No.

She choked on a sob. "My sister-in-law is dead, too, isn't she? Is that what you've come to tell us?"

Instead of confessing his ignorance, he asked, "Where did she go last night?" He already knew where she went. It was after the disruption of the American's scream that he'd lost her again.

The widow shrugged. "Who knows where? Umit used to go with her sometimes. Meryem had to go alone last night."

"Did your husband never tell you about their night-time business?"

"He said they read fortunes for the *gadje*. That's what gypsies do."

"Do you know whose fortunes they read?"

"As long as the customer has money, it doesn't matter who they are. They're all the same."

Yaziz pulled out the broken beads. "Do you recognize these?"

She shielded herself with the baby and let out a soft gasp. "Where did you find them?"

"At Anit Kabir. The day your husband was murdered there. These beads belonged to your *eşek*, didn't they?"

"I...I don't know. They all look alike. Maybe they belonged to the ox that was stolen last night, from the yard below, right under our neighbor's nose, the baker."

Yaziz jotted down notes, but there was nothing he could do about those problems just then. "Meryem and the *eşek* were with your husband that day he was murdered, weren't they?"

"They were supposed to be working their rounds."

"And now they're gone."

"You don't think...but she couldn't have killed him."

"Did your husband and sister-in-law take the *eşek* with them at night when they read fortunes?"

"Sometimes."

"Do you know why these beads are broken?"

"The beads have nothing to do with reading fortunes."

"They would crush, don't you think, if someone stepped on them?"

"I suppose so, but what does that have to do with my husband's murder?"

"Think, Bayan Alekci. Who were your husband's customers?"

"I know nothing."

"Who else might know, if you do not? It is important. If we are ever to track your husband's killer."

"You think where Meryem went last night to read fortunes is where my husband's killer was?"

He shrugged again. He doubted the general had done it, but he could not account for where the sister had gone after she was done at the general's. After he'd lost her. "How did they find their customers?"

"You think Meryem knows who killed Umit?"

"Yes," he lied. "We must find her, if we are to find your husband's killer. Where did they get these beads?"

"Well... I suppose you could ask Ozturk Bey."

"Ozturk Bey?"

"Yes. He's a merchant near the bazaar."

"I know where he is." Yaziz tensed. "What is your connection to him?"

Her eyes widened, and she shrank backwards a step or two. "Nothing. He's a wise one. A *hoça*. He knows everything."

"He's not a *hoça*, Bayan. There is no place for such religious men today in Atatürk's Republic. But Ozturk Bey does sell beads like these. Is that where these came from?"

"Yes! Yes! That's how we know him. That's all."

Clearly, that wasn't all. Yaziz pocketed his notebook and took his leave. He'd already thought of Ozturk Bey while on his roof that morning, as a possible source of the opium bribe. And if it hadn't come from him, then that old poppy farmer would know where else it had come from.

But what he hadn't understood, until the matter of the beads just now, was why Ozturk Bey should have an interest in seeing the police drop the investigation of a gypsy. He still did not know why, but for some reason, Ozturk Bey was protecting this family.

That's why he'd given them blue beads. When the widow saw them broken, she'd known her protection had shattered as well as her world.

Chapter Thirty-Nine

In the leather interior of Ahmet's car, a white Mercedes recently imported, Anna felt a growing unease. Aside from the events of the last two days, something else wasn't quite right. She couldn't put her finger on it.

Ahmet's knuckles stood out against the grip-wrapped steering wheel. They sped a bit too fast, in her opinion, down the hill and onto Atatürk Boulevard.

It didn't feel right to head off somewhere like this, without Priscilla. Or her purse. She'd only needed the house key, when they'd left to call on Ahmet, and she'd tucked it in the pocket of her skirt. Next week, when Priscilla would go away to school, Anna would have plenty of time to explore. Not yet.

She leaned back in her seat and tried to relax. "You said your father was military attaché in Berlin. That must've been interesting. Were you there, too?"

Ahmet chuckled softly. "My mother was German. I grew up there, until the Sultan needed Father on the home front."

"After your father's death, you returned to Germany with your mother?"

"No, she went back alone. I am Turkish, not German. I stayed on here with my aunt and uncle."

"And became both a merchant and head of police. An interesting combination."

"I am not the head of police."

"Administration, then, that oversees the police. Does that answer your German half? And selling rugs, your Turkish half? How do you manage both sides at the same time?"

He took his eyes off the street. Glanced at her. She watched the road for him as they sailed past a donkey laden with sticks.

"One job is good for the other," he said, slowly turning his attention back to his driving. "There are official matters with the Americans from time to time, and the rug shop allows me to establish a better...how would you call it? 'Rapport,' I think. Yes, that is it."

"Did you have a rapport with my sister? Did she buy her rugs from you?"

"Yes, she is a good customer, as are many of the Americans."

"I expect you know a lot of them. Fran Lafferty, perhaps."

Ahmet laughed, which helped to break the strain of nervous energy in the air. "Fran? A smart woman. I will send for her as the representative from your embassy to advise me of the accident last night."

Anna stared out the window at the palatial compounds that lined the street. "Regarding those accidents," she said, "would you say that they're normal? Detective Yaziz says that trouble seems to follow me around."

"Yaziz said that?" This time his eyebrows arched to sharp points as he glanced at her.

With his curiosity aroused, Anna had to say something. So she told him about the incident in the shop the day before, when someone had tried to steal her purse after hitting her over the head.

Another coincidence, she thought, that the detective had

mysteriously rushed to her rescue. Three times, now, Yaziz had intervened for her.

"Wherever you have large crowds," Ahmet said when she was done, "there is always a greater chance for crime. But they're thieves, not killers. As long as you are careful, you will remain safe. We are a safe country. It is only those troublemakers who wish to upset the status quo that we have to worry about."

"Who are they? I understand there's talk of a coup."

He whipped around to look at her, even though they'd joined more traffic of taxis and buses the closer they approached to downtown. "Where did you hear such a preposterous claim?"

"At the party last night." She waved away her words as casual chatter. "It was just gossip, which you said you wanted to hear. I thought you could tell me if it's true or not."

A sour moodiness descended over him as he turned his attention back to the road. "We will have elections next May, and then we will see if Menderes remains in power as Prime Minister."

They drove on in silence, a queasy ache spreading at the pit of her stomach. She wondered what had provoked his apparent unhappiness—Menderes, or the need for elections? Or was it something else? Something that concerned her presence. She'd made a mistake, coming along today, and now she wasn't sure how to recover.

Downtown, buildings squeezed closer together, taking on a bland, gray sameness. Ahmet turned off the boulevard onto a narrow side street, a more crowded place. Blocky buildings towered over them as they sailed past a neon sign for the *Republic News*.

"What do the newspapers report?" she asked. "There must

be some news of unrest if there's talk of a coup, whether or not it's true."

"It's not true. Not even the brother of my future wife believes it is true, and he is a troublemaker who works back there."

"At that newspaper office we just passed? Is he a reporter?" She wondered if Emin had ever worked there too as a photographer.

Ahmet scowled. "You will find no information from him, because there will not be a coup. Now then, you can rest more easily."

If only she could. She remembered that Paul and his friends had said the night before something about a press law that restricted reporters from reporting anything negative. Hints of a coup. Still, she wondered what people in the business of digging up information—reporters, like Ahmet's future brother-in-law, or perhaps photo journalists, like Emin—what they might've found out. Was that why Emin had died?

Perhaps she shouldn't dig too hard for answers to the troubling questions that engulfed her. She could become the next victim. Her breath caught in her throat.

The car weaved through enough turns that Anna no longer recognized which way they headed. With each turn, the streets narrowed and the crowds of pedestrians thinned.

"I am driving around to the back," Ahmet explained, "where there is a private entrance to my shop. That's where I usually park."

They drove into an alley and parked next to a cart filled with rolled-up rugs. No one was in sight, only the ox, patiently standing hitched to the cart. Ahmet turned off the ignition and slapped the steering wheel. He mumbled a few words in

Turkish under his breath, then turned to Anna.

"New merchandise arrives," he said, "and no one is here to protect it. Any thief could help himself." A vein throbbed at his temple. He sprang out of the car and raised his voice, yelling something in Turkish.

Anna climbed out of the passenger side as a young, skinny man ran from the building and into the alley. He stopped in front of Ahmet, who unleashed a torrent of Turkish. Oaths, she imagined. The youth listened to him with his head lowered. The scene reminded her of last night, when Fran scolded the photographer. Anna blinked, pushing the memory from her mind.

Then Ahmet must've realized the spectacle he'd made, and he turned to Anna and wagged his head. "I'm sorry. The man is impudent, but I must forgive him. He is working alone today in my store, since the brother of Emin, your unfortunate photographer, did not arrive to work. I must speak with him in private. Would you mind waiting inside the shop? I'll only be a minute, and then I'll join you. If any customers arrive, or any thieves to steal my merchandise, just call out." He smiled, but the vein still throbbed in his temple.

Anna agreed, eager to escape the stressed air of the alley. She hurried down a half flight of steps and through the door Ahmet's skinny employee had exited. She found herself in a cramped storage room, behind the beaded curtain to the main area of the shop. Clicking through the beads, she strolled out into the showroom, stacked to each side with carpets. Carpets, hanging from hooks, defined the perimeters of the shop and gave her a snug feel, wrapping her in a heavy smell of wool. She didn't feel very snug, though. She ran her fingers along plush fibers and waited.

She'd smelled a hint of wool only moments before the attack on her yesterday. Her attacker must've worn wool. Or else carried the scent of wool. Maybe he worked in a rug shop, such as this one.

What on earth was Anna doing here?

She waited, but Ahmet did not join her. She wandered to the front end of the shop, which opened onto a street of small shops. In spite of the chaos of movement around her, from feral cats to veil-swathed women, she felt alone. In her western dress, she hardly blended in. She scanned the cobbled street. It looked the same to her as what she'd seen the day before. Was it? She wondered which way were the shops she'd visited with Priscilla. Ozturk Bey's evil eyes, jewelry, and copper must be nearby. Just down the hill was the covered bazaar where they'd bought the slippers with the curled up toes.

The beads tinkled behind her, and she whirled around. The skinny employee returned, and without looking at her, he busied himself, counting rugs in a stack.

Any minute, Ahmet would follow. His familiar presence would dissolve the lump forming in her chest. He was probably unloading the rugs from the ox cart all by himself. He'd only be gone a minute, he'd told her.

He did not appear.

She stumbled along the aisles between piles of rugs. At the back of the store, the attendant kept counting rugs.

"Where's Ahmet?" she asked him.

He cocked his head at her, at first not understanding. Then he pointed to the door into the storage room and resumed his task.

She slipped past him and pushed through the beads. The

door to the alley stood open. Outside, the ox waited, and the cart stood there with its load of rolled-up rugs. But the Mercedes was gone. Along with Ahmet.

* * * * *

Meryem lay crushed on the floor of the *asker's* room, where he held her as his prisoner. No longer saved, she anticipated joining her brother. She willed herself to die.

She did not die.

She did not feel the pain anymore. She'd used it all up long ago, and now there was none left to feel.

She did not know when was now.

But eventually, a crash, then another one, somewhere in the distance, but not too far away, drifted to her consciousness. Only because the *asker* lifted himself from his torture of her body. Breath crept back to her ruined body.

"What?" the *asker* said with a growl, standing up. "What are the Americans up to now?"

It took all of Meryem's strength to open her eyes. From her position on the floor, her gaze fastened onto one of the windows of the *asker's* room. Through its glass smeared with grime, she saw the yellow stucco house next door like a slap in the face. She rolled into a fetal ball, as much as her bindings would allow, and pressed herself against the wall.

Someone moved through an upstairs window of the Americans' house. She'd seen that clean-shaven face before. Somewhere. That face with the coward's look of desperation lived somewhere in a distant memory. She searched her mind, her memories, and then it came to her. He was Stork. The partner of their liberator-savior-rescuer. He had abandoned them long ago. And now he'd finally come back.

The *asker* watched through a crack he'd opened in the door. The line of his body went rigid, and he cursed. Then he shut the door with a click and turned back to Meryem.

"What did you tell the secret police, whore?"

"Nothing!" Meryem made a whimpering noise.

"Don't lie to me. What's he looking for?"

"I don't know what you mean." Pain stabbed with each gasp, and she welcomed the sensation, for pain meant the absence of numbness.

"He's looking for something the Americans have, and you sent him there."

"Maybe he's there because of what you did to the American woman last night, that one who screamed. That's why you're worried."

"You talk too much." He snatched up the kerchief gag and lunged for her. Again.

With fire flowing back into her, she bit his fingers as he struggled to wrap the scarf around her.

* * * * *

Anna clattered down the steps into the back door of the rug shop. She whisked through the beaded curtain, tinkling its glass pieces as she moved. "Where did he go?" she asked Ahmet's employee.

The skinny Turk glanced up from his task of counting rugs and frowned. He shrugged and gave her a look of sympathy.

"I mean, did he say when he was coming back?" Of course

he was coming back. It was pointless to speak in a language that was not understood. She summoned what her scattered memory of college French had taught her, and she tried her questions again.

It didn't work. The man responded in Turkish, a harsh, foreign sound that only made her feel even more isolated. Panic gnawed at her insides. She was not familiar with being helpless. It was a sensation that did not warm her.

"Is there a telephone I might use?" she asked, pantomiming a phone call to make Ahmet's employee understand her. She'd phone Paul. But what was his number?

"*Yok*," said the employee. No. No phone.

She glanced around the woolen cocoon of the rug shop. Back at the beaded curtain. Then at the employee. He seemed to have forgotten her as he counted his rugs.

Patience drained away. Why in hell had Ahmet abandoned her this way?

She stalked out of his rug shop and into the cobbled street, where her brief flare of anger evaporated into the exotic sights and smells. Women under head scarves. Carcasses of meat hanging in doorways. Children and cats darting through the crowds.

She had no purse. No money. How would she get home?

If she was lucky, she would stumble across Ozturk Bey's shops. Maybe she'd get even luckier and Yaziz would rescue her again.

Just then she caught sight of a trio of boys, about eight to ten years old, snaking past shops and weaving around people filling the streets. They wanted to carry shoppers' bags, Priscilla had told her. They fetched coffee for customers. One of them, with a shaved head, held out his hand to a likely target.

Then the shaved boy saw Anna watching him. He must've recognized her instantly, for he bolted away from his two companions.

"Hey!" Anna shouted. Without a second thought, she took chase. "Come back!" she cried out, but the boy melted into the crowd and darted uphill.

She followed, her Keds pounding along the uneven cobbles. "*Hayir*!" she thought to yell, although it hardly made sense to yell "no."

A few heads of those nearby turned and gave her quizzical stares.

"I just want to talk to you!" No one understood her.

The two other boys spread out, separating into side streets, but Anna didn't let them distract her. Continuing uphill, she ran through narrow, winding streets, up the sharp slope of the cone-shaped hill of Ulus. At the top of the hill, under a gate, she paused to gasp for air.

Nearby, a broken column lay on its side, looking as if it could've come from a Roman ruin. It tweaked enough interest on Anna's part that her scan of the area lingered there a moment. Long enough to glimpse the crown of a nearly bald head, barely protruding above the column.

With her soft soles, she soundlessly crept around behind the boy who crouched behind the fallen column. At the last instant, he saw her and sprang to his feet. But she pounced on him faster than he could sprint away, and she pulled him out of his hiding place by his collar. Her fingers twisted around the fabric of his coarse shirt in a grip she'd perfected on a couple of occasions with unruly students.

The boy's arms flailed about, but her arms were longer, and she held on, at distance. He screamed at her, and she imagined what the oaths meant.

"You're the one who stole my purse, aren't you? Did someone hire you to do that?" But it was pointless. He didn't understand her. Finally, she remembered one of her Turkish words. "*Nerede?*" Where?

Her strength weakened as his thrashing grew more wild, and she knew she couldn't hold him much longer. Their raised voices drew attention, and curious onlookers closed in on them. The closer they approached, the more they babbled and scolded, and the more panicked the boy's face became. Finally, he stopped fighting her, and he reached into a pocket and pulled out Rainer's silvery medal. He dropped it at her feet and used her flash of surprise to twist free from her grip.

The white sapphire winked up at her as the boy disappeared into the crowd.

Chapter Forty

A commotion outside the toilet broke through the lice of Meryem's memories. Arguing voices. No, only one of them carried a querulous tone. The other...

The *asker* flung open the door of her toilet, and blinding light stabbed the dark interior. "Get up. The general wants you."

Sniffing an opportunity, Meryem anchored herself against one wall and pushed herself up.

He reached for her, and she pulled away. "Come here," he said, then swore at her as he grabbed her bound wrists and worked at the knots.

Suddenly, a deep voice rumbled from behind the *asker's* shoulder. "What's this?"

"Pasha! A thousand pardons. The girl does not cooperate."

"What have you done?" The general's hearty voice grew to a roar. "I only wished to speak to her. Such treatment as you have given her is not necessary, and I will not tolerate it in my house."

"But pasha, since she has been waiting for you out here, in my quarters—"

"Silence! You will untie her at once, and leave us. I will deal with you later."

"Yes, pasha."

The *asker's* fingers trembled as he undid the knots. Freed, Meryem rubbed her raw wrists. Her liberator had come for her, as she'd always known he would.

Stalking past the *asker*, she spit in his face. She float-stepped across the room to the general, although her joints protested with brand-new aches. The general stood over her and surveyed her silently while the *asker*, shooting glances of hatred at Meryem, flounced past them. As soon as he left for the garden, slamming the door behind him, the general spoke.

"This is an outrage," he said, his gaze sweeping across the torture room. "You have been held here against your will, and I won't have it. Regardless of who you are."

"He did not pay me what he'd promised for my dance." When Meryem realized she did not know when she'd danced for the general—only the night before or many nights ago?—a sinking feeling of panic flitted through her.

"He is a crazy old man whose mind has turned, but I did not think he would harm anyone. We will send for a doctor."

"No! I mean, that's not necessary. I'll take my money and go." She had to find the gun. Before the gunman did anything foolish to Mustafa.

The general's bushy eyebrows knotted as he frowned. "About last night—"

"I heard nothing."

"Of course you didn't. There was nothing to hear. A few of my closest friends were invited to dinner. Sometimes the raki makes men imagine things. Especially in the heat of their excitement. But they are only stories, you understand?"

She nodded, and her glance darted to the door. She thought she saw movement at the window. The *asker* was prowling, trying to listen. He was good at that—spying.

"You will need new clothes," said the general, pulling her attention back to him. His steel gaze drifted from the cut on her cheek to the tears of her costume. "And a bath. I will have my maid prepare a room for you in the house."

"No! I mean, that's very kind, but...I must go."

"Of course. Your family must wonder what's happened to you." His hand thrust into a trouser pocket and withdrew a wad of bills.

She watched carefully as he counted out five of them. He paused with his thumb in place between the fifth and the sixth bills and looked at her once again. "And what will you tell them to explain your absence?" he asked.

She shrugged. "I could tell them that I danced for very important men, who—"

He counted out five more bills.

"Who no longer hold any positions of power, and so no one pays any attention to what they say."

"Excellent." He handed her the ten bills.

"But in their fever of excitement, as men can become, they ruined my costume, which is my only means of income..."

Swiftly, he thumbed out five more and handed them over.

"On the other hand, I could say I fell asleep in the fields on my way home, but that would not explain my injuries, which will surely cost a hundred more lira for a doctor to heal."

He pushed more bills into her hands and gave her a frown, besides. "Is that all?"

"There are my friends next door, who might be interested to know—"

He grabbed her arm and squeezed hard. "How do you know the Americans?"

"I have clients." She stomped on his foot and glowered at his hand. "You are hurting me."

He released her at once and, without counting, pulled a handful of bills from his diminished wad and passed them over. "You will say nothing to them or to anyone, do you understand?"

She shrugged. "If you wish."

"It is not as I wish, it is as I command. And my man will escort you home, to see to it."

No! Quickly, she sidestepped away from the general and slipped out of range of his lunge, which followed a heartbeat too late.

She sprinted for the door, praying that she wouldn't slam into the *asker* as she rounded the corner. She didn't. He wasn't there, but his scythe leaned up against the wall of the cottage that had served as her prison. She grabbed up the iron tool, whose awkward length was half as tall as she was, and she pressed herself flat against the rough prickles of stucco.

And waited. For the opportunity to lash out with her weapon. She would not hesitate to use the scythe, while the *asker* had only threatened her with it.

Bah! Men and their hollow promises.

The general didn't follow her around the corner of the *asker's* cottage. Instead, he marched to the back door of his pink palace, yelling all the while for the *asker* to come with him. She threw down the distasteful weapon. Thought about the other one.

The gun.

It really was not possible that someone had followed her across the fields from Anit Kabir. She would've noticed. Therefore, someone had accidentally stumbled across the gun, after she'd hidden it away inside the hollow stump.

Another vendor, hawking his wares up and down the street? Possibly. Others must use the vacant lot with the water hole to rest, as she and Umit did. Her mind skimmed over the milk man, and the bread man, and the vegetable man, and...

Then she remembered the turtle.

The red-haired American child—Priscilla—hunter of turtles.

Meryem darted along a garden path, to the retaining wall at the corner of the general's property. She climbed up onto the rim of the wall and stepped across the wire fence, onto the creaking roof of the American children's shack. She jumped down to the ground, landing in a dust cloud of aches and pains. So many bruises already knotted her body that she could not determine if this jump damaged anything new.

Wincing, she slid aside the board that served as a door and crawled inside the smelly, sandy hideout. Something more in the air, this time. Fear. Holding her breath, she sank onto the sand, soft as silk after her bed of cement in the toilet. She sifted her fingers through the sand. Dust rose in the air from her scrabbling search, tickled her nose, and forced a cough from her.

Then her fingers bumped against smooth metal. She pulled the gun out of the sand.

* * * * *

White light of a poker-hot, midday sun blinded Anna. People surrounded her, buzzing with questions she didn't understand and couldn't answer. Her head spun. She wasn't sure where her flight, chasing the boy, had taken her, except to the top of the cone-shaped hill.

Ulus, where Paul Wingate had warned her not to go.

She didn't care where she was, because she had Rainer's medal again. She closed her fingers around the silver piece, gripping it tightly. Her heart raced. Breathing slowly, she tried on a smile of reassurance, more for herself than for the curious Turks who paused nearby.

"Everything's all right," she said, backing away, but not knowing exactly where to go. She slipped her hand into her pocket, dropping the medal inside, clinking it against her house key. "Thanks very much. *Teşekkür ederim.*"

She pretended to be a tourist, studying the ruined wall that followed the contours of the hilltop. Eventually, the curious onlookers gave up, muttering under their breath. Crazy American, she imagined was what they mumbled.

Soon, the flow of people resumed as they went about their business. The boy was gone by now. Or else hiding from her, watching her. He hadn't been Mustafa, Umit's son. She wasn't sure why that information pleased her.

Exactly *where* in Ulus had her chase taken her? She evaluated her position on the hillside overlooking Ankara. The panorama of the city spread out below like a crust where none should exist, across dusty, rolling terrain, a sandy brown. The faint sound of hammers floated across the gap from the new part of the city away in the distance to the old city, up here on the hill. Ruins crumbled around her.

She'd read about some of these ruins in her guidebook. There was a fortress crowning the hill, and it had been used by the Byzantine, Roman, Hittite and many other cultures to defend against their enemies. Here was the center of their old power, and she absorbed some of that radiating strength now.

Her pulse rate evened, and time slowed around her. Yes, she did feel something. Maybe not power, but timelessness. Nearby, Turkish women balanced pitchers, presumably of water, atop their heads as they glided silently past her, never missing a step over the rough cobbles. For how many centuries had this same scene of activity gone on, without change? Anna could almost hear echoes of the voices of lives long past. History breathed in the air, as alive as she was. For an instant, she had to remind herself that this was 1957—A.D., not B.C. She was living in the midst of live history.

Under other circumstances she would want to explore further, but now she shook herself out of the spell that the reminders of history always cast about her. What was she going to do? She needed to find her way back to Priscilla, and she had no means to do so other than her own two feet.

If she headed downhill, she would eventually intersect Atatürk Boulevard, and if she just followed that main artery of the city, she'd eventually get home again.

Home! Had she called it that?

She picked her way carefully down the steep slope of the cobbled lane, no wider than a donkey's path. Choosing a route that appeared to follow the general direction she needed to go, she soon dropped from the exposed crown of the hill into cool shadows, where the winding lane tunneled through dilapidated buildings that tilted this way and that. Narrow porches hung out over the street on their supports of long poles and looked as if they could come crashing down atop her head at any minute. She hoped there were enough hours of daylight left to find her way, as she had no idea how far she would have to trek or how long the journey would take her.

Damn that Ahmet!

Descending deeper into the canyon of buildings that framed both sides of the narrow alley, she remembered that the Alekci family lived in an apartment on a lane like this one. Anna wondered if she could find them again in this maze. Mustafa wasn't the boy who'd hurt her, and she wished she could make amends for having believed he was.

As long as she was already here, in the neighborhood, she searched for the leaning building with the stork's nest atop. She called into her mind the butcher's hastily sketched map and oriented herself to the slope of the hill.

She surprised herself when she actually found the stone portal leading off the street. She stepped into its cool shade and gazed up the wooden steps into the darkness of the upper floor, where the Alekcis lived. No wailing floated down the steps today. Instead, a slice of light from an open doorway up there let out the sound of soft voices. She wished she could understand what they were saying.

She thought she recognized one of the voices as Mrs. Alekci's. And a man's voice. What man? There were no other men in the family, now that Umit was gone. There was a visitor today.

Curious, Anna crept up a few steps. Then a child's voice spoke to her from behind, stopping her in mid-step. She whirled around and saw the boy standing in a puddle of light at the edge of the courtyard, watching her. She felt her cheeks flame, and she was grateful for the dark interior of the stairwell.

"*Merhaba*," she said, a little too forcefully. "You're Mustafa, aren't you?" She could tell that he was. Although his head was nearly bald from his close haircut, he was shorter than the boy she'd tackled, the coffee-carrying boy who'd hit her over the head and run off with her purse the day before.

"I was about to visit your mother," she continued. "*An-ne.*" She remembered the word that Ahmet had taught her and pronounced it slowly.

Ahmet! He was responsible for her predicament now, and she cursed him again under her breath.

Mustafa curled his finger, motioning for her to follow him. He was the one Alekci who might know the boy thief. Perhaps he knew who had hired him. She tiptoed down the stairs and followed him through the open portal. A dusty yard squeezed between the jumble of buildings, and in its center, a donkey grazed on dried weeds. Mustafa ran to the donkey and rummaged through a basket strapped across its back. When she caught up to him, she spoke in English, even though she knew he couldn't understand. She illustrated her words with pantomimes of being hit over the head.

"Who was he?" she asked, shrugging her question and rubbing her fingers in the gesture for money. "Who paid that boy to steal my purse?"

Her efforts appeared to be in vain, though, as Mustafa wasn't paying her any attention. He kept glancing over his shoulder as he dug farther into the donkey's basket. He spoke rapidly, breathlessly, but she didn't understand his words any more than he'd understood hers. He must want money, she decided. He wouldn't give her any information until he saw her money.

She had no money with her, and she doubted that he would understand her promise of money. But she *did* have something of value: Rainer's Saint Christopher's medal. How fitting to use the medal as payment for the information she wanted. Information, she realized, was actually more valuable to her than Rainer's medal. She pulled the medal out of her pocket and dangled it on its chain before Mustafa.

"Who was he?" she repeated.

Mustafa's wandering attention focused on the dangly piece, and he licked his lips, withdrawing his hand from the donkey's basket and reaching out for the medal. But Anna pulled it back, out of his grasp. "No, you tell me first who he was, and then I'll give this to you."

But then she realized the coffee boy had ended up *not* handing over the medal to whoever had hired him to be a purse thief. Maybe there'd been no such person. Perhaps she'd been wrong all along. It had just been a random act of thievery. Hayati had been right.

"Never mind," she said, dropping the necklace into Mustafa's outreached palm. "You keep it, anyway. I don't want it anymore."

Just then, a door slammed. A woman's voice screeched from the second floor, and footsteps pounded downstairs. Mustafa clenched the medal between his fingers and darted away, back across the yard, and into the passageway. He nearly bowled over a man in sunglasses, standing in the shadows at the edge of the portal.

Chapter Forty-One

Relief swept over Anna. She charged through the weeds of the courtyard, toward the newcomer. "Ah, Mr. Yaziz! Fancy meeting you here."

"I could say the same for you, Miss Riddle." He leaned against the wall of the arch and scanned the yard, as if looking for someone other than Anna or the donkey behind her.

"You're just the person I hoped to see," she said, breathless as she reached the detective's side. "Do you have any information for me?"

"I think perhaps it is *you*," Yaziz said, "who has information for me, instead. What is your interest in the girl who did not return home after her brother's death? Does she have more letters for you from your Lieutenant Rainer Akers?"

The gypsy girl, he meant. Anna understood. "No, of course not." A flush from the lie crept up to her cheeks. She wasn't supposed to have her own letters, which Umit's sister had sold to Cora. They now rested safely in her desk drawer at home, thanks to Fran. Anna took a deep breath, inhaling the pungent odor of animal sweat. "But she's still not home? Do you know yet who might've killed her brother?"

"Have no fear. We in the police are asking our questions. You need not concern yourself with our matters. You can go about your own business. Did you come to Ulus to shop? I see you have no purse. Have you lost it already?"

"I didn't bring it with me this time."

A wrinkle lifted his brow, and she went on to explain. She told him about Ahmet and how he'd brought her here and suddenly left. An emergency had taken him away, she thought. Yaziz's chin tilted up, showing more interest, and she finished her story. She'd taken a walk and gotten lost. Carefully, she avoided any mention of Rainer's Saint Christopher's medal. And the boy, Mustafa.

"How convenient that you found your way here," Yaziz said.

"Yes, and how convenient that you happened by, again. Look, are you following me?"

The ends of Yaziz's mouth turned down. "You are not wise to take matters into your own hands. Leave it to us."

As if she had a choice. She'd had enough of this. "Will you take me home? I have no money for a taxi, and I must get home." Besides, she had to get back to Priscilla, the sooner the better.

"You have no more questions?" Yaziz said, grinning.

"No, detective. I want to go home. I have a terrible headache."

"Very well, Miss Riddle. But first I have one more visit to make. Perhaps you would like to assist with my interrogation of Ozturk Bey?" He chuckled. He was laughing at her.

She swept past him, leading the way through the tunneled passage to the street, such as it was. It was more like a winding donkey lane. "Interrogation, Detective? I mustn't keep you." She waited for him to catch up, although by now she knew the way to the copper and trinket shops. "Is he a suspect, then? What did you learn last night to make you suspect Ozturk Bey?"

"Ah, your English words are all the same. Perhaps 'interview' is a better choice of words."

"I think you knew exactly what word to use." He was still teasing her, she thought. "See here, I didn't choose to become...I don't know, some sort of junior detective. It's not my fault that I've become embroiled in your police matter. I wasn't the one who gave my letter to Umit Alekci, and I didn't ask for any of this trouble."

"Then, why?" Yaziz said, limping along the slippery cobbles. "Why do you continue to invite trouble? Why do you not leave the investigation to the police?"

"Perhaps I would, if you were making some sort of progress in your investigation, rather than sending your goon out to spy on *me* instead of tracking down the guilty party."

"You, Miss Riddle?" He tipped his head sideways, but she thought he understood her perfectly well. "Ah, but you see, we have to make certain our American guests remain safe while they visit our country."

"I only want to know the truth." She chose her words carefully. All this trouble was because of Rainer. "Why can't we be honest with each other? Why must we keep so many secrets? If we could only share more truth and honesty, there'd be far more trust in the world."

She realized she wasn't referring merely to the two deaths in the last two days but about a world of injustice, rampant throughout history. Somehow Rainer had become a party to that injustice, when he'd set out at the beginning of the war to combat injustice. Where had his sense of justice changed along the way? Or had she been wrong about him all along?

"You ask for truth," Yaziz said, "but you do not give truth yourself."

She opened her mouth to protest. Protest had long been her automatic response. But she realized he was right. She thought of all the years she'd spent building walls around her, protecting the privacy of her emotion, her personal history, when what she'd really been doing was suppressing truth. The truth about Rainer. She was doing it still.

She let out a long breath and said, "All right. You're right. I can tell you now what I did not wish to speak of before." She glanced over her shoulder, first in one direction, then another, but she did not know what she was looking for. The scene of the crowded street, teeming with its daily business, appeared...well, normal, she supposed. If life in Ulus was normal.

"It's about my ex-fiancé," she continued, lowering her voice to a whisper. "Rainer Akers. He didn't die in the war. He's *here*. Here in Ankara."

"Yes, Miss Riddle, I know."

"You...*know*?"

"We are not as stupid as you seem to think we are."

"No! That's not true. I don't think that."

The sunglasses stared at her silently.

Finally, she couldn't wait any longer. "Well?" she spit out. "Are you going to tell me how you know that? What's Rainer doing here?"

"Exactly our question. We hoped you might be able to answer that for us."

"He wouldn't tell me."

"Then you have seen him?"

She nodded. "Last night. Before Emin died. And then again, after." She shivered. Rainer was involved in that matter.

Yaziz said nothing for several heartbeats. Then he touched

her arm. "I am sorry. This will not take long with Ozturk Bey, and then I will take you home."

"Why did Emin die, detective? Do you know yet?"

Yaziz frowned. "Our Doctor Vardarli has not prepared his report yet."

"But you don't think it was a heart attack, do you? That's what people at the party were saying. But they didn't get to see his body, as I did. Emin died after having some sort of convulsion. Poison would cause that." The *asker* knew about poisons. He'd poisoned Priscilla's kitten.

"And many other conditions, too."

Rainer had been about to visit the *asker* in his shed when Anna first saw him the night before last. And then he had been present at the Wingates' party when Emin died. Goosebumps ran along Anna's arms, where Rainer had touched her.

Rainer, the connector in two deaths in two days.

Yaziz shrugged, apparently taking Anna's silence as a conclusion to their conversation, when in fact, she felt too stunned for more words. He turned and continued along the way, but Anna hung back, searching for her words, staring at the street scene but seeing nothing.

Finally, she found them, and she ran after him. "Detective!"

Yaziz stopped at the threshold of the shop and waited for her.

"You still haven't told me how you knew that Rainer is here in Ankara. I didn't know it myself. I swear I didn't know that at Atatürk's Tomb, when Umit was shot holding my letter to Rainer."

Yaziz shifted, looking as if a great weight rode his shoulders. "Miss Riddle, it is my duty to do my job *and* to uphold the laws of our supreme leader. Sometimes they are not always one and the same." Color flamed to his cheeks, and he ducked inside the shop, calling out to Ozturk Bey.

Anna watched him go, wondering what on earth he'd meant. It seemed that she could never get a direct answer from the man. He appeared embarrassed, as if he regretted having said too much. But about what? Perhaps his boss had told him one thing, but the laws of his country directed another course of action. Paul Wingate had mentioned the name of Yaziz's boss as Bulayir, who was apparently the police chief who answered to Ahmet. Perhaps the conflict was between them, and Yaziz was caught in the middle.

Or... Ahmet lived in the neighborhood where Rainer assumed his Hungarian identity. Maybe Ahmet knew Rainer aka Viktor. Ahmet always seemed to know more than he let on. Then, Yaziz would have found out about Rainer through his work. Through Ahmet.

Not that it mattered, really. Yaziz was a detective. It was his job—his duty—to find things out. Maybe he would solve this crime after all.

Still, Anna couldn't leave the questions alone. They haunted her now, along with the knowledge that Rainer had been alive all these years, running for his life, hiding, while Anna had lived in relative comfort. Anna's troubles were no more serious than what her eleventh graders could give her.

All that had changed now. She stared glumly at the street scene around her. It had appeared so colorful only the day before. Today it was appearing...slightly less foreign. She could never go back to the comfortable way things used to be.

* * * * *

Yaziz carefully lifted the copper lid of the brazier. He'd seen Ozturk Bey withdraw a hidden package for the Burkhardt child from this very place.

Nothing.

Not that he expected to find anything. The old merchant was no fool.

Still, where there had been one, there could easily be another. A similar package could be tucked away anywhere among this copper and brass clutter where Emin Kirpat and Umit Alekci had worked, more or less together, before their deaths.

"The boys who work for you," Yaziz called out to Ozturk Bey who puttered at the back of the shop, "do they get along?"

"My nephews do what they are told."

"And the others...they do not?"

"There are no others. We are all family."

"You have many nephews?"

There was no response, which meant no denial. Yaziz pictured a shrug of affirmation. He wandered through the shop, picking up a pot here, leaning over a pan there. He glanced behind the crates that displayed the wares. He ducked through the beads at the back and stole a glance at Ozturk Bey's wife, minding the sister store, the one that sold beads and jewelry and evil eyes. "Are there more boys to fill the places of those who go missing?"

"Is there something specific that you are looking for, *efendim*?" Ozturk Bey lifted his rag from the pot he was polishing and narrowed his eyes.

Yaziz scowled and continued snooping through the shop. The merchant had not cooperated from the first moment of his forced greeting. The broken beads could've come from his shop, he'd agreed, or from a hundred other places as well. His evasiveness made the detective wonder if there was more than just opium that was hidden somewhere on the premises.

What were the other absent nephews doing now, a work day, away from the shop? Delivering more packages of opium to locked apartments for their uncle?

It was a little faster than he wished to proceed, Yaziz thought, but he had many more duties to fulfill before his day was done. So he leapt into the heart of the reason for today's visit. "I regret, Ozturk Bey, that I must bring you information of the unfortunate news of last night."

Yaziz's colleagues at headquarters, despite their grumbles in tracking down the information first thing this morning, had told Yaziz that Emin's name was not among the list of those in trouble with the Press Law. Therefore, Yaziz could inform the old man—for now—that Emin's death was the result of tragic, natural causes.

But Yaziz knew better. His instincts seldom failed him.

Still, an accident, he told Ozturk Bey. The young man's heart had given out unexpectedly. Sometimes it happened, even in one who appeared so young and healthy.

The tactful caution Yaziz used didn't seem to matter, as no surprise registered on Ozturk Bey's face, nor in the tilt of his head. He revealed no remorse at losing one of his boys. Instead, he went back to work with his cloth, rubbing the same spot on a piece of brass until it gleamed a fierce gleam.

"Did you know about his other work," Yaziz asked, "as a photographer?"

Ozturk Bey shrugged. "He was a journalism student."

Yaziz gave up his examination of the merchandise and pulled his worn notebook from a pocket. He flipped it open and pretended to study a page. "Emin worked here part-time. He also attended school, and he photographed American parties. What else did he do?"

"I think he was stealing from us."

"You *think*?" That would explain the absence of his remorse, Yaziz thought.

"He used his camera to photograph information, which he then sold to those who would be interested."

"Such as?"

The ends of Ozturk Bey's mouth turned down. "Here, it was designs that my artisans use for their finest work. Who knows what he stole someplace else? Practice, he claimed it was when he took his pictures. But my son-in-law was watching him all along."

"Then, I should speak with him. Where is your son-in-law?"

"Helping my wife in the other shop."

"No, she is there alone."

Ozturk Bey shrugged again. "The young. Who knows what they do?"

Yaziz frowned. "I understand you also employed Umit Alekci. Was he one of your nephews, too?"

Ozturk Bey dropped the pot he was shining with a loud clang and wheeled around to disappear into the back room. Yaziz followed, limping, and repeated his question.

"No. Of course not." The old merchant gave an angry tick of his tongue, smacking off the roof of his mouth. "*That* one was gypsy."

"But you gave him work at times?"

"Some of my customers asked him to go to their homes and take care of the copper and brass that they bought from me. It was their choice, not mine. I have no more dealings with a gypsy than that."

"Nothing more?" Either Yaziz was wrong that Ozturk Bey had been protecting the Alekci family or else the old merchant was hiding something. His opium trade?

Ozturk Bey shrugged, his shoulder rising up to his ear. "I pass along what my customers tell me they want, and everyone is satisfied."

"Who is satisfied the most? Which of your customers was most interested in Umit Alekci?"

Ozturk Bey lifted an eyebrow at the detective, then fussed over a pile of rags, a stack of newspapers, and a row of jars reeking of polish. But he remained stubbornly silent.

"The same ones," Yaziz persisted, "who asked Emin for his photographs?"

"No, no, that is a different matter."

"But an important one in finding the killer of Umit Alekci." Perhaps the same one, Yaziz thought, who'd produced the "natural causes" of Emin's death.

Bumping sounds came from the front of the shop, along with footsteps. Ozturk Bey glared once more at Yaziz, then pushed past him and rushed to greet his customer with smiles creasing his face and a gush of welcoming words. Yaziz trailed along behind. Miss Riddle had finally decided to give up her sight-seeing and follow him inside the shop.

Ozturk Bey fussed over the unfolding of a chair and insisted that she sit.

"No, really, it's quite all right," she said, waving him away. "I'm not staying."

Ozturk Bey ignored her protests and held up only two fingers to one of the coffee boys patrolling outside. It was an intended slight for Yaziz. Then he dragged a table from the back, placing it in front of his customer.

"Without your purse," Yaziz told her, "you will have to open an account here."

Ozturk Bey picked out a copper samovar, a brass bowl and some cups, which he arranged atop the table in front of his customer for inspection. Then he surveyed his shop, selecting more pieces for display.

"I didn't come to buy anything." Yet, she oohed and ahhed, admiring the copper and brass before her.

Yaziz limped to the back of the store where the old merchant balanced atop a crate. He was reaching for some trays on a shelf high above their heads.

"It does not look good for you," Yaziz said in Turkish, which the American did not understand, even if she could overhear. "Two of your boys died under suspicious circumstances in the last two days. Will I have to take you in for further questioning? I have colleagues who will be happy to interrogate you for me, and I warn you that they will not be pleased if you do not tell them something interesting."

Hopefully, an interrogation would confirm Yaziz's suspicions—that Ozturk Bey used unskilled youth to smuggle his opium for him.

Suddenly, a brass coffee grinder tumbled off the shelf above. Yaziz ducked to one side, and the hand crank caught the rim of his glasses, then stung his arm. He grunted, swallowing the pain.

"A thousand pardons," said Ozturk Bey, jumping down

from the crate.

A welt throbbed on his arm where a bruise already took form. Yaziz doubled over, cradling his arm.

His tinted glasses lay broken on the floor.

Chapter Forty-Two

Behind a barricade of brass and copper, Anna spied one certain large pot, covered with a lid, sitting on the floor in a far corner of the shop. It looked like the one Anna had seen the day before, the one that held the package Ozturk Bey had tried to pass to Priscilla.

A surprise, Priscilla had called it. A package of spices for Fededa, but Anna had spoiled the surprise.

Now, Anna glanced at the beaded curtain to the workroom, where Ozturk Bey and Yaziz had disappeared. They were nowhere in sight. Anna rose from her stool and tiptoed across the shop, threading her way around tables displaying copper and brass. She knelt down and lifted the lid. Inside, there was—

"What have you found now?" said a woman's voice in English from behind her.

Anna glanced over her shoulder and stumbled to her feet. Fran! "I didn't hear you come in."

"Obviously." Fran nodded at the copper lid Anna still clutched. "What have you got there?"

"Nothing." She peered into the pot. There was nothing inside it today.

Fran snorted. "You expected to find something."

"Yesterday, Ozturk Bey kept something inside this pot. I'm pretty sure it was this one. He wanted to give it to Priscilla."

"It didn't belong to him," said Fran.

"How would you know that?"

"I don't. I'm guessing. What did it look like?"

"It was a small package, about the size and shape of a pocketbook, wrapped in newspaper and tied with string. Fededa kept one like it in the broom closet at home."

Fran's gaze flickered past Anna. "Don't worry about it. We'll take care of it for you."

Anna started to protest that she wasn't helpless, but just then, something crashed in the workroom that connected Ozturk Bey's two shops. Sounds of metal clattered. There was a yelp of pain followed by a breath of silence. Then, a rush of voices.

Anna dropped the lid back onto the copper pot with a clang, and then ran to the cramped space of the workroom. She blinked a few times to adjust to the dim light filtering through the thick glass of a narrow window.

"Fededa!" Ozturk Bey was shouting and waving his arms. He hovered beside Yaziz who doubled over, waving away any assistance. Ozturk Bey shouted a stream of Turkish, either at the detective or at his absent wife, who failed to appear. Anna didn't know.

"*Hayir,*" Yaziz mumbled, among other mumblings. He flung his arm up to block his head. His sunglasses were missing. Without them, his face looked naked. The twisted frames lay on the floor, and their tinted lenses sprinkled in pieces beside a brass coffee grinder. Spots of blood speckled the back of his hand as he shielded his face.

"You're hurt!" Anna said.

"No, it is nothing." Yaziz waved her away and squinted

hard, keeping his eyes closed. He groped his surroundings as if he were a blind man.

"But you got hit with a piece of brass," Anna said, shuddering. "That's what happened to me."

"In this case, no one hit me. This was an accident." Yaziz broke free of their attention and dropped to his knees. He picked up shards of glass and stuffed them in his jacket pocket.

"Let me help," Anna said, kneeling next to him.

"It's done." He rose, pulled his handkerchief from another pocket, and dabbed it against his brow. Crushed, blue beads spilled to the floor from his handkerchief.

Anna scooped them up. "Are these the same beads you showed me the other night?"

"They came from here. That's what I was asking about when that brass fell off a shelf and conked me on the head."

Ozturk Bey shouted once more for Fededa, who finally pushed through the beaded curtain from the trinket shop. She jabbered something back at him in a scolding tone of voice and passed a damp rag to Yaziz.

Fran swept aside the strings of beads hanging in the doorway of the copper shop and stood there, watching.

Ozturk Bey snapped out instructions to his wife, who glanced nervously between Anna and Fran and muttered something in return. She scurried away, back into the trinket shop.

Ozturk Bey jerked his head backwards and ticked his tongue. He glared at Yaziz, then bowed a greeting at Fran and fussed over selecting a chair to unfold for his new customer. Still bowing, he carried the selected chair into the copper shop, set it up next to Anna's, and motioned the women into their seats.

Anna lingered in the workroom, trying to examine the cut on Yaziz's forehead, but he kept dodging her efforts. At least it didn't seem to be bleeding anymore.

"It took me a while to find a place to park," Fran said, "but I see that I'm in time. The gang's all here. What's wrong with your face, Detective?"

"An accident, I regret." He broke away from Anna and limped past Fran into the copper shop.

"All in the line of duty, I presume," Fran said with a deep chuckle. "Did you come seeking more information, or was it merely to break the sad news to Emin's employer? I see that he's heart-broken."

"I have a job to do, Miss Lafferty. Perhaps you will tell me what brings you here?"

"To shop, of course." She trailed after him. "This is a shop, is it not? And I always buy something from my favorite shopkeeper. How can I make amends? I feel responsible for Emin's untimely death, since I'm the one who talked him into being the photographer last night."

"Doesn't the embassy have its own cameras?" Anna asked, remembering the equipment she'd found in Mitzi's hatboxes.

Fran stopped next to a stack of trays and whipped her attention from Yaziz to Anna. "Why on earth do you ask such a thing?"

Anna tried to keep her voice steady. "I found an old camera at home and thought it might have come from the embassy. Perhaps it was misplaced." She didn't want to confess that she'd been snooping. Hatboxes seemed an odd place to store a camera. Now, Fran's sharp reaction made her suspicious, but Yaziz cleared his throat and interrupted.

"Why did you offer him the job?" the detective asked.

"My boss, Paul Wingate, wanted me to find someone. Everyone else that the embassy uses was booked, as it turned out. It was all rather last minute. Then I remembered Emin."

"How convenient that he was available," Yaziz said.

Ozturk Bey held up another finger to the coffee boys crowding the doorway. Then he rearranged copper pieces and dragged another table beside the chairs where he intended his customers to sit.

"Yes," Fran said, lifting an eyebrow as she watched Ozturk Bey bustle around the shop. "Our friendly shopkeeper here was planning to dismiss him, you see."

A hush fell over the room, and Yaziz looked up. Now Anna saw the problem requiring sunglasses. The detective had one brown eye and one blue eye. "You are in his confidence to know such a plan?" Yaziz said.

"Naturally, Detective." Fran gave a sigh of exasperation. "On account of the opium he was smuggling."

Anna gasped. "*Opium?*"

"That package you saw. It was a cube of raw opium. Paul and I suspect that's how your sister got her supply." She turned to Yaziz. "Well, Detective, go ahead. Aren't you here to arrest him?"

* * * * *

Anna felt ill. Her knees gave out, and she wanted to collapse into the nearest chair, but Fran grabbed her, holding her upright.

"I'm all right," she said, grateful for Fran's support. The

initial shock had come the night before, learning of her sister's addiction.

Fran steered her out of the shop, into the blinding sunlight of the street, leaving Yaziz to deal with Ozturk Bey. The sounds of wavering voices and clip-clopping hooves swam around Anna, hammering her head.

Now she understood why Paul had wanted her to fire Fededa, who'd been the link between Mitzi and Ozturk Bey's opium. Were there still more hidden packages somewhere in the Burkhardts' house?

Anna's concern focused on her niece. There was nothing she could do to help her sister. Henry was taking care of her. Meanwhile, Anna had to make sure Priscilla remained safe. Steeling herself, she allowed Fran to drag her along. She stumbled over cobbles as they wound their way along side streets to Fran's parked car.

"Why couldn't Henry have warned me of all this before they left?" Anna said as Fran opened the passenger's door for her and guided her inside.

"Maybe he thought that if he removed Mitzi from the scene, there would be no further complications." Fran slammed the door behind Anna and then crossed around to the driver's side.

But Rainer was already here, Anna thought, charading as Viktor Baliko. Henry had known. He should've expected complications.

All along, she could've asked *Henry* about Rainer's fate after the war.

"Thank you for telling me last night," Anna said, once Fran climbed in behind the wheel. "You didn't have to say anything about Henry and Rainer, that they'd worked together during the war, but you did, and I'm grateful. What I don't understand is why Henry never told me. He knew Rainer and I were to have been married. Why didn't he say anything?"

"I believe it has something to do with guilt," Fran said. "Besides, none of them ever knew the real names of the people they worked with, people on whom their lives depended. Maybe he never realized who his partner was."

Anna didn't believe it.

"Anyway," Fran said, "it's all classified."

"It couldn't have been very classified, not if he told *you* about it."

Fran concentrated on starting the car and pulling out into the street. She said nothing.

"You're one of them too, aren't you?" Anna asked.

But Fran continued to pay attention to her driving. She steered past an ox and cart, like the unattended one filled with rugs that had annoyed Ahmet.

"Classified," Anna said. "Right? You can't tell me."

Fran smiled and looked in the rearview mirror. Anna glanced over her shoulder, too, but she didn't see anyone following them.

Anna sighed. "You don't think you can make me wait until Henry returns, do you? Because you can't. I'll confront him, you know, whether I have to take Priscilla and go track them down in Switzerland myself, or whether I wait until they come back on their own. No matter which, I'll force him to tell me all about his association with Rainer. So if you know anything about it, you might as well tell me right now. He won't keep that kind of information from me much longer."

Fran opened her mouth to speak, but Anna beat her to

it and said, "Don't tell me it's classified. I have some rights, too. Besides, after all these years, it shouldn't still be classified, should it?"

"Whoa," Fran said. "I've already told you all that I know."

"No, not what you know. You've only told me what you think you're permitted to tell me. There's a whole lot more than what you're letting on."

"You're imagining things."

"No, I'm not one to imagine very much. I overheard you with Paul Wingate last night, and I can put two and two together. There's talk of a revolution, and that photographer knew something he wasn't supposed to know. Now he's dead. Henry is still spying, that's why he's been assigned here to Turkey. Is he spying on this revolution that's in the works? Or is he just spying on the Soviets who are geographically so close? Maybe the revolution has to do with the Soviets? Anyway, regardless of what it's all about, I can guess why Henry hasn't said anything about it. If he confessed about an association with Rainer, a known spy, that would blow Henry's cover here. Right? That's why it's classified information. And you can't talk about it, not because you don't know, but because you're a spy, too. I'm right, aren't I? Never mind, you can't say."

Fran burst out laughing. "You really believe all that? I think you underestimate your powers of imagination, and you've been reading too many spy novels."

"Actually, that's not my type of reading," Anna said. She chuckled along with Fran, although her heart felt heavy. Fran's lack of denial told Anna she was right. She wondered if she'd blundered into things she shouldn't know, things that made young, healthy photographers die of so-called natural causes.

She changed the subject, hoping to steer them into safer waters. "I know I'm right, even though I realize you can't admit it. For now, at least tell me why you gave me the letters last night at the party?"

"I guess I felt sorry for you, but anyway, they're yours, aren't they? What do the police need them for?"

"What if Paul Wingate finds out that you didn't do what he asked you to do?"

Fran shrugged. "Those letters won't tell the police anything they don't already know. Odd, that they surfaced after all these years."

"Umit's death must've made his sister want to get rid of them."

"But how did Umit get them in the first place? That's the real question."

From Rainer, Anna thought, but she still wasn't sure she could trust Fran enough to tell her the truth about Rainer and what he'd told her—how the Alekcis nursed him back to health. And that he was *here* today in Ankara. Maybe Fran already knew that, as Yaziz did. Probably. Still, it was safer to change the subject. "Last night you assumed at first that I was looking for opium. In Cora's bedroom. Are you implying that Cora has an addiction problem, too?"

"Cora and Mitzi are in the same bridge group, and they meet several times per week."

"Maybe they just play cards?"

"Maybe. Their latest venture is into belly dancing with their private instructor, Tonya Baliko."

"Belly dancing!" Anna clenched her jaw, whether at the reminder of Rainer's supposed wife or having found the belly dancing costume in Mitzi's hatbox, she couldn't be sure. "But why were you so certain that I wouldn't find any...opium... among Cora's things?"

"Paul already searched."

All these years, they'd lied to her. Henry had lied as well as Rainer... It was too much for her to absorb.

"Don't be so hard on Henry," Fran said, reaching from the steering wheel with one hand to pat Anna's arm. "What you've got to understand is that everything changes with war. War causes people to make mistakes that can fester inside them for years. Maybe Henry was only trying to make amends."

Anna wasn't sure she could ever forgive Henry for the lies, or Rainer for his betrayal, but maybe it was true what Fran suggested. War was the pollutant that modified history beyond repair.

They drove the rest of the way across town in silence. The feeling of intimacy that had blossomed between them, smothered.

At the Burkhardts' house, Anna thanked Fran again and climbed out. She watched her new friend drive away, then turned to the house.

She thought it odd when she noticed the side door standing open to Priscilla's playrooms. This door, which she had never seen used, now stood wide open. Priscilla must have come home from Gulsen's house.

Anna would have to speak with Priscilla about leaving doors open like this. She hurried inside. "Priscilla?" she called.

But all that answered her was a stack of old newspapers, ruffling in the breeze.

Chapter Forty-Three

Steam wrapped around Yaziz like a wet cloth and filled his nostrils and lungs. Clogging carefully in his wooden sandals across wet tile, he entered the hot room of the Turkish Bath and scanned through clouds of vapor for Bulayir. He hated disturbing the chief at the *hamam*, but Bulayir himself had instructed him to keep him informed.

He spotted the chief, his vast, hairy belly spilling over his loin cloth, seated on a bench in one marble corner. An attendant was scrubbing one of Bulayir's arms, coating him with a soapy lather.

Yaziz clumped over to the chief's corner, then stopped short, not daring to continue without an acknowledgement first.

Bulayir glanced up and snickered. "No glasses, Veli Bey?"

Yaziz gave a soft tick of his tongue. "No, *efendim*. They're no good here."

"You have something to say that cannot wait?"

"That's right."

Bulayir waved the attendant away. "That's enough for now. Let me sweat a while."

"As you wish," said the attendant, backing away with his soapy mitt.

Yaziz remained standing, as Bulayir did not invite him to sit. His bad leg ached, either from too many hours on his feet,

401

or the moist air hanging thick under the domed ceiling, a shock on his body after the dry air of Ankara's high plateau.

"I have found the ringleader," Yaziz said. Then he described the comings and goings at the general's house the night before, a gathering of military men, all of whom had reason to feel dissatisfaction with the current regime. Although he would not go so far as to mention the presence of his old friend, Murat. Loyalty counted for more than that. And he was careful to avoid the problem of the gypsy woman, who'd luckily led him there for surveillance, once Yaziz had finally found her.

"And the evidence?" Bulayir asked, interrupting his report.

"A roll of film. I am on my way now to collect it. But first I must stop off at the lab." He *would* find the film somewhere in the Wingates' yard, he knew he would. Perhaps it had rolled to the Burkhardts'.

Bulayir nodded. "Good. And the reason for your haste that required you to interrupt my bath?"

"Sir, it's a matter of great urgency. I believe their plans are to be put into effect tomorrow, which is the date that is coded on the envelope we collected. On the other hand, I am at a loss of how to warn you."

"You? Veli Yaziz, the *koreli*?"

"I fear that one of your own men has the potential to... betray you."

Bulayir straightened from his slouch and snatched the towel from beside him. "Me? Who would dare?"

"Erkmen was one of the general's guests last night."

Bulayir took a deep breath. As his chest rose and fell, soap suds glistened on his skin under the thin light that streamed through star shapes cut out of the domed roof. "Anything else?"

"*Efendim?*" Did his boss not care that his own lieutenant conspired to bring down their lawfully elected government? No, that was not possible.

Bulayir, then, must be holding something back. Either he knew of Erkmen's association with the plotters, and therefore approved it, or he'd sent Erkmen there to infiltrate. Yes, an undercover agent. That made better sense, especially considering that Erkmen had crossed the street to the assistant minister's house after leaving the gathering at the general's house the night before.

Erkmen was reporting to Bulayir's boss, *his* boss, too.

But why had Bulayir brought Yaziz into this? Why insist that Yaziz break up the plot if he already had Erkmen working on the case?

"There is more," said Yaziz, and he told him of the ill-fated photographer and the damning photographs he had taken. Yaziz waited now for the lab to confirm his suspicion that Emin's death was due to a fast-acting poison. There were many possibilities—ricin, wolf's bane, strychnine. They would find that, too.

He left it unsaid, but obvious, that he suspected Erkmen responsible. That would bring the golden boy down.

And there, Bulayir had it. Yaziz would arrange for the old opium smuggler to be brought in yet this afternoon, while Yaziz attended to collecting the damning film. By that evening, or as late as tomorrow, interrogations would bring out the old merchant's part as well in the murder of Umit Alekci, and—

"No!" Bulayir sprang to his feet. Yaziz thought his boss was going to charge out of the *hamam*, wrapped only in his loin cloth and towel.

"Did I not tell you to drop the matter of the gypsy? *Tshinghiane*, Veli Bey. That's all they are. Do not waste our resources on this matter. That is final. Understand?"

"Yes, *efendim*." But what Yaziz understood now was that Bulayir's order sounded very much like the note that had accompanied the raw opium inside his locked apartment. Yes, there was a hushed-up plot, all right. But now Yaziz feared that it involved more than just a coup against the government.

* * * * *

"Priscilla?" Anna called, a feeling of dread creeping into her from the empty house. "Where are you?"

She hurried through Priscilla's playrooms, up the half flight of steps into the kitchen, and out to the dining room. No one was here. The French doors stood open to the verandah, and Anna stepped outside and surveyed the empty backyard.

The *asker* moved in the general's yard next door. The gate to the Wingates' yard swung, creaking on a broken hinge.

A shiver tickled the back of Anna's neck. She turned and raced up the wooden steps to Priscilla's bedroom. Clothes, toys, and books—what looked like all of Priscilla's possessions—lay strewn across the floor. Drawers were pulled open. The top of the dresser had been cleared bare. The mattress twisted askew, half off the box springs.

Anna gasped. Priscilla hadn't come home and done this. Someone else had been in the house. A burglar. He'd broken into the house and torn apart Priscilla's room while Priscilla, thankfully, played at Gulsen's house. He must've left the playroom door standing wide open when he fled.

She hoped he was gone, but what if he wasn't? He would've heard her pounding steps up the stairs. He could be hiding somewhere, waiting for... What? The police to arrive? Logically, he should be gone by now. If he'd heard her, then he would've run out. Maybe by way of the balcony. Its door stood open, too. Or was that how he'd gotten in?

Moving more cautiously now, she crept out onto the balcony. No one was there, except for the *asker* looking up at her from the general's garden. Looking up, expectantly.

"Did you see anything?" she whispered to him.

He said nothing. Turning on her heels, she ran back through Priscilla's room, into the hall, and up the half flight of stairs to her room.

Night stands and the dresser and her desk had been turned over, drawers pulled out, their contents spilled across the floor. She pawed through her piles of garments, her papers, her fountain pen and bottle of ink. She could not find her bundle of letters. The ones she'd written to Rainer years ago, and Fran had returned to her last night. She'd put them in the desk drawer after Rainer left.

Rainer.

He'd been searching for something in her bedroom the night before. Had *Rainer* come back today to do this?

Rainer, the man whom Priscilla thought was chasing her daddy... And maybe he really was. Was there unfinished business left over from the closing days of the war? Rainer and Henry and the Alekcis had all become mixed up together, and now Umit and Emin were dead.

A knot twisted in Anna's stomach. If she phoned the police, would that undermine whatever secret had made Rainer go undercover? He'd made her swear to keep his presence secret, although she did not know why. She did not trust him anymore.

She would phone the police, but what if Yaziz was still out of the office? She'd need Priscilla to explain for her.

She needed Priscilla. She needed her here with her, at her side, within sight. In case... What? She didn't know.

Or maybe she should phone up Paul first. Let him handle the police. He'd told her to call anytime, after all. Yes, that's what she would do. But first, Priscilla.

She hurried back down the stairs, out through the front door this time, past Henry's car, and up the hill, around the corner.

At the Aydenlis' house, the driveway remained empty. Ahmet's white Mercedes was still gone. The reminder of his having abandoned her at his shop wrenched her again.

She knocked on the door. No one answered. She knocked again, louder.

Finally, Bahar opened the door.

"*Merhaba*," Anna said. "I've come for Priscilla."

Bahar frowned at her, evidently not understanding. A look of compassion filled her plump face, pooled in liquid, brown eyes, and she responded in Turkish.

"I'm sure the girls have had a wonderful time together," Anna said, "but I must take Priscilla home now. I'm very sorry."

Then Gulsen appeared behind Bahar, and the two of them conversed.

"Honey, would you tell Priscilla that I'm here?" Anna stepped across the threshold and bent down to Gulsen's level.

Gulsen shied away, said "*hayir*," and some other things Anna didn't understand.

"What do you mean? Isn't she here?" Anna's heart skipped

a beat. "Where is she, then? *Nerede*?"

Gulsen pointed at the street. Bahar smiled warmly at Anna, clearly not understanding her.

Anna spoke louder, more slowly, as if she could will them to understand her language. "She left already? When?"

Bahar and Gulsen returned blank stares, and Anna tried again. "How about your dad, honey? Where's he? Ahmet Aydenli."

Gulsen and Bahar exchanged looks and spoke again in Turkish. Their rapid dialogue carried a hint of anxiety.

For Ahmet? For Priscilla?

A strand of Anna's hair tickled her cheek, having worked its way out of her bun. She felt as if she were coming undone, piece by piece. Frustrated, she turned away and leaned against the doorframe to ponder what to do. Across the blazing pavement of the street, Tommy Wingate rumbled down the sidewalk on roller skates. He paused to watch a car turn into the general's driveway.

"Tommy!" she called, straightening from her slump. "Can you please come over here a minute?"

The children adapted better, Fran had said at lunch the day before. And at the party last night, someone had said how easily the children learned this language.

Tommy skated across the street and scrunched to a stop in the Aydenlis' empty driveway. "Yeah?"

"Have you seen Priscilla?"

"We didn't do nothing."

She took a deep breath, wondering what the children had been up to. She would have to save that for later. "Right now it's very important to find out where Priscilla is. You know Turkish, don't you? Please ask them for me how long ago Priscilla left. And where is Gulsen's father?"

She waited, biting her lower lip, while Tommy rolled up the sidewalk to the front door, then spoke in halting Turkish. He stumbled over his words a little more than Priscilla usually did.

Finally, he rolled back. "They said she left a little while ago to go home. Isn't she at home?"

Anna's heart hammered. She felt numb, her mind stuck on a single thought.

Priscilla had surprised whoever was breaking into the house.

Tommy carefully repositioned his skates to roll away. "You want me to go get my mom?"

"Not yet," Anna said, shaking her head. So far, Cora only seemed capable of making matters worse. "I need to call your dad, instead. He's at work, isn't he?"

Tommy brightened. "I know what! I bet Prissy is hiding. Let's go look in the clubhouse. C'mon."

Anna, not sure which of the goodbye words in Turkish she should use, picked one of them. She nodded at Bahar and Gulsen and gave them reassuring smiles. Then she followed Tommy, who scraped and whirred his rollerskates across the street and down the sidewalk. When he reached the yard that skirted the side of their house, he whumped across the garden to the backyard.

Anna stepped more cautiously. This place had been the scene of a suspicious death, a possible crime, only hours ago. Now that the yard filled with natural light and was empty of police, party guests, and servers, Anna felt distanced from those events, as if it had all been a dream.

Anna hoped and prayed that Tommy was right and Priscilla had just run off to hide. That's what she would've done if she'd surprised a burglar. Especially, if that burglar had turned out to be the man Priscilla thought was chasing her daddy. Anna felt certain. And besides, Rainer wouldn't hurt her.

Tommy shouted with excitement as he rounded the corner of his clubhouse.

Anna hurried her step. She looked over to the general's garden, but the *asker* was out of sight. The wheels of the wiggling boy's skates disappeared through the opening of the shack and into its shaded interior. She ducked down low to follow him inside. Daylight trickled in through the cracks between the boards, casting an air of gloom over the pit of sand. It was enough light to reveal a woman—not Priscilla—crouching in a far corner.

Chapter Forty-Four

The woman looked more like a child, Anna thought, and a wild one at that. Her tangled hair tumbled out from under a black head scarf.

"Her name is Meryem," Tommy said. "She left last night, but now she's back. She's our secret, and you have to promise not to tell!"

"Meryem?" Anna whispered. Umit's sister. That's what Yaziz had said was her name. "Last night? She was here? During your parents' *party*?"

"Yep. She was running away from the general. He was having a party, too. Prissy and I like to spy on him, 'cause he's someone important, and he has lots of secrets, and we're going to find out what they are. We're going to be detectives when we grow up, or maybe spaceship captains. But you can't tell that, either!"

In a flash, Anna wondered if Priscilla's absence was due to another game. Maybe she was pretending to be a detective. If she'd walked in on the burglar in the midst of his search of the house, maybe Priscilla had followed him.

Then, she should've returned by now.

She hoped Priscilla's disappearance wasn't due to the trouble that had caused Meryem to run away from the general.

"Tommy," Anna said, "ask her if she knows where Priscilla is."

"Tom-my!" a woman's distant voice called. Cora.

Tommy scrambled around, flinging sand in Anna's face. Meryem tensed, her wild-eyed gaze darting back and forth from Tommy to Anna.

"I've gotta go," Tommy said, crawling toward the opening.

"Wait," Anna whispered. "First you've got to ask Meryem about Priscilla. Go on, hurry!"

He paused and frowned at Anna. Then he sighed and spoke words Anna couldn't understand. Meryem responded with anxious whispers and gestures that pointed east, south, and then finally aimed west.

Tommy listened, and then reported. "She says she saw her going away with a man, that way."

"A man?" Anna's heart skipped a beat. "What man?"

"Maybe I should call my dad," Tommy said.

Anna frowned, not sure she could trust Paul Wingate, either. *Get rid of him*, he'd ordered Fran last night. Anna trusted Yaziz more than Paul. Not that she had much confidence in the detective, either.

"Tom-my!" Cora called again.

"I'd better go," Tommy said, springing back onto his knees.

"One more thing," Anna said. "I won't give away your games, but you've got to promise you won't say anything about Priscilla to your mom. Not yet." She couldn't risk anyone's endangerment through Cora's blunders. "I'll take care of everything."

"You? But you're just Prissy's aunt from the States. You're not even a mom. What can you do?"

Anna bit her tongue. She needed to find Priscilla soon.

"One...two..."

Tommy slipped out of the clubhouse. His roller skates thudded away through the grass as Anna contemplated Meryem. She knew something. Anna could tell, the way she slunk into her dark corner. The tang of fear radiated off her as she clawed nervously at the sand, flinging dust into the air. Had she come here to the children's clubhouse to hide because of what she knew? Her presence here last night also convinced Anna more than ever that there was a connection between Emin's death and Umit's. This woman, his sister Meryem, had to know what it was.

She reminded Anna of a wounded animal, the way she pawed at the sand, burrowing into a hole to recover from its injuries. Meryem took shallow, rapid breaths as she dug, scraping her fingers. A buried object clunked, and she pulled a can from her hole.

"What on earth is *that* doing out here?" Anna asked, recognizing the name printed across one side. It was a brand of powdered milk from the commissary.

The can rattled as Meryem handed it to her. She spoke in a stream of rising hysteria.

"This isn't powdered milk," Anna said, tugging at the lid. "What's inside?"

With a jerky motion, Meryem grabbed Anna's arm with one hand. She said something about the *asker*. With her other hand she pointed in the direction of the general's house, and then she lunged for the clubhouse opening.

"Wait!" Anna cried, crawling after her. "What about Priscilla? Is the *asker* the man Priscilla went with?"

Meryem ticked her tongue. No. "*Leylek*," she whispered, and then she crawled outside and ducked into the same weeds where Rainer had disappeared the night before.

Leylek? That meant "stork" in Turkish.

Puzzled, Anna sank down onto the sandy floor. She would have to call for help, but she wasn't sure whom to trust. She turned back to the can of powdered milk and pried its lid off the rest of the way. Rolling loose inside were four film canisters, ready to be developed.

* * * * *

A telephone rang, a distant sound coming from her house. At first Anna didn't react, as she stared at the can containing film. Not milk. Finally, the bleat of the phone's ring penetrated the fog that numbed her mind.

Maybe it was Priscilla calling.

Anna sprinted across the backyard, clutching the rattling can all the way to the kitchen door. The telephone continued to ring.

She flung open the door and pounded inside. The phone was still ringing in the dining room. She dropped the can onto the table and lifted the heavy receiver.

"Hello?"

Silence. Then a dial tone.

Odd. Slowly, she replaced the phone. Whoever had called had let it ring, waiting until she picked up before disconnecting. Alarm blossomed within her and hammered at her. Someone was watching to make sure she was back in the house. Before... what?

The can with its rolls of film caught her eye. She wondered what photos the film would reveal. Was *that* what her burglar had been looking for when he'd ransacked the house? Before Priscilla went missing.

All of this was connected. Somehow.

She thought of the camera she'd found in Mitzi's closet. The *asker's* interest in—or distaste for—the goings on in this house.

Had Mitzi been photographing the general?

And now someone was after that film. Anna swept up the milk can. Glanced around the room. Where could she hide it?

The phone rang again.

She ran into the kitchen, removed the film from the can, and dropped the four canisters into her deep pocket, hidden beneath the gathers of her skirt. Then she shoved the can onto a cupboard shelf, along with other canned goods, displaying it in plain sight. The phone kept ringing. Someone wanted to make sure she was still inside the house.

She ran back to the phone and picked it up. "Hello?"

This time she caught the faint sound of breathing, then a click. Then the dial tone.

She left the phone off the hook. Next time he called back, he'd get a busy signal.

She wondered what was happening outside that her caller— if he was the same person watching her house—didn't want her to see. Tiptoeing across the room, she crept over to the French doors to the verandah. Maybe he could hear her movements as well as see her. She had no idea where he was hiding. She kept thinking of him as a "he," but was he?

She thought of Meryem, small and delicate as a child, and discarded the thought.

From behind the protection of the filmy curtains, she peered out across the verandah and into the backyard. A strip of grass needed mowing. Lawn chairs scattered across the grass. Priscilla's bicycle lay abandoned under the quince tree. Beyond, a periphery of tall weeds lined the fence. Nothing out of the ordinary.

Meryem had crawled into those weeds. Was she out there still? She'd handed over whatever evidence those roles of film contained. Why? What did she know?

What was the significance of "stork"?

Emin had been killed for the photographs he'd taken the night before. Was it *his* film that hid now inside the milk can?

"Get rid of him," Paul Wingate had said. Rainer had been there, too. He'd heard it. She hoped he hadn't been the one who carried out Paul's directive.

Should she call Paul? Something told her no.

Think!

A chill crept down Anna's spine as she stared vacantly across the backyard. There was an apartment building on the other side of the vacant lot to her left. Rainer, aka Viktor Baliko, lived there with his fake wife. Blocky and modern, it was tall enough at four stories, near enough, with an unobstructed view across an empty field. Empty except for weeds. A stalker could easily watch her movements from an upper-story window.

Rainer?

Maybe Priscilla had followed him there.

Anna shrank away from the French door. Turned and sprang back across the living room, bolted up the step into the dining room, past the phone off the hook, and sailed out the front door. She had to believe that Rainer wouldn't—*couldn't*—hurt Priscilla.

* * * * *

Anna raced down the hill, choking on her breath by the time she reached the apartment building. She pounded up the concrete steps and pulled open the heavy, central door. Just inside the entryway, she scanned the row of buzzers that conveniently displayed the residents' names in small hand printing. V. Baliko. There it was. Fourth floor.

She plunged into a modern stairwell, so new it smelled of fresh concrete. Treading lightly, she raced up the stairs. If Priscilla was in danger, she could not risk announcing herself.

The climb forced her to slow, and she paused on each landing to catch her breath before racing on. On the fourth landing, she caught the sound of raised voices, floating to her on a current of dusty air. A central hallway pierced through gloom to a back stairwell. She tiptoed down the hallway, scanning the numbers for Rainer's apartment. The paper-thin walls muffled the bursts of voices, but couldn't entirely block out arguing voices.

She found Rainer's apartment on the east side of the building, the side that faced Anna's house. Thudding sounds came from inside, and voices.

"We must hurry," said a woman's voice in broken English. "Not much time left."

No doubt they used English to keep their Turkish neighbors from understanding them. Language would work as their protection from paper-thin walls with ears.

Something slammed inside, a man's voice cursed, and footsteps beat across the floor.

Anna lunged toward the back stairwell, hoping she could reach it before he came bursting out of the apartment. The footsteps died, and she backtracked, stepping softly, creeping closer to the door where Rainer pretended to live as Viktor Baliko.

"Please," the woman said. "We must go now." Mrs. Baliko.

"Not yet," said a man from within the apartment. It must be Rainer, but Anna didn't recognize him, not with the tightness of anxiety in his voice.

"But the police, they are coming any minute. Why do we wait for them to come?"

"If we pull out now, it'll ruin everything. Is that what you want?" Hatred seethed along with his clipped words. It couldn't be Rainer.

If it was, then he was not the Rainer that Anna had known.

Mrs. Baliko laughed a high-pitched wail, or perhaps it was a cry. "Is already too late. General will not stop the revolution. We can still save ourselves. I know a place where we can hide in Bolu Mountains, then go up to Black Sea. From there, across to Russia."

"You want to run, go ahead. I'll meet you in Bolu. I've got to take care of the kid first."

The kid? Did he mean Priscilla? Anna lurched forward, ready to break down the door and whisk Priscilla away. But then she stopped, realizing that Priscilla must not be here after all. They wouldn't argue in English in front of her, wouldn't argue about running away, not if Priscilla was here. Anna forced herself back into the shadows. Forced herself to wait.

"No, Viktor," the woman pleaded. "Leave her out of this."

"Too late. She knows."

Anna felt her knees grow weak. It wasn't true. Priscilla knew nothing.

"She is an unnecessary complication," Rainer said. "We took the house apart, and the film wasn't there. Now the minister will have to take care of it."

Film? Minister?

What minister? This was a Moslem country. Unless...did he mean...someone like their neighbor, the assistant *minister* to the Interior? Ahmet Aydenli?

"But no one will find her at Roma Hamani," the woman wailed. "No one goes there."

"Shut up, I told you!" Rainer's voice snapped, and then came the sound of smacking flesh. He'd hit her.

Anna recoiled, as if *she* was the one who'd been struck. Dizzy, she swayed on her feet. She tried to make her mind work, but her thoughts tumbled around loose inside her head.

Priscilla... Held hostage by Ahmet Aydenli? And Rainer, somehow in league with Ahmet... That's why Ahmet had abandoned her downtown today at his rug shop. To return home for Priscilla, conveniently left behind with Gulsen. It was hideous.

Mrs. Baliko sobbed. "What if they do not bring it to you?"

"They will if they want her back."

Then the pieces fell together. It was the *film* they wanted. In exchange for Priscilla. She'd been snatched in order to force Anna to turn over the film. They knew she had it. They did not know where.

Anna brushed the side of her skirt with her hand and felt the lumps that indicated the canisters of film still lodged in her pocket.

Her stomach roiled. Roma Hamani. They'd taken Priscilla there, to the ruins of the Roman baths.

Somehow, she had to get there. She groped for the wall for support and stumbled down the hall. Tripped down the steps. No longer cared about the noise she made. On the second floor, her legs felt stronger, and she ran. Down to first. Out to the street.

She didn't stop running. Tears choked her, streamed down her cheeks. Her lungs were on fire. She sputtered and coughed and ran on. Up the hill.

Anna didn't know how, but she would get there, to Roma Hamani. She would get there fast, and she would save Priscilla.

Chapter Forty-Five

Anna only knew of one way to get anywhere very fast. She would have to drive Henry's stick-shift car. Never mind that she didn't know how.

She raced into the Burkhardts' house. There was no time to lose, searching for Henry's car keys. She started with the telephone table, where the menacing, black receiver still lay off its hook atop the lace doily. Yanking open a drawer of pencils and notepads, she saw no keys among the clutter.

Her vision swam before her. She wasn't thinking properly. She must call the police instead. Why hadn't she realized that sooner? Choking on her breath, she snatched up the receiver and stabbed with her finger at the hang-up button, pumping it several times. Or, maybe she should call Paul instead. After all, Mrs. Baliko had said the police would be here any minute, as if she'd known that they were already alerted. But were they really? And anyway, they wouldn't know to go to Roma Hamani, instead of coming here, the opposite side of town. Although, Anna didn't know if she could trust the word of Rainer's spy partner.

It was better to let Paul handle things, even if she didn't trust him, either. At least he worked on her side, although she couldn't be sure what side that was anymore. She dropped the receiver back into place in its cradle and shuffled through papers, searching for Paul's number at the embassy.

The phone rang.

Each bleating trill pierced her, and she flinched, as if it had come alive and had stung her.

He was still watching her. He'd watched her run up the hill. He knew she was back inside the house. No, she scolded herself. He only knew that someone had hung up the phone. That's all. She stood frozen in front of the table, her hand extended in mid-reach. If she answered, she would listen to his breathing, which would tell her that he knew her every move.

The air shifted behind her, and a footstep swooshed across the thick pile of Mitzi's rug. Before Anna could whirl around, an arm encircled her, pressing her spine against a solid body. She opened her mouth to scream, and a hand slammed against her face, cutting off her shout to a gurgle. The hand shoved her head backwards, snapping hard against prickly whiskers.

They were the strong fingers of a man's hand, and they pressed hard under her nose, bruising her jawbone. They reeked of day-old sweat.

"Where. Is. It." His words strained, as if through gritted teeth, under a heavy accent.

The film, oh God, that's what he wants. Anna willed all of her mental strength to force herself to go limp in his grip, to keep from fighting to reach for her skirt pocket. To keep from revealing the presence of the film.

But if giving it up would get Priscilla back, then she would gladly hand over the film.

Not yet. Not until she saw Priscilla safe. Until then, the film was her ace, and she would not hand it over.

His grip on her loosened the barest amount, probably in response to her submission, or maybe because of the steady ring of the telephone. In that instant, she twisted and squirmed and tried to lurch away. In a flash, one of his arms squeezed around her, tight enough to take her breath away. A cold, hard, blunt tip dug against her back.

"Stop," he said with a growl.

He had a gun! She stopped struggling.

The phone kept ringing.

"Where's Priscilla?" she tried to say, but her words gargled in her throat, muffled by his hand.

The blunt end of the gun pressed steadily against her back, but the man slid the fingers of his other hand from her mouth, up to the bun atop her head. He yanked, undoing the pins that held her hair in place. A few of her black hairs came loose from her scalp, but she didn't mind the wrenching pain, as she took that opportunity to scream. It was a loud, blood-curdling scream. Surely someone would hear. Cora. The *asker*. Another neighbor. A hawker in the street. Surely someone would run to her aid. Or at least telephone the police.

Riiiing.

"Shut up," he said, tossing her aside, aiming the gun at her.

Biting off her scream, she tumbled onto the woolen carpet. A black scarf wrapped around the man's head like a hood and shifted across his shoulders as he backed towards the phone. The gun still pointed at her. She could not tell who he was, dressed in his faded black suit. Dust the color of sand splotched the cuffs of his pants and his worn, scuffed, brown leather shoes.

The scarf slipped away from his face as he lifted the receiver to his ear. Right away, she recognized his thick mat of hair that curled into the shape of a V. Like a bird's nest, she had thought before. He was the policeman whom she thought Yaziz had assigned to watch her house. The same man who'd followed her to the bazaar the day before. There must be some terrible mistake. He was pointing a gun at her as he spoke into the phone in Turkish and then paused to listen.

"You're making a mistake!" she cried. "Call Mr. Yaziz. He'll tell you. It's not me you want. I'm innocent."

He switched to English, mumbling into the phone, but she caught the words "you can come now" before he hung up. Then he turned a deadpan look on her. "Where is it?"

"I don't have it. The police have it."

"You lie!" He sprinted forward and slapped her cheek with the back of his hand not holding the gun. "*I* am police. You think I don' know?"

There was police, Paul had said, and then there was secret police. This man couldn't work for Yaziz. She'd made a mistake. *Her* detective was only incompetent. Not corrupt.

He slapped her again, a dull force thudding her face. Something warm trickled across her upper lip. Blood.

"Wait!" she cried, panting. Gasping. "Okay. I'll tell you where it is. I...I hid it. Somewhere safe."

"Where?"

"Somewhere that no one would find." Where could she tell him? She had to think of a place far away from here, a place that traveling there would buy her enough time.

But then he would kill her.

Because he was worse than corrupt. Anna realized with

a wave of terror engulfing her... This man had already killed at least once before. He aimed a gun at her now. What would stop him from killing again?

She sprang to her feet, lurching first to one side and then to the other. If he was going to shoot her, then let him try. Running, she had a chance. A bad one, but still a chance. Maybe she could dodge his aim.

She screamed again. Where was that help who should be on its way? He slammed into her, knocking the wind out of her and cutting off her cry in mid-scream. He wrapped his arms about her, quickly immobilizing her struggles, and pinched off her breath with a foul-smelling hand. He threw her to the floor and sat atop her.

* * * * *

She couldn't breathe. *Please*, she tried to say, but she had no breath left. Her ribs felt crushed from his weight. Dead weight on top of her. She felt on the verge of passing out.

A door squeaked open.

"Aunt Anna!"

Priscilla's voice sounded far away. Her voice was like music filling Anna's heart, flowing strength back into her. She shuddered for air as the man rolled off of her.

"*Efendim*," he said.

"You idiot." It was Rainer. "What the hell are you doing?"

Priscilla sobbed. "Let me go. I want Aunt Anna!"

Anna sucked in a deep breath of air. Pain fired through her ribs. Blood streamed from her nose.

"You weren't supposed to hurt her," Rainer said.

The secret police mumbled something in a language she did not understand. She assumed it was Turkish, but she didn't think Rainer understood Turkish any better than she. Rainer...

"You!" Anna gasped and managed to spit out some words. She pushed herself up onto one elbow. "It's been...*you*! All along. Hasn't it?"

"Annie...you don't know what it was like. I had to survive. Everything I did, it was all for us. For you."

"Don't put your blame on me," she said, struggling to stand. "You're responsible for your choices, not me. It was *you*, wasn't it? You killed Umit. You hired the boy to hit me over the head. How can you say you didn't want me to be hurt? And now this! Kidnapping Priscilla."

"I borrowed her, that's all, and it worked, didn't it? I knew you'd come looking for her. You think I didn't know you were standing outside in my hall a few moments ago? Tonya and I, we staged that little disagreement, all for your benefit."

Something broke inside her. His lack of denial concerning Umit's death was as good as a confession. How had it come to this? The man she had once loved...a murderer.

And now he had her darling niece, the only one who mattered anymore. "Let her go, Rainer. If there's anything left inside of the person you once were, you'll let her go."

His arms sagged in an apparent moment of hesitation. Priscilla squirmed, pushing away from him. She ran to Anna's side and hugged her tightly. "You said he's a good guy, remember? That's why I went with him. *He* said you needed my help."

"And she still does," Rainer said, tossing her a

handkerchief. "Don't you see? Umit was going to reveal my identity, and we can't have that, not if we are to succeed."

"We already won the war," Anna said. "You didn't have to do it. None of it."

"Your war, perhaps. Not mine. I had to survive, Annie. For us. You've got to believe me."

"Don't include me in your scheme. What about people's lives? And Emin. You killed him, too, didn't you? Did you use the *asker's* poison? Is that why you were visiting him the night before last?"

Rainer ignored her and strode across the room to the secret policeman. He held out his hand, acting as if he was in charge. The Turk shrugged and handed over his gun.

"We couldn't allow him to record the general's meeting," Rainer said, as if suddenly remembering Anna now that he held a gun in his hand. "Now, be a good girl and hand over the film. No one's going to get hurt." He turned to face Anna, the gun aiming at her feet.

Her heart leapt. He wouldn't actually shoot her, would he? She clutched Priscilla tightly, nudging her around to her backside. "I...I don't have it."

"You've always lied poorly, Annie. Truth is, you told Erkmen you have it. He told me so. Where is it? Don't make me make you. Just hand it over. You've got the kid now. That film doesn't belong to you."

"It's my mommy's film," Priscilla shouted, twisting around the side of Anna's skirt, "and I took it! It's not yours, and you can't have it. Don't tell him where it is, Aunt Anna."

Rainer laughed, sounding amused. The aim of the gun crept up her thigh, zeroing in on the pocket of Anna's skirt.

Her arm tingled, as if wanting with a will of its own to move toward her pocket where the film hid, but her mental strength overruled and forced her arm to still.

Priscilla went on shouting. "I don't care if you don't believe me! Mommy was taking pictures of the general, and some bad man gave her candy for her film. It was making her sick, I could tell, so I hid the film, so she couldn't get any more. You can't have it. I don't want you to give her more candy when she comes home again." Sobbing, Priscilla burrowed into the gathers of Anna's skirt.

Anna bent down to cradle her. "Oh, honey," she whispered. *Opium.* That was Mitzi's "candy."

"Erkmen started this badly," Rainer said, waving the gun in the direction of the secret police. "He could not even handle a simple tape recording for the minister. Now I must finish it. I will tell you once more to hand over the film to me, and then we will say nothing more about it. The minister will allow you to quietly leave the country, never to return."

"The minister?" Anna said. "Ahmet, is that who you mean? Is he one of your spies, too?"

Rainer grimaced. "We couldn't operate without his, shall we say, facilitation."

A shadow danced into the room behind Rainer. Anna's hope soared, and she tried not to look over there. Someone must've heard her screams. Help had finally arrived.

Then she saw the heavy gun, swinging up and pointing at Rainer. It wasn't police, come to her aid. It was Meryem, with a gleam of fire in her eyes. Both hands wrapped around the handle of her gun, too big and clumsy for her delicate fingers.

"No!" Anna shouted, dragging Priscilla down to the floor.

Pain shattered through her damaged ribs, but nonetheless, she would die protecting her niece.

"*Leylek*," Meryem said calmly, the instant before the gunshot exploded over Anna's head.

The sound reverberated through every cell of her body. She continued to breathe, with only the sharp pain from her ribs stabbing her with each breath. She opened her eyes and dared to lift her head from Priscilla, who shuddered and sobbed beneath her. Nearby, Rainer lay on the floor. Erkmen bent over him. Blood trailed across the floor. And Meryem...

Where was Meryem?

The front door burst open just then, letting in blinding light. Two men rushed in against the backdrop of light. Their footsteps scuffled, and voices shouted. Yaziz, wearing a new pair of tinted glasses, limped to Anna's side. His partner aimed a gun at Erkmen.

Chapter Forty-Six

Even in death, the pretense continued. A simple service was held several days later in the JUSMMAT auditorium for Viktor Baliko. Rainer had vanished once again, but Anna preferred to think he had never come back. She attended the service along with a dozen or so others from the American community, sprinkling across the first three rows of folding chairs. Anna sat in the second row with her new friends, Hayati and Fran, at either side. Priscilla was at school.

Words of the sermon echoed through the cavernous chamber, nearly empty. She only heard the rhythm, reverberating like a scolding harangue against the evil forces that had taken the life of one weary journeyer whose escape from the Iron Curtain had been cut prematurely short.

Hardly.

Anna wondered if Rainer's luck had run out when he'd lost his Saint Christopher's medal. The Alekcis somehow had recovered it, she wasn't sure how, but it seemed to have brought them luck in the form of passage to their future here in Turkey. She could only hope it would promise a bright future for the boy to whom she had given the necklace.

Gossip raged around her on the downbeats of the sermon's echo. Whispers speculated on the whereabouts of "Mrs. Baliko." The pregnant widow wasn't here.

In the hospital, the whisperers assumed. The stork was coming early.

But Anna knew the truth.

There was no stork, neither the baby-delivering kind nor the turncoat spy. *Leylek*—Stork—had been Rainer's code name. Tonya, the Stork's partner, was probably back on Soviet soil by now.

Meryem had known him as *leylek*.

Survival, he'd claimed, had made him switch sides, but something much deeper must have turned his mind to make him resort to such crimes. Had it been the war and its atrocities?

Lost in her thoughts, Anna let her friends cue her through the service and steer her outside afterwards. Afternoon sunlight reflecting off the stone buildings and the street made her blink, bringing her out of her somnolent state that the sermon had induced in her.

Its cadence kept echoing in her mind long after the words had ceased. New sounds—their clicking heels on pavement—hammered away the last of the rhythm. She was done with the pretense. It was time to move on.

Hayati was squeezing her elbow and telling her something about a museum.

"I'm sorry," she said, squinting into the sun, "what did you say?"

He winked at her. "You'll like it, when I show it to you tomorrow."

"But..." Interest fired in her, but she didn't remember agreeing to the plans. "I have to be home by the time school is out." Kidnappers didn't lurk behind every bush for Priscilla, but it was too soon for Anna's piece of mind to allow her niece to walk home alone from the bus stop.

"Don't worry," said Fran, "he can't take all day for his lunch break."

They walked on in silent camaraderie. The warmth of anticipation spread through Anna.

Yaziz waited for them on the street, beside Fran's parked car. He pulled his hands from his pockets as they approached, and all of them eyed each other in somber contemplation. After allowing them several minutes of drinking in a newfound gratitude for the simple pleasure of enjoying another day, he passed an envelope to Anna.

"What's this, Detective?" she said, pulling her hand back, wary now of taking just anything offered to her.

"It's yours, Miss Riddle. We have recovered it from Erkmen. You may have it now."

She recognized her own handwriting on the envelope. It was the letter she'd written to Rainer so long ago, the one that Umit had offered her in death. She glanced past Yaziz's shoulder up the street, but there was no shooter out there now, no one to shoot him for offering the letter to Anna. Rainer was dead. She snatched the envelope from Yaziz and stuffed it into her purse along with the rest of them.

"Thank you, Mr. Yaziz. Do you have news about Meryem? Have you found her yet?"

His head tilted back, although not quite a gesture of "no," as his new sunglasses appraised her. He was a blend, this man, between east and west. "I regret that she has not yet turned up."

"Gypsies have a way of disappearing," Fran said with a laugh.

"What about Ozturk Bey?" Anna said. "Have you asked

him? What does he have to say about where she might've gone?"

Yaziz sighed. "Miss Riddle, are you in competition for my job?"

The heat of a flush rose up her throat. "Of course not. I just thought that since Ozturk Bey was their patron, he might know where she's hiding."

"Not exactly." A small grin showed beneath his frames. "Ozturk Bey was willing to act as patron for a price. He only followed the instructions your Henry Burkhardt gave him."

Of course, Anna thought. It had been Henry all along. The Alekcis had healed Henry—not Rainer—all those years ago. Ever since, Henry had been trying to return their kindness. While Rainer had gone on to betray those closest to him.

But all that was behind them now. Anna smiled. "I'm having a little barbecue party later this evening at my house. It's the least I can do to show my thanks." She glanced left to right, from Fran to Hayati. Her new friends were her community now. "Will you join us?"

Yaziz dipped his head, and his new sunglasses shifted against the bridge of his nose. She supposed that was an acceptance, but she couldn't be sure. He was an enigmatic man to her.

So unlike Hayati, who held open the car door for her and beamed with pleasure.

Fran gave her a lift home, but when they arrived at the yellow stucco house, she declined an invitation to come inside for a lemonade. It was still a workday for Fran and Hayati. They would see Anna later that evening at the barbecue, Fran promised, and then drove away.

Inside the house, Anna found Fededa and Bahar in the kitchen, with preparations for the feast well under control.

Anna tried out the few new words she'd learned in Turkish from Hayati. Whatever they were preparing, it smelled delicious, savory with spices from the bazaar. Spices wrapped in newspaper bundles...

She refused to let the reminder of Rainer pummel her recovering spirits. He'd compromised Ozturk Bey's spice packages with opium for Mitzi.

Bahar was looking for more work now that Gulsen had moved to her great-aunt and uncle's horse farm while her father was away. Detained temporarily, Yaziz claimed. On the other hand, Hayati said that Ahmet had fled the country in disgrace, that he'd tried to direct Yaziz's boss, and when that failed, he hadn't wanted to become a Soviet puppet.

Anna wasn't sure whom to believe, but the fact was that Ahmet was gone. Meanwhile, she appreciated the extra help from Bahar. She'd planned the barbecue party for this evening to show all of her new friends her appreciation for their support. A community had to bind together when it found itself so far away from home.

Besides, it would be another opportunity to see Hayati again. As well as tomorrow, during his lunch "hour" at the museum.

Before then, Anna still had some unfinished business. She headed out the back door where the barbecue grill was already set up. One of the women had laid a fire, and a woodsy-scented cloud of smoke billowed into the air. Anna unclasped her purse and withdrew the bundle of letters she'd written to Rainer so long ago. Without a second's hesitation, she flung them onto the smoldering bed of embers. The paper caught and flared into flames. She stared transfixed, watching as the paper blackened and curled.

When the flames licked up the last wedge of paper and then died down again, she headed back inside. She marched up the stairs, straight for Mitzi's room. In her sister's closet, she found the hatbox high on the shelf, and she pulled it down. She lifted the lid and removed the veiled hats, laying them carefully on the bed. The loose rolls of film clattered around inside the box, where she had placed them after that harrowing day when she'd tried desperately not to reveal their presence in her skirt pocket. Three rolls were Mitzi's, and the fourth had been added by Priscilla and Tommy. They'd found it in the weeds by their clubhouse the night of the Wingates' party. Anna replaced the lid and carried the hatbox downstairs.

Outside once again, the heat of the sun had dropped its intensity by perhaps as much as a degree. Cooler days, relief from the heat, lay ahead. Swinging the hatbox, rattling its contents, she strode out the driveway and headed up the hill.

She pieced together the various bits of information that she'd learned in the short time here in Ankara, which wasn't so very unlike her job back home. In the classroom, she had to thread together pieces of history in order to present the overall picture.

So many players here. But once she understood whom she could trust, it wasn't so difficult to see the pieces fall together. She'd even learned from those she couldn't trust. Ahmet had taught her that not everyone was satisfied with Atatürk's reforms. His faction wanted the current government to continue drifting away from western reforms. On the other hand, the general, who'd served under Atatürk, was trying to bring back the reforms his revered leader had started.

With Yaziz, Anna had understood the rest.

It had started with Ahmet, and his anti-Atatürk fervor. Through his spy, Erkmen, he found out about the gypsy and the bids the gypsy had solicited for a "valuable" piece of information.

Evidence for the brewing coup, Ahmet thought. In reality, Umit was only trying to feed his family by selling the treasure originally belonging to Rainer—his Saint Christopher's medal.

And then Anna entered the picture.

She would have plenty of time later, when Henry and Mitzi returned from Switzerland, rehabilitated. She would decide then if there was any point in confronting Henry about having kept her letters all these years. The letters were gone, so did it even matter anymore?

Anna marched up to the general's front door and rang the bell. Nothing happened. She tapped on the glass pane and peered through it.

Finally, a maid, not the *asker*, opened the door. Anna breezed past the maid. "I came to give my regards to the general," she said, even though the Turkish woman couldn't understand. Anna's lessons with Hayati hadn't progressed far enough for her to translate any of that, but it didn't matter. She knew where to find the general. After all, she'd seen him enough times, across the garden, from the vantage point of Priscilla's balcony. She knew he spent his afternoons in his second-floor study.

The maid said something that sounded like a protest, but Anna continued up the marble stairs, pausing only long enough to admire the chandelier. There must be hundreds of crystals cascading over the curve of the steps.

The maid hovered behind her as she tapped on the door to

his study. A grunt responded, and she swung open the door.

An imperious man, the general sat behind a desk fit for a president. Medals twinkled from his uniform. He removed reading glasses from the bridge of his nose—a very Turkish nose, Anna thought, the way it bumped out in the middle. Like the beak of a feared bird of prey. His eyes opened wide, and his glasses clattered to the shiny surface of his desk. He bolted to his feet. Thrust back his shoulders. Chin up. Nostrils flaring.

"*Merhaba*," Anna said, striding across thick carpets to stand before his desk. "I'm Anna Riddle, your next door neighbor, and I thought it time we meet. Besides, I have something that I think belongs to you." With a whump and a clatter, she set the hatbox down atop his desk, lifted the lid, and turned it upside down. Canisters of film skittered across the glass-topped surface.

It wasn't for her to destroy the evidence of his secret meetings, meetings that in one sweep would change the course of a country. Let *him* do it. Or not.

She had other matters on her mind just now. A party. New friends. A place that was feeling more like a home. And all of that put together left her feeling rather happy. Not just content. There *was* a difference.

* * * * *

Author's Note

This is a work of fiction. Any resemblance to real persons, living or dead, is unintentional.

Real events serve as the framework of this story, inspired by the author's personal experiences in the 1950's as a dependent of a Foreign Service officer with the International Cooperation Administration. ICA was the U.S. agency giving economic assistance to Turkey at the height of the Cold War as a result of the Truman Doctrine and the Marshall Plan following World War II. ICA, along with the Joint United States Military Mission to Turkey, formed an ambitious United States Overseas Mission to Turkey during the 1950's. The authors have attempted to depict as accurately as possible the ambience of a real place and time within history, but the immediate events of the story and its characters are a product entirely of their imagination.

About the Author

Sue Star and Bill Beatty are a writing team from Colorado who lived in Turkey during the Menderes era. Sue writes the Nell Letterly mystery series and other stories of women's suspense. Bill writes historical crime with a darker edge. Short stories about Veli Yaziz appear in the collection, *Making Their Own Law,* and in Fiction River's *Hidden in Crime.* Please visit dmkregpublishing.com for more information.

APR 0 9 2018

CPSIA information can be obtained
at www.ICGtesting.com
Printed in the USA
LVOW10s1821150318
569991LV00011B/1111/P

9 780989 357876